T5-CQD-771

46

David Andrew Saint

THE WINNOWING

THE
WINNOWING

DAVID
ANDREW
SAINT

TOPSAIL PRESS, INC.

PUBLISHED BY TOPSAIL PRESS, INC.
Akron, Ohio

FIRST EDITION

Limited

Library of Congress Catalog Card Number: 98-90112

Saint, David Andrew.
   The Winnowing / David Andrew Saint – 1st ed.
     p.   cm.
  I.   Title.

ISBN 0-9662818-0-2

Printed in the United States of America

To Carolyn

*For her encouragement
and unwavering support.*

PREFACE

All persons, places, and events except customarily recognized locales are fictitious.

The early history of HIV/AIDS as portrayed in this book is a fanciful creation of the author's imagination, however, the plague's proliferation since 1980 is based on commonly held but not universally accepted conclusions. Prophecies are the writer's extrapolations deduced from the epidemic's status in mid-1997.

Considerable effort has been expended to be scientifically sound but where medical accuracy inhibited plot development or jeopardized telling a good story, poetic license reigned.

David Andrew Saint

THE WINNOWING
by
DAVID ANDREW SAINT

"Sheer numbers dictate that famine, war, pestilence, disease–and more recently pollution–have eroded, are eroding, and will continue to erode, the quality of life upon the Earth."*

John H. McDonnell
Governor of the
State of Ohio

*Excerpted from a speech presented to an educational conference at the University of Toledo, Ohio. Dec. 3, 2001

"Whether they are beneficial or detrimental, time sanctifies religious ideologies, making it difficult to separate debatable premises from God's will.

"Control thy numbers lest the Earth become overburdened and your progeny fail to thrive.

"Prophets–especially those with dire warnings–are seldom heeded, for their message often conflicts with human desire."

Preston Millwright
Founder, Universal
Pragmatic Church

PART I

GERMINATION

"Perhaps plagues are visited upon the Earth by a much wiser god than we can comprehend."*

John H. McDonnell
Governor of the
State of Ohio

*Offhand comment in response to a student question while serving as a guest speaker at Oberlin College, Oberlin, Ohio. Nov. 16, 2002

1

Initially simple, over eons life evolved with prodigious complexity; aggressively probing the seas, meandering about the land, and borne aloft by capricious winds, engulfing the planet. Whether created during chance encounters of receptive proteins, spontaneously begat by an atmospheric electrical discharge, placed on Earth by divine intervention or one of myriad other possibilities, the organisms were life for life's sake. Once viable, however, single cells and combinations thereof pursued similar goals: survival, reproduction, and the assimilation or elimination of competitors. The battle for continuance and domination was joined. A need to exist, any desirability of purpose, or the organism's sophistication level was not relevant. Nor did it matter that in order for one to live another must die because factors contributing to success were amoral: luck, persistence, overwhelming numbers, the ability to dominate, and uninhibited aggression.

The virus was perfectly suited to enter such an arena. Emerging into an intricate world of microorganisms, flora, and fauna, it found itself ideally situated in the netherworld of the fictional undead with a potent ability to invade a vulnerable cell, implant its genetic code, replicate, then move to the next unsuspecting host. Omnipotent, yet oddly fragile, by stealth and careful adherence to very narrow conditions, the invader thrived until denied the victim's lifeblood, whereupon its tenuous existence ceased. Science fiction is replete with fascinating examples of similar anomalies and the terror they unleash.

. . .

Kostahk lived along the east bank of an emerald river that one day would be named the Rhine. While hunting, he became lost. An encounter with a hostile tribe suggested he had ventured into unfriendly territory. After several aborted attempts to flee—his hasty retreat creating confusion–he followed the afternoon sun and eventually spotted a familiar rise a day's journey from the river. Reoriented but exhausted, he feasted on indigenous red-black berries and spent the night under a protruding rock-shelf.

Upon arriving home the next evening, he fished. Unsuccessful, he dug a few scrawny roots from the sparse hillside soil. After rinsing them in the cool waters of the river, Kostahk–just fourteen–ate the Spartan rations and fell asleep hungry.

He was born and raised in an established clan. Life was good and uneventful until some months ago when, under duress, he chose to leave. Exploration led to his current location. The serenity of still water away from rushing currents undercutting the opposite bank pleased him, while the river bend provided a modicum of security. Caching his meager belongings high in the fork of a tree, he settled in.

Solitude held no terrors, for even as a toddler, he resisted his mother's efforts to cuddle and pet him. Eventually resigned to her eldest son's aloofness, she nurtured more receptive little ones, picking lice from their heads and otherwise grooming them. That was fine with Kostahk who felt unfettered, not unloved or unwanted.

His father likewise ignored him, for siring little ones was infinitely more pleasurable than tending those born. However, as Kostahk matured, hunting and fishing lessons were provided to promote his survival. A natural predator, he grew to be healthy and strong.

Kostahk's youthful years were unremarkable until he was presented with his first sexual partner. Displaying normal adolescent curiosity, he examined her in detail, but was not aroused and remained a virgin. The rejected female, secure in her sexuality, reported their lack of consummation to his father and mother whereupon the young prince came under extreme parental pressure to perform. It was abundantly clear the two were to spend the coming night together, and he was to execute his rite of puberty.

Twilight found them intertwined, Kostahk exploring between her thighs and enthusiastically sucking her mammaries. Stimulated nipples firmed and, while not discernable in the dim light, darkened. Several times she spread her legs while gently guiding his erection, but he successfully evaded each maneuver. Finally, confused and frustrated, she pushed his head away, retrieving a tender nipple. Kostahk would have preferred to continue feeling and examining her, but not if required to participate in what she obviously had in mind. The act, rather openly performed by other males and females, had no appeal to him.

The next morning, his carnal failure communal knowledge, his embarrassed father was good-naturedly, but painfully, ridiculed. Submitting to firm paternal coercion, Kostahk reluctantly agreed to spend the coming night with a different girl, one sporting huge breasts and solid buttocks, which in truth *did* arouse him. After fondling her generous endowments, he rolled her over and attempted to penetrate further back than she anticipated. Her alarmed screams brought the villagers running, and Kostahk soon found himself in darkness at the edge of the clearing. By pleading inexperience or navigational error and allowing the female to direct him into the proper opening, he would have been welcomed back, but chose to walk away.

Days were spent foraging, playing in or near the water, and occasionally thinking about shelter, as nights were becoming increasingly cold. While preferring to maintain his independence, but considering the advantages of joining a group, providence solved his dilemma by selecting him for a bolt of good fortune. Little did he suspect that from conception, he was also predestined for a uniquely grave misfortune.

During an exceptionally violent thunderstorm, with pelting rain rendering him miserable, fire from the sky felled a giant tree not a hundred feet from the river. Lightning jaggedly seared the bark, sending splinters and sparks in all directions, filling the air with smoke and the unfamiliar smell of ozone. His ears rang for hours. Recognizing the event as a gift *and* an omen, Kostahk piled brush and stones against the massive trunk to create the windward side of a dwelling. With equal success he wove branches a few feet away to erect the opposite wall. The back quickly followed, and employing meager yet intuitive engineering skills, a cave-like structure took shape. But when he tried to span the sides and form a roof, it collapsed; hence, he settled on a smaller enclosure. Over the next two years Kostahk strengthened his crude abode by interlacing vines and small branches where it remained permeable. Windblown debris helped seal it. Summer rains continued to leak through, but once iced over in late fall the hut was weatherproof. Winters were hard, but not life threatening. By obtaining fire from the nearest clan and huddling under animal skins, he avoided freezing.

On balmy days he was sorely tempted to let his blaze die for it was a nuisance gathering wood and tending it; nevertheless, he learned the first winter what a mistake that could be. One morning then, at the end of a January thaw, he awakened to temperate rays dancing in iridescent pools of yellow and orange along the forest floor. The sun moving imperceptibly through the trees promised warmer temperatures by early afternoon . . . another halcyon day . . . no need to think of fire. Mesmerized as the sun sliced more directly though the forest, Kostahk watched as shimmering pools of light ballooned into irregular patterns, encroaching upon the shade and overlapping one another, leaving only the shadows of trunks and branches on the ground.

Thus preoccupied, he failed to notice a foreboding overcast appear on the northwest horizon. The dark turbulence creeping surreptitiously overhead, previously stationary treetops began listing in the intermittent wind ebbing and flowing across the valley. Finally aware as menacing storm clouds rolled into view, and light snow started falling, it was too late to rekindle the dying embers.

The temperature plummeted. Gossamer flakes turned heavy and wet, drifting over the hut and packing against the windward sides of tree trunks. Sleet clung to branches, and ice crystals formed in the placid water by the sandbar.

With no heat, Kostahk realized he must seek other cover or perish as numb fingers and toes signaled initial stages of frostbite. He feared venturing into the blizzard, but animal skins wrapped around his shivering body were failing to ward off the cold. Filled with trepidation, but having no choice, he journeyed to the nearest clan in hopes of survival. The exertion elevated his temperature, blood pressure, and heartbeat, therefor, saving his extremities and life, as temperatures fell below zero by the dawn.

Warmed, fed, and recuperated, he departed on the first day that was calm enough for fire to be carried without the wind extinguishing it. Arriving home and experiencing loneliness for the first time, he spent the remainder of the winter pondering its resolution.

Summer arrived. A sparse diet of berries and fruits was supplemented by meat from small animals warmed over the fire, a practice conducted during the winter months. Discovering a year round preference for partially cooked food, Kostahk recalled that his family had occasionally heated game, though with so many to feed, the carcass was usually eaten before it cooled. Edible leaves and roots rounded out his diet. Life was good, but as the season progressed, he continued feeling oddly unsettled and anxious. That inexplicable emptiness persisted.

Toward fall, a young male and female arrived. Offering roots and skins, they indicated a desire to stay, and when he neither objected nor blocked their way, they moved in. The female tended the fire while the male secured and shared food. Wary of the intrusion, Kostahk was torn between tolerating them for their assistance and companionship, or evicting them for invasion of privacy.

The indecision prevailed until one evening when, without prior notification, the male failed to return. Alarmed as the third day of absence progressed, Kostahk vowed that if the man reappeared, he would ignore him less, perhaps even accompany him on a foraging expedition.

Mercifully at dusk the familiar footsteps approached through the gloom; and close behind the young hunter's heels, muffled by the sounds of his greater bulk and larger feet, were the barely audible footfalls of a much smaller person. As they came into the flickering glow of the fire, Kostahk saw the silhouette of a young girl. Illuminated by the dancing light of recently prodded coals,

5

she was presented by the male. Kostahk viewed her suspiciously. He did not want another being around; but then, he did not want to offend his . . . friend.

Reluctantly accepting the additional intruder, he felt a responsibility to sleep with her to provide warmth. As shyness abated she aroused him by fondling his penis. When she started licking, the sensation was so pleasurable, he submitted to her guiding him between her thighs.

Predictably, within weeks her tummy swelled. It became awkward to lie on her, and good as the penetrations were the act felt unnatural. As she reached for him one night during her third trimester, he spontaneously pushed her away, sufficiently brusque to make his wish to be let alone painfully obvious. She ceased trying to seduce him, and he never entered her again. With the arrival of spring, the young girl delivered his only child, a boy, well formed and healthy.

The mother never became infected, and since she remained free of the virus, the infant was spared. The mutant strain remained a prisoner in Kostahk's body, unable to bridge the gap from male to female, neither harming him nor infiltrating any other being.

In succeeding years, others joined Kostahk. Each summer fertile females bore babies, the result of primal urges and close confinement during the preceding fall. Few offspring survived the ensuing winter, but that was of no consequence as enough lived to assure the clan's perpetuation.

Watching the obvious if transitory pleasure of copulating couples, Kostahk resumed occasional foreplay with his son's mother and some of the more active females but, despite his urges, never consummated the act. Avoiding penetration, he retreated and finished the job himself, experiencing diminished satisfaction, but no sense of unease. His aroused and deserted partner had little difficulty locating an accommodating male to mount her and finish in a flurry what Kostahk had commenced at leisure. Eventually, he ceased excursions into the heterosexual world.

During Kostahk's twenty-seventh year, winter loomed with intimidating power in what posterity would call early November.

A fierce storm raged across the land, its gale-force wind faltering at the escarpment, inverting and depositing snow in deepening windrows upon the hill. Sequestered day and night, the clan strove to survive, venturing outside only to replenish depleting firewood or replace dwindling food supplies. Attempts to better enclose the dwelling for heat retention failed, but winter accomplished what the group could not. An alar wedge formed above the entrance, warding off the wind and making the chamber remarkably cozy. As drift piled upon drift, the opening shrunk to an igloo-like passage maintained by the females' repeated visits to the root shelter and everyone's trips into the forest to relieve bodily functions.

It was into this uterine world that Mok came. As with Kostahk, his rejection of females incensed his father. A stymied attempt to touch a male resulted in a severe beating and expulsion into the inhospitable and potentially fatal winter. Days later, debilitated and frostbitten, he stumbled upon the fresh tracks of Kostahk's hunters. Retracing their steps, Mok presented himself at the enclosure. Had he been healthy or older, he might have been repulsed, since supplies were short. However, due to his frailty and the unrelenting cold, the males permitted entry, and the females warmed, fed, and nursed him back to health.

One evening, with vigor returned and several couples sexually involved, he noticed Kostahk crouched at the back of the hut stroking himself. Fascinated, he watched for the briefest moment before hurrying to bring his new chief to climax by a most pleasurable method. A life-long union was forged.

Over the next few weeks the inclement weather subsided. Days grew longer, and more snow melted than fell. The ledge sculpted by the winds over the snow-entombed shelter collapsed, requiring the emaciated inhabitants to wrestle it out of the way before venturing outside. Though suffering severe malnutrition, all would recover except Mok, who–infected by some strange malady–became progressively weaker as the virus sapped his strength. Kostahk vacillated between devotedly tending him and, unable to cope, disappearing for days on end.

The villagers were puzzled by the youth's unfamiliar illness. Unlike typical ailments where the victim either got better or quickly died, Mok lingered, month after month, one symptom leading to another without remission. To compensate for his misery, he was fed the best berries and choicest fruit, and provided with the warmest pelts as fever wracked his feeble body. And yet, it was to no avail, for mid-winter of the third year, he died. Kostahk carried the emaciated corpse to a swale where wolves would pick it clean. After milling about for what seemed an eternity, he returned in sad resignation to the village before hypothermia threatened his life as well.

The group flourished. Fire burned year around. Babies arrived in such profusion that the weaker males and most females were abandoned at the swale to ensure survival of the best. As clan elder, Kostahk was ritually offered maidens for sexual initiation and to perpetuate his seed, but as anticipated, he deferred to his son.

One winter day, years after Mok's demise, Kostahk and several clansmen hunting near the escarpment flushed out an impressively large boar. Intuitively it darted down the slope seeking more maneuvering room. A lagging hunter, anticipating its move, launched a brutal, but unsuccessful, swing. Unscathed, the panicked animal reversed direction and ran up the hill.

The hunters skillfully steered their confused quarry to a sheer section of the promontory. The ring tightened; clubs were poised. In desperation the boar, charging blindly at its adversaries, became momentarily entangled in a briar patch. The nearest hunter lunged, driving his club at the top of its skull. Blood spewed from an ear as lungs expelled precious air. Staggered, yet standing, the beast squealed the attack, darting under an adjacent tormentor's legs, causing him to pitch forward into the brambles. Out of the cordon, it raced for low ground. Kostahk, moving from the flank to intercept, tripped over a vine and crashed heavily to earth, striking his unprotected head.

A crimson stain seeped through rumpled hair. His head, crushed at the left temple, lay concavely cupped over a protruding rock. Rivulets of red melted surrounding snow as warm blood flowed through to the frozen ground beneath. Kostahk had been rendered instantaneously unconscious.

Valiantly, his heart beat, but instead of pumping life, it hastened death. The wound at his temple began pulsing as the heart, sensing his body failing, redoubled its efforts to provide sustenance. Quietly, Kostahk's life ebbed. The mutant virus that had benignly infected him and ravaged Mok, disappeared into the snowpack and expired with its host. It would have to wait for another spontaneous generation or the revitalization of a dormant cousin before wreaking havoc upon the human species.

. . .

Uncharted and sparsely inhabited, central Africa's luxuriance in the thirteenth century belied its fragile nature. Gargantuan trees received supplemental support from neighbors' ensnarled branches as their own partially exposed root systems clung tenuously to shallow, infertile soil. When disease or catastrophe denuded a section, torrential rains eroded the precious loam veneer, leaving only a persistent scar.

Variegated birds soared above and flitted through the foliage, singing in harmonic counterpoint. Solo voices penetrated the din; celebrating life, advertising for a mate, or shrieking death. Camouflaged snakes draped over tangled branches feigned drowsiness while lying in ambush to feast on slow-witted meals. Chattering and scolding primates hung by hands and feet or dangled adolescently from prehensile tails when not racing playfully about their communal jungle. Consuming vegetation and each other, trillions of creatures thrived or perished in their embryonic, insect and disease-ridden world.

The veldt awaited the onslaught of the Boers with the civilization and conflict they would bring. Diamonds lay deep within the earth destined to unleash murder and intrigue upon discovery and extraction. Seemingly endless savannas accommodated game that one day would attract white hunters bearing such awesome firepower that extinction would befall dozens of species and millions of individual animals. Sluggish rivers spawned life; carnivorous fish and hungry crocodiles coveted splay-legged giraffes drinking at their banks.

Prince Henry had yet to send his navigators–more concerned with safety than discovery of the unknown–bumping along the

Atlantic coast. Vasco da Gama wouldn't sail for two and a half centuries. Arabian and Indian traders were plying east-coast waters but not venturing inland to disturb the ecological and sociological balance. Elephant carcasses were not rotting tuskless in the subtropic sun as jackals and vultures jousted and feasted. Slavers were not trading a few barrels of rum for one's neighboring tribesmen.

Into this improbable world of plenty and famine, safety and peril, peace and terror, exuberant life and vile death, the virus reemerged.

. . .

The cattle stirred, nervous and disorganized. A panoramic sweep of the area by the young herdsman revealed nothing, yet their agitation coincided with an alarmed lowing urging him to rise and once more search the horizon. Nothing . . . nothing . . . no, wait! The morning sun was blinding but there seemed to be a shape.

Shading his eyes with a cupped hand–the other involuntarily tightening on the spear–he espied a lion canting its head, feigning nonchalance. Only a nervous, irregularly twitching tail betrayed the tension of its stalk. The beast yawned, ponderously studied a paw, licked it, and lay down facing north. Clearly visible now, this small but mature male, wise and wary, expected success. The cat arose, glanced noncommittally at the herd, turned tail and sauntered over the knoll.

Cognizant of the ruse, the youth commenced jogging toward his charges, simultaneously scanning the hill, confident the predator would return. Suspicions were confirmed when he detected motion south of the lion's last location and more directly downwind. Crouching down, convinced he was undetectable with the sun to his back, the cat was slinking with deceptive feline speed toward the nearest cow. The young man broke into a run, and the lion, abandoning pretense, did likewise.

Blind courage propelled the youth toward certain mauling and possible dismemberment and death. The lion closed rapidly with huge leaping bounds, silently raising dust with each impact. Eyes locked on the slack throat of his targeted victim, he ignored the frail human racing to challenge him.

The predator leaped as the youth sped in front of the cow, ramming the lance's base into the ground while positioning its tip in the path of the descending feline body. Though momentum carried him from danger, the boy's shoulder struck the earth, re-injuring a wound incurred the night before during a good-natured tussle with an older brother.

Belatedly sensing vulnerability, the lion violently twisted and contortedly retracted its haunches in a futile attempt to change trajectory. The spear impaled his neck, severing the spine between two vertebrae. Dead before hitting the ground, the cat crashed to earth at the feet of the befuddled cow, which trotted a few yards before resuming its grazing on spindly vegetation.

Arterial feline blood spurted onto the victor's lacerated shoulder as fear and rational processes replaced bravado and adolescent testosterone. Shaking and wincing, but incredibly proud, he dusted his cloak and wiped intermingling human and animal secretions from his abrasion.

Hours before the lion's ill-fated attack on the Masai herd, it had spied a sickly, unattended baby monkey. A loping run; a graceful pounce; and it secured a small, tender meal. The virus invaded through a fissure in the beast's mouth and remained viable until fate provided a better host. By year's end, multiple diseases wracked the unfortunate lad. Always slender, he became little more than skin and bones before sores erupted, resisting all treatment.

His death thwarted the disease until 1498–the year da Gama sailed around Africa–when a viral carrier in the Congo married his betrothed. Retiring to a mean hut at the edge of the clearing, they consummated their union. Villagers rushing to indulge their communal penchant for voyeurism were rewarded with muffled sounds of conjugal joy followed by a burst of climatic utterances. Raucous cheers erupted outside while the newlyweds smiled and tightly embraced, but now she too was infected.

However, their marriage was not blessed with children, and since she did not seek impregnation from another, though his brother offered, and he refused a cousin of his wife, commitment to monogamy contained the disease.

. . .

11

Another three centuries lapsed before the malady reemerged when, in the early decades of the 1800's, several mysterious deaths occurred. All were suspiciously similar, unlike any known ailment, and geographically confined to the vast Congo basin. After a brief remission, numbers held steady the remainder of the century with the world medical fraternity blissfully unaware of the impending malaise.

The virus gained its long sought foothold in the south-central jungles of turn-of-the-century Africa. A young boy, destined to be sexually insatiable, was bitten by the sickly monkey he was tormenting. His puncture wounds healed, symptoms failed to develop, and the incident was relegated to the forgotten memory of all such childhood mishaps.

Keokoshee blossomed into a handsome youth, surreptitiously helping himself to all available females. As word of his prowess spread, so too did the legs of village maidens; except for Fala. Since her disinterest affronted Keokoshee's royal manhood, he specifically made his wishes known and invited her to his hut. She tactfully declined. He ordered her to come; but she didn't. In a weak moment he begged; only to receive a polite refusal. As retaliation, he spread the word she was unclean.

For a while Keokoshee sublimated his urge to bed Fala by accelerating his sexual activity with the bevy of the willing. Unfortunately, Fala continued to dominate his thoughts–especially during climax. Finally, he could tolerate it no longer. He was the son of the chief, and Fala would submit!

Determined after a sleepless night, he invaded her hut at dawn and brusquely shook her awake. As drowsy eyes opened, a hint of a smile flickered across her face only to be quickly replaced by anger, but Keokoshee would have none of it. He demanded she report to his hut at sundown.

To his surprise, she acquiesced, carelessly letting her night robe fall away, allowing Keokoshee a fleeting glimpse of the most alluring patch of pubic hair he had ever beheld. Flustered and flushed with anticipation, he muttered some inappropriate, incoherent orders, and stumbling over adolescent feet, departed.

He spent the day in total confusion, walking aimlessly about the village, encountering her twice. First, she avoided his gaze, but the second time flashed a shy smile that set his loins on fire. It took rigid self-control to resist finding a girl to relieve the pressure. But no, that would spoil his explosive climax inside her that night.

Fala arrived early, wearing a thin fabric wrapped twice about her hips, once over nubile breasts and protruding nipples. Displaying a demure smile upon entering the hut, she brushed his cheek with willing lips, then slowly removed the wrap to reveal youthful cleavage. Transfixed, he stared at her ripening beauty, deep, dark-brown haloes encompassing maturing nipples. The final two layers fell away, rendering her naked. Awestruck, he tentatively reached for her breasts, but she gently diverted his hands to the outward curve of her sculptured hips, guiding his palms over her buttocks. His fingers curled against small dimples where delectable cheeks met the tops of velvet thighs.

Oozing seminal fluid dampened his loincloth. He begged her to lie down. Fala nodded assent; but first, might she wet him to prevent his enormity from hurting her? It was, after all, her first time. Oh, great and good goddess of fertility! She smiled, kissed him lightly on the lips, then fell to her knees and took his throbbing glans into her mouth. He felt the first bump of climax, tried desperately to stem the flow, knowing it would surge, and then she simultaneously bit down and cuffed his testicles!

Pain ricocheted though his groin, radiating to the small of his back and down his legs. His involuntary scream pierced the early evening air as he collapsed to the mats holding his crotch, too terrified to look. Fala quickly inspected him, satisfied herself no major damage had been inflicted and kissed him gently on the mouth. Gathering her wrap, she left the hut to intercept converging villagers.

Keokoshee fled into the jungle, mortified and humiliated. He, the great Keokoshee, sire of half the tribal children under four, son of the chief, had been rejected. How could he show his face again?

Late the following day, as he sat morosely on the bank down-river from the compound, jumping at every sound for fear it was a villager, Fala soundlessly slipped up behind him. Startled, with no time to feign anger or superiority, he listened to a proposal of monogamous marriage. If he accepted, she was prepared to demonstrate the carnal delights she had to offer. Any breach of their agreement and he would never lie between her thighs again. Acquiescence came quickly and humbly–but wait, what of his shame? She assured him the villagers believed it was nothing more than a shoulder bitten in frenzied ecstasy.

The end of the incubation period for some of Keokoshee's early conquests coincided with his and Fala's nuptials. By the time Fala turned twenty-two, the epidemic prompted a decision to gather her immediate family and flee. After many days journey through unfamiliar jungle, they encountered a friendly, compatible tribe, and following negotiations with the chief, settled in.

Years passed with no incidence of the disease, convincing Fala she had been wise. Only after her oldest child married did the first case develop. Approaching middle age with nowhere to flee, they lived to see their adopted village ravaged. When Keokoshee died at sixty-one, the unrecorded worldwide death toll surpassed the fifteen hundred mark. It was 1951; and the virus was firmly entrenched.

. . .

By 1978, cases outside central Africa were reported, and files thickened at medical facilities around the world. There was no name for the disease, for it might be a variation of a known illness or perhaps no ailment at all, just sickly individuals.

Most reports originated in undeveloped areas. What did natives know? It wasn't as if the data came from Cairo or Monrovia or Johannesburg. Witch doctors. A tribal belief in a curse. Voodoo. Psychologically susceptible people developed real symptoms, and some died. It happened in Haiti, why not Africa? Medical professionals added haphazardly to their files and waited. No research teams were formed, nor money appropriated. No doctor displayed any special interest–except one, and his involvement predated the disease's official discovery in 1979 by ten years. Twenty-six and a graduate of Ohio State University, in 1969 he began serving an internship at the prestigious Northcoast General Medical Center in Cleveland, Ohio.

14

The disorder, casually mentioned in a lecture during his sophomore year of medical school, fascinated him. The topic centered around diseases that predominately attacked one race and/or were geographically confined such as Tay-Sachs, which afflicted eastern European Jewish infants, and HTLV, entrenched in southern Japan. This ailment seemed to predominately affect blacks. He was black.

It took a month of searching to locate Northcoast Medical's sparse file, which surfaced at the back of a folder on rare, unnamed viral diseases in the influenza section. Four sheets, nine years old. Whoever started it must have lost interest or was no longer associated with the hospital.

He initiated a letter campaign to facilities that might have information, convinced it was a new and distinct infection. He wrote to the government of Zaire. Personnel were helpful, though guarded in their response. It was flattering to have someone in the mighty United States interested, quite another to acknowledge a strange scourge indigenous to their countrymen. He contacted top immunologists, corresponded with leading virologists, read and reread every account of unusual death, gleaning a point here, a lead there. Before his internship was completed, Dr. William Fairchild possessed the most inclusive files on the disease in the world.

. . .

Elders reminisced about a time when village clearings required constant attention to prevent the encroaching jungle from reclaiming hard-won space. Late middle-aged individuals remembered the slash and burn era as an ill-fated attempt to feed a burgeoning population. Those in their late thirties and early forties vividly recalled the sad futility of it all as starvation and civil war snuffed more lives than accidents, disease, or advancing age. All the young knew was devastation. Hundreds of square miles of virgin jungle that once demarcated the savannas from the veldt ceased to exist. Those two words–more properly descriptive of the current landscape than any former terms for the sprawling Congo basin–became increasingly interchangeable and were applied to the entire region by news media the world over. The only common frames of reference among generations were the malaise and the presence of United States Army Omega units dotting the African continent. Swarms of helicopters spewed forth daily from each base, carrying teams of medical specialists to aid and treat skyrocketing numbers of afflicted. Descending en masse upon a village, they spent hours performing triage and dispensing food, medicine, and supplies; then departed in a mechanical flurry, evacuating individuals in need of hospitalization.

As the decade of the nineties neared its end, a fourth mutation was detected, its explosive proliferation imminent. While Type 4 could no more survive prolonged exposure to air than any other form of the virus, avenues of transmission were greater, and its life expectancy outside a fluid medium was sufficient to render containment questionable.

PART II

PROLIFERATION

"If He (God) wants us to control it (AIDS), He will provide a cure. If not, the population of the world–now wildly out of control–will be decimated beyond our comprehension."*

John H. McDonnell,
Candidate for President
of the United States

*Response to a question at a Born Again Baptist Convention in Louisville, Kentucky.
July 2, 2003

2

It was dusk when the medevac helicopters neared the field. Normally in a widely spaced, higher altitude formation to reduce the particulate density of rotor-generated vortices, they approached in tight single file, flying low to compensate for fading light. Their mission had run hours longer than expected, triage a nightmare as steadily rising numbers of severely ill conflicted with overcrowded conditions at the base hospital. Every building was bursting its seams with patients lining narrow halls and overflowing into anterooms and examination areas despite the consolidation of numerous offices to free space for additional makeshift accommodations.

The situation was traumatic, but soon the decision of whom to transport and whom to abandon in the stricken countryside would be wrested from medical personnel. With no more room, all treatment would be in the field. Increasingly, doctors and nurses were asking themselves and each other why it mattered. They all die!

Sensing familiar pulsations, the pretty nurse looked through the window and spotted the landing lights of the returning squadron. Knowing the mission was behind schedule, she had worked late, skipping supper in order to dine with her special friend. Now that he was back, she was determined not to miss one precious moment of the remaining evening. Hurriedly slipping out of uniform and pulling on a pair of tight jeans, she inhaled deeply and fastened the top snap, closing the zipper with a final tug. Donning an oversized tee shirt, she cast a dissatisfied

19

glance at her image in the mirror, shrugged at the futility of doing anything creative with her hair, muttered, "Hopeless," and headed for the landing zone.

The air was foul. Bad enough when the choppers converged from higher flight levels, this twilight maneuver in the absence of a dispersing breeze guaranteed maximum atmospheric pollution. Propelled by rotor downdrafts, churning debris enveloped the camp as one by one the helicopters touched down. A weary pilot exited the lead Huey, and striding through the encroaching darkness, broke into a tired grin when he saw the young girl standing at the edge of the field.

"Hi, honey," he greeted, lips gently brushing her cheek.

She returned his kiss. "You look exhausted."

With the mission flight log tucked under his arm, he took her extended hand, and together they walked toward the lighted complex of buildings designated Omega 22.

"Don't you have to check in?"

"I reported by radio. I'll do paperwork before lift-off tomorrow."

That knowledge visibly upset her. "You have to go out again?"

"The medics barely made a dent."

"So much for our day off," she observed, not bitter or whining, but deeply disappointed.

"Sorry. You eat?"

"I waited for you."

"Thanks."

They stopped outside a nondescript bachelor officers' quarters.

"Give me ten minutes to shower and change," he requested, kissing her squarely on the lips, a little hard and territorial.

"Mind if I come in?"

The pilot stared for several seconds at his winsome paramour. She was svelte–except for the big tits. Dark, almost black hair, tossed into casual waves by the rotor, surrounded her face and fell about her shoulders. Cute and pretty, with nicely proportioned features, she had enough Italian blood to be sensuous without effort.

20

Openly lecherous, he finally said, "If you want."

"I'll cover my eyes when you're naked."

After detouring through the Officers' Club to obtain beer, they re-crossed the commons and entered another look-alike building housing the mess hall. Acknowledging mission colleagues already assembled, they selected light meals before seeking as private a table as the austere facility provided.

Preoccupied, neither showed much interest in food. She picked at her salad, realizing anything consumed this late would leave her uncomfortable if not a little nauseous.

"Was it worse than usual?" she asked, sensing his dismay.

"No," he lied, "just longer. How was your day?"

Exhibiting a noncommittal expression, she started to answer, "Fine," then abruptly changed her mind. "Terrible. We can't surrender another square foot for patient beds and have sufficient office, lab, and treatment areas in which to function. I'm working out of a closet," she exaggerated.

The pilot stared blankly into space. "Won't matter soon," he commented. "Compared to six months ago, there's hardly anyone left, and those we find are so sick, it's pointless treating them. When current patients die, there won't be replacements."

"It's the end of the world, isn't it?"

"Maybe not everywhere; it sure as hell is here."

"Any idea when you'll be back tomorrow?"

"Fourteen, fifteen hundred. Not late."

She gave in to a sigh of resignation. "Could be worse. Want my salad? I don't feel like eating." She pushed the bowl across the table.

"Thanks."

"Let's turn in early. I'll make it worth your while."

"You always do."

"Flatterer."

"Works, doesn't it?"

. . .

Eight miles outside of Manila, on a dusty, heavily traveled road off the highway, a diverse convoy of aging trucks and battered vehicles was lining up at the entrance to Burial Facility 3. Drivers remained in their cabs, anxious to unload and not

21

fraternize with other operators whose cargo might be more putrid than their own. At first, only hearses transported bodies, but over time their use diminished, as larger, more efficient carriers were required. Gutted buses and covered tractor-trailers now performed the bulk of the macabre task.

Conventional transportation could be afforded by the wealthy, but due to shortages, most caskets, instead of matching the hearse's elegance, were Spartan boxes hastily constructed from cheap materials. The poor, praying they could find any container or conveyance prior to decomposition, coped and endured.

Before the infection reached epidemic proportions, family, friends, and clergy were present for graveside services, but now the dead were lucky to have anyone in attendance.

Individual burials were yielding to stacking as backhoes dug excavations, and front-end loaders filled the holes after the third body was in place. Mass graves were under consideration, and only the most naive felt they could be forestalled much longer. Awaiting legislative authorization for mass necropolises, earth-moving equipment was already requisitioned and available in motor pools near the graveyards.

The Graves' Registration branch of the Philippine army had been expanded to handle interment and record keeping. Even so, senior military officials privately conceded uncertainty over the exact burial location of many victims, and discrete discussions were held to consider replacing individual grave markers with a roster posted near each facility's entrance.

Unfenced cemeteries were surrounded by yellow tape to warn people away, and as an additional health precaution, bodies were stripped of valuables to forestall exhumation and robbery. Because established burial parks filled rapidly, suitable farmland adjacent to population centers—thereby minimizing transportation distances—was acquired through military fiat or eminent domain. Although new grave locations were chosen to reduce physical and psychological health hazards, monitoring contamination of underground water supplies remained a high priority since sanitation standards were mercilessly reduced or ignored.

The population had decreased dramatically over a decade

with the majority of losses occurring during the last two years. Relatively few babies, predominantly those born to young girls impregnated by neighboring boys in outlying districts, were disease-free. Flight from the cities well underway; citizenry in infection-free rural pockets were heavily armed, killing anyone that approached unbidden. Official communiques predicted burnout in 2008 with attrition over ninety percent. Only the isolated few would survive.

A signal indicated the cemetery was open. The first truck passed the gate and, following instructions from a man directing traffic, turned left on the interior road. The quiet countryside echoed with sounds of starting engines belching fumes into the still morning air, masking the smell of death.

. . .

Several time zones away in Georgia, that former republic of the old USSR, a family was discussing the erratic behavior of their third and youngest son. Always gregarious and pleasant, he had grown to be a charming and socially adept young man.

Recently, however, he had undergone a marked personality change, becoming distant and absent-minded. Nineteen-years-old and possessing an enviable scholastic record, he remained–in spite of apparent problems–remarkable, although it did seem odd he spent an inordinate amount of time with a handful of effeminate young men, most from outside the immediate area.

Because of his impressive musculature and strength, the family was initially concerned, then alarmed, as he progressed from one affliction to another. Coupled with a noticeable weight loss, his deterioration commanded attention. But though he was often the sole topic of conversation, not one family member had an inkling of his true condition until a fortnight later, when the local hospital administrator called informing them the diagnosis was AIDS. They had little knowledge of the disease, and mercifully, no idea how it was transmitted.

. . .

A solid looking man just under six feet, with a tendency for a heavy beard and possessing strong weathered hands, President John McDonnell belied an erudite background. Pre-occupied this morning, he stared through the windows of the Oval Office at the

23

descending gloom. Winter, late in arriving, but now firmly entrenched, showed few signs of abating. Weather conditions were dismal, even for Washington in February.

Addressing the only other person in the room–his immaculately barbered, manicured, and attired aide–he commented, "Bob, like everything else I've inherited with this job, AIDS research is chaotic."

Harrison, noting the President's stance, recognized a soliloquy about to commence. His function was to listen until it was over, then assume the role of antagonist.

"Everywhere I look," McDonnell continued, running his fingers through his thinning, receding, gray hair, "there is duplication of effort with only perfunctory communication within the research community. The most basic discovery is jealously guarded, and I've yet to get a straight answer on what anyone is doing and hopes to accomplish.

"I wouldn't care if everyone was busting ass, but they aren't. During my tour through research facilities last week, I walked unannounced into the office of a department head and caught him reading a goddamned newspaper–the sports section, no less. Little I know about science and less about AIDS; however, it's obvious until someone takes charge, issues orders, and kicks ass, we're never going to make progress. It's as bad as in education–and I should know, having been a professor for thirty-two years, when in a burst of insanity, I let some influential people talk me into becoming a politician. Worst damned decision of my life!" Without turning, the President paused to stretch. "Where was I?"

"About to bemoan the sorry state of education."

McDonnell cast a sidelong glance, indicating Harrison's sarcasm was not appreciated.

"So I was," he acknowledged, returning full attention to the blackness beyond the security lights. "*Fucking* educators reinvent the wheel every ten to fifteen years and have the audacity to call it innovation. When I retired, pontificating assholes traveled the country collecting outrageous fees for conducting seminars on ideas discredited when I was in college, for Christ's sake!"

"Yes, sir."

McDonnell spun around, visibly annoyed. "Yes, sir? All

24

you can say is, 'yes, sir'?"

"Would you like me to say, sir, that you shouldn't digress?"

The President's temper flared until he remembered why he selected Bob. This man was a lightning rod, detecting and dissipating irrelevancy.

"My point, Robert, concerns disorganization and incompetence. Without direction, chaos reigns. Doesn't matter if it's in education, business, or medical research. We need a take-charge person who can cut through bullshit, sift out promising leads, and ruthlessly enforce decisions."

"Begging to differ, sir, researchers won't take kindly to that, and I'm not sure your approach is scientifically defensible."

"Oh, you aren't? Well, damned little has been accomplished in the last twenty years! I'm telling you, Robert, I refuse to condone the status quo. AIDS is my *number one* priority, and as President, I have the clout to get the research ball rolling!"

"I'll call Atlanta and Walter Reed. Even Toronto if you think it will do any good."

"What for?"

"To compile a list of candidates for your . . . research czar."

"Do you have any idea who we'd get? Closet politicians masquerading as research specialists! Forgive my analogy, but I watched this fester in education for three decades. Pseudo-intellectuals, bereft of ideas to enlighten their cerebrally vacuous young charges, fled the classroom to goldbrick in some inane staff-development job. If just *one* had admitted he was burned out and couldn't stand the self-centered little bastards another moment. Those with an ounce of mettle stayed in the trenches and slugged it out or retired to give young blood a chance."

"Sir."

McDonnell raised his hand to stay subordinate censure. "I'll get back to my point, *which is*, I don't want some bureaucratic incompetent included on the list because he or she politicked, ass-kissed, clawed, manipulated, or *fucked* his or her way to the top!"

"Then, with all due respect, how should I go about selecting candidates?"

"No need to. I've already picked someone."

Harrison raised an eyebrow. This was quite arbitrary, even for McDonnell. "Does he or she have a name?" he inquired, piqued that he hadn't been informed.

"*He*. And do be careful, Robert. Diplomacy may not be your strong suit but a little pandering wouldn't hurt your career. God, I love that word. Be forever indebted to Tsongas for using it so adroitly."

"I'll begin pandering immediately," Harrison smirked.

"God, you are an arrogant, impudent pain in the ass."

"Thank you, sir."

McDonnell broke into a broad smile. "Dr. William Fairchild. From Cleveland's Northcoast Medical Center. Remember him?"

"No."

"He was one of the specialists I summoned to Washington my second week in office to ascertain the state of our research. A subsidiary motive was to select a 'czar', as you so aptly termed the position. Dr. Fairchild has been thoroughly investigated and exceeds my criteria. Intelligent, dedicated, superbly organized, he has been on the trail of AIDS his entire professional life. In short, one impressive son of a bitch."

"Will his colleagues at more prestigious institutions accept him?"

"They have no choice."

"Why not?"

"He's African-American. After the fallout that settled on the Senate Judiciary Committee investigating Clarence Thomas, who would have the effrontery to challenge him?"

"Suppose he refuses the appointment?"

"See to it he doesn't."

"*Sir*, with all due respect . . ."

"Stop using that insipid expression!"

Harrison unsuccessfully fumbled for an alternative phrase. "Sir, *you* should handle this."

"You want clean hands if he turns out to be incompetent as an administrator?"

"*No, sir*, not at all!" Harrison was legitimately distressed.

"Have him here Wednesday at 10 a.m. Set aside the rest of the morning. And plan to sit in."

. . .

Fairchild's intercom chimed.

"Line one, Doctor," a pleasantly competent voice reported, "a Mr. Robert Harrison, Office of the President."

"Thanks . . . of what?"

"The United States."

"Oh."

. . .

Most people receiving an unexpected request, to meet for an unknown purpose with the President of the United States, would be nervous, conceivably exhibiting a reaction similar to a student called in by the principal or an employee summoned by the company's CEO. Congressman Charlie Grant had no such emotion.

The middle-aged representative from Ohio felt only curiosity as he approached the Oval Office, for President McDonnell was a lifelong friend, fellow northeast Ohioan, educational colleague, and most importantly, mentor during the Congressman's undergraduate years over two decades ago. It was hard to think of John Harvey McDonnell as anything but a gentle academic, who vacillated between withdrawn introspection and a curious extroversion years of teaching instill in the shyest of people.

McDonnell had entered politics via the back door, having been aggressively recruited as a dark horse by a well-oiled party machine desperate to find an untainted candidate–a la Ross Perot–with presidential possibilities from a populous Midwestern state. Party elders wanted someone with homespun charisma to attract votes and naive in political machinations so he could be manipulated. In short, they envisioned a modern Lincoln to lead America from the fray rather than into it.

McDonnell's secretary smiled and rose as Grant entered the reception area, wondering anew what it was about him that commanded attention.

Quiet and unassuming, he was a study in blandness. Of average height and weight, he possessed mousy brown hair, a medium complexion, and regular features. Comparable attired, he would never be picked out in a crowd, and yet, up close, he projected an undeniable presence that riveted. Perhaps it was his innate decency lurking within sleepy, hazel eyes. That alone made him different, as concern for others was a rare commodity among the self-seeking elected and non-elected predators that peopled the halls of Congress.

"He's expecting you," she commented, moving from behind her desk.

"Representative Grant of Ohio," she quietly announced, before silently closing the door behind him.

"Charlie, it's good to see you!"

The new President exploded from his chair and quickly came around the desk to pump Grant's hand. Maintaining his grip, he pulled the congressman several steps closer to one of two other individuals present. Vaguely familiar, looking burdened and fatigued, the man ponderously rose to his feet.

"Meet Dr. William Fairchild, chief of AIDS research at Northcoast Medical."

"Which Northcoast?" Grant inquired, extending his hand.

"The eastside one near the Cleveland Clinic," the doctor answered. "We're independent."

"Bill just flew in from CDC in Atlanta," McDonnell stated.

Grant looked blank.

"Centers for Disease Control," the President supplied. Charlie's expression indicated acute embarrassment at failing to recall those universally recognized initials. "Don't let it bother you, you're as tired as the rest of us. Bill, this is Charlie Grant, former protege and long-time valued colleague."

"Pleased to make your acquaintance," the doctor greeted. "I've seen you from time to time on the evening news."

"Hard to avoid publicity," Grant modestly responded.

"Inherent in your chosen profession," observed the big African-American. "Of necessity your career thrusts you into the limelight, whereas mine relegates me to perpetual oblivion. Which, I might add, is extremely advantageous most of the time."

Smiling, the President focused attention on the fourth member of the group. "And you remember Robert Harrison, invaluable aide-de-camp and trusty guard dog."

Charlie nodded. The slender, effete man in his mid-thirties–handsome by male or female standards–rose and shook hands.

"Welcome, Representative Grant." With no further exchange of courtesies, he resumed his physical and psychological distance.

"Sit down, Charlie. Sit down," McDonnell urged, retreating behind his desk. "The three of us have been discussing an issue of the utmost importance... the rampant proliferation of AIDS... not only in America, but all over the planet. Dr. Fairchild is the world's foremost authority."

"I thought I recognized you," Grant stated. "You're the new national HIV research coordinator. Sorry I couldn't place you."

"No reason to be embarrassed. Perhaps my fame is premature."

"If Bill worked out of Toronto, CDC in Atlanta, the Cleveland Clinic, or some other equally prestigious place, he'd get more press," McDonnell surmised, "but he chooses to remain where he started, and I support that decision. Bill was learning about AIDS before anyone knew it existed. When it burst on the scene in 1981, he had been hot on its trail for eleven years. Longer, if you count suspicions in college. Travels all over the world for consultations."

"Usually only to Toronto," Fairchild clarified, then casually admitted; "though in truth I use touching bases with their research teams as an excuse to further explore an enchanting city."

"My wife likes Toronto, too," McDonnell confided. "Hopes we can continue to visit now that I'm President. Insists the heterogeneity of the populace will facilitate our blending into crowds, but personally, I doubt we can ever travel incognito again. Unfortunately, she's not comfortable with our new high-profile status or the power of this office. Tells me I'm aptly suited for both. Wonder if that's a compliment or a criticism?"

Noticing his aide's mildly censorious expression, the Chief Executive abruptly changed tack.

"But to the point. You wonder why I've summoned you. Certainly not to reminisce or socialize; none of us has time for that. Charlie, I want you to head an intelligence network on AIDS." McDonnell, noting Grant was nonplussed, held up a hand. "Let me finish before you speak. I've already briefed Dr. Fairchild on your talents and the essential role you can play, so forgive me if I dispense with reiteration.

"Your mission is to become the world's most informed source on the progress of this catastrophic disease. You will supply to Dr. Fairchild and me whatever data we request as accurately and promptly as possible. Currently, only rumors, suppositions, and highly suspect body counts are available. We need to know precisely who has AIDS, for how long, with what symptoms, where they live, and how it is transmitted. Raw data must be collected, codified, and interpreted. You will work closely with the three of us and have the clout of this office at your disposal. Money is no object.

"Perpetuation of the human race depends on your unerring statistical accuracy upon which this man," he indicated Dr. Fairchild, "will guide research and I will make global decisions. At the risk of redundancy, if we fail to find a cure or immunization for AIDS, extinction of the human race is a possibility."

Startled by the proposal and feeling unqualified, Grant said, "I'm flattered, Mr. President, but surely there are others better suited for this position. My knowledge of AIDS is extremely limited."

"What you need to know we can teach you. You won't be determining strategy; Dr. Fairchild and I will. The missing link is intelligence. That will be your domain . . . interested?"

"Do I have a choice?"

"Hell, yes! Do you think I want a half-hearted commitment?"

"He means, 'half-assed'."

Before Grant could react, the President indicated support of Harrison's interpretation while telegraphing the need for more discretion in his choice of words.

"Robert has a tendency to be blunt, Charlie."

"Merely emphasizing a point, Mr. Grant."

"Take my offer under advisement. Talk to Sarah. If you accept, you won't be home much. And see what arrangements can be made with your staff. I can't exempt you from regular congressional duties and constituent responsibilities, but I can ameliorate your committee work. Mostly bullshit, anyway. People on the Hill waste incredible amounts of time rehashing the obvious and preening before cameras. Protects them from doing any real work. Sleep on it, Charlie. Mull it over, then call me."

The dismissal was obvious. As Grant rose from his chair, McDonnell held his gaze. "There is one more thing. This will put you in the national spotlight. The 'good people' . . . those who vote . . . don't want to hear about AIDS. In fact, less than a decade ago, they convinced themselves it was going away. Even if all goes well, and this atrocity is conquered, you may not become a hero and rise in prominence. Failure is more likely, and your career could be tainted. Does that matter?"

"Yes, but I never expected to get this far."

"A healthy attitude. Call me before the weekend."

. . .

Situated in a quiet, upper-middle class neighborhood, the Grants' stately French Provincial sat further from the street and at a higher elevation than any home for blocks around. No larger than adjacent houses, it exuded an unmistakable superiority of design, materials, and workmanship, and served as a mute architectural reminder that egalitarianism was a sham.

The only illumination at 2:20 a.m. on this moonless night emanated from widely spaced streetlights and a gas fixture strategically located near the juncture of the front walk and driveway. Entry lamps were extinguished and timer-controlled accent units had turned off at midnight.

All the houses were dark, even the elegant brick, unless one were at the rear of the wooded lot looking up at the middle floor. There, masked by heavy decorator drapes, a faint glow betrayed a nocturnal presence.

Exhausted, and sitting on diagonally opposing settees in their small walnut-paneled library, Sarah and Charlie were engaged in a deep, pragmatic discussion.

"Some things don't have a good solution," she commented, then fell silent once more. Disheveled, wrapped in a mint-green terrycloth robe frayed to the point of ruin by their mischievous dog, Sarah sat drained of her usual vitality. Even her frequently expressive face was drawn and troubled. Charlie, never a model of animation, looked worse.

A half-empty wine glass rested on the bookshelf beside a

31

patinated bronze elephant purchased on impulse their first year of marriage. More beer cans sullied the beveled-glass coffee table than either cared to acknowledge.

Sarah was distraught. Aside from not wanting her husband involved with AIDS in any manner, she was dismayed by the prospect of her frequently absent spouse being home less. Too bad the offer was such an honor, the job crucial, and the potential career leapfrog so obvious. But years were flying by, and the outlook for normalizing family life had just grown bleaker. Was her husband's future role in AIDS eradication worth additional family sacrifices? Misgivings abounded. And she wasn't at all convinced AIDS was as rampant as everyone seemed to think!

Granted, drug users and inner-city types were afflicted; thoughtless, selfish men continued to transmit the disease to girlfriends, if that was a properly descriptive term for such casual sexual partners; and HIV-positive women repeatedly bore doomed infants, but Sarah wasn't sure she cared what happened to those people. It *was* tragic for the babies.

She glanced at the clock. In four hours, the kids would be up and another seventeen-hour day would commence. Sarah looked across the room at the man she loved, depressed by the further erosion of time together this job was going to precipitate.

"You have to do this, don't you?"

Their eyes met.

"Yes."

"I agree."

"I'll miss you." He looked so sorry.

"Me, too." A lone tear rolled down her cheek. "I support, you, but I worry about us, the effect on our marriage, the impact on Matt and Jennifer."

"D.C. is only an hour by air. I'll come home at every opportunity, if only to tuck the kids in and sleep with you. *Damn any expense to the government!*"

"Just be careful. Look what happened to Sununu."

"People will have to understand."

"They won't."

Grant acknowledged the wisdom of her remark. "I'll make that a condition of acceptance and put it on the record. More than that..." His voice trailed off and then he defiantly added, "And damn what people think!"

Sarah crossed the room, held out her hand. "We'll manage, we always do. I can't keep my eyes open. Let's go to bed."

Entangled and sharing a pillow, Charlie whispered, "We'll talk more tomorrow."

"No, we won't. Make your call."

3

Four a.m. is a hellish time to rise, and Charlie could not adjust. Barely functional an hour later, he kissed his sleeping wife and children goodbye, then drove through moonlight to the airport and mindlessly boarded the Washington National-bound jet. After leafing through *USA Today* while awaiting takeoff, he closed his eyes and was fitfully asleep before the sun probed the eastern horizon at eighteen thousand feet.

His body never ceased rebelling. Bone weary with queasy stomach and aching head, he tried unsuccessfully to convince himself that life in the fast lane compensated for perpetual misery.

At least this Monday was different. Instead of vying for a cab to his congressional office, a limousine would be waiting to take him to the White House for intensive instruction on HIV/AIDS. Whatever time it takes, the President had said. When he was sufficiently versed, events would be set in motion to establish his new department.

. . .

Small and sparsely furnished, the utilitarian ground-floor room seemed woefully inappropriate for the start of a momentous journey. Symptomatic of the entire structure, the aging West Wing revealed its years in the confined space McDonnell allocated for his training.

A young doctor casually occupying one of two chairs rose as Charlie entered. While appearing capable, he could not have been more than three or four years beyond internship.

"Representative Grant?"

Charlie nodded.

"Thank you for being prompt, a characteristic some members of my profession might emulate. I'm Dr. Harold Taylor from Walter Reed."

"Nice to meet you."

"You, too. Make yourself comfortable, we're going to be here awhile. My instructions are to educate you on the human immunodeficiency virus, aka, HIV. What we know; what we need to learn. I am at your disposal until you feel comfortable discussing AIDS with anyone, including a research scientist, and can comprehend and contribute to the conversation. Erudition is not expected, but reasonable academic facility is. Does that correspond to your expectations?"

"Absolutely."

Grant removed his coat and hung it on the back of the door.

Taylor sat and said, "We'll work until 11:30 or one of us needs a break. Our afternoon session will resume at 1:30 and continue until we complete the scheduled topic. Oh, before I forget, President McDonnell wants you to join him for lunch."

"I was notified on the way over."

"Then let's get started. In the absence of questions, I'll assume comprehension."

"Fair enough."

"I am going to break this down into various categories such as chronological progression; the definition and description of a virus; associated diseases; T-cells; symptoms; causes. Do you follow my logic?"

Dr. Taylor slipped easily into a command instructional mode for one so young. Charlie surmised it must have something to do with the personalities of people who enter the medical profession.

"We don't know when HIV evolved," Taylor proceeded. "It could have been thousands of years ago or during the last century. For the record, AIDS was first observed in monkeys in equatorial Africa, although the specific date is debatable. Not identified as a known disease or labeled a new one, it wasn't perceived as a threat, or concerted action might have been initiated.

"Postdating this, also at an unknown time, the simian virus invaded humans. Fortunately, geographic isolation continued for decades, possibly until the late seventies when it was assumed one or more individuals transported the disease to Haiti. Or New York. There is disagreement about where HIV surfaced in the Americas.

"Regardless, once rooted it spread rapidly across western Hispaniola largely due to voodoo practices that included mixing human and animal blood and urine, which provided fertile new conduits for transmission. We also believe a more potent mutation evolved at this time. In New York... "

Charlie interrupted. "How did it get from Haiti to New York? Or vice versa? Haiti is hardly a tourist Mecca."

"I was coming to that. In the late seventies/early eighties Port au Prince was an erotic smorgasbord for New York City homosexuals. Availability of sexual partners for affluent big-city gays rivaled that of countless teenage girls soliciting heterosexual males in Juarez and other Mexican border towns. The point is, AIDS allegedly found its way from Africa to the Americas. The destination of the original carriers hardly matters because at virtually the same time, 1981-1982, cases were diagnosed in Miami, logical since Dade County is the unofficial capital of the Caribbean. What we can say with certainty is that HIV was entrenched in the Americas by early 1983."

"Confined, though, to homosexuals?"

"Not necessarily. That's difficult to determine from meager empirical evidence but, while not everyone concurs, I suspect because of its prolonged latency, the disease was already prevalent in heterosexuals, albeit fewer cases. Regardless, during this time associated diseases showed a dramatic increase. Pneumocystis for example... pneumonia to the layman... and Kaposi's Sarcoma, which I'll subsequently refer to as KS. Epidemic in Uganda, KS became common in Miami and though uncorroborated, probably New York as well."

"What's KS?" Grant asked.

"A term for a specific skin or lymph cancer."

"Sounds grim."

"Everything about HIV is grim."

The morning progressed rapidly, with Taylor tracing the proliferation of AIDS as it leapfrogged from drug-infested homosexual pockets of New York City, Port au Prince, and Miami to similarly blighted areas in every major urban center. Poverty as an acceleration factor was explored along with race and sexual orientation. Its sudden explosion in San Francisco while cities such as Cleveland and Chicago remained relatively chaste, bolstered the latter contention. Transmission through medical procedures was examined. Any possible path, its plausibility and probability, was scrutinized.

They were so engrossed neither noticed the time until the phone rang, and the President politely inquired whether the next day might be better for lunch. Since it was a breach of protocol to stand up the President, even if he was an old friend, Grant excused himself and hurried to the designated dining area.

. . .

Having exhausted the facts and assumptions concerning the origin and propagation of AIDS before lunch, upon Grant's return, Taylor quickly plunged into an analysis of pathology by starting with a definition.

"Pathogens: any disease-producing organisms; such as bacteria, fungi, protozoa. And naturally, viruses."

"But unlike the others, viruses aren't technically alive," Grant injected, proud of his erudition.

His error was reflected in the doctor's expression.

"They aren't, are they?" Charlie was suddenly unsure.

"A somewhat common misconception," Taylor suggested, careful to protect his charge's ego. "I should have anticipated that and explained earlier. A virus is a nucleic acid with a protein coating which can exhibit growth and reproduction only within a living cell, whereas a bacterium is an organism able to exist independently. Is that clear?"

"Sort of."

"Suffice it to say there is scientific disagreement as to whether viruses are vital or merely mimic life. For research purposes one must assume mortality. Otherwise, why bother? Along with the literary undead, viruses haunt a limbo between life and death, functional, but belonging to neither. Viral research shares a fictional dilemma in that assumed lethal options include the usual methods of elimination, but in variant or highly specific ways.

"For example; animal and avian creatures can be killed by drowning, but not fish, and water applied to the Wicked Witch has the bizarre effect of melting her. And consider all creatures die from impalement with any kind of wooden stake except Dracula, in which case the wood must be . . .?"

"Ash."

"Very good! And in the case of the Wolfman, the bullet can't be any old material but must be . . .?"

"Silver. I'm beginning to understand. Not that it's impossible to destroy HIV, we just aren't sure what to use."

"Haven't a clue is more accurate, but you are getting a handle on how complex the problem is. Let's continue. Whether HIV is alive or aping life, we are able to accomplish the following: Inhibit the virus; AZT and various medicinal cocktails do that...at least for a while... along with several other promising compounds. Also, we can lower the probability of access to human tissue by monitoring the blood supply, educating anyone in the drug culture willing to listen, encouraging condom use, and preaching abstinence or fidelity. In addition, there are several ways to destroy AIDS if we are willing to kill the host cell as well. Chemotherapy and radiation do that. And maybe it doesn't have to be killed, just neutralized."

"How?"

"No one knows, but it opens explorable possibilities. AIDS is a retrovirus which turns an invaded cell into a virus factory. Perhaps that process can be further interrupted, a line of research currently being pursued by Dr. Fairchild in Cleveland. He theorizes that if the protein membrane can be broken down, cell penetration will be stymied, thereby eliminating reproduction."

"Is that possible? To destroy the envelope?"

"Certainly. It's easily dissipated by heat, numerous simple chemicals... soap, for example... and ultraviolet light. Even exposure to room temperature."

"So, what's the problem?"

"We can do those things outside the body, where it dies anyway. The dilemma is how this feat can be accomplished once a cell is violated. You see, we've returned to the starting point.

Kill AIDS, and the breached cell and patient die with it."

"Frustrating."

"But not hopeless. This is where antigens come in."

"Antigens?" Though recognizing the word, Charlie was unable to think of its precise definition.

"Targeted antibodies. They represent an extremely fertile area of investigation in which Dr. Fairchild is also involved. You look tired."

"I have a headache."

"If you can endure a few more minutes," Taylor suggested, "we can begin examining T-cells tomorrow."

Grant rubbed his shoulder muscles while nodding his assent.

"Thank you. I'll be brief. Even if we are ultimately successful in interrupting the life cycle of AIDS, anything short of killing it... ash stake through the heart, bucket of water on the Wicked Witch, that sort of thing... may be futile.

"One characteristic of HIV and similar viruses is their ability to regenerate after long periods of dormancy. Years, even. Herpes and some cancers can be in remission, seemingly cured, then flare.

"You *do* look uncomfortable. It's late and I'm tired, too. Tomorrow at 9:00?"

"Nine-thirty."

"Fine."

. . .

"Well, Congressman, have you assimilated yesterday's rather prodigious amount of information?"

Charlie smiled faintly. "I'm working on it."

Dr. Taylor extracted a bulky manila folder from his attache case and placed it on the thick oak table. "Don't be intimidated by this. I dug through my files last evening and made copies of material that might help you. Take it home. Keep anything beneficial and discard the rest." He settled in the chair opposite Grant. "This morning we tackle lymphocytes. Let's determine how much you remember from high school. What are they?"

"White blood cells," Grant answered.

"Close enough. Their function?"

"Fight infection."

"In what part of the body are they produced?"

"Bone marrow."

"Excellent! Where else?"

Grant shrugged.

"The thymus. Do you know its function and location?"

Charlie was surprised he remembered. "A gland in the upper thorax. Sort of disappears as one matures. Don't know what it does."

"That is partially correct. It produces T-lymphocytes, the 'T' designating thymus. We'll henceforth refer to them as T-cells, which act as sentinels, commanding generals. They roam the body looking for invaders, then summon troops if any are found.

"Let's back up. The body also produces B-lymphocytes... 'B' for bone marrow... those white cells you mentioned. B-cells are soldiers, attacking anything they are ordered to: common colds, chicken pox, measles, even transplanted organs because they are foreign to the body."

"Then why don't T-cells send B-cells to kill an AIDS virus?"

"They do until it hides."

Grant frowned.

"AIDS is similar to stealth aircraft, or more correctly, pretends to be something else. Like Dracula turning into a bat."

"It can do that?"

"In a manner of speaking, yes, but more on that later. First, let me elaborate on T-cells. There are two types: 'helpers' and 'suppressors.' Helpers activate B-cells, and suppressors dampen them. In a biologically normal individual, the T-cell ratio of helpers to suppressors is two to one.

"Enter HIV into this closed world. The alien virus is detected, and the attack commences. How do we know? Because tests indicate the presence of specific antibodies. Soon, however, the helper/suppressor ratio reverses, thwarting the immune system while AIDS simultaneously masks its presence by adopting the genetic code of host cells and/or altering its protective coating to confuse B-cells programmed to destroy specific, but no longer recognizable, targets.

"For the record, HIV is not the only disorder to neutralize the body's defenses. Arthritis is a case in point . . . as is Herpes, which causes the same T-cell/B-cell reversal as AIDS. The difference with herpes is when symptoms disappear within days or weeks the cell ratio reverts to normal. Once a person contacts AIDS, the ratio remains inverted forever. Ergo, it is fatal one hundred percent of the time because the patient is eventually exposed to one too many unrelated diseases the body is helpless against."

Captivated by the intricacies of the disorder and riveted by the unfolding horror, Charlie concentrated on every word, assimilating a surprising amount during the first hour. Nevertheless, burdened by the spate of information, he requested a recess.

Upon returning to their cloistered environment, Taylor suggested tabling further analyses of the virus's unique properties to devote the remainder of the morning to less technical and taxing topics. It seemed an appropriate time to delineate symptoms.

Grant recognized most: enlargement of lymph nodes in the neck, armpits, and groin; fatigue, both chronic and debilitating; persistent fever as the body amassed habitual defenses; weight loss; muscle aches; sore throat; skin disorders. The discourse confirmed what any alert individual could glean from the daily news.

Quickly satisfied with his student's absorption of the simple material, Taylor launched into the next explorable area.

"Is there a genetic cause? The profession concurs everyone is susceptible so we need not torment ourselves over why some become infected while others do not. Husbands and wives, for example: where one is HIV-positive, and the other is not. Given proper biological access for the type of AIDS present, the infection-free partner contracts the disorder. It is unproductive to learn why a mate is disease-free. More worthy of investigation is why HIV develops at different rates in different people."

Taylor proceeded to analyze other possible origins and accelerating factors.

"Drugs? Nonsense. Shared needles? Yes. Physiological and/or emotional overload? Certainly, because fatigue weakens the body's defenses as does chronic mental turmoil. Sperm

41

deposited in places other than where nature intended? Hardly."

"You mean AIDS-free sperm entering a fissure in the lower intestine causing HIV?"

"Diplomatically stated. A foolish idea perpetuated by bigots to make the gay community look worse than it is and accept more blame than deserved."

"What about oral sex?"

"Husband and wife?"

"Yes. Is it safe?"

"How can I be delicate, and put your mind at ease? There *is* no way to be delicate. Animals have been licking their own and other's genitalia since the beginning of time. It's safe and natural... for animals. Human beings? Well . . . the utmost hygienic care should be exercised before any such activity, and danger exists if one partner is HIV-positive and a breach is present in the tissue of the mouth or vagina or rectum; any fissure will permit viral entry. On the bright side, the worst a monogamous, herpes/AIDS-negative couple can contract from oral sex is a bladder, sinus, or yeast infection. Most consider any or all worth the price.

"Let's backtrack," Taylor suggested as he rose from the table and began a confined pacing. "There are two schools of thought on the origin of HIV. It is either a mutation of an existing virus... believable... or an entirely new one... possible. Fortunately, we can dismiss both theories as irrelevant and concentrate on why an immune system malfunctions and how to reactivate an impaired one.

"To facilitate investigation of these approaches, researchers consider the following: Are there any observable and/or contributory demographics? That's where you and your soon-to-be-selected team come in. By the way, I'll be teaching them, also. Can an AIDS-precipitated immune dysfunction be reversed or prevented? Several facilities are exploring this area, including Northcoast Medical. Do personal habits contribute as smoking causes cancer and alcohol damages the liver? The literature has documented now obvious factors relating to the acquisition and proliferation of AIDS. Is there anything else? And finally, genetics. I can blithely state some lines of research are absurd, but good technique necessitates a thorough examination of everything. Look at HTLV."

"I've forgotten what that is."

"Human T-cell Leukemia Virus."

"Right! Southern Japan."

"And there has to be a reason why HTLV was historically present there, and AIDS, a related disease, was not... until recently." Taylor glanced at his watch. "If we work through dinner, we can finish today. Are you willing?"

"Absolutely. I'd like a couple of days to catch up on my regular duties and get the hell out of D.C. early Thursday."

"I'll have something sent in." Taylor picked up the phone and placed an order, then said. "Let us review until the steward arrives. Can the virus be detected using ordinary optical instruments?"

"No, only through an electron microscope."

"Describe its appearance."

"Grainy, a charcoal color."

"How many actual cases before 1995?"

"One hundred million, mostly latent, but few believed it."

"Why did the number increase so rapidly?"

"Because AIDS reproduces so fast."

"Another reason?"

"Unlike most diseases which are contagious for a short time, AIDS viral particles are produced and shed in body fluids for a lifetime."

"Name specific fluids," Taylor drilled.

"Saliva, semen, urine, vaginal secretions."

"Which virus has the closest link to human?"

"Simian."

"How long has medical science known about retroviruses?"

"Ninety years."

"How many have been conquered?"

"None."

"Is there natural immunity to a retrovirus?"

"Not that we know of."

"Are there any promising vaccines on the horizon?"

"No."

"Does the body produce antibodies?"

"Yes, but they don't do any good."

"Explain," Taylor demanded.

"The mutation rate is high. Every infected person has several strains. The outer viral coating changes so quickly, antibodies can't recognize the invaders they were sent to destroy. Your examples were stealth aircraft and Dracula."

"How many strains have been catalogued by researchers?"

"Hundreds."

"Can the body's defensive mechanisms sense HIV?"

"Initially, yes, but by genetic alteration they become indistinguishable from normal body cells before the targeted attack is consummated."

"Have any compounds proven effective against AIDS?"

"No."

"What about zidovudine?"

"Commonly known as AZT. Similar to DDC. Not curative. At best, they prolong life and even that is debatable."

"What is unique about HIV-3?"

"Usually confined to heterosexuals."

"Explain."

"Possibly related to vaginal sex. It may be the only type gaining entrance that way."

"Does it exhibit any similarities to HIV-1 and HIV-2?"

"Yes, basically similar."

"Describe HIV-4."

"Aggressive, kills rapidly, becoming epidemic. Transmitted as easily as the common cold. Only sure protection is avoiding the infected. Central Africa nearly depopulated by Type 4."

"What precautions can medical personnel take to protect themselves?"

"Standard operating room procedures."

"Congratulations, Representative Grant. By early evening, you will undoubtedly be laity's foremost AIDS authority."

. . .

Charles Grant pulled into his driveway shortly before midnight Thursday evening. His day had not gone well. Processing backlogged legislative proposals necessitated taking a later flight, which in turn was delayed by inclement weather and repeated de-icings. His only comfort was not spending another night in that damned D.C. apartment.

"Hi!" Sarah enthusiastically greeted him with a warm hug and kiss, diplomatically avoiding any mention of his awful appearance. He must have aged five years since Sunday. "Are you hungry?"

"Just a light drink. Split a beer?"

Shoes off, tie loosened, suit coat tossed casually over the desk chair, Charlie sprawled on the loveseat by the window. After reporting family news, Sarah broached the subject of his private seminars with Dr. Taylor.

"What did you learn about AIDS?"

Avoiding her gaze, Grant stared out the window at falling February snow. Gusts blew a tree branch near a motion sensor, activating security lights. Large flakes shone brightly in the sudden illumination, reflecting a wonderland of sparkling white diamonds descending slowly against a still backdrop of barren, sturdy trees.

"It's hopeless," he uttered without emotion.

4

Bill Fairchild's secretary glanced through the glass partition, noted the time, and wondered what he and research specialist Dr. Eric Li were discussing, for the intensity and duration of the meeting were unusual. Normally, staff conferences were conducted at workstations for document and specimen access and to subliminally emphasize her boss's preferred role of facilitator rather than supervisor.

Oh well, everything that transpired eventually passed over her desk or was shared by the doctor. Roberta returned to her computer as Fairchild rose and resumed a nervous pacing.

"What you're saying, Eric, is you want to transfer all findings and supporting evidence on inhibiting reproduction to Feldstein and exclusively research T-cells."

"That's correct. I feel strongly it will be more productive."

Fairchild sighed, watched his secretary access her word processor's medical dictionary, then turned to Li with a frank admission. "Last summer I was interested in investigating T-cells and felt you were best qualified to supervise research, but decided against it."

"What changed your mind?" If the reason could be determined, perhaps he could undermine Fairchild's reluctance.

"Let's just say, political pressure. There is a desire in Washington to avoid duplication of effort. You must admit to a certain logic."

"The new administration appointed you czar, allowing you great latitude and, I would think, sufficient stature to pursue a pet

46

project."

"Look, Eric, we both know I can authorize any reasonable line of inquiry, but you're evading the issue. Others are doing a fine job, and I have neither the time and energy, nor the desire, to ignite an inter-facility squabble over territorial rights." Fairchild looked at Eric, saw a friend and valued colleague, and gently asked, "Do you understand?"

"Please."

"You are like a goddamned pit bull!"

"It's *your* idea and *you're* the one that came to me!"

Fairchild sat heavily in his chair, and after a long pause, quietly replied without anger or sarcasm, "What makes you think you can do better than teams that have been in place for months . . . years?"

"Focus. No one else is, or will, get anywhere because of his or her incorrect approach. Everyone is trying to alter T-cells to make them more sensitive to chameleon-like HIV, and that won't do any good. Even if it's possible to create a T-cell that recognizes a specific type and strain, the targeted virus will cloak itself in a new 'invisible' form. Asian flu has been doing it since the middle of the last century. Every damned year a new vaccine, and every damned year thereafter, a new strain."

Fairchild probed, "What do you propose that is different?"

"Find a naturally occurring, intrinsically superior T-cell, replicate it and inject the clones into volunteer patients."

"What I alluded to last August, based on cancer research in the nineties."

"Right. Look, I understand some insecure son of a bitch may complain if his area of expertise is invaded, but there is more at stake than some pompous asshole's feelings! You have a moral obligation to try anything that might work!"

Fairchild pondered a moment, opened his office door and asked his secretary for the latest T-cell file.

"Do you want that pulled up on your screen?"

"You know I hate that thing. Please get me the folder."

"Won't take a minute."

"You really ought to become computer-literate, Bill. Once you're familiar with... "

"I *am* computer-literate, and you are in *no* position to suggest *anything* to me!" Fairchild sharply retorted.

"Sorry."

Waiting in the doorway until Roberta retrieved the documents, he thanked her, returned to his desk, and began flipping through the pages, engrossed by their contents. After several minutes, he pushed the packet across his desk. Li made no attempt to reach for it.

"Aren't you interested in your counterparts' progress?"

Li shook his head, ignoring the touch of sarcasm. "I already know what they're doing."

Fairchild leaned back in his swivel chair, closed his eyes, and worked his head from side to side trying to relieve chronically sore neck and shoulder muscles.

"Describe *specifically* what you propose to do," he instructed, "omitting *nothing*. Convince me this would be worth the bullshit I would have to endure."

Li smelled blood, psyched for the kill.

"First, we amass statistical evidence that while AIDS is inevitably fatal, survival times are wildly divergent, thereby proving people exhibit varying levels of resistance. If that was not true, there would be a standard period of incubation and duration as in childhood diseases."

"'Suggesting' might be more clinically accurate than 'proving,' but continue."

"HIV is similar to carcinomas in this regard. Both have unpredictable onslaughts after inception and periods of remission. With some cancers, however, a cure occurs or the remission is so long, something else kills the patient . . . like old age. I'm joking, but only a little. If we can achieve dormancy for decades, in a way we will have 'cured' AIDS."

"Fascinating premise. Not entirely original, but noteworthy."

Li acknowledged the compliment.

"AIDS, on a continuum, is simply the most resistant to natural defenses. The body loses one hundred percent of the time, but out there, somewhere, are people with genetically superior T-cells."

"Or something in the immune system."

"Granted, but we have to limit this and start somewhere. I propose selecting a statistically random study group, meticulously researching and verifying their medical histories, and analyzing their T-cells. Genetic variations must account for differences in longevity."

"And what is your goal after isolating the most effective?"

"Further genetic modification to create 'super-cells'."

"Let's say you *are* successful in producing better ones. What then?"

Hesitant as he was to become involved in a project fraught with fratacidic peril, Fairchild began considering newly opened options.

"Replicate and inject them into patients with lower HIV resistance."

"How can you be certain super-cells will replace natural ones?"

"They don't have to. Immunity will increase by virtue of a bigger and better army."

"Not a given, but intriguing."

Li smiled. Victory was imminent.

"However, that is only half the solution," Fairchild objected. "The T-cell ratio must be reversed."

"I can't prognosticate, but what may be present in patients with superior resistance is less interference from suppressors."

"That doesn't seem to be the case."

"I can't answer your objection until we're further along with the research."

"You're assuming approval."

Li leaned forward. "Dr. Fairchild, you are too good a scientist to let this go." He sincerely meant it.

"On one condition, Eric. B-cell structure must be simultaneously examined."

"Done! You won't regret it."

Li pumped his supervisor's hand.

"Undoubtedly, I will. I'll meet with Feldstein today. If he's agreeable, we'll get together and reallocate personnel."

Alone, Fairchild slumped in his chair, deep in meditation. More of a long shot than Li acknowledged, this project had definite possibilities, and he appreciated Eric's enthusiasm and persistence. Not wanting to evoke a jurisdictional dispute over a personal project, Fairchild had been hesitant to initiate action, but now that someone else . . . a gentle tap at the door stirred him.

"Sorry to bother you, Doctor," Roberta apologized, "but it's almost one, and I'm going to lunch. Can I get you anything?"

"No, but thank you for asking."

"I may be awhile. I'm going to walk to University Circle, grab a sandwich, and eat it on the way back."

"Be careful. This neighborhood deteriorates by the minute."

"I'll be okay. Kelly's going with me."

Fairchild drifted back into his reverie. Futility dampened the rush generated by Li's eager embrace of his theory as the real reason he had not re-approached Eric intruded. The odds for success were slim, and if this concept failed, he was bereft of ideas.

. . .

It was quitting time before Li was summoned. Tired and concerned, he sat stiffly in a green vinyl office chair waiting for his boss to speak.

Without looking up, Fairchild said, "I talked with Feldstein."

Eric squirmed in his seat trying to get comfortable. "And?"

"Just a second." Fairchild activated his intercom. "Ms. Curtis, please inform Dr. Feldstein I'm ready for him."

"Right away."

"And join us when he arrives."

"Will do."

Returning to Li. "Feldstein, cantankerous son of a bitch that he is, has reluctantly agreed to accept your current project in addition to his own oppressive work load, providing you give him two technicians and relinquish some space. Be thankful he's a workaholic."

"I can't spare anyone."

"*Spare* them. It took most of the afternoon and a substantial list of budget-busting concessions to work this out. It's the best deal I could cut."

Li was firm. "I'm going to need all my people, and more space. And additional computer time, plus operators."

50

"*Make do*," Fairchild interrupted as Roberta approached with Dr. Feldstein in tow. He waved them in.

"Aaron, Eric has consented to transfer two individuals and relinquish twenty percent of his space."

Startled, Li was about to object when, unseen by Feldstein, Fairchild sternly gestured for quiet and compliance while verbally stroking his colleague. "That was very gracious of you, Eric."

"And necessary if I am going to assume responsibility for your current project," Feldstein affirmed.

"The least I could do," mumbled Li.

"Paperwork to accomplish this transfer will be completed no later than . . ." Fairchild turned toward Roberta.

"Thursday."

"Thursday. And all changes will go into effect Monday morning. Now, what can I do to facilitate this?"

During the next hour details were hammered out. The last major bone of contention was achieving consensus on personnel transfers, but after that was attained, Li and Feldstein were dismissed, leaving Roberta and Dr. Fairchild alone.

"Go home," he ordered. "You haven't been out of here before 6:30 all week."

"I might suggest the same to you, Doctor. The word is out you often stay until midnight."

"I slow down in the evening," he answered defensively, "and there's no one at home."

"You are *avoiding* the issue. You need *rest*. You're going to leave before 7:00 if I have to walk you to your car!"

Fairchild smiled.

"That won't be necessary. We'll go now. Satisfied?"

"For the time being."

. . .

While Dr. Fairchild and Roberta stood in the employee parking lot recalling the day's events and bidding each other good night, the editorial staff of Moscow's major newspaper was making final changes on an article for the next day's edition. They thanked the Russian people for heeding the advice of their government and the medical profession on controlling the spread of Acquired Immune Deficiency Syndrome. Sound sexual practices, immediate exile of suspected homosexuals, and the certain swift execution of all convicted drug dealers, regardless of age, was successfully combating the plague. Old Bolshevik tendencies were serving them well.

Simultaneously, at Murmansk, a Bahamian-flagged freighter carrying an international crew of malcontents was docked beside a rusted and rotted pier. The captain was anxious to unload, take on cargo, and weigh anchor, but unpredictable Russian red tape and less than energetic longshoremen were stretching the process.

Shore leave was essential, for a surly and mutinous crew could make a horror of any voyage. Even so, the captain hesitated granting leave as it would be impossible to retrieve his crew from the bars and hotel rooms on short notice. Wresting a paid-for bottle from a drunken tar, or pulling a man who had not experienced sex for two months off of even an ugly woman was a formidable task. When multiplied by twenty, it was tantamount to impossible.

The captain solved his dilemma by granting renewable twenty-four-hour passes commencing and ending at 1200 hours. Stragglers could be located, sobered up, or dragged from bed.

. . .

Nicholas Menshekov, the freighter's meticulous first mate, walked the harbor streets without locating any promising establishments. Equally unsuccessful at his last port of call and in urgent need of sexual release, he was little different than other sailors confined to the ship. However, Menshekov's mates were straight; they had no women. Menshekov was gay; he had no man.

Frustrated as midnight approached, Nicholas returned to his cabin in a highly agitated state. Fully clothed, he lay upon his bunk listening to the Arctic waters lapping against the steel hull and shipboard rats scurrying along bulkheads throughout the hold. He smoked a cigarette–it did not help–then read until his eyes rebelled. Mercifully, at 0300 hours, he lapsed into a fitful sleep only to be prematurely jarred awake by a nerve-shattering alarm clock reminding him to report to watch at 0800 so the captain could go ashore. Relieved by the second mate in mid-afternoon, Nicholas retired to his quarters and rested until early evening.

Refreshed and optimistic, he returned to shore. Having had little breakfast and no lunch, Nicholas was famished. Locating a cafe where it appeared the food would not poison him, he ravenously ate. Thus fortified, Menshekov prowled the most promising haunts visited the night before. After striking out once more, he began a methodical coverage of the few remaining places that offered a reasonable chance of success.

Past 2300 hours he was beginning to panic, but shortly before midnight his diligence was rewarded. In the same manner a man and woman sense mutual sexual attraction, Nicholas knew moments after entering the waterfront cafe he had found a willing abettor. After the decent preliminaries any couple would engage in before a tryst, they left for the man's apartment.

At fifteen hundred hours on the following day, a relaxed, satisfied first mate stood on the freighter's bridge, ready to weigh anchor.

. . .

When Menshekov's Murmansk companion kept his appointment for a routine medical exam six months later, he had no idea that within hours he would be arrested. The vaguest hint of physical harm caused a veritable eruption of the names and addresses of numerous sexual partners. Unfortunately, each man supplied a list of comparable length. The burgeoning roster was a source of great mirth among the officers until it grew so long the squad was forced to work on weekends.

To the authorities' chagrin, many of those individuals, either through practiced guile or use of numerous aliases, maintained no regular residence and were untraceable. Official anger was further fueled when it became apparent that they would never determine the identity of the errant merchant sailor. His paramour, still in custody, never knew his name and could not remember the date of their encounter. Authorities were fairly certain that that was true, for they had taken to beating the man with regularity and enthusiasm. Diligent as they were in administering punishment, they were unable to ascertain which freighter was involved, how long it was berthed, or its country of origin.

To assuage part of their anger and frustration, Menshekov's comrade that fateful night was summarily shot. The report listed suicide. Authorities then regretfully informed Moscow that AIDS was not only present in the isolated port, but was, in all probability, epidemic.

. . .

As he delved deeper into the highly restrictive trade bill, President McDonnell felt a familiar surge of hostility and disbelief. For decades even friendly countries had erected tariff barriers and stringent quota systems while the U.S. maintained a policy of relatively equal and unrestricted access to American markets. Did his predecessors and the public believe industry was so firmly entrenched that no country could successfully challenge the United States' manufacturing superiority?

Such a premise was possibly true, but the President felt it was more crass than that. What he suspected was; the selfishness of the rich, plain stupidity so rampant in the masses, and the shortsighted, greedy ignorance of virtually everyone. Americans hadn't just sold their neighbors–and ultimately themselves–down a river of economic ruin; it was their progeny as well. In order to obtain cheap consumer items in the eighties and nineties, eco-nomic serfdoms were created overseas while domestic industries withered and died.

McDonnell read the severity of the trade proposals he had initiated with a twinge of revenge and a touch of glee. Congress had damned well better hang tough and pass this legislation, or the rest of the world would usurp what little domestic manufacturing remained. Ulysses' Siren, which had sounded the Good Life while sucking our life-blood, must be silenced.

. . .

Virtually unknown in Japan during the eighties and early nineties, HIV had insidiously infiltrated the population and, once entrenched, AIDS became epidemic. Lacking erudition of the disease, the Japanese turned to America.

The precedent of compassion set by Douglas MacArthur after World War II–part of their twentieth-century heritage–left them at a loss to understand the newly elected President's reluctance to help. They needed medical expertise and the continuity of foreign sales to provide financial resources to purchase food, petroleum, and the plethora of other things not produced by their sagging economy.

Furthermore, rumors abounded that if they did open their markets, Americans were no longer willing to sell. If true, that attitude was totally beyond the grasp of the Japanese mind, for the Empire had always been pro-Western, selling products overseas at a lower cost than to Japanese citizens. Market dominance was sound business practice, not an anti-American stance. And lately, a new rumor began circulating that McDonnell was considering nationalizing foreign ownership in all fifty states. While such a coup de maitre was impossible, that the idea even existed was incomprehensible. Barring a miracle, the sun was about to set forever on the Land of the Rising Sun.

. . .

Intent on stemming the precipitous decline in population, China went further than its recent abandonment of a decades-old policy of one child per couple. With propaganda and tax incentives, it encouraged large families and subsidized the relocation of carefully screened, non-infected couples into the western mountains. Refugees approaching a clean village without proper clearance, identification, and spotless medical records, were ordered to retreat. Noncompliance resulted in execution. In the midst of the plague, China was striving for survival in a less-populous world.

. . .

The minister postponed the funeral until 11:10 a.m. To delay longer would be cruel, for with each episode of grief, the mother's fragile hold on sanity diminished. But it had to be done soon or her tenuous self-control might dissipate, and she would have to be removed and sedated, thereby, missing the service and burdening her with more anguish later.

The couple's only daughter was dead, and there was no possibility of having another. With two active boys under the age of six, the twenty-five-year-old parents deemed it wise, at the birth of a perfect little girl, for the husband to have a vasectomy. Family finances strained, it seemed logical and intelligent. How were they to know that AIDS would claim their precious daughter?

At 11:15 the mother was sufficiently composed to sit through the macabre funeral service, but the closing of the tiny coffin exceeded her ability to cope. Screaming, she was removed and sedated.

The father, all grandparents except the baby's maternal grandmother, and close friends proceeded to the cemetery. No one–the parents, statisticians, or the President of the United States–knew or would ever know that little Lauren, nineteen months and four days, was victim number 800 million of Acquired Immune Deficiency Syndrome.

After the service the toddler's father stood alone beside her tiny grave, sobbing as he read and reread the inscription he and his wife composed for their baby's tombstone:

LAUREN MARGARET MOHLER
APR 2003 - NOV 2004
SISTER OF ROBERT AND BENJAMIN

He wanted to kill someone, but he didn't know whom.

5

Key members of Charlie Grant's AIDS statistical staff were assembled in the conference room of his 14th Congressional District offices.

"I spent the morning with the President," he announced, opening the proceedings. "He asked me to relay his appreciation for your initial efforts and assure you he understands how traumatic this must be to deal with day after day."

That said, he turned to a young woman seated at the far end of the conference table. "This is Marcie Warner," he introduced. An attractive brunette projecting a quiet self-confidence stood. Athletic looking, though thoroughly feminine, she seemed intelligent and polished, yet somehow unsophisticated. A deep tan hinted at prematurely aging skin.

"As you know, Lisa Pierson resigned to care for her mother. Marcie is on loan from GAO for as long as we need her. Please welcome our new chief statistician." Grant paused as polite applause rippled about the room. "As with Lisa, she'll make intelligible to President McDonnell and me, the voluminous statistical data all of you so diligently and efficiently provide.

"She's from Jamestown, New York and graduated summa cum laude from Cornell in 2002. When I asked the President for the best available person to replace Lisa, he called GAO on the spot, and she was immediately recommended. We are very lucky to get someone of her caliber on short notice."

"What Representative Grant didn't tell you," Marcie smiled pleasantly, "was that when we first met, he hustled me out of his office and called the President to complain about my age and lack of experience. But as you can see, it didn't do him any good."

"*That's* not true," Grant objected.

"Certainly it is," she insisted, "but I would have felt the same." Looking directly at Grant, and then about the table before resuming her seat, she confidently said, "I *am* young to have such a responsible position, but I'll work hard to earn your respect."

"Thank you, Ms. Warner." Grant graciously conceded the truth of her disclosure and moved on with the agenda. Within an hour, all reports had been rendered and the meeting adjourned. Todd Simmons, Grant's congressional aide, entered the room as the statistical people filed out.

"Got a minute, Charlie?" he asked.

"Sure." Grant always made time to listen.

"I just got a call from the Secretary of the Interior. Rumor has it a coalition from both parties, plus some independents, are going to block-vote to kill your park appropriations bill, and I know how much it means to you. If we don't get the measure through, the Cuyahoga Valley Recreational Area and most of the other parks close to population centers are in jeopardy."

"Goddamn it, we had the votes, and it was supposed to be settled!"

"Not any more."

"Goddamn it! Who's spear-heading this?"

"I can guess, but I'm not sure."

"I want *names*."

"We can put the heat on those we suspect are defecting, but I doubt it will do any good."

"When's the floor vote?"

"Friday."

"Fuck!" Grant sat back down and indicated to Simmons to do likewise. "I *want names*. Call in favors; twist arms."

"I'll try, but time's short, and I don't think anyone will talk. These people want to remain temporarily anonymous and push for a quick defeat. Then, if their constituents bitch about it, they can say they felt pressured to dispose of the measure and get on to higher priority things."

"Which they'll also find a way to dodge."

"Probably. Anything to avoid incriminating debate and media scrutiny."

"Cowardly bastards. This is the same shit we had to put up with in the late nineties when the parks were falling apart."

"I suspect they're also using this as smoke to hide their opposition to the President's austerity program and Far Eastern trade bill. They're afraid of offending the Japanese. I'm guessing they intend to point to this and say, 'we cut expenditures'."

"Goddamn it! Deceitful, nickel and dime mentalities frost my ass! Billions for defense, Medicare, and Social Security and pennies for the environment. What really pisses me off is we haven't had a formidable enemy for twenty years, and senior citizens are the most affluent demographic group on the planet. Goddamn it! No one has the balls to confront the Japs or cut the military or entitlements!" Usually unflappable, Grant rubbed his brow in consternation. "I want names."

Simmons looked helpless. "I'll try."

"No." Suddenly calm and calculating, Grant rose and strode the length of the room. "Do this: Get on the phone and round up the big civilian contractors that do park work. Call the EPA and all environmental groups of register. Tell them what's going on and to start blitzing Capitol Hill in support of my bill. Notify any other interested lobbyists and have them collar the suspected leaders of this and tell them in a diplomatic fashion that if the proximity park system gets dismantled, I'm going to have the President line-item veto every fucking pork-barrel project in their district until hell freezes over."

"Can you do that?"

"No… but as devious as these bastards are and as close as I am to McDonnell, they'll believe shit like that."

"Anything else?"

"Stay in touch."

"Will do." Business taken care of, Simmons asked, "Who's the girl?"

"What girl?"

"The last one to leave."

"Oh. She's my new statistician. You were out when I interviewed her. Lisa quit."

"Good looking in a denim sort of way."

"What do you mean by that?"

"Just that she looks like she belongs in jeans."

Grant shrugged.

"Pretty short skirt." There was no reaction. "Nice legs."

"I didn't notice."

"Bullshit! You be careful, she's dangerous."

"I don't even know her."

"You will because she's ready, and she'll see to it."

"Go do your fucking job! If the park bill goes down in flames, your ass goes with it!"

"Just trying to take care of you, Charlie."

Grant gathered his notes, closed his attache case, and entered the hall.

"Hi." Marcie was waiting outside the door.

"Hi." Her smile was enchanting. "Is there something you want?"

"As a matter of fact, there is. Can I take you to lunch?"

Charlie glanced at his watch. "I don't have time. Will a rain check do?"

"Not really."

"Well... do you mind grabbing a bite in the basement cafeteria?"

"Not at all."

"Well... come on."

Moments later, sitting across a small worn table, he said, "I hope I didn't embarrass you by listing your credentials."

"Not at all. And I'm sorry I put you on the spot about your hesitancy to hire me. It was rude to make that public."

"It was rude to excuse you and complain to the President, too. He wanted you, and it was his call. So we're even. What was it you needed to see me about?"

"Nothing specific. I just wanted to get to know you better before I started to work and got busy."

"That was nice, but I am in a hurry."

"I shouldn't have insisted on lunch. I apologize."

"No need to." She seemed remorseful, and Charlie felt sorry for her. "Your approach was very professional, and I appreciate your enthusiasm. Meet me in my office at eight tomorrow morning, and we'll get acquainted and go over your duties."

"Thank you. I didn't want to lose touch, and I suspect you often travel. It's important to know you and exactly what you expect of me."

Grant was impressed. This girl deserved a bit of his time. "We'll talk at length tomorrow. For now, be assured we'll stay in constant communication. You'll have a desk at my congressional offices and the AIDS Statistical Center. I'll arrange for a secure line from both places to my private office, and if I'm out you can page me." Charlie rose. "I have to go. See you in the morning."

"I'll be there. Thank you."

As Charlie reached the exit, he glanced back at his new statistician sitting with her legs crossed. She smiled and waved. Her skirt *was* pretty short for business. If she wore one like it tomorrow, he'd say something. He stole one last look. Or maybe he wouldn't.

. . .

Sarah Grant kissed her children, hugged and thanked her mother, then quickly departed before being re-summoned by Matt and Jennifer into their night-lighted chamber. Anticipation of a thirteenth-anniversary second honeymoon tempered maternal guilt over leaving them. While driving home, it occurred to her this milestone was joyful yet alarming, for it seemed only yesterday she had been a carefree, neurotic teenager, and now she was the mother of two and wife of a U.S. congressman. Hardly old, Sarah suspected she wasn't particularly young, either. Nevertheless, according to her husband, she still possessed three remarkable features: extra-ordinary eyes promising intelligent companionship; a sensuous, invitational mouth; and a captivating ass, rounded and soft, suggesting erotic delights to a lucky embracer. Sarah delivered on all fronts.

She and Charlie met at a political rally during her senior year in college when he was on campus campaigning for the House of Representatives. He was attracted to her unique beauty, she by his maturity, sophistication, and aura of impending power. They went to bed on their first date and wed fifteen months later.

Her daydreaming resulted in late braking, sliding on the wet pavement, and overshooting their driveway. Turning around next door, she garaged the sedan, then secured the house and hurried upstairs to join Charlie in bed to get what little sleep she could.

. . .

The pulsating tone rudely wrested them from a sound, entangled sleep. Charlie released her breast and rolled over in the dark, attacking the alarm with a vengeance usually reserved for political opponents.

"Fucking clock," he mumbled.

. . .

Packing completed and about to depart, Sarah inquired of her husband, "Where are your pills?"

"On the dresser."

Carefully placing the vials into a satin pocket of her cosmetic case, she closed the lid and commenced zipping the adjacent garment bag as Charlie carried the first load of luggage to the car. Nice automobile, but he felt guilty every time he looked at it. No wonder few jobs remained when even he–a congressman–owned an import! That was disloyal to his Midwestern constituency.

Sarah joined him with the last of their baggage.

"Did you lower the thermostat?" she asked.

"Fifty degrees," he answered.

"Are the doors and windows locked?"

"Yes."

"Did you check the timers?"

"The timers are fine."

"Good!" She reached up to kiss him. Their lips lingered, the tip of his tongue caressing hers as hands drifted from her waist to relish the soft feel of her cheeks.

"Happy anniversary, darling. Nice ass."

"Thank you." Easing into the front seat, Sarah flipped down the visor vanity mirror to fuss with an errant stand of hair, then turned to her husband. "Are you sure we have everything?"

Charlie nodded, checking for traffic before pulling onto the street.

"Tickets?"

"Yes, dear," mocking her concern.

"AIDS-negative certification?" She was determined to be

sure.

"Affirmative."

"Birth certificates?"

"Oh, *shit!*"

Rapid deceleration generated squeals from protesting tires. Using the nearest driveway to reverse direction, within seconds they were rocketing back to their house.

"Where are they?" Sarah inquired, unfastening her seat belt as the car rolled to a stop by the front sidewalk.

"On the desk."

The answering machine being deactivated for their lengthy absence, she was greeted by a demanding telephone. After hurrying through the foyer to answer, she hesitated, thinking, "No! It's probably one of Charlie's constituents wanting to bitch about something. Not today, thank you!" She grabbed the birth certificates, returned through the foyer, and pulled the locked door shut as the caller gave up.

"Right where you said," she smiled upon reentering the car.

Minutes later, they merged into the traffic flow of I-76 east. Light snowflakes threatening to pummel the windshield were captured by the slipstream and darted over the vehicle at the last millisecond.

"Nice of your mother to watch the kids," Charlie stated.

"She enjoys it. With Dad gone it gets kind of lonely." A touch of sadness flickered over her face.

"I'm sorry."

"It's okay."

Sarah's father had died the first week in June, and reminiscing brought a collage of poignant memories. Charlie tactfully remained silent as she turned toward the window for a modicum of privacy. Moments later, her composure regained, she said, "Going to Nassau was a *great* idea. Thank you."

He reached over and squeezed her knee.

Truck gardens rolled by, their black loam fallow until next season. A rusty old tractor sat abandoned in the middle of a large field. Summit Lake eased into view. Charlie recalled his grandfather's nostalgic accounts of an amusement park that used to be on its east shore in the days before King's Island, Cedar Point, and Disney World. There were dodge-um cars, a roller coaster over part of the lake, paddleboats, a mechanical gypsy lady that laughed grotesquely from inside a glass case, and a merry-go-round with vintage Wurlitzer that today would be a collector's dream.

"Did you stop the papers?"

"Called Thursday," Charlie answered.

The defunct Akron Brewing Co., an intact reminder of a bygone era, loomed on the left, and blocks beyond it sat the once abandoned and now mostly renovated B.F. Goodrich complex. Charlie wondered what it was like before the industrial decline, with bustle, noise, middle-class prosperity, and full parking lots twenty-four hours a day, six days a week.

The central interchange loomed ahead. Charlie maneuvered into the right lane and moved quickly onto I-77 south, a vacation mood enveloping him. He needed time alone with Sarah. God, she was attractive, thirty-five years old and improving. He wondered how many times he, at forty-two, could perform, given optimum conditions. Maybe he would find out if the Caribbean half-lived up to its reputation as a vacation paradise . . . if Sarah wore those seductive panties with the scanty triangles front and rear and–he was suddenly snatched from carnal reverie.

"Charlie! Behave!"

"I am behaving."

"No, you have that *look*."

"How do you always know?"

"I just . . . know."

"Honey, I never looked at your ass until we got married."

"Just drive and cut the bullshit . . . and try not to look so smug!"

A semi thundered past, its slipstream rocking the car. Sarah abruptly altered the mood. "Do you really think it's safe?"

"Flying never is. Every trip to D.C..."

"I mean leaving the country. You know, AIDS."

"Oh . . . where is safe? The Bahamas are as safe as anywhere. Less than ten percent of the population... "

"That's bullshit! Unreported cases; juggled statistics. Departments of tourism relentlessly protect their turf. Look what happened in Mexico. Cancun should have been closed two years ago when… "

A sudden sea of brake lights near the airport exit short-circuited their conversation.

. . .

"What were you preoccupied with on the way down?" Sarah asked as they peered across the tarmac from an observation window.

"Besides your ass?"

"Shh!"

"Our vacation and having time to consider something other than AIDS."

"I was thinking of Matt and Jennifer. Do you miss them?"

"Probably not as much as you." It was a candid reply.

"I envy that. I know you love them, but you can put your feelings on hold. Or block them out. I can't. Like at night. You never hear them."

"I do the few times you're not home."

"That's good. But I still don't know how you can be so deaf when I *am* there."

"It's a gender difference."

"You are *so* full of bullshit. Societally conditioned, macho-instigated and encouraged *bullshit*."

Charlie shrugged, hoping to avoid embroilment in a battle of the sexes on their second honeymoon. "I think that's our plane," he said, trying to divert her attention by pointing at the far runway. A DC-9 was touching down, tires smoking, wings flexing slightly under the strain of sudden impact.

They arrived at the boarding lounge as the jetway's doors opened, permitting weary passengers to deplane.

"Looks as if they're glad to be home," Grant observed.

"So will we be in a week," Sarah sagely commented.

"Excuse me."

Easing past in the narrow aisle, the flight attendant's hips unavoidably brushed against Charlie as he placed winter jackets into the overhead compartment.

"Nice ass," he whispered into Sarah's ear.

"Mine or hers?"

"Both."

"Honestly!" Sarah slid into the window seat and noted the typical Ohio snow squall was abating. Despite the dismal day, she felt at peace.

The plane taxied to the end of the runway, engines spooled up to a high-decibel whine, compartment vibration increased and with brakes released, NACON flight 147 quickly gathered speed. Exceeding one hundred sixty miles per hour with over three thousand feet of runway remaining, throbbing, brute propulsion lifted the craft. The ground rapidly fell away, resulting in the miniaturization of the airport complex and traffic moving along I-77. Topping winter turbulence at eleven thousand feet, they hung suspended over a convex charcoal mantle extending to the horizon in all directions. Sunlight streamed through the windows, brightening the cabin while simultaneously warming the sands of Paradise Island a thousand miles away.

Charlie reached over and touched his wife's hand.

"I know, Charlie. You, too."

Engines were throttled back at cruising altitude almost seven miles above the earth, leveling the canted aisle. Outside air at fifty degrees below zero hissed over the red, white and blue fuselage as the craft rammed through sub-stratospheric air. The pretty flight attendant paused for their order.

"Scotch and a bloody Mary."

"Just scotch," amended Sarah, leaning back and closing her eyes. "I'm cold. Will you get me a blanket, honey?"

From the overhead compartment Charlie retrieved a cover and tucked it around his wife as the stewardess delivered his drink. She hadn't completely turned to serve the couple across the aisle before Charlie's eyes were focused on her ankles and working upward to linger on enticing hips. Sensing lechery, Sarah placed her husband's hand under the blanket and positioned it between her thighs.

"*Scope* the redhead," she whispered, "*I'll* reap the benefits."

. . .

Rays of sunlight refracted by a crystal vase on the antique

pedestal table near the window probed the President's face. His eyes opened to a squint. What day was it? Oh, yes . . . blessed Saturday. Half awake his mind shifted into kaleidoscopic overdrive, wondering what terror the world concocted as he slept. Would it be a new crisis in the economy, another ecological disaster, or the disintegration of the health care or Social Security system? Could even be a new economic threat from the Land of the Rising Sun. Influenced by recent failed negotiations, President McDonnell increasingly perceived the Japanese as unscrupulous, self-serving, and devious! Or maybe AIDS–lurking, malevolent, omnipotent–would ruin his day. Cynically, the President wondered what pitiful rationalizations the churches would eventually devise for this affliction. Though not expected to provide answers, they seemingly couldn't resist offering them.

Dancing sunbeams flickered on Karen, who muttered something unintelligible, sighed deeply, then resumed slow, rhythmic breathing. Longing to make love, he wished she would waken. Last night, she had been exhausted, and he did not have the heart to suggest it. She involuntarily cuddled closer. Momentarily content he lay still, enjoying the soft familiarity of her body, but it was no use, for once awake, he could not remain idle. Careful to avoid disturbing her, he slipped quietly from bed, only to trip over a lurking slipper. Swearing under his breath, he moved to the nearest window.

Briskly moving cumulus clouds cast mobiles of shade across the White House lawn which lay covered by heavy morning dew sparkling brilliantly in sunlit patches. Traffic, moving slowly along Pennsylvania Avenue outside the fence, occasionally braked to avoid jaywalking sightseers. McDonnell was glad the street was open again. *Damn* the lunatic fringe that might try to assassinate him! Living in a fortress sent the wrong message to the American people, many of whom were gathered outside the gate for a tour as professional protesters in Lafayette Square across the street warmed up for another busy day of accosting an apathetic public. And here he was, inside, looking out. Amazing! John H. McDonnell, President of the United States, a semi-retired college professor and, until middle age, a political novice whose only qualifications were being mayor of Cleveland and governor of the

State of Ohio–one term each–won by the narrowest of margins.

His party was deadlocked over major contenders in the summer of '02 until his name surfaced. A nonentity outside of Ohio, he was the perfect dark horse: scandal-free and from a populous state. His image could be groomed to fit any situation. An abrasive bluntness and intractability didn't surface until after his election. Before inauguration, he managed to alienate a coalition of naturalized Hispanic and Mexican immigrants demanding bilingual education by telling them to learn English or be prepared–outside of Dade County and Mexican border areas– to fail economically in America. And that would be doubly true for their children!

Vatican enmity was incurred when he was asked if he felt the pontifical stance on birth control made feeding the world's hungry more difficult. Presidential staff members were appalled at his candid reply: 'What other conclusion could there be?' Catholic laity, practitioners of birth control by the millions, rose tentatively to his defense, as the papal hierarchy remained apoplectic. Someday, his mounting critics swore, he would go too far.

Karen stirred. He crossed to the bed, leaned over and kissed her. "I almost woke you."

"You could have."

"Thought you needed the rest."

"That's sweet. Come here." She pulled him onto the bed, hugged him close, and whispered, "What's the matter with now?"

. . .

"Here's your coffee." Karen offered a steaming mug. "What's on today's agenda?"

"Budget reductions . . . and AIDS. I'm calling Fairchild for an update."

"How's the budget going?" She wished to avoid discussion of the AIDS trauma.

"Terrible, but that's to be expected."

"I'm surprised the PAC's aren't pressuring you."

"They are. I ignore them, as I do the Japanese."

"You'll never get reelected."

"Does it matter?"

Without hesitation, "Not if it doesn't to you!"

"Karen, I'm looking three years down the road. My goals ... besides conquering AIDS...are to balance the budget, reduce the deficit, decrease imports, and halt foreign investment. If someone destroys my achievements after I leave office, whether its 2008 or 2012, so be it. I refuse to make decisions with 'electability' in mind."

The certainty of three more years in the White House with the possibility of seven gave the First Lady pause. "Any thoughts about how we can get away from here once in a while?"

"This is a bit premature, but a Key West estate may become available."

"Wonderful!"

"And if not, we have a potentially acceptable alternative. There's a smaller complex north of Clearwater worth looking into."

With hope renewed, Karen brightened. "I have to get cleaned up. Somewhere under this frumpy old exterior is the President's wife." She pecked his cheek and went to shower.

. . .

"Did you see this, John?" Karen handed a folded page from the *Washington Post* across the breakfast table. "It says fourteen percent of babies born in New York City are infected. Can that be right?"

McDonnell put his *Times* aside.

"Probably low. The same here in D.C."

"Well, I don't believe it's God's punishment for homo-sexuality or chemical abuse or anything like that, but it certainly seems that way."

"I agree."

"On the other hand . . ." Thoughtfully stirring her coffee, uncertain how her next statement would be received, she commented, "I do wonder if it isn't *God's will*. That's an entirely different matter. Perhaps He has a grand plan to depopulate the Earth and start over."

Intrigued by her last statement, McDonnell's intense stare put his wife on the defensive. "Why are you looking at me like that?"

"I'm wondering if you aren't right. It's a fascinating premise. If true, we should be careful who's saved even if a cure is found."

"John, that's terrible!"

"Still, an interesting theory."

"If God provides a cure, I doubt He intends it to be selectively administered!"

Alien concepts were coursing through his brain. "But what if there wasn't enough serum to go around? Then we'd *have* to be selective."

Karen skewered her husband with a jaundiced expression. "That's *not* what you meant!"

McDonnell averted his eyes to avoid her gaze. Depopulate the earth. Return the planet to the flora and fauna. Man *did* seem responsible for the majority of the problems. If that's what God wanted, He picked one hell of an impressive way to accomplish it.

"I have to go," he stated.

"Can we fly to Camp David this weekend? Anything to get away from here."

"I'll make arrangements. Is two o'clock, okay?"

"That's fine. John . . . you don't *really* think we should let people die, do you? If we can prevent it?"

His reply was strangely distant. "We have no cure, Karen. It's academic."

"What if we did?"

He answered with a gentle rejoinder. "I'm not an unfeeling monster."

"But the way you acted . . . and looked."

"*Karen.*"

"I'm afraid, that's all. The world is in a big enough mess without us making it worse!"

"I couldn't agree more."

McDonnell paused momentarily in the hall before heading for the West Wing. A seed planted minutes before was rooted and spreading tentacles through his mind.

. . .

Infected Islamic pilgrims flocked to Medina and Mecca as moths to the flame. Ill-equipped for a catastrophe of such magnitude, cleric-dominated Arab governments revived a medieval response, ordering corpses placed in the street for collection by stake-body trucks, the modern equivalent of horse-drawn carts.

Bulldozed pits, reminiscent of the Nazi pogrom, served as massive crypts after cremations were outlawed because putrid fumes, wafting unpredictably, fouled the air. An anticipated counter-exodus to the desert failed to materialize, for people accustomed to urban comforts were unwilling and not prepared to live an austere, nomadic existence.

Meanwhile, affluent Americans felt reasonably secure, as the potential for calamity hadn't materialized outside the ghettos and drug culture. So long as AIDS minimally impacted mainstream society, it was relegated to being a disturbing presence, briefly discussed over cocktails and condemned as unfortunate, but never dwelled upon. Society's powerful elite–self-appointed paragons of virtue–possessing material wealth, an outstanding level of health care, and isolated playgrounds in the Caribbean, steadfastly refused to worry over tiresome people dying in troublesome places. With the population of south Florida severely infected, most Americans ventured only to relatively safe Orlando, the Keys, and the Gulf coast. So long as southern Floridians made no attempt to migrate north–and they indicated no propensity to do so–there was little reason for concern.

. . .

McDonnell acknowledged Kim's signal on the intercom.

"I rang Dr. Fairchild's home," she reported, "but all I got was his answering machine. Do you want me to page him?"

"No. Leave a message at Northcoast that I'll call Monday morning between 9:00 and 10:00. Make a note so I don't forget."

"Yes sir."

"And ring the First Lady."

"Right away."

"No, wait. I'll do it myself."

"Whatever you say, sir."

McDonnell sat meditating, unsure a weekend in Maryland was advisable, for he shared his wife's aversion to Camp David. On the other hand, if both took something enjoyable, they could relax, using nature as a backdrop for truly relished leisure activities. Ambivalently, McDonnell punched the button that connected him with the presidential quarters and informed Karen that Marine One would be standing by after lunch.

6

Dr. William Fairchild rolled his head from side to side in a persistent attempt to ease tense trapezia. A general discomfort coursed through his legs and lower back, culminating in knotted shoulder muscles, while pressure behind his eyes made it difficult to resist their involuntary closure.

Hoping to alleviate his morning misery with a steaming cup of coffee, he rooted unsuccessfully through the refrigerator for cream before locating a can of condensed milk in the cupboard. More asleep than awake, Fairchild searched the gadget drawer for the device which punched holes in lids, one for air–guaranteed to scum over before the container was empty–another to pour from. Of course, it was not there.

After his wife died and he acquired a housekeeper life became a continuous game of hide and seek, with him always "it." Using the electric opener to half-sever the top, he poured a healthy measure into now cool coffee. Thirty seconds in the microwave at full power fixed that!

Slumping onto a kitchen chair, Fairchild was thankful it was Saturday and his housekeeper would not be arriving until ten. Though she picked up after him, vacuumed twice a week–once more than his wife had done–did the laundry, ironed, loaded and unloaded the dishwasher, and prepared dinner Monday through Friday, he resented the intrusion.

But perhaps he should quit bitching about misplaced items for he vividly recalled the first few weeks after Coletta's death when meals were limited to microwave dinners and anything in a boilable bag. Loneliness, mediocre food, and the exponentially growing mess fueled the necessity for household help.

Mrs. Romano, an acquaintance of his late wife, lost her husband to an aneurism shortly after Coletta succumbed to breast cancer. Having lived in fully integrated neighborhoods all her life, she had no qualms about working for a black man.

Fairchild retrieved his morning paper from inside the storm door, a service worth those outrageous tips he gave the carrier to put it there! Scanning the weather report, he noted intermittent snow squalls were expected, ending early, with four to six inches in the snowbelt east of Cleveland. With Coletta gone there was little to do at home, so after work he planned to drive to Sandusky to check on his boat before the marina winterized and stored it.

Perhaps Roberta Curtis would like to ride along. A month after his wife's funeral, she had invited him to lunch–her treat. It wasn't provocative, just an act of compassion and friendship from a secretary consoling her boss. He wanted to reciprocate, but he could not bring himself to ask. What if she was glad their token lunch was over? Not certain he wanted to know that, he resolved the problem by eating in or skipping lunch altogether.

But lately he found himself watching her for extended periods, thinking how attractive she was. Did he have a carnal interest in her? No! Just male appreciation of a beautiful girl… woman. Well, *maybe*.

Roberta was a late-thirtyish divorcee. The marriage, during her early twenties, had lasted only a couple of years–that much he knew–but he wondered why so short a union and why not try again? Certainly opportunities were available.

With her light complexion and many Caucasian features, it surprised him he found her appealing, for Coletta had African features–like his–and dark brown skin, the epitome of beauty and allure.

What if he asked Roberta out, and she declined? Her outward behavior was completely professional. Why did he think she would accept a date? Were undercurrents there or merely products of a lonely man's imagination? He was reluctant to embarrass himself and make her uncomfortable by asking.

A truck stopped out front, probably the lawn service. He made a mental note to call their office on Monday to order tree trimming along with new sod for the tree lawn next spring.

He went into the bedroom to dress. Cargo pants, sweatshirt, docksiders–habitual Saturday attire. Dissatisfied after inspecting his image in the mirror secured to the bedroom door, Fairchild opened the armoire and selected a more stylish sweatshirt in a color that coordinated with his pants. A handsome reflection assured him he was still a bit of a buck at sixty-one.

A leaf blower started outside. Passing through the kitchen, he unplugged the coffeemaker, then exited to the adjoining garage. As the Buick backed smoothly out of its shelter, the landscaper passing nearby thoughtfully re-aimed the discharge chute. Fairchild waved thanks and turned on the radio. Classical music from WCLV filled the air.

Since his wife's passing, Fairchild frequently found himself depressed, reliving the graveside service and missing the children they never had. Although both had been tested, their fertility problem defied diagnosis. When Coletta suggested adoption he pleaded lack of time–promising to discuss it later–or pretended not to hear, and she finally gave up. Not adopting was his fault and must have hurt her deeply.

He was tormenting himself to no avail! Assuaging guilt, real or retributive, was counterproductive now. All things considered, Coletta had a good life. Rather than being better off with children, she might have been worse. And him, too, for not everyone was cut out for parenting. If they had really wanted children, then damn it, one of them would have acted!

Fairchild pulled into the parking lot wondering if Roberta had arrived. His pace quickening upon entering the lab, he went to her cubicle only to find she was not there. He was disappointed, far more than he cared to admit. Quickly greeting several technicians, he retired to his office. On the table beside his desk, were stacks of analyses from Li's Friday blood cell harvest. Why bother to look?

He sat down, swung his feet onto the desk and meditated, reviewing avenues being explored by teams nationwide. Kill the virus... weaken it... dissolve its protective membrane... prevent cell invasion... stop replication... isolate it... alter it... strengthen the body's defensive mechanisms... gene therapy.

His neck hurt. Attempting to ease the persistent discomfort, he closed his eyes and gently rolled his head from side to side.

"Good morning, Doctor."

Roberta's voice was manna from heaven.

"Hello! I presumed you weren't coming today."

"Car trouble; that's why I'm late. My brother brought me."

"You can't be late on a day off."

"Certainly I can, because you depend on me. Did you have breakfast?"

"Coffee. That's not breakfast, is it? I usually stop at McDonald's on Saturday. It's not a dietician's dream, but a tasty repast. This morning I passed those beckoning arches before realizing it."

"Good." Roberta, who seldom brought treats, for both of them were frequent dieters, presented a box of donuts. "Which do you want?"

"Anything with chocolate."

Of the two she offered, he selected the one with more icing. Double fudge frosting hung in glacial folds over the edges, and cream oozed enticingly from inside.

"Yum," uttered Fairchild. "Sit down."

"Thank you." They ate quietly for a minute. "What's on today's agenda?"

"Checking petri dishes. One never knows."

He studied his secretary of six years. Wearing a fitted–not tight–sweater and a pair of conservatively tailored slacks, she was indeed beautiful by white or black criteria. Her fine features were hardly African yet her ebony hair showed no trace of Caucasian blood.

"You want the truth?" he suddenly inquired.

"About what?"

"Why I came in today."

"Go ahead."

"To get out of the house."

"I'm sorry. . . . Is it still difficult?"

"Not like it was." He was surprised to be saying these things,

75

but felt no embarrassment.

"Want to talk about it?"

"Not really, but thank you."

"Maybe later?" A door left open.

"You are very nice." Oh, Jesus! Did he really say that? He looked for signs of discomfort but could not read her expression.

"Thank you. I try to be."

He felt compelled to redirect his drifting mind. Scarcely realized fantasies could ruin their professional relationship or worse, result in a sexual harassment suit! "You are very nice." Unbelievable! Sophomoric. Next he'd be telling her how pretty she was and how long he had thought so!

"Anything you want me to do?"

"Pardon?"

"Do you need help?"

"Oh." Fairchild collected his wits. "No, thank you."

"Then I have things to catch up on."

She excused herself, leaving him feeling more than a trifle ridiculous . . . and a little guilty. Coletta had been gone less than a year, but then, she wouldn't mind if he displayed interest in another woman. Of course, she'd mind . . . especially since this woman was so much younger and bore no resemblance! What a terrible thought! Coletta had been very attractive. God knew he was no prize. What an absurd line of reasoning!

Roberta had started working. He should do the same. Selecting a sample tray from the storage locker, Fairchild reluctantly crossed the lab to the scanning electron microscope. Minutes later he reappeared in Roberta's doorway.

"Did Eric say anything yesterday?"

"About what?"

"Do you have a minute?" He looked so serious.

"Sure."

"Come here. I want you to view something." Bill led Roberta to the monitor. "Tell me what you see."

"T-cells . . . what am I looking for?"

"Anything unusual."

"I don't know. Do you want me to call one of Eric's assistants?"

"No, just describe what you see."

Roberta shrugged. "Lots of T-cells."

"More than usual?" Fairchild seemed excited.

"Based on my few previous observations . . . no."

"Damn! Li altered the medium to attempt accelerated replication. I thought this sample indicated some success."

"Maybe it does. Your judgment is better than mine."

"Not necessarily."

For the next ninety minutes Fairchild remained sequestered in his office, reviewing Eric's most recent reports. Finally emerging, he asked Roberta if she was ready to go.

"After I straighten my desk. Yours, too, if you don't mind."

"Not at all. I appreciate it when you do."

"Did you find anything encouraging in Eric's notes?"

"I'm not sure."

Retrieving his jacket, Fairchild draped it over an arm, then froze, mesmerized by her ripe beauty displayed as she stretched across the desk for a paper clip.

"How are you getting home?"

Now why did he have to ask? Twenty-two employees reported to him. He was not responsible for their transportation!

"The bus. There's a stop close by . . . and it's not very cold."

"Oh . . . I'm going to Sandusky . . . to check on my boat."

"It's very impressive."

"You've seen it?"

"You brought in pictures after taking delivery... was it three summers ago?"

How tacky, he thought . . . showing off an expensive cruiser to someone on a secretary's salary.

"Yes . . . well, goodbye."

"See you on Monday."

Hesitating at the hall door, Fairchild noticed Roberta bending over the work sink, rinsing a flower vase.

"Let me take you home," he stated after retracing his steps. "It's not as warm as it seems."

"It's too far out of your way."

How did she know where he lived? . . . Oh, yes, the department Christmas party he hosted. My God, that was four

77

years ago!

"Please, I want to." More words he might live to regret. "I may need a ride someday."

"Well . . . okay! I can straighten up later. Your office, too. I promise. Let me get my coat. It will be good to get out of here before eleven."

He helped her with her wrap, wondering why he never detected her perfume before. Just a hint, when she was close.

. . .

Snowflakes were accumulating, creating a wonderland of ermine white, clean and fresh-looking.

"What a gorgeous day," she beamed, as the steel exit door slammed shut behind them. "I love snow."

Many months had elapsed since he last opened a car door for a woman. An unexpected surge of excitement originating in his groin, warm and insistent, refused to go away. Pressure built against his fly. Not wanting this sensation to ebb, he felt the urge to let it develop, to experience satisfaction. No harm, as long as she did not know. He brushed snow from the windshield, opened the driver's door, and settled deeply into the seat. The delicate scent of her perfume filled the interior.

"What a nice car. Is it new?"

"Yes. No! It's an '02, but I still think of it as new."

He felt foolish, was flustered by her proximity and his engorgement. How could she not notice the bulge?

"It's very pretty, plush."

Except for her necessary directions they rode the rest of the way in silence. How pleasant it was to have a woman beside him. He had not realized how much he missed the company. But he did not know what to say.

"Third unit on the left," she indicated.

"Lovely apartments."

"They are nice. I don't need a house. And couldn't take care of one. However, it does get lonely. And confining. I go for a lot of walks, especially on weekends."

He pulled into a vacant space. She opened her door, faced him, and smiling, held his eyes. "Thank you. Have a pleasant afternoon."

"Do you have plans?" he wondered.

Her answer was self-assured, yet matter-of-fact. "I'll probably call a girlfriend and go shopping."

"Have fun."

"I will. Be careful driving."

She crossed in front of the car, waved, then turned and inserted her key into the lock. Her smell lingered.

Fairchild panicked. He didn't think–he reacted–exiting the car with a demonstration of quickness unseen since his basketball days.

"Roberta?"

"Yes?"

He was too disquieted to notice if she was surprised, confused, startled, or pleased.

"Will you ride to the lake with me? I'll show you the boat. And there's a nice waterfront restaurant about halfway, at Vermilion, although I can't remember its name."

She looked pleased. "I'd love to."

"You would?" Flustered again; by the situation, her answer, her presence.

"How sweet of you to ask. What time will you be back?"

"An hour and a half?"

"I'll be ready. See you at…" checking her watch, "12:30."

And she was gone.

It took a moment to realize what had happened. It was not just a ride to the lake; it was a *date*, complete with dinner! He climbed into the car, let the wine leather mold around him. Testosterone surged. He felt sixteen years old.

Roberta placed her purse on the hall table, leaned against the door and said aloud, "Thank you, God."

Picking up the phone, she called her brother to check on the car. Repairs had been delayed because the replacement part was backordered, but he offered a ride to work Monday morning. Graciously declining, she told him she had one.

. . .

Under reduced thrust, the Grant's DC-9 glided through frag-mentary cloudbanks on its final approach to Atlanta's Hartsfield

International. Geometrical housing developments drifted in and out of view, forming a monotonous mosaic of drab, suburban sprawl intermingled with industrial park ugliness. Miles away the narrow cluster of tall buildings that demarcated downtown jutted from the Georgia plain. It reminded Sarah of the Land of Oz when Dorothy first saw it at the end of the Yellow Brick Road. Surrealistic flotation during descent yielded to the brief, unnerving upward rush of the ground as landing became imminent. With the runway speeding beneath, a correcting surge of power prolonged touchdown by a split second. "Thank God," thought Sarah as the wheels made smoking contact, and rapid deceleration vibrated the airframe. When they rolled to a stop, she summoned the nearest flight attendant.

"Pardon me. Will we be on the ground long enough for me to make a phone call?"

"You can call from here."

"I need to stretch my legs."

"If you hurry."

"Thanks. I won't be long, Charlie. I want to reach Barb."

Moving rapidly through the jetway, Sarah crossed the NACON lobby and followed the concourse to a bank of public phones. Quickly sliding her credit card through the slot, she punched in the number and tapped her foot impatiently as the double-pulsing ring went on and on.

Barbara Collins was one of her dearest friends. They had attended high school and college together, sharing a dorm room their senior year. Marrying and settling within a few miles of each other helped maintain a solid friendship. When Barb's husband was transferred to Atlanta, Sarah felt she had lost a sister.

"Damn!" Cursing under her breath, she hung up.

"Any luck?" Charlie asked as she scooted over him and settled into her seat.

"No, and I'm worried. She's never home when I call, and she hasn't answered my letters or E-mail for a month."

"Maybe she's busy."

"Well, I can't worry about it now." Sarah leaned back and adjusted her skirt. "We're going to smother in Nassau. We might have been wiser to freeze in Akron than roast upon arrival."

The Grants sipped drinks and catnapped their way across southeastern Georgia's pine forests and over northern Florida. The pilot's carefully modulated voice invited them to look down at Cape Canaveral as they passed overhead, and in a surprisingly short time the Bahamas came into view.

The ocean, indigo blue to jade green, was magnificent. The shallow reefs of varying depths, coupled with a variety of undersea plants and schools of brightly colored fish, marbled the sparkling waters. Narrow bands of crystalline sand–blends of tide-crushed coral and rock–matted New Providence and the north side of Paradise Island.

A large, shallow body of water–more an untainted swamp than legitimate lake–dominated the western portion adjacent to the airport. Nassau anchored the eastern end. Random groups of dwellings, roofed in royal blue, white, or scarlet–reminders that this had been a crown colony of the British Empire–clustered together in strips along the coastal roads. The lustrous greens of subtropical vegetation and the mellow ocher of the earth completed the picture.

As the plane slowed to make a U-turn, Sarah noted grass on the runway, its presence about as comforting as the quaintly dated terminal.

"Please remain seated," the captain urged, "until the plane has come to a complete stop and the 'seat belt' light is extinguished. Have your birth certificate, return ticket, and AIDS-Negative certification ready for customs. You are in a foreign country. Exercise more than normal care of all documents. Thank you for flying North American Consolidated."

As the Grants approached the terminal, they observed bleary-eyed and exhausted departing tourists heading for the jet. Having found escape from the confinement and regimentation of work, they now wished to be free of the tyranny of unstructured leisure pursuits. Nocturnal hours in the casino; debilitating, capricious schedules; and frenetic attempts to cram a fortnight of vacation experiences into a week, eroded the meager stamina with which they had arrived days before. Intestinal havoc caused by unfamiliar foods combined with extensive alcohol, consumed too early each day and too late at night, overburdened body and mind. It would be good to get home, unplug the phones, and pass out. Conversely, the wide-eyed new arrivals anticipating sand, sun and fun, were eager to debauch their bodies and anesthetize their brains.

Calypso strains from a three-piece band greeted them as they entered the sultry terminal and were shuttled toward a somewhat brusque but surprisingly efficient customs officer.

"Birth certificates," he curtly demanded, followed by a cursory look to verify they were originals.

"Return tickets."

Sarah handed them over.

"Purpose of visit?"

"Vacation," Sarah replied.

"Declarations?"

"None," Charlie responded.

"Medical verifications."

Sarah simultaneously returned the tickets to her purse while extracting their lab reports. Properly organized, she retrieved them with little delay.

"Next!" ordered the inspector.

Merging without yielding to the horn protestations of an oncoming taxi, the hotel's shuttle driver threaded aggressively through a transportation armada of mostly older cars and vans lining both sides of the narrow access street. Speeding down the egress lane from the terminal, he turned right onto the main road, then accelerated rapidly east.

The blue-green ocean admired from above blended to a more uniform turquoise at sea level. Houses drifted by, punctuated by hibiscus and poinsettia in vivid colors and great profusion. In varying stages of disrepair, they appeared more worn than decrepit. Sun-bleached, salt-sprayed, and hurricane-pummeled, these weather-beaten soft pink, white, and faded yellow island dwellings had housed too many for too long . . . but that was about to change.

The van shot up a connecting street and swung left, racing along an avenue parallel to Nassau's main thoroughfare.

"Please notice our government house," the driver intoned,

"the original sailor's church, and many magnificent old mansions. Some finely restored, but others, alas, waiting for rich Americans to salvage a bit of history while contributing to our fine economy."

Contrasts were severe. Some buildings were renovated to a condition never enjoyed in their prime, while others were mere shells, with broken timbers, sunken or fallen roofs, listing walls, and crumbling foundations. People on the sidewalk reflected the pattern.

A loop in the street and the van was moving cautiously toward a precipitously high and narrow bridge spanning the intracoastal channel between Nassau's waterfront and Paradise Island's sheltered, but beachless, southern shore. Shaped like an arched feline spine, the camelback allowed unimpeded passage below to the largest of watercraft. Sloops with furled sails rode calmly at anchor or were lashed to ancient piers. Wide-striped umbrellas displaying randomly blended colors mingled with others of very narrow bands beside veritable mountains of conch shells.

On the island, the GMC passed a modest plaza housing tourist boutiques, a road on the left leading to Club Med, a grand-looking high-rise on the right, and then rolled to a stop before the casino hotel.

Charlie and Sarah entered the lobby, an elaborate replica of the sweeping veranda. Wicker-laced, bamboo-framed settees and chairs, reminiscent of the Humphrey Bogart and Sidney Greenstreet era, formed randomly placed conversation groups. Deep-cushioned, floral patterned seats and backs, decorated in vibrant tropical colors, invited guests to linger. Amid the dated splendor, the registration staff exuded lethargy and apathy.

"Laid back island charm," Charlie commented on their demeanor with amused disapproval. "I'll check us in."

Emerging on the fourth floor, the bellhop preceded them down a long, deserted hall.

"Weird," whispered Charlie, "it's deathly quiet."

"Maybe it's siesta."

The porter admitted them, turned on the AC, and parted the drapes, exposing a small balcony overlooking a large, panoramic expanse of ocean and beachfront. He waited professionally by the door, neither begging his tip nor planning to depart without one.

Charlie handed him a generous amount, asking, "What time does the pool close?"

"Eleven, though it's seldom enforced," the porter replied.

The door closed discreetly behind him.

Sarah opened the sliding glass enclosure and stepped onto the balcony, her husband close behind.

"I'm surprised you're out here. We're pretty high," he observed.

"Notice I'm not at the rail. Look out there. This could be addicting."

Far out to sea an Olympian cruise ship, sailing to Miami at thirty knots, appeared motionless. Near the shore, a powerful motorboat towed a parasail, the connecting catenary-shaped line secured high amidships to a swiveling eyebolt. Scattered shrimp boats and numerous unidentified craft speckled the waters in between.

"This is *great!*" Sarah exclaimed.

Grant lifted his wife's hair and brushed the nape of her neck with a kiss.

"Will you get some ice while I go to the bathroom?" she asked, resting her head against his chest. "I'll make it worth your while."

7

Unable to recall a single incident during the drive from Roberta's apartment, a euphoric William Fairchild arrived home. He had left a scant four hours ago, entertaining middle-aged fantasies of a date with a beautiful, young woman, and here he was less than an hour from their culmination. The previously depressing quiet encountered upon entering his house was now perceived as serenity. No longer the grieving widower, he could not envision what the future might hold, but he felt hope, some sense of direction, and an anticipatory excitement.

Delayed by heavier than usual traffic, he needed to change, gather refreshments, and depart as quickly as possible. Habitually well-organized and methodical, he became a study of inefficiency, wandering from room to room to do something or get an item and often as not, arriving at his destination totally confounded. Somehow, he managed to change clothes and fill a cooler with a liter of wine and a six-pack of beer.

Fairchild had donned a nautical ensemble: sea-blue and white striped rugby jersey, navy cargo pants, and blue-black docksiders. Natty! From the hall closet he extracted an off-white canvas jacket and on impulse reached for his captain's hat ... a bit affected, but what the hell! By prominently displaying the hat on the car's rear package shelf, his image might be augmented.

The hall clock chimed. Gathering the cooler, Fairchild checked the lights preparatory to locking the door.

"Money!" he exclaimed to himself.

Dear God, how stupid he'd look without enough. The top

bureau drawer netted two fifties, four twenties, and a ten, a sufficient amount to cover meals, gasoline, and incidentals. In an emergency, he could use plastic.

. . .

"You're early," Roberta greeted him. "Please come in. I'm almost ready."

"Traffic was congested going home. I thought it might be coming back. Didn't want to be late."

"That's sweet."

A friendly kiss on the cheek, natural and noncommittal, unnerved him. Warm and flushed, he noted she was wearing a fitted, teal sweater of soft lamb's wool, which snugly followed the upper contours of her breasts, then fell away to her midriff. Protruding nipples left no doubt as to their exact size and location.

Confidently aware of her impact, she cheerfully commented, "The weather's improved." Then, moving aside to admit him, she added, "Bet it'll be sunny during most of the drive."

Struggling for composure and an asexual mental focus, he remarked, "The snowbelt got a couple of inches. Probably melted already."

"That often happens. Please sit down. I'll be right out."

Roberta turned and moved gracefully toward what he presumed to be her bedroom. Designer jeans, molded to the supple lines of her hips, thighs, and calves commanded his attention. She paused in the doorway.

"There's beer in the refrigerator," she offered.

Compulsively, he scanned her narrow, model's waist, and earthy, sensuous hips. The slightest outline of high-cut bikini panties was visible through her jeans, covering less than half of her–he quickly averted his eyes. Clothes fitting like a second skin had erotic power far in excess of anything he was prepared to handle.

Roberta disappeared into her bedroom. Alone, he felt like an intruder, for he could not recall being in a woman's apartment before. Coletta had moved directly from her parent's home to theirs. Though some of their generation slept over or lived together, they had never spent a night under the same roof before their honeymoon.

With Roberta not present to rivet his attention, he looked around. The living room was a casually elegant blend of styles and accessories. Knowing her preferences, he would bet she designed it. He felt welcome, but awkward.

Upon her return, he was more comfortable. Oddly, her presence legitimized his. As she approached, he detected the addition of a delicately scented perfume.

"Your apartment is lovely. I'm guessing *you* decorated it."

"A few consultations, but yes. It was fun. I like to feel comfortable yet be surrounded by beauty."

The statement was an equally accurate description of her wardrobe. Her carefully tailored suits, dresses, and sports clothes reflected conservative good taste. Roberta was exactly as she appeared, honest and without pretense; but with a touch of feminine guile he would appreciate in time. His libidinous stare embarrassingly obvious, she nevertheless seemed flattered and faintly amused. She was probably used to men scoping her in this very room. That thought made him uncomfortable and was oddly annoying.

"My house is sort of nondescript," he volunteered, to get his mind off unwanted rivals. "It could be elegant; the outside suggests that, but if I like something I buy it with little regard as to how it fits in. Don't suppose anything goes with anything else. Probably a decorator's nightmare."

"I don't remember it that way."

"You've seen it?"

"Your Christmas party four years ago."

"Oh, yes . . . I forgot."

"Your wife was very gracious."

The mention of Coletta precipitated an awkward silence, which Roberta salvaged.

"Sorry, I wasn't thinking."

"No, no. Don't be. I'm adjusting." At a greatly accelerated pace, he might have added, as of the last few hours. "But I do feel strange being here. It's difficult making the transition from you being my secretary to my... " Fairchild hesitated, not knowing what to call their afternoon together.

"Date," Roberta supplied with a matter-of-factness he was

not prepared for.

"Date," he parroted.

"By the way," she asked, "what would you like me to call you on our dates?"

Dates? Was that plural a simple error, a Freudian slip, or an intentional expression of a desire?

"By my name, I guess." Fairchild was getting flustered.

"All right... William."

"No, not William. My . . . Coletta called me that."

"All right, then... Bill."

"Can we sit down?"

Roberta motioned to the sofa and curled up at the far end.

"Because I haven't dated in... we won't talk about that," he smiled, regaining some composure, but then fell silent.

"What's bothering you?" she gently asked, wanting to get whatever was troubling him out in the open.

"I'm your boss."

"Anything else?"

"I feel guilty."

"Because of Coletta?"

Fairchild nodded.

"What else?"

"I worry what our co-workers would say if they knew."

Feeling he was finished, she said, "I understand your discomfort. That's a pretty intimidating list."

"Strange, you would use that word because it brings up another problem. It exactly describes how I feel. I'm *intimidated* by you."

"Whatever for? It should be the other way around. *Was*! For longer than you'll ever know."

Wishing he'd never started this conversation but committed to explain. "You are incredibly beautiful. I'm not used to being with an attractive woman in this . . . setting."

"But we've worked together for years," she protested, simultaneously flattered and incredulous.

"That's the point. At work you're my secretary. Here you're a . . . woman."

"I'm a woman at work, Bill. Doesn't it help that I've been

your confidante for years? Though I'm your secretary with the… implicit gulf and formality… I've been your friend."

Remaining uncomfortable, Fairchild nevertheless smiled an acknowledgement of friendship, and suspecting he would regret this entire conversation Monday, took the plunge. "I have wanted to ask you out for weeks. Almost did several times."

"I know." She said it ever so softly.

"You do?"

"Shall I list the times, dates, and places?"

Mulling that over, he admitted, "I always lost my nerve because… because I feared rejection, the effect it might have on my male ego. And I wanted to avoid placing you in an awkward position at work." He was past the point of no return. "And because… this is really difficult… because if I had a daughter, you are almost young enough to be her age." Fairchild was suddenly miserable. "Correction, you *are* young enough to be my daughter."

"Bill," she assured him, moving closer to take his hand, but not invading the protective cocoon he was weaving, "if it doesn't bother me, why should it bother you?" When he did not answer, she placed both hands around his. He felt her warm softness. "Would it help to know that if you didn't ask me out soon, I was going to ask you?"

Fairchild was speechless. Reality was outracing his day-dreams. He wanted to kiss her but did not dare. It was a wonderful moment.

"Why are you so surprised by my interest in you? You're my friend. I like you, and you're very handsome."

"I guess it's mostly the age thing."

She squeezed his hand and held on. "Bill, I've been a big girl for more than twenty years. That qualifies me as an adult. If I didn't want to be with you, would I have accepted your invitation?"

"No."

"That's right… and the subject's closed! Come on; it's 1:30. I want to see your boat." Ending the conversation, she led him into the kitchen where she presented a wicker basket. "Carry this! Some wine, cheese, and a few other snacks."

"I have wine in the car. Thought you might enjoy it. And beer. I don't know your tastes."

"Wine *and* beer? Really, Dr. Fairchild, you weren't planning to take advantage of me . . . *were* you?"

. . .

By 2:30 they were rapidly rolling west on the Ohio Turnpike, halfway to the yacht club near Sandusky. Rural Ohio sprawled in all directions. Comprised of an occasional town, fields of combined wheat, and windrows of trees demarcating property lines, it was nevertheless mostly empty, pastoral space. They were silent, enjoying each other's company in a relaxed, unstructured atmosphere new to them. Music from WCLV played softly over the stereo, a violin concerto both recognized.

"What a gorgeous day," Roberta observed as the last visible clouds drifted east. "I'm so glad you invited me."

"My pleasure. It's not a long trip, but it seems so when I'm alone. You make it delightful!" Fairchild began to feel brave. "I can't imagine why you never remarried."

"No interest."

"It's difficult to envision you home on a Saturday evening."

"I would have been tonight."

"I didn't mean to pry." But, of course, he did. "Men must constantly vie for your attention."

"Honestly, Bill, sometimes you sound like an Arthurian novel." She felt him stiffen. In spite of his personal and occupational success, he had a typical fragile male ego. She would have to be more careful in the future. Taking a deep breath, she sighed and turned to face him, left leg folded beneath her. "You give me too much credit. I don't go out very often. Men who ask me... present company excepted... are either white, seeking the thrill of dating a fair-skinned black girl, or black, using me as a surrogate for a white woman that wouldn't give them the time of day. I'm too black for a serious white suitor and too white for most blacks. And . . . I hope this comes out right . . . I frighten nice guys."

"You scare me."

"I rest my case."

. . .

"It's me," Charlie announced, entering from the hall and attaching the safety chain.

"Out in a minute!"

"Whisky and seven okay?" he inquired through the bathroom door.

"A light one."

Grant prepared two drinks, sipped from each before adding a dash more Black Velvet to his.

She emerged, clad only in a tiny bra and pubic patch attached by strings riding low about her hips.

"You like?" she inquired, flaunting her tits.

"Turn around."

Sheer fabric between her thighs disappeared, then fanned into an elongated wedge.

"*I love you.*"

"You love my ass, but that's okay! I like your buns, too."

Prone on the bed they kissed and petted, familiarity not diminishing their passion. Charlie lavished kisses and caresses on each bare cheek, then rolled her over and nuzzled the tiny triangle unsuccessfully containing lush, dark curls of pubic hair. Thoroughly aroused, he pushed the lace aside, and Sarah felt his tongue where it gave the most pleasure. Abstinence due to a busy schedule prior to departure and the absence of children propelled her rapidly to climax.

"Fuck me! I want you to fuck me!" She spread her legs, guiding his penis smoothly into her.

"I won't last long."

"That's okay. Just pump me hard."

Charlie gave himself to the moment, feeling the delectable thrill as his penis swelled, then throbbed with contractions.

"More!" she breathed heavily, lifting her ass. "More cock!"

With love and caring, Charlie sustained a final series of strokes with his now uncooperative manhood as Sarah massaged her erect nipples.

"Ahhhhh! Ahhhhh!" Spasms rippled, wave after wave. "It's so good, so good."

She became aware of her surroundings with Charlie still inside, warm and sweet and wet. "Charlie, you are *such* a good fucker," she complimented, then asked, "Get enough?"

"Uh huh. Did you?"

"I'll let you know after dinner."

. . .

The weekend at Camp David was better than expected.
Pleasantly cool weather greeted the McDonnells, and a protective
staff managed to stay or deflect interference. Over cocktails John
expressed optimism on acquiring a Florida retreat. He wouldn't
say what caused his reevaluation since breakfast, only that he had
a plan. Immersed in a sweet alcoholic glow, Karen vowed to try
harder to like this place. The telephone warbled.

"Yes?" the President answered.

"Sir, I'm sorry to bother you... "

"It's Bob Harrison," McDonnell whispered to his wife,
momentarily muting the instrument. She noted her husband first
appeared annoyed, then became increasingly agitated before
finally exploding. "Those fucking sons of bitches! Call me back
when you confirm." McDonnell slammed down the phone and
gulped the rest of his drink.

"What's wrong?"

"Apparently the Japanese are offloading a shipment of cars in
San Francisco in violation of quota."

"Sorry, dear." Karen rose and took his glass to the wet bar.
"Let me freshen your drink."

"This will *not* spoil our weekend."

"But, of course, it will. You're the president, remember?"

He managed a feeble grin. Pouring a double shot over ice,
she returned to pat his forearm as he offered an apology. "I'm
sorry, dear."

"It's a twenty-four-hour a day job; I accept that."

McDonnell nodded appreciation of her tolerance before
lumbering into the library to await his aide's return call, which
came soon after he lapsed into introspective silence.

"Harrison, sir. Besides refusing to comply, they're threatening to go to court for an injunction if we interfere. There's a
distinct possibility... "

"Bullshit! Tell those unprincipled, blood-sucking, yellow
bastards to obey the law and stop unloading that fucking ship, or

the Boston Tea Party will pale in comparison to the San Francisco Car Party!"

"Sir, I'm not sure… "

"Tell them, Bob!"

"Call you right back, sir."

"Shouldn't take long," McDonnell thought. Unable to relax, as the minutes ticked by his anger rose to unprecedented heights. "Amoral bastards! They weren't…" the phone interrupted his silent diatribe.

"Sir, the ambassador has agreed to a delay, provided he's granted an audience first thing Monday so this matter can be resolved. He ordered the captain to resume unloading at 6 a.m., Tuesday, regardless."

"We'll see about that. Notify me of any changes."

"I will, sir."

McDonnell hung up. Primed for combat, feeling invigorated and alive, he rejoined his wife. "Karen, let's take a walk!"

"Do you know why you enjoy being president, John?" she asked, donning a sweater.

"You sound as if you know the answer."

"You love to fight."

"You're probably right."

"And the dirtier the better!"

He'd have to mull that one over.

. . .

Conversation flowed easily between Roberta and Bill the remainder of their journey. Tentative testing, so much a part of first dates, had largely been avoided as their maturity and a well-established work relationship compressed the normal pattern of behavior between two people in similar circumstances. They left the Turnpike at Exit 7 and followed a series of two-lane roads and highways, passing through assorted towns and hamlets of significance only to residents. After several miles, Fairchild turned into an upscale condominium complex, reminiscent of the many waterfront developments from Virginia Beach to Key West.

"We're here," he unnecessarily announced. "When the developer discovered the demand for slips was greater than for year-round homes in this price range, he restricted condo construction to expand the cove, then built modest single-unit dwellings across the road for the local market. It's a contiguous and integral enterprise, drawing from an entirely different population segment."

Amused, Roberta smiled a tolerant acknowledgement of Bill's analytical explanation. "How like him," she thought, "to make ordinary conversation sound like a college thesis."

"What's so funny?" he demanded.

"You, but it's a compliment."

"I don't understand."

"I know. Trust me, I'm not making fun of you."

Following the curving main road, they drove slowly through the well-appointed, repetitious development. Suddenly facing an embankment of earth and riprap, which protected the structures from encroaching storm waters, they veered right onto a gravel parking lot. One side bordered the rear lots of a succession of staggered condo units; the other, a huge marina accommodating several hundred vessels of all descriptions—sail to power, trolling skiffs to high-powered ski boats, pontooned houseboats to family cruisers. There were even some whose sole function was to serve as a floating bar. Fairchild parked next to the embankment, opened the passenger door and took her by the hand.

"Come, I want to show you the lake." Invigorating gusts tingled their faces as he led her along a well-worn path.

"Feels good to stretch," Roberta observed.

At the shoreline large waves slamming into rocks shot fluid pillars skyward, cascading cold mists over them. Gray, murky water smelled clean, but "fishy." The midafternoon sky was becoming overcast as a Canadian front drifted over the lake from the northwest, preceded by a light, frigid drizzle—a harbinger of snow. Fairchild felt Roberta shiver.

"Let's go back," he suggested. It would be a good afternoon to snuggle warm and dry on board the boat. "I just wanted to show you the magnet that attracts me."

"It's certainly impressive, Bill." The raw wind, the harshness of the lake with winter approaching did have an exciting, masculine appeal. Fairchild guided her back over the revetment.

"My boat is docked at the closed end of the marina. Do you

mind walking?"

"I need the exercise. Aren't you going to get your hat?"

He was pleasantly surprised she had noticed. "Perhaps later."

"So many boats. Okay, captain, which one is yours?"

"Come, I'm dying to show you. Watch your step!"

They started down a narrow pier, two docks from the horseshoe sweep around the headwaters of the marina. Gulls sailed mutely overhead.

"When I bought my boat, all the desirable slips were leased so I had to settle for this one."

"Is that a problem? They all look alike."

"Just inconvenient. On a busy day there are minor traffic jams. And the waves intensify at this end of the cove. Notice it's funnel-shaped. Compression makes them stronger and higher."

"Like the Tidal Bore in the Bay of Fundy."

Fairchild was impressed. They neared a noticeably newer, broad-beamed cruiser with a flying bridge.

"That one?" she asked, knowing the answer. Pride oozed from Fairchild's every pore. It was a classic example: man eternally showing off for woman. "Oh, Bill, how magnificent!" she gushed. "No wonder you love it. Pictures didn't do it justice."

"Did you catch the name? From one of the pictures?"

"No."

Firmly gripping her hand, he led her along an even narrower walkway past the end of his boat. "Be careful, some boards aren't real solid." There, across the stern in blue lettering outlined in gold, were the words, "Sweet William."

"That's precious."

"My one touch of vanity. Or so I'd like to think."

"That and your captain's hat," she teased. "I did notice some pretty creative names as we walked along. And more than a few suggestive ones."

They were standing on a precipitous part of the pier. Fairchild guided her back to relative safety. Climbing on board first, he assisted her over the gunwale by placing both hands on her waist, easing her onto the deck. Their faces only inches apart, her subtle perfume enveloped his being. Neither seemed in a hurry to move.

Cushioned, built-in seats lined the perimeter of the rear sun deck. Amidships, one flight of steps led up to the bridge; and another down into the forward cabin. Fairchild took Roberta to the bridge. Sitting in the captain's chair, she spun the wheel and looked out over the prow.

"How do you know where it is?" she asked.

"Pardon?"

"How do you know how close you are to anything? Even up here all I can see is the front deck."

"Oh, you just . . . know. Remember when you first drove a car? How the right fender seemed over the berm or half on the sidewalk?"

"Vaguely."

"Well, it's a similar situation. You just learn it isn't."

"If you say so." She was not totally convinced.

The salon elicited the most "oohs" and "ahs."

"It's like a motor home, but wood and brass instead of plastic and chrome. What's in there?" She indicated the left forward door.

"The head. Those bi-folds hide the galley. Really just a big closet with appliances."

"The head?"

"Nautical bathroom."

"That's right," she nodded, remembering the terminology.

A third, short set of steps led down into the master suite. Tucked under the rear deck, it had limited headroom and shared space with an equipment compartment. A large double bed secured to the back wall monopolized the chamber. Roberta perched on its edge, while checking its firmness.

"Sleep over often?"

"Occasionally."

As she mounted the steps to the main cabin, Fairchild was once more keenly aware of the fit of her jeans. Settling onto the starboard couch, she offered compliments. "This boat is a work of art. What a great place to spend weekends."

"Especially during the summer. Make yourself comfortable. I'll move the car and bring the coolers on board. The head... bathroom... is right there."

"I remember, both the name and location. Take your time."

With Bill gone, she studied the salon. It was done in sepia-tones, with asymmetrical furniture placement, wine-tinged carpet, and plum-colored leather and fabrics. Impressive as that was, it was the accessories that were the most stunning. There was a pair of stylized breeding cranes–one preening, the other proudly standing by–and a freeform wine decanter with several long-stemmed glasses on the bar. Strategically placed vases–one containing reeds, pheasant feathers, and carefully selected dried flora drew her appreciative eyes. Futuristic tables and bar stools complemented the arty, masculine décor creating a room that exuded a quiet, self-indulgent ostentation.

Roberta recognized the delicate, understated touch of an exceptionally talented decorator. The overall effect accurately reflected Bill's taste, but his self-furnished home, as best she remembered, stood in contrast and mute testimony to his inability to design and create such aesthetically pleasing accommodations.

The sun was nowhere in sight as Fairchild exited the Buick after moving it closer, but the cloud deck was lifting, and it appeared the threat of snow had diminished. A couple he recognized, but whose names escaped him, waved from two docks away. He raised a hand and smiled, then, armed with the containers, returned quickly along the pier, climbed onto his cruiser, and rejoined Roberta.

"That didn't take long," she observed.

"I managed to run the errand with only a nod and a wave."

"I've been admiring everything. This is a great room."

"I think so."

She wondered if his first impressions of the vessel–acquired at the IX Convention Center in Brook Park–were similar to hers. That was doubtful, the boat being in a building and all, but if so, they were very much alike. No matter, for she was seeing a side of him only sketchily glimpsed before, and she liked it. Of his dedicated drive to conquer AIDS, she knew better than anyone, but regarding his artistic bent and his adopted love of the water and cherished cruiser, she never would have guessed.

. . .

The wine Roberta contributed had been consumed; the bottle

Fairchild brought contained less than a glass. It was dark outside, the salon lights were on, and the cabin temperature was rapidly falling.

"You must be starved," he commented, downing the last of the beer.

"*Drunk*... is a little more like it. How many 'sheets in the wind' do you have, captain?"

"We should eat, Roberta. It's almost seven."

"How many bells is that?"

"I haven't the least idea," he replied, amused by her condition, aware his was not much better.

"I think . . . captain . . . the last time I had this much to drink, I was sixteen, threw up for hours, and had a headache that lasted two days. My mother found out and grounded me for a month. Are you going to ground me, captain?"

Surprised and mildly flustered by the innuendo, he deflected her question. "We have to eat, or we'll be sick. There's a nice restaurant in the hotel downtown. It's in a century building and is very quaint. The food's not great, but is decent."

"Sounds good." Regaining a modicum of sobriety, she headed for the bathroom. "Let me freshen up. I'll be right out."

While waiting, Fairchild turned on the heater and set the thermostat to seventy-two degrees.

"If we aren't careful we'll both end up in the water," he cautioned, as they stepped onto the unstable flooring of the dock. Supporting each other and a bit unsteady, they wove their way toward the parking lot.

"Are you sure you can drive?"

"I'll be fine. It's only a few miles. I'm really sorry about the change of plans."

"Shush! I've had more fun today than I can ever remember."

"I'll be okay after dinner. We'll be home by midnight."

"Is that why you turned on the heater?"

8

Lounging at poolside, the Grants felt unpressured for the first time in months. Rested might come later.

"Charlie."

"Huh?" he mumbled, half asleep.

"Have you noticed how few people are here? It's *creepy*!"

Hedging, "Not really."

"This place is deserted. Every room should be full, and I don't think half the suites on our floor are occupied."

"Maybe it's the season."

"This *is* the season."

"The airport was busy."

"With passengers from our plane. How many other jets did you see land or take off?"

"Maybe it's a slack week."

"I don't think so. Something's not right. The staff seems preoccupied, and the ominous expressions on those departing at the airport . . . they knew something we didn't."

"You're paranoid, Sarah. They were just tired."

"It's AIDS. I *know* it. I *feel* it."

"*Oh*, honey."

"Don't 'Oh, honey' me."

"I think you're jumping… "

"It's out of control, and the Chamber of Commerce doesn't have the decency to quarantine the island."

"Quarantines aren't necessary."

"They are with Type 4. What if that's here? Look at

99

Cancun."

"Cancun didn't have Type 4."

"That's not the issue. AIDS was epidemic months before they shut down." Her observation went unchallenged. She was confirming what he felt since the bellhop escorted them to their room.

"I'm going to ask the bartender." She was up and moving.

"Ask him what? Sarah!" She did not break stride. "Well, at least get us a couple of pina coladas," he called after her. AIDS, yes. Type 4? That could never be kept secret. Charlie settled back on his chaise.

"Hello," Sarah beamed broadly at the bartender, a tall, handsome part-British, part-black man about her age. Blessed with the best of both races, the combination begat a strikingly handsome individual. Deep-tanned skin, brown with a moderating tinge of orange, he had fine English features, which bespoke of aristocracy. With soft, wavy black hair, thin expressive lips, and pronounced forehead, he exhibited few features that were not considered classic. "Two pina coladas, please."

After pouring ingredients into a blender, he turned and looked directly into her eyes. "Tab or cash?"

"Is this enough?" she asked, presenting a ten-dollar bill.

"Don't you think it should be?"

Change not forthcoming and uncertain if he was toying, Sarah extracted a dollar tip from her purse and placed it on the makeshift counter.

"Thank you." Smiling urbanely, the bartender ignored the money, filled both glasses and placed the icy, milk-colored coconut drinks before her. This situation was not developing as planned. Instead of probing fertile ground, she felt mocked for incomprehensible reasons. Finding no way to initiate the intended discussion, her only option was to leave.

Several paces away, drinks in hand, she abruptly turned and confidently retraced her steps. "You were in the band at the terminal," she stated.

"Very observant," he replied.

"And you're the bartender here," she continued, as if to ask, *who are you really?'*

"One does what one must. The life of a musician . . ." He let the statement hang, unresolved. "I also play here at the hotel . . . parties, weddings, by this pool. At eight, the rest of the band arrives. Perhaps you'll catch us after dinner."

"I'll ask my husband." Recognizing a coveted opportunity to pick his brain she asked, "Will you join us? He's over there."

"For such a pretty lady, it would be an honor."

Encouraged and determined to maintain her advantage, Sarah offered to buy him a drink. His response implied she had blanched at the cost of the two she carried. "At these prices? I will buy you one later, and one for your handsome husband." This man was infuriating! His impudence bordered on rudeness, but one with such candor might supply the answers she sought.

Grant opened his eyes as his wife and the dashing Bahamian approached.

"Charlie, this is... I don't know your name."

"Reginald."

"Charles Grant."

Without rising, he offered his hand.

"Steele," returning the courtesy of a surname. "A stage name. Even my mother has forgotten who sired me... if she ever knew."

"I'm Sarah Grant."

"I am honored."

"Honestly," thought Sarah, "he's either the most cultured musician she'd ever met or a flaming, cocky pain in the butt." Regardless, she intended to glean some information.

"Mr. Steele was... "

"Reginald," the Bahamian politely interrupted.

"Reginald was part of the trio at the airport. He'll be playing here later tonight."

"We enjoyed it. Nice welcome."

"Pap for the tourists, but thank you."

"Sit down. Business slow?"

"Your lovely spouse is my only customer."

Amused, Grant was going to like this man.

"My wife and I were just discussing that. Bad week?"

"Every week is bad. The hotel is bathing in red ink. Even the casino is slow, and it draws from other island hotels and the cruise ships."

"Why?" Sarah bluntly inquired.

Steele studied her face. "Curious tourist lady, you do not want to know."

Certain of her position, Sarah got right to the point. "AIDS," she emphatically stated.

"Your wife is not just another pretty face, Mr. Grant."

Sarah doggedly pressed for confirmation. "How bad?"

"What do you want to know? Numbers? Percentages?"

"Either will do."

"Ten percent."

"That's the official admission."

"And you insist on the truth?"

"I have a right to know."

"Since you are our guest, that is probably so. And not hard to discover if one is persistent," he conceded, implying she was.

"What *is* the truth?"

"The truth . . . the truth is no one knows."

When Sarah started to object, Reginald raised a hand in appeasement and continued. "No one knows except ten percent is too low. Accurate statistics are hard to come by."

"What percentage would *you* estimate?"

"Fifteen. Certainly not twenty."

Sarah looked doubtful, suspicious of his answer.

"Does that surprise you . . . Sarah?"

Trying not to appear offended by his increasing familiarity, she responded, "I thought it would be higher."

"We could not function if it was."

"Are there any Type 4's?"

"Heavens, no! Do you think this is Africa? Do I look Negro?" Sarah flushed. "Do not be embarrassed, pretty lady, it's a legitimate question. No, I guarantee you, no Type 4. I wouldn't be here if that were true, for how could it be confined on so small an island?"

"Well, that's a relief."

"Where did you say you were from?"

"I didn't. Ohio."

"I have relatives in Detroit. They are much lighter than me,

102

barely able to pass for," he lowered his voice, "African-Americans. Isn't that a fright? Trying to be black in this world? It is unwise to be too white in Detroit... especially in my relatives' neighborhood. Where was I? Oh, yes, we have AIDS on New Providence; you have AIDS in Ohio. It may be more prevalent here. We undoubtedly exceed fifteen percent."

"It must be destroying the island's economy," mused Charlie.

"Leave it to a man to link human deaths to a balance sheet," thought Sarah.

"Oh, it is not so bad as it seems. We have guests. *You're* here! You will see them on the beach tomorrow. They rest for dinner now. Siesta. Sales are down on Bay Street, but the shops survive. The casino remains full until the wee hours, one just doesn't have to wait for a slot machine or sidle sideways through the aisles. *We* know; customers don't."

"They know or you'd be full," Sarah reasoned.

Instantly capitulating, "You are right, of course."

"I interrupted. Sorry."

"Do not apologize. You are a guest; a rich American." It was a gentle jab, with no malice intended. "Even when we are at capacity, some never go near the beach, so you would have to examine the bookings to know how bad business is. People are perverse, wouldn't you agree? Spend all that money, yet ignore the ocean."

Feeling he was drifting, Sarah prodded. "What about the locals? How are they reacting?"

"No panic. There are no houses boarded up or anything, just people missing. A father here, a child there. It is very sad. Add in cousins, nieces, nephews; few families have been spared. From the street all is well. Children in the yards, old people sitting outside in the evening. Only now there are five children where once there were six; now grandma rocks alone. Very sad. But for you, less congestion, a place at the tables, better prices at the Straw Market."

Sarah was visibly upset by his implications. "That's terrible. We aren't callous."

"I never meant you were. The problem is you are from Ohio."

Sarah, who felt the man was infuriating, was becoming angry. "How is that significant?"

"It's the heartland. Were you from Miami, Los Angeles, or New York, you would better understand. Nothing happens in the Midwest. Death comes in bed at old age, surrounded by distraught, loving relatives. In the world at large, death comes at any time, from many things, often alone. Gunfire; starvation; a needle; the government. Now it comes from a virus. Is that any worse?"

Neither Grant was prepared to answer.

"Such things scare you. We are used to it, more or less. We never get much out of life except most of the troubles. Last season we were completely booked, then word leaked out. 'AIDS is on the island! Those niggers have AIDS!' Our authorities could not hide it because the importation of medical supplies increased, and familiar faces behind the desks and in restaurants were missing. We rely heavily on regulars; people who return to the same suite, same week, year after year. After they learned of our plight we lost them, at least for this season. That is the reason the top three floors of the hotel are closed off. But I am depressing you. Would you care for a drink on the house?"

"Sure." Grant's immediate response was followed by Sarah's refusal. Reginald Steele headed to the bar and was soon out of earshot.

"Charlie, we have to get out of here!"

"I don't think we can. It's unlikely they would change our tickets, and obviously the number of flights has been reduced."

"This is *awful*."

"We won't get it, Sarah."

"How can you say that? The Bahamians serve us. We've already had several drinks. You just ordered another!"

"It's not transmitted that way."

"That might have been true, once. Now it's *bullshit*!"

"Honey, we run the same risk at home."

"Like hell! Suppose he's lying! Suppose there *is* Type 4!"

Charlie felt under siege. "Honey, it's not my fault."

"I'm not blaming you; I'm just scared. That awful man at Customs had the nerve to check our medical records. We should have checked *his*!"

"Shh. Here he comes."

"On the house."

Grant graciously thanked his benefactor.

"What is your name? I have forgotten."

"Charles Grant."

"Forgive me. Too many to remember. Let us change the topic. Your lady does not look well."

Sarah assured, "I'm okay, but I would like to know why you stay. You're a musician. You could go anywhere."

"Miami?"

"Why not?"

"Because it is worse there. Your government just won't admit it."

"Is that right?" Sarah glared accusingly at her husband. In a sense he *was* the government; collection and interpretation of statistics being what McDonnell appointed him to do.

"Numbers are hard to come by." Charlie was lying.

"Then it is worse," she concluded.

"Only in some parts of the city."

"Rich Miamians love it, pretty lady. They figure that some day Dade County will be given back to them just like it used to be. Before the Latinos; the Haitians; before drugs. Who can blame them?" Reginald rose to leave. "Don't be frightened. You are safe. Me too, for I inhabit the same sterile tourist world you do and would no more think of going some places on this island than you would frequent slums in your cities on the continent. Especially since last summer."

"What happened then?" Charlie wanted to know.

"Nothing to be concerned about. We thought we had a Type 4, but he died unconfirmed in September. An isolated case. None before; none after. Do have a pleasant evening."

. . .

Perusing the menu, Roberta mentioned a craving for seafood, then abruptly changed her mind, for a Midwestern, small-town restaurant was no place to order fish. "Filet mignon, medium rare," she told the waitress, reluctant to order red meat but feeling no viable choice.

"Two," Fairchild amended.

Fresh air during the ride to town, consuming a full meal and the simple passage of time served to sober them. After sharing dessert and a pot of coffee, she looked directly into Bill's eyes and smiled. "Thank you for dinner."

"No need. Your presence added elegance to an otherwise mundane dining experience." Then, suddenly awkward and unsure, his easy eloquence and aplomb dissipated before her eyes. "Roberta?" he hesitantly asked.

"Yes?" she replied, wondering what could possibly account for so precipitous a shift in demeanor.

"May I see you tomorrow?" His words were spoken uncharacteristically fast.

She reached across the table and gently held his hands. "If you let me fix you supper."

The cabin was warm when they returned. Roberta stood before him, searching his eyes. "This is so nice," she softly murmured.

Leaning down and gently kissing her lips, he reluctantly suggested, "We'd better go."

With the lights out, the distant glow from high-pressure sodium luminaries bordering the parking lot washed through the cabin. Her features–soft, radiant, demurely outlined–riveted him. He kissed her again, no pressure, only the sensation of touching. Her breasts firm against his chest, thighs touching his, she detected the beginning of an erection. Long and lingering, their first passionate kiss filled her with satisfaction, him with anticipation. Lips parted.

"We must go," he asserted.

"Why?"

"Because it's late, and if we don't leave soon, I'll be too tired to drive."

"That would be a shame." She kissed him ever so lightly.

"Roberta, if we stay, I'll keep kissing you."

"What's wrong with that?"

"It won't end there."

"So?" Reaching up, she found willing lips and slowly, deliberately slipped her tongue between them, tentatively probing his mouth with a kiss he had never experienced. "Is the car locked?" she whispered.

"No."

"Is it safe to leave it open all night?"

"Probably not."

"Go lock it."

While he was gone, Roberta turned on the lights, then closed the salon's venetian blinds and overlapped the curtains in the master suite to guarantee their privacy. Returning to the upper level, she adjusted the dimmer until the room was bathed in a dusky erotic glow. Bill entered, closed and secured the cabin door. If he hesitated in the seductive atmosphere–and she thought so–he recovered remarkably well.

"You sure you want to do this?" he asked, encircling her waist.

"Are you?"

"I'm sure I want you. I'm not certain we should."

She kissed him tenderly, experimentally. As he relaxed, Roberta slightly opened her mouth, teaching, inviting his tongue to probe between her parted lips. Soon he was kissing more passionately, his tongue touching hers, never too deep, never too long . . . a touch, a withdrawal, a promise of more. Silently, she led him down the steps into the master suite. Disrobing to her panties and bra while he undressed, she readjusted her bikini, then stretched out on the bed gazing up at him. Her skimpy lingerie intensified her allure.

"You are beautiful," he breathed, lying beside her.

Merging in a sweet, prolonged embrace, his mouth drifted to her ears, eyes, flawless cheeks. Probing lips brushed an offered neck, then moved along velvet shoulders to kiss the tops of supple breasts where they spilled over her low-cut bra.

"Take it off," she urged.

Bark-brown nipples emerging from chocolate haloes highlighted magnificent pliable mounds.

"Suck them," she demanded.

The tip of his tongue traced the areolas of both.

"Put your mouth on them, Bill!"

Fairchild suckled willing flesh, taking her right nipple into his mouth, drawing the firm, leathery flesh in until it rested between his teeth.

"Oh." she moaned, rearing her pelvis. "Suck the other. Even it out!"

In rapture never known, he filled his mouth with the succulent delight of her flesh as her encircling fingers embraced his penis, precipitating the first pulse of seminal fluid.

"Take my panties off!"

Lush, tightly curled pubic hair covered her swollen and beautiful crotch. Bill mounted her, then paused before penetrating. "I don't have a condom . . . Do you?"

"No, and I don't care."

"But... "

"It doesn't matter," she insisted, thighs parted in invitation.

Aching for release and never having attained this level of arousal, the lack of a condom ceased to be a problem.

"Roberta, it hurts."

"Put it in. I'll fix it so it won't hurt."

His glans touched her vulva, electricity discharging between them.

"I love you, Roberta," he whispered.

"I love you, too."

Kissing her lips, he began a slow, steady penetration. Feeling he would erupt with each gentle push, he fought desperately to stay the inevitable and when fully within, paused, savoring the unparalleled thrill of the initial penetration of a beautiful woman. Ejaculation seemingly under control, he resumed careful thrusting, wishing to prolong the sensation forever.

"Uhh!" she cried. "Bill, it's so good!"

Her pleasure pushed him to the brink. He quit stroking, fighting the ecstasy that would end their first union.

"Don't stop," she pleaded.

"But I'll come."

"I don't care! Don't stop!"

She grabbed his buttocks and pulled him tightly against her crotch. His response was a flurry of pulsating thrusts.

"Now?" she gasped, sensing the first contraction. "Now?"

"Now," he uttered, pounding with incredible power and rapidity. "Now! Now!" Animal sounds emanated from deep within his throat. Climax overwhelmed him.

"Get it, Bill. Get it all."

"I love you, Roberta. I love you, I love you, I love you."

"Get the pussy, Bill! Get it! Get it all!"

Cradled between her thighs, her vise-like legs encircling him, his penis throbbed with relief.

Quietly they clung, kissing and caressing. Roberta broke the silence. "Just because we were being intimate, you didn't have to say you loved me."

"I've been in love with you for months. I needed time to be psychologically prepared to express it, and think you might be receptive."

"Was I receptive enough just now?"

"You know what I mean." Something occurred to him. "You didn't have to say it either."

"Say what?" she coyly asked.

"That you loved me."

"Did I say that?"

"Roberta, that's not fair."

"You're right, it isn't. I said it because I meant it. Bill Fairchild, I love you, for a lot longer than I am supposed to have, and ages before thinking I'd get a chance to act upon it. What just happened has been brewing for months."

"I'm sorry I didn't last longer."

"Shh! Don't go away."

She rose from the bed and walked naked to the steps, her undulating bare ass mesmerizing him. He savored the vision, anticipating her return.

Tentative footsteps muffled by the salon carpet, she suddenly appeared at the top of the stairs, then cautiously descended, for her eyes had not recovered from the bright lights in the head. Slow-motion movements provided him extended time to examine her lithe body. A second erection stirred.

"Where are you," she asked.

"Over here. Be careful."

She crossed to his voice, breasts sagging slightly, more from size than lack of firmness. Constricted pupils began to dilate. "There you are. Lie back." A warm, soapy washcloth was applied to his genitals, then in masturbatory fashion on a damp hand towel wiped the length of his penis. "Scoot down," she ordered.

Compliance was prompt.

Little by little the world returned. Pulling the sheet from the tangle at the foot of the bed, he covered her. From the closet he selected a lightweight blanket, spread it over the sheet, crawled in and snuggled close. Roberta gave him a kiss.

"Good night, Bill."

Spooning, with his flaccid penis pressed against her cheeks, he encircled her waist and cupped a breast.

"I love you, Roberta," he murmured.

"Uh," she sleepily acknowledged.

Sexually and emotionally satisfied, they fell asleep.

9

From the murky shallows of a troubled sleep, Sarah's first perceptions of a new day were the muffled sounds of her husband fumbling through her cosmetic case in search of a painkiller to quell a debilitating headache. Unwilling to enter the infirm world glimpsed last evening and buffeted by dreadfully unpleasant dreams, she retreated to the spurious security of her blankets, praying the poolside conversation had been hallucinatory.

She thought of her children and, for the first time, hated gays for the horror they had unleashed. Homosexual by choice or genetics, their sexual deviations were decimating the world Matt and Jennifer were supposed to inherit.

"You okay?"

A familiar voice penetrated her sanctuary.

"Honey?"

Peering over the cover's satin-bound edge, Sarah stared at the unshaven countenance of her husband. Rage, at gays and a heinous disease wildly out of control, stemmed the tears that welled.

"What's the matter?" Charlie asked.

"Nothing you can fix."

"Last night on your mind?"

"Yes. How do you feel?" She needed to change the subject.

"Rough."

"I can't imagine why. All you had yesterday was a beer, three or four scotches, two pina coladas, and a Seven 'n Seven."

"Sarcasm will not heal my head."

"Nor will the effects of all that alcohol wear off very quickly. Did you take a pill?"

"Just now."

Determined to cleanse her mind of Type 4 stalking the island, Sarah attempted to console her suffering husband. "You poor intemperate thing. It's getting so one can't indulge in a little harmless debauchery anymore."

"You aren't funny."

"Certainly I am. Lie down while I get a cold compress."

From the chrome rack on the bathroom wall, Sarah selected a heavy napped face cloth. As she had done so many times before when Charlie suffered his migraine attacks, she held it under the cold water faucet. To her surprise, the flow warmed. Life in the tropics was going to require innovation. The thought occurred that water in the ice bucket might still be cold; and it was. With practiced fingers Sarah placed the damp cloth across Charlie's forehead and against his temples, gently pressing cool relief into his stricken sockets.

"Better?"

"A little."

"Stay there. I have to pee."

Pain throbbed under the numbing cold. The misery did not stop, but was mitigated. Lying quietly for several minutes, he was almost overtaken by sleep when he sensed Sarah's presence.

"Don't remove the cloth," she cautioned. "I'm going to open the drapes.

"It's nice out," she reported, returning from the sliding glass doors. "I'm going to get cleaned up. I feel yucky."

Sanitized, Sarah sat cross-legged on the bed, touching up her nails. She leaned forward to plant a good morning kiss. "Your turn."

Reluctantly removing the compress, Charlie trudged into the bathroom in an attempt to get presentable. After showering, he cracked the door to vent accumulated steam, as Sarah, who had been on the balcony for some early morning people-watching, crossed the room and leaned against the jamb. Her husband looked younger without stubble. Specks of gray creeping through his beard were neither flattering nor distinguished. They made him look "old," and Charlie was not.

"Do you think that man was putting us on last night?"

"Who?"

"Reginald."

Grant glanced from the mirror, studied Sarah's face, then looked at his own reflection, pondering the answer to her question. "No," he finally decided.

"Do you think he exaggerated?"

"No."

"Me, either. . . .Are you sure we're as safe here as at home?"

Charlie rinsed his razor, placed it on the counter to dry, and splashed on aftershave. "Positive."

"Doesn't say much for home, does it?"

. . .

Travel brochures, prone to embellishment, could not do the sand justice. Fine, ecru, and free of debris, it sifted through one's fingers, compacted firmly underfoot. Composed of fragmented coral–not rock–it left no dirty residue. One shook it off, rather than bathe it away.

The beach, wide and deep, was pleasantly crowded. Spreading her blanket, Sarah stretched out on her tummy and reached back, unhooking her bra. No stark, white strap lines would spoil her tan! Charlie relaxed on a stubby legged beach chair. Squinting out to sea, he absorbed the panorama for which the islands were famous. A speedboat towing a parasail wove back and forth, lifting an apprehensive or ecstatic thrill-seeker with each round trip.

"Want to try that?"

"Try what?" Sarah asked, eyes closed, almost asleep.

"Parasailing."

"No way!" She held her bra in place and rolled over to roast her front. Backs got tanned when one walked around. "You can if you want."

Offshore to the northeast a small cay baked in the sun. Palm trees permanently bent northwest by prevailing winds formed a pillared, umbrella-topped wall of trunks and fronds that lined the beach. An occasional gull sallied out to sea on some instinctive mission. The heat and sun were delightful. *Damn* that Reginald or whatever his name was! He may have spoiled last night and part of the morning; he was not going to ruin the entire week!

. . .

Early afternoon found the Grants exiting an eleven-year-old Cadillac taxi, paying a per-mile rate that would make a New York City cab rider blanch. Starting at the east end of Bay Street, on what promised to be a long shopping expedition, they crisscrossed the thoroughfare, browsing in or bypassing shops at their whim. Jaywalking with impunity–few pedestrians heeded intersections or designated crosswalks–they skirted surreys and an eclectic collection of motor vehicles. The only apparent threat to their safety was numerous scooters–operated by inept riders that had never driven on the left and had not been on two wheels in twenty years–darting in and out of traffic. Fortunately, other motorists were cautious, patient, and deferential.

"The streets are full. You'd never know, would you?" Sarah remarked.

The leisurely paced fun, more infectious than the disease lurking in the back streets and Spartan housing of the populace, temporarily enabled the Grants to forget the viral veil descending upon the island.

"There it is!" Sarah exclaimed. "Across the street."

The famed Straw Market was a rambling, partially enclosed warehouse, open at the center with its surrounding roof in obvious disrepair. Random shafts of sunlight probed brightly through fissures, dancing unexpectedly in the aisles and playing delicately on counters piled high with the wares of a burgeoning cottage industry. The varying shapes, patterns, and colors masked the sameness of it all. While Sarah browsed, Charlie found a hat with a two-inch pliable brim and dark blue floral band. He prided himself on striking a good deal.

"Great value," he facetiously informed her. "Instead of four times, I only paid twice what it's worth."

Torrential rains erupted with minimal warning and explosive force. The shopkeepers, exhibiting unsuspected speed, splashed through aisle-blocking puddles to unroll plastic sheets over their displays. They weighted down the corners with bricks before seeking shelter for themselves.

Lasting only minutes, the flash storm swept out to sea, racing in the direction of the Florida coast. Since storm sewers were nonexistent and low-curbed sidewalks blended with the street, the water ran off the island's surface to the sea from whence it came. The noonday sun reappeared before the last drops fell to earth, boiling away moisture from hot streets and sidewalks, tile and corrugated roofs. Relative humidity shot to one hundred percent, and as sultry air closed in, conditions became more oppressive than before.

. . .

Voices of early risers tending their boats or planning a crisp fall sail on the waters of Lake Erie intruded into the master suite and etched a message of morning on the subconscious mind of the sleeping Fairchild. Sounds of cushioned feet treading the weathered dock commingled with protesting creaks and stresses of aging boards underfoot. All were in stark contrast to penetrating screeches from hungry gulls gliding overhead in search of a meal. He had slept long and soundly. Devils were put to rest, and cares kept at bay, as only the tender ministrations of a loving woman could accomplish. He wanted to roll over and spontaneously kiss her good morning, but then it wouldn't be spontaneous, would it?

Shy and hesitant, desirous yet in awe of this woman, he dared not move. What if she was asleep? Or worse yet, wide awake and tensely wondering how she had gotten herself into this mess? Able to stand it no longer, tentatively, apprehensively, he rolled over to discern her state of awareness, and with luck, her mood.

She was not there! Oh, God! The police would arrive any minute! Sexual harassment would be mild compared to this. *This* was sexual bombardment! She had probably been gone for hours, walked to town and caught a bus back home, or had banged on the door of a condo, told an expurgated version of the whole sordid affair, and obtained a ride to the depot. Whichever, the chances were she had returned to Cleveland hours ago.

The tragedy was she had liked him, and he had ruined it for a piece of ass! You could not wait, could you, William? You had to have it on the first date! You deserve her scorn. What was that? The aroma of coffee wafted through the companionway, followed by Roberta–all smiles–noiselessly descending the carpeted steps into the bedroom.

"I thought I heard you stir. Good morning!"

"Good morning." Thank God she was there!

"It's after 9:00. Aren't you the man that can't sleep past 7:30?"

"Must have been the late hour."

"I slept like a log. The fresh air, the boat . . . it rocks like a cradle. I made coffee."

"Smells good."

"I needed a robe and found this in the closet. Hope you don't mind."

She was wearing one of several shirts kept on board for those rare occasions he dressed to go out. Fairchild noted the tails barely covered the tops of her thighs while the vents ran far up her hips in French-cut swimsuit fashion.

"Why would I mind?"

Roberta sat on the bed dangling one leg over the edge, curling the other beneath her. The shirt fell away into an upside-down "V" exposing her lower abdomen, pubic hair, and the inside of a thigh. He was not very successful keeping his eyes on her face.

"I've only been up twenty minutes. I was exhausted, too; crashed as soon as my head hit the pillow."

"Listen, about last night. Please don't think..."

"I don't."

Slipping out of the shirt, she gracefully lifted the covers and, kissing him soundly on the lips, snuggled naked beside him.

"I was afraid you were gone. Worse yet, that you hated me."

"Oh, Bill. This isn't sudden. Why do you think I asked you out to lunch? Why do you think I've been so solicitous?"

Roberta pressed closer, the swell of her breasts firm and full. He engorged, felt her vulva settling over his glans. Fairchild was on fire.

"I promised myself if you were here, we'd date a while before doing this again."

"We dated at the office; you just didn't know it. This is okay because I love you, and care for you."

He instinctively picked up on the reversed order of

significance. The love was understood.

"I care about you, too."

"Bill," she said, sitting upright and flexing her vagina, "I know what you're worrying about, and Monday morning will just be fine."

His response was to move slowly, strongly, under her.

"Hold my ass," she requested.

Her breasts bobbed down as he thrust and sprang back to conical as he partially withdrew. Soon on the verge of climax, he tried desperately to hold back a sensation so intense it was almost pain.

"You can come, Bill. It's okay. Hold my tits."

She pushed down hard, taking all of him as he ejaculated an enormous pulse. Out of control, lost in pleasure, he pumped and shot, pumped and shot. Roberta rode him with abandon, embracing his cock, squeezing and extracting every drop, then leaned forward, flattening her breasts against his chest. It was affection, not lust.

"Now, William Fairchild, did you get enough?"

"Umm."

They lay quietly, almost drifting back to sleep.

"What are you thinking?" Roberta asked.

"That everything will be fine in the morning."

. . .

"How careful do I have to be with water?" Roberta called through the bathroom door before stepping into the shower. Fairchild responded that within limits it was like home as the vessel carried a huge auxiliary fresh water tank.

She emerged into the salon wearing only his dress shirt, folded over instead of buttoned, more for warmth than modesty.

"Your turn," she said brightly, disappearing down the companionway steps into the master suite.

Warm water pounded his chest. Shutting it off, he lathered and shampooed his hair, then turned it back on, adjusting to a hotter temperature. He had not felt as rested or at peace since . . . since he was a kid.

After toweling dry, Fairchild brushed his teeth, shaved and splashed on cologne. Pulling on yesterday's underwear, he remembered the remainder of his clothing was strewn about the bedroom. With no alternative, he opened the door and stepped into the salon.

Roberta, fresh and lovely, occupied the same spot on the couch she had found so comfortable the day before. He felt naked in her fully clothed presence.

"You look nice," he complimented.

"Wish I'd brought a second outfit... but how would I have known?"

Roberta had found clean sheets in a storage unit, bagged the dirty laundry to take back, straightened the room, and carefully laid out his clothes. "I could get used to this," Fairchild thought.

"Thanks for changing the bed and picking up."

"I assumed partial responsibility for the disorder." Was that innuendo and understatement accompanied by a smirk? "By the way, I stepped out on deck to see what was going on, and it's freezing!"

"That's not unusual in the morning."

"Can we go for a boat ride?"

"It's rather late in the year," he lamely protested, hoping to avoid the nuisance of taking the craft out.

"A cruiser left the marina while you were dressing. A big silver one."

"The Russells. They're crazy."

"Can't we be crazy, too?"

. . .

Perched high in the pilot's chair, wearing his captain's hat that Roberta insisted on retrieving from the Buick, Fairchild checked fuel levels, ventilated the hold, and cranked the engines. Roaring to life, they idled synchronously. Shifting the transmission into reverse, he expertly backed out of the slip.

"Are any of the islands worth visiting?"

"Several. South Bass: in particular. It has an airfield for light planes, wineries, an Old Town section facing a big commons, a marina, and the longest bar in the world. At least that's how it's advertised."

"Can we go?"

He would have to refuel. What the hell!

Correctly reading his expression, she kissed his cheek. "I knew you'd see it my way!"

Increasingly, he found himself doing just that. She looked younger, face aglow, the wind buffeting her hair. He wondered if he did. Probably not, but who gave a shit? If she did not care, he did not either. He certainly *felt* younger.

As they entered open water, Fairchild eased the throttles forward. The engines changed pitch and emitted a deep-throated, well-muffled rumble louder than before, but insufficient to interfere with conversation or mask the swish of water knifing by the bow and cascading along the sides.

"I thought it would be so noisy we couldn't talk," Roberta remarked, only slightly louder than normal.

"Noise is for those hoping to convince others their boats have more power than they do. People that buy these boats don't want to hear anything but ice tinkling in their glasses. Would you like to take over?"

"Sure."

Fairchild stood up, maintaining his grip on the wheel as Roberta climbed into the vacated chair. He showed her enough about the controls to operate the craft, then relinquished the helm and settled into the companion seat.

"Have fun!"

"Can we go faster?"

"Go ahead."

Roberta abruptly advanced the throttles. The cruiser jumped as twin screws bit into the water. "Wow! No wonder you're hooked. Does this ever wear off?"

"Not so far."

Fairchild reached over and placed the captain's hat on her head. Within minutes they approached the public pier lined with aging fuel pumps along the waterfront of Port Clinton. The deck leveled as Roberta throttled back. "You better take over."

"There's a rope coiled in the port corner of the rear deck. Throw it to that kid standing on the wharf."

Roberta descended to the aft deck, found the line, and after picking up a length she hoped would reach, stood by the gunwale as the cruiser came alongside the first pump. The transmissions reversed the propellers, and the craft settled in as the young man ran to meet them. She tossed him the hawser and in two swift motions, he had it secured.

"Hi," he greeted Roberta, vaulting on board and climbing the steps to the bridge. "Morning, Doctor. You're out late this year." He scampered across the forecastle, picked up the other tether line and flung it onto the dock. "Have you tied down in a minute. How much gas do you want?"

Fairchild checked the gauges. "Two hundred dollars. Is the store open?"

"No, but Dad's here. He'll let you in."

Roger leaped onto the dock, lashed the forward end to a piling and zeroed the fuel pump. Bill climbed over the gunwale and reached up to help Roberta. "Squat down so I can get a hold of you." His hands firmly gripped her now familiar waist. "Jump!"

"How do we get back on?"

"Roger will help us."

"You bet, Doctor!"

She jumped.

"Come on. Let's get provisions, beer and chips or… "

"Two hundred dollars?"

"I only wished that filled the tanks."

"Expensive hobby, *Doctor*."

. . .

Roberta's eyes swept the scene. Pedestrians peacefully coexisted with cyclists on the walkways and streets surrounding the multi-acre commons. Facing them across the lawn was a single row of attached and free-standing buildings.

"This looks like Chautauqua," she commented.

"I've never been there."

"I'll take you some time. You'll love it."

Up close the buildings that fronted Main Street exuded less charm than from afar, but their flaws imparted a certain character. Roberta made an observation. "Seeing this, it's hard to believe what's going on in the world, and what we do for a living."

"One needs to forget."

"Does it bother you that we make so little progress?"

"Yes, but I don't dwell on it."

"You seem confident. Our technicians think you're God."

"A facade for the troops."

"You impart a sense of holy mission."

"A crusade?"

She nodded.

"I suppose it is, isn't it? A holy crusade against an evil, non-discriminate infidel. Only this time the infidel is a mindless thing. If there is a reason, I don't even want to think about it." Then, in the intimacy of the moment, Fairchild admitted thoughts he had never voiced. "I'm afraid, Roberta, afraid we aren't going to make it. I'm gambling that whatever we develop will be effective against all current types of AIDS as well as future mutations, but that's lousy science. Charles Grant's reports are enough to take the heart from you. The Orient is reeling, India is under siege, central Africa nearly depopulated . . . " Fairchild trailed off, unwilling to continue the litany of annihilation.

"That makes me feel guilty, blacks dying throughout Africa while you and I sit here with . . . relative immunity."

"Perhaps white blood is a factor. You have a lot."

"You must have some. To be black in America is to have at least *one* Caucasian ancestor."

"A fourth. It doesn't show. If I had children, it might appear in them. My maternal grandmother, a French girl in World War I."

Roberta was confused. "So you *do* think that's part of it? Being Caucasian?"

"I was being facetious."

"Oh. Well, there is one beacon on the horizon." Fairchild looked askance. "Eric's test results... my God, was that only yesterday? A lot has happened." She leaned over to give him a kiss. He met her halfway. "You were riveted. Maybe a palliative for AIDS is waiting for us at home."

His response was noncommittal. "I plan to sit down with him Monday."

"Nobody can blame you for being reticent. The last time you got burned by the media."

"I'll never forget. You hadn't been at Northcoast a year. After a single false positive, one of our junior technicians called the paper and told them we had made a great leap forward."

"And when they learned it wasn't true, they blamed *you*."

"Human nature. High expectations were dashed. After that, Washington buried me under paperwork."

"Buried *whom*? Who was still keyboarding when you went home at 7:00?"

"Touche. I should have provided you with help."

"Don't feel badly. Who else could have read your writing?"

They walked the short main street, holding hands, trying to absorb the events that had taken them from a professional relationship to this one–whatever it was, wherever it might lead.

"Roberta, please don't think I'm pessimistic. I desperately hope we'll conquer AIDS. I just don't believe we are close in any current research, including Li's."

"My uncaped crusader. By the way, I never paid much attention in history class. How did the Crusades end?"

"After two hundred years . . . total failure."

. . .

Exhausted from the day's activities, the Grants returned to their hotel room for a late afternoon siesta. Charlie, a frequent but short napper, woke first. Gingerly pulling the sheet over Sarah's shoulders to prevent chilling, he donned sunglasses and went onto the balcony. Propping his feet on the extra chair, he flipped through the pages of a crossword puzzle book to his current project. 'Guido's note.' With no inkling who Guido was, how could he hazard a guess about his fucking note?

Uncaring, he placed the book on the discolored concrete deck, pencil folded inside. Surveying the scene, he felt the Siren pull of a subtropical isle. The pace was slow; the landscape serene; the repetitious, ceaseless waves and predictable tides reminders of a very real eternity.

The sliding glass door snagged on a track imperfection, then reluctantly retracted behind the fixed companion glass.

"Hi!" Sarah greeted, closing the door to preserve the cool conditioned air in their room. "Whatcha doing?"

"Contemplating the meaning of life."

"Come to any conclusions?" She stretched, squinting in the unaccustomed glare.

"Work sucks!"

"That's original."

Grant smiled. "This is a great place."

"Want to relocate?"

"I wouldn't mind." He moved his head from side to side.

"In your dreams! You'd find Government House a bit primitive after the halls of Congress." Sarah kneaded the muscles of his neck. "Where does it hurt?"

Grant pointed to the base of his head. Sarah directed the massage upward.

"May I go off on a tangent?" he asked.

"Be my guest."

"More and more I feel… you're going to think I'm weird."

"Tell me something I don't know."

"More and more I feel that God… " Grant broke his train of thought and digressed to a corollary. "I dislike that word because our interpretation seems outmoded and archaic. We… the human race, not you and I… have an infantile view of God. An eternal progenitor that dispenses good fortune if we are devout and adversity if not. And if we are subservient… and non-heretical… salvation. That really burns me. All this egocentric concern with salvation."

"What brought this on? Did the church ask for an increase in our pledge?"

"I'm serious."

"So am I."

"AIDS brought it on. God has had it with us. Apocalypse AIDS. Instead of the chosen ones going to heaven they get to stay on a cleansed Earth."

"All this from the man that thinks no religion can withstand analysis?"

"I didn't say everything was nonsense, just our two-thousand-year-old fairy tale. What do you think?"

"That I won't sit too close to you at dinner this evening."

"Might get smote?"

"If that's all that happens, I'll be lucky."

"How about a date tonight? Catch the stage show?"

"Only if you promise to take me to that French restaurant we passed earlier. Word on the street is you can't afford it."

10

"Shut her down," Fairchild called to the bridge while snubbing the forward line.

Roberta handed down the coolers and laundry bag before climbing over the gunwale without assistance. She did it rather easily, Bill observed.

"I liked it better when I had to help," he dryly commented.

"You're allowed to touch without an excuse."

. . .

At a quarter past six they pulled into Roberta's apartment complex.

"Come in and have supper," she insisted.

"I should be heading home."

"Not before eating a decent meal. I won't allow you to pig out on beer, chips, and God knows what else!"

"I planned on beer and peanuts."

Ignoring his remark, Roberta unlocked the door and flipped on the lights before escorting him inside.

"I can fix something quickly. The bathroom's down the hall, and here's today's paper."

There was no use arguing, so he made himself comfortable in an easy chair and turned to the op-ed page. It had been a long time since he enjoyed the luxury of sitting and reading, while a woman he loved prepared his meal. Roberta reappeared under the kitchen archway.

"Would you care for a beer?" she asked.

"No thanks. You know, I could get used to this."

"So much for any shyness you had left. Will you come in here? I need you to set the table."

. . .

"Dr. Fairchild . . . Dr. Fairchild!"

From somewhere in the cavernous depths of an ancient somnolent grotto, Bill Fairchild heard a familiar voice reverberate off the walls and ceilings, compounding false echoes and contradictory signals.

"Dr. Fairchild! It's time to get up!"

The grotto dissipated as the voice at the bottom of the stairs began ascending, and Fairchild was rudely thrust into reality. Suddenly, someone was standing in the doorway of his bedroom.

"You have to get up! Breakfast is almost ready. You're going to be late!"

The world snapped into focus.

"Mrs. Romano. Thank you for waking me."

"For a moment I wasn't sure you were alive. I've never known you to sleep so soundly." She seemed relieved.

"What time is it?"

"Six thirty. I just assumed you were up."

"Got back late from Sandusky. I'm awake now."

"I'll keep breakfast warm until you're ready." She returned downstairs to the kitchen, leaving him to shower and dress in privacy.

After only a single night with Roberta, he found it difficult to sleep alone. Although she had invited him to stay, suggesting they get up early and stop at his place so he could change clothes, upon reflection both felt spending the night together might be unwise. How would Mrs. Romano react? Would their new relationship become obvious at work? How could they suppress their newly found intimacy when appropriate with increased familiarity?

He had tossed and turned more than an hour, unable to relax without her cuddling beside him. Wondering how she slept, he would have been disappointed to know she dropped right off. Mrs. Romano called maternally from the foot of the stairs.

"Dr. Fairchild, you didn't go back to sleep, did you?"

"No, it's just difficult getting started."

She mounted the steps and returned to his bedroom doorway. "You don't have to go in on time. You *are* the boss."

"It's tempting, but I must. My secretary's car is in the shop, and I promised to pick her up. It would be unfair to make her late."

"Miss . . . I can't think of her name."

"Curtis. Roberta Curtis."

"That's right!" Her face broke into a broad smile. "Such a pleasant woman. And good looking, too. She was so attentive at Coletta's funeral."

"She was?"

"You were too distressed to notice, but she never let you out of her sight; she was like a daughter to you."

That hurt. If that's what Mrs. Romano thought, so would others.

"You should pay more attention to her. It would be nice if you took her to lunch... no, dinner. She wouldn't misinterpret your motives."

Feeling an unknown conspirator, Fairchild thought, "No, Roberta wouldn't misinterpret my motives."

"I'll consider it."

"I wish you would. You're alone too much. It's time you got out. Coletta wouldn't mind. Enough time has gone by and Miss . . . "

"Curtis."

"Miss Curtis can help you break the ice so you can look around for someone appropriate. There must be lots of older ladies at Northcoast who are widowed or divorced that would love to date an eligible man like you."

"I'm sure there are," Fairchild agreed, uncertain whether to be amused, chagrined, disconcerted, or some combination of all three.

"And don't be shy about looking around at church."

"A good idea."

"Here I am carrying on about your personal life and making you even later. Tell me five minutes before you want breakfast served."

Fairchild got out of bed, stretched, scratched an itch in the middle of his back as best he could–Roberta could easily reach the spot–closed the bedroom door and picked up the phone. He started to punch in her number before realizing he did not know it. "Isn't *that* great!" he thought. He knew she had an elliptical birthmark the size of a quarter high on her left thigh, but not her phone number. It was a bad idea, anyway. What if Mrs. Romano overheard, especially if the conversation turned intimate? It was hardly proper for his housekeeper to discover he was fucking Roberta's socks off before inviting her out for a friendly dinner, in preparation for dating "appropriate" women.

. . .

Roberta was waiting outside her apartment, enjoying the cold morning air. She opened the passenger door before he could help and got in, curling up on one leg, half facing him, in a now familiar pose. "Good morning, Doctor. Sleep well?"

"Not especially."

"What's the matter, Doctor? Something on your mind?" The erotic overtones in her voice and manner blatant, she reached over and planted a quick, affectionate kiss, loaded with tenderness and innuendo. "I missed you, too." Sitting back on her leg, locking his eyes with hers, she broke the spell by adding, "Hi."

"Hi."

"Thanks for picking me up. My brother said it might take until Wednesday to get my car repaired. I'm willing to trade supper tonight for a ride again tomorrow."

"May I take you out instead?"

"That would be nice."

"We'll discuss details on the way home."

"The weekend was fun, and I love your boat. We don't have to go out; it's so expensive. Want to stop after work and get steaks instead?"

"Do you always switch subjects so abruptly?"

"If I'm happy and have a lot on my mind… yes."

"Mrs. Romano thinks I should take you out."

"Your housekeeper? How did my name come up?"

"When I told her I was giving you a lift to work, she suggested it was time to start dating."

"See? I'm not the only one that thinks so!"

He wanted to relate more of his discussion with Mrs. Romano, but several things did not bear disclosure. One was Roberta's greater than normal concern for his well being during Coletta's funeral. It bespoke of a romantic interest predating anything he was prepared to handle. Another was Mrs. Romano's observation about the abundant supply of middle-aged ladies that he should be investigating as appropriate social companions. And then there was that 'daughter' reference. Actually, little remained of the conversation that would not put Roberta on the spot or focus on an age difference he did not want her thinking about.

"Should we explain why you are riding with me?" Fairchild asked as they neared University Circle. Severance Hall appeared on the right and just beyond, the Art and Natural History Museums.

"No. I don't think any explanation is required." Roberta was amused that Bill's reticence about their new relationship was creeping back as time together in the lab approached. "At work it's business as usual. You can treat me as your secretary... which I *am*, remember?" She flashed her most subservient smile.

. . .

"President McDonnell's secretary called Saturday morning after you left, Doctor," reported lab assistant Louis Khoury as Bill and Roberta hung up their coats. "She wanted to make sure you were aware of the message she left on voice-mail. I put a note on your desk. Morning, Miss Curtis."

"Good morning, Louis."

Roberta began sorting the department mail, a mindless chore enabling her to gear up for more important tasks.

"Since you are here, Louis, tell Eric I'd like to talk with him."

"Sure, boss."

Fairchild entered his office, retrieved his electronic communications, and waited for Li to report.

. . .

Eric ambled from his supervisor's inner sanctum.

"That was short," Roberta commented.

Her intercom buzzed before he could respond. "Please come in here." Bill's abruptness exuded an urgency she had never heard before. With a wink, Eric continued down the aisle.

"Right away, Doctor."

In ten steps, she was there.

"Close the door and sit down."

Fairchild's voice sounded different, its forced modulation serving only to attract attention to the nervous undercurrent permeating his manner and gestures. Roberta took a seat beside his desk as he began.

"With every passing second, five more people, worldwide, succumb to AIDS. While that aspect of the problem cannot immediately be resolved, if Eric and I are correct, we can buy precious time to continue our search for a cure or vaccine."

"Bill, that's wonderful!"

"The more rapid T-cell replication I suspected, in the enriched medium, has been confirmed. Once we isolate superior cells, we can produce them in quality in an acceptable length of time."

"You must be so proud! This entire approach was your idea. You'll be in the history books with Pasteur, the Curies, Jonas Salk."

"Well, that may be a bit premature, but if we can impede HIV's progress, the probability of destroying it becomes more plausible."

"Are you going to tell the President?"

"Not yet. Besides successfully isolating the superior T-cells before I call, I want all tests replicated, results correlated, valid double-blind procedures developed, and sufficient numbers of HIV positive volunteers injected with the super T-cells to make our research creditable. It may take awhile," he said, facetiously, "so we'd best get started. Please get your steno pad."

"Be right back."

Roberta returned and with legs crossed, dutifully waited. Her shorthand, almost a lost skill, saved Bill from intimidating encounters with dictation equipment gathering dust on the credenza behind his desk. Leaning back in his chair, eyes half closed, he dictated a revised lab schedule. As in the case of Roberta sorting the mail to collect her thoughts, it was something mundane for him to do while pondering the momentous.

" . . . subject to change on short notice," he concluded. "The usual heading and signature block. One each and normal bulletin board and file copies. Can you have that distributed by noon?"

"No problem, boss." Roberta rose, straightened her skirt, and pushed back the chair.

"May I take you to lunch?" he asked.

"What happened to discretion?"

"I only meant for a couple of hours. Pick a nice place and make reservations. Please."

"I'll use your phone. *More* discrete."

"Roberta, in forty-eight hours my life has turned around. We're on track to developing a promising AIDS treatment, and I've fallen in love. Roberta Curtis, *I love you*. If I can say that here on a Monday morning, it must be true."

"That's sweet. I wasn't wrong about you."

"What do you mean?"

"I'll tell you at lunch."

. . .

"Bill, how are you?" boomed the Chief Executive.

Fairchild informed the President he was well and inquired the same of McDonnell.

"How are things at home? Are you enjoying that big boat?"

"As a matter of fact, that's where I was this weekend."

"God, I envy you. And miss Ohio. Karen and I spent the weekend at Camp David. *Dreadful* place. I felt like an aging Boy Scout. The only alternative was to stay home, and neither of us could bear that. A few blocks from the Capitol are slums that make any moderately sized city in the Midwest positively utopian. There's been little time to make an impact, but believe me, before I leave office these ghettos will be eliminated. I won't witness this on the next generation."

"It certainly would be a blessing, Mr. President."

"I'll get right to the point, Bill. How are you doing?"

Fairchild wanted to be candid, but the accelerated division and growth of a few cells hardly constituted an earth-shaking accomplishment.   While withholding information from the President bordered on treason, he absolutely refused to endure another media fiasco the magnitude of the last one.

" . . . We are making . . . progress, Mr. President. You can be sure I'll notify you the minute we have anything . . . substantive."

"Day or night. On second thought, *don't* call at night; a few more hours won't make any difference. You know, Bill, as awful as this sounds, until AIDS permeates mainstream Western society, no one in authority will panic. We've all but lost Africa and much of the Third World. The Far East can't bury them fast enough. And you know what? . . . Few care. With destruction of the drug culture imminent and the nearly complete eradication of indigents, I've actually heard people say this is good. Winnow the chaff from the seed."

"I don't doubt that for a minute. Who can fathom a continent depopulated? At this point, all I am trying to do is save humanity from extinction."

"Well, I have the utmost faith in you, Bill. By the way, I hear that woman you were with over the weekend is gorgeous. Where did you meet her?"

"How did you . . . who . . .?" One could not confront the President. "She's my secretary, sir. We..."

"I'm not interested in details about your personal life, Bill. I'm just complimenting your taste in women."

"How did you know?"

"Secret Service."

"Secret Service?"

"A man of your stature requires protection. Bill, you're the most important man in the world. Hell, a hundred people could do what I do. Probably more! But I doubt there's another soul on Earth that could fill your shoes."

"Thank you for your confidence and concern, but that . . . that puts a damper on my social life."

"Nonsense! You and your lady can have a normal courtship. We never go near the bedroom. That's movie stuff. Call me if there's anything I need to know."

"You'll be kept informed."

"Goodbye, Bill."

"Goodbye, sir."

"He knows *exactly* who she is and what we did," Fairchild thought, "and that's fine, because *nothing* is going to change!"

McDonnell was his boss–in a manner of speaking–but certainly not the arbiter of his morality or determiner of his leisure activities. He wondered what he should tell Roberta.

The President shut off his speakerphone. "Fairchild's found something." His comment was directed across the Oval Office desk to his aide-de-camp, Bob Harrison. "He hesitated before responding, was a mite too careful choosing his words."

"Then why the denial?"

"No doubt that unfortunate media situation several years ago. He wants time to be absolutely certain before being thrust into the national spotlight."

The phone rang. After identifying himself, McDonnell listened quietly for more than a minute.

"I'm sorry you feel that way. It would be wise to reconsider."

Without saying goodbye, he hung up. Harrison studied McDonnell's sober and disappointed expression for a clue to the nature of the call.

"That was the Japanese ambassador, expressing regret and canceling his request for a meeting. In diplomatic terms he just suggested I do something to myself that's not anatomically possible. Have General Shaw dispatch a detachment to impound that ship and detain its captain."

Harrison nodded, reached for the phone and punched in the appropriate number.

"Oriental *reprobates*," McDonnell muttered. "Bill Fairchild isn't the only one who's going to get fucked tonight."

. . .

Flying low, the Huey's grass-rippling downdraft disturbed a small pride of lions milling about a fresh kill. One magnificently maned male, monopolizing the feast, batted an impertinent cub harmlessly away. Tumbling head over tail, the youngster regained its feet and growling contentiously, bounded back. Either from pride or glut-induced lethargy, the adult delivered a final gentle swipe at the callow offspring, then abandoned the prey. Snarling victory but losing interest, the kitten yielded to its mother and commenced nursing in a most awkward position. His occasional, immature growl reminded the world who it was dealing with.

132

With the scene fading from view, the observer returned his attention to scanning the terrain ahead. Noting him adjusting his binoculars, the pilot throttled back.

"Spot something?"

"Naw. Keep going. One more pass and I'll mark this quadrant negative. How much fuel's left?"

"Fifty minutes."

The helicopter swung through a wide arc and then cruised north to conduct a final east-west reconnaissance. Upon reaching the eastern boundary of an adjacent sector, the captain brought the tail around, simultaneously ascending and gaining speed before heading northeast toward the base, twenty minutes away. The rhythmic beat of the large rotor, coupled with the craft's inherent vibration, lulled the observer into a relaxed reverie.

"Ever wonder why we are here?" he asked.

Not prone to introspection, the pilot answered obliquely, "In six and half months, I won't be."

"Been here long?"

"Long enough to miss my kids . . . and the wife."

The captain's tone and manner were unconvincing.

"My wife is here. A GS-9 with Procurement. Liaison to Ordnance."

"How does she like it?" The pilot was disinterested, but felt obliged to ask.

"As long as they provide us with air conditioning, hot showers, and cold beer, fine. She's enchanted with Africa, convinced it will become more beautiful every year." He stared pensively at the vast expanse unfolding below. "And I think she's right. It's returning to a primordial condition; great to look at, exciting to explore, but potentially lethal." The observer paused momentarily, looking away from the panoramic landscape to his pilot. "Sort of like strange pussy."

. . .

"Why would anyone want to be closer?" Sarah asked as they were seated at a table one row from the horseshoe-shaped runway. The casino show was about to start.

Charlie shrugged, thinking of several good reasons.

"They aren't really bare-breasted, are they? Some of the kids in here are pretty young."

The opening curtain removed all doubt concerning that supposition. A statuesque beauty posed motionless in cerise spotlights that mellowed, with altered filtration, into sepia tones. Nude from the waist up, with exquisite, tubular, chocolate-brown nipples capping symmetrical, perfectly formed breasts, her only attire was a tightly encasing full-length wrap-around skirt and ornately flowered turban. With patrician features, she personified a classic prototype of a future commingled race, the consummate amalgamation of humanity. A disco sound track–supplemented with a handful of live musicians–burst through the still cabaret. Coming to life, she oscillated, undulated, and haughtily preened.

"She's firmer naked than I am in a bra!" Sarah lamented in hushed tones. "Not an ounce of fat or a day over twenty-two."

Flowing with the music in a tasteful burlesque, the regal beauty shed her sarong. Wearing only a headdress, G-string, and four-inch spike heels which attenuated slender ankles and accented her calves, she tempted and tantalized while maintaining a psychological distance that forbade anyone from violating her or interfering with the act. A chorus line joined the star attraction, exploding from the wings and filling the stage with frenetic motion and ostentatious color.

Next, a magician materialized with the obligatory over-endowed assistant. Two cages wheeled from behind the curtains were positioned at opposite sides of the stage. To the left, a confined Bengal; on the right, one of the scantily clad chorus girls. The enclosures were covered, powder flared, and when the satin was lifted, the occupants, as expected, had exchanged places.

For his finale, the illusionist led a huge African elephant on stage. Bowing and smiling, he ignited phosphorous, which sent billowing smoke to overhead kliegs. Through the dissipating haze, the audience saw that the elephant had vanished, replaced by the show's magnificent star, ready to bestow one last heady look.

"Her G-string is so far up her crack you can't see it!" Sarah whispered with vehement disapproval. "Do you know how uncomfortable that is?"

Enrapture inhibited Charlie's response but did nothing to stem contemplation.

"Remember that obscene teddy you bought me last year?"

"Uh huh."

"Oh good, you can talk. It's so uncomfortable I can't wait to get out of it."

"I can't wait to get you out of it, either."

"Oh, *honestly*."

Abruptly the cabaret was plunged into darkness. The clear, whispered vibrato of a solo trumpet slowly crescendoed as a pinpoint of light lasered center stage, then expanded to caress the beauteous headliner of Nassau's finest show. In pagan prayer she raised her arms, reaching for the heavens with supplicating, provocative hands. A sudden blinding luminance seared scores of attentive eyes as crimson smoke obscured the girl. The narrowly focused beam held steady, knifing through the blackness of the cabaret. She was gone.

Outside, weaving through the casino crowd to an exit, Charlie offered detailed personal observations of the beautiful star's body.

"Honestly, Charlie, if someone heard you, they'd think you'd never seen a woman's ass before!"

"I'd never seen hers," he said in mock defense.

"That is *so* tacky and *so* old."

Sarah was right concerning the French restaurant–they could not afford it. But the dinner was a wonderful extravagance. The food was exquisite, and the service was faultless.

Too tired for a poolside nightcap and with Sarah determined to avoid that depressing guitar player, Reginald, the Grants went to their room. It seemed a good idea to sit on the balcony and enjoy the tropical night. Shortly after 1 a.m., happy and content, they collapsed into bed, made love, and kissed good night.

Lori Tomasini would have traded a year of her life to share one such evening with Ed.

11

An emerging sun turned night into day. Omega 22's squat military buildings–transgressing upon the African landscape–cast staggered shadows. The surface temperatures of whitewashed eastern walls would soon be sufficient to blister unprotected flesh. By midmorning the solar heat would tax rumbling multi-ton air conditioning giants to their limits, wearing at components as it ate at people . . . searching for, attacking, and breaking the weakest.

Distant thermals would weave whimsical mirages and create illusory lakes and unstable apparitions. The hospital and other flat-topped buildings seen from departing helicopters would seem topped with amorphous pools. It was easy to understand how heat-induced paranoia fueled the desert folly of pursuing a receding, equidistant shoreline in hopes of quenching one's thirst.

Eighty yards west of the largest edifice, a block structure that served as the hospital, sat a row of medevac and reconnaissance helicopters. Poised like mutant cloned dragonflies, they awaited their pilots, ready at the turn of a switch to wrench themselves into the air.

One of those men, Capt. Edward Reynolds, emerged from the back door of a small facility marked "Nurses Quarters." Raising dust with every step, he strode at a leisurely pace around the hospital, past a fuel tanker with a BP logo, and approached the air traffic control operations office.

Dressed in a light-weight, khaki flight suit and traditional patent leather billed hat–in lieu of the more common baseball-style cap preferred by most of his fellow pilots–Reynolds entered the building. After stamping dust from his shoes as a Midwesterner might attempt to rid his footwear of snow on a blustery winter morning, he turned to the PFC on duty and bitched, "Jesus Christ, it's hot. I figured by leaving at dawn I'd be airborne before it got so fucking miserable!" Scanning the room to further vent his spleen on anyone else unlucky enough to be around, Reynolds noted the presence of a recently assigned Spec 4 he recognized, but with whom he had never flown.

"Who are you?" he demanded.

"Specialist Fourth Class Paul Michaels, *sir*," the young soldier responded, snapping to attention.

"Where's Jack?"

This question was directed to Capt. Benjamin Essell, wing commander, who was double-checking the day's mission assignments on a computer screen.

"Sick bay," he responded, without looking up.

"Does Michaels know what we are getting into?"

"Ask him."

Reynolds returned his attention to the medic, expecting an answer without the courtesy of repeating the question.

"Follow-up recon mission, possible pickup, sector 43, *sir*."

"Ben, is he aware of standing procedure if... "

Essell quickly glanced up to forestall completion of the query. "No, and it shouldn't come to that. The survivor appears in good health."

"What if he isn't?"

"Avoid the situation."

"Suppose I can't."

"You have your orders, Ed. Justify them."

"Swell. Come on, kid, let's get out of here before it gets any fucking hotter."

"Yes, sir!"

As he left the building, the young man paused in the doorway and, in a low voice, asked the commander, "Is he normal?"

"I certainly hope not," Essell philosophized.

Paul Michaels hurried out, trotting to catch up.

"Fucking heat!" bemoaned Reynolds, reaching for a web safety belt to strap himself in while keying the radio transmitter.

"MV-27 checked out and operational. All systems go. Flight plan: November 27-2004-1. Ready for liftoff. Over."

"Acknowledged and cleared for vertical ascent, MV-27. Flight level one-zero. Status check at seventy-five miles and upon arrival; every twenty minutes during recon. Over."

"Roger. Out."

As the aging Huey's rotor collected speed, the cockpit floor trembled, and skin sections rattled around worn rivets. When the composite blades changed pitch to commence the arduous task of lifting the chopper, the sensation on board became one of being buoyed atop a bubble. Dirt flew and, one by one, camp buildings were obliterated until no signs of civilization remained.

"Poor fuckers eat that shit fourteen hours a day," mused Reynolds, pointing at the percolating haze they were creating. "It's obscene, Michaels. MV-27 to base, Omega 22. Over."

"O-22. Go ahead."

"Let's park these birds further out, Ben. You people shouldn't have to breathe dust all day. Over."

"Taken under advisement. A sudden stroke of altruism, Ed?"

"Negative, Captain, just hate to see a pussy ground job fucked up. Clear."

The altimeter wound past nine hundred. Coming around to a heading of zero-one-two, the helicopter continued to ascend, then rapidly accelerated to an air speed of ninety-five knots as the indicator steadied at one thousand feet.

It was a routine mission. Yesterday a recon team spotted an adult male frantically waving one hundred fifty miles north. Upon notifying base, they were instructed to avoid contact, but to videotape the subject and his surroundings, including any easily recognizable landmarks, and to record the precise location using their differential global positioning system.

During crew debriefing, a review of the tape indicated the subject was black—hardly a revelation—around thirty, and did not appear ill or injured. He kept pointing and gesturing as if others were nearby. Orders were issued for the team assigned to MV-27 to fly out in the morning, locate the survivor, pick him up if necessary, search for his family or friends, and deliver those requiring medical attention to the hospital.

Twenty minutes after liftoff, Reynolds and Michaels were cruising thirty miles north of Omega 22. Pleased by his decision to depart early, Reynolds planned to complete the mission and return to base before the heat became debilitating. With luck he could lunch with Lori.

"Sir, isn't sector 43 designated potential Type 4?" Michaels nervously asked.

"That's the rumor."

The young man was appalled at the implied risk.

"And we have to transport him?"

"Son, nobody in their right mind transports a Type 4, voluntarily or otherwise."

"But we won't know until we get him to the hospital and run tests."

"Well, son, you are making two rash assumptions. One; that this person needs to be transported and two; if he does, we're going to do it."

"You mean we aren't bringing him back, regardless?"

"Bingo!"

"But we have orders."

"*Bull......*shit!"

The medic lapsed into a contemplative, confused silence. On a selfish, primitive level he felt relief, harboring no burning desire to nurse a doomed Type 4 for an hour and a half. On the other hand, if they were going to abandon a man in need of assistance, why bother to locate him?

Dropping down to six hundred feet, they followed a zigzag course for twenty miles, maintaining a nominal northerly heading. Sensing his subordinate was disturbed, Reynolds pontificated, "Out here, son, there are orders and then there are orders. Order number one is to not convey anyone that might infect the camp."

"I never read that."

"Yeah? Well, you fucking won't, either."

Despite the displayed insensitivity, Michaels accepted his logic and found he could not dislike this particular pilot who was little different from the others. There was no civilizing the men that helicoptered missions throughout Africa. Assigned by temperament and molded by duty, all were frighteningly similar.

They drank too much, occasionally before missions; were dedicated to flight, not saving lives; and grew more callous with each passing week.

They willingly abandoned families for months to staff hardship areas. No sacrifice was too great to gain airtime over unfamiliar terrain. Emotionally stunted at twelve or thirteen, they possessed the eye-hand coordination of gifted athletes and the intelligence of successful candidates for the most demanding disciplines. An amalgam of contradictory characteristics, they were primitive and sophisticated; childlike and adult; disciplined or unruly–depending on their mood and the requirements of the job; and living for the fix flying provided.

Marrying late if at all, they were blessed or cursed with a powerful sex drive. At home–their wives willing and the time of the month permitting–they engaged in daily intercourse. During hardship tours they sublimated their urges to aviation until– fraternization rules be damned–establishing a liaison with a receptive and available woman. Demanding frequent and immediate satisfaction, single or married, they were seldom without at least one if not several compliant partners.

"Are you married, Captain?" It was a not so innocent question triggered by Michaels' train of thought, for he was aware of Reynolds' liaison with the young nurse.

"Three daughters. Why?"

"I read someplace that pilots sire sixty percent girls."

"Where the fuck did you read that?"

"A medical journal in the day room. It was based on a 1988 study of military pilots and astronauts. A Ph.D. candidate in sociology updated the earlier investigation, examining the records of four hundred pilots between 1988 and this year. The percentage held."

Reynolds, with his female brood of three, expressed a genuine interest. "No shit!"

"The conclusion was that g-forces caused stress that inhibited development of male sperm, thereby increasing the probability of siring girls. You think that's possible?"

"Are you shitting me?"

"No, sir. What were you flying before each of your girls was conceived?"

"F-14's."

"See!"

"Interesting."

"A second conjecture predates 1988. You'll like this one."

After a pregnant pause Reynolds urged him to continue.

"A theory was developed during the late seventies or early eighties... I'm not exactly sure when... that frequency of intercourse has a significant effect on sex determination. Male sperm swim faster than female, so if intercourse... "

"Fucking."

Ignoring the correction, Michaels continued, " ...is infrequent and the woman ovulates, male sperm will get to the egg first."

Reynolds felt a pleasurable swelling coupled with an urge in his groin.

"However, a male sperm quickly dies, so if no egg is present, a surviving female sperm may impregnate a late egg or... and this is the good part... if a couple has intercourse often, there are always sperm around. The chances are the longer living female determinants are in the uterus, ready to pounce on the egg when it's released."

"You're telling me I fucked myself out of a son?"

"Sure looks that way, Captain."

"Damn!"

With the image of his cute little nurse from hospital records dominating his thoughts, the urge in his groin grew insistent.

"Therefore, macho men have daughters. Jocks with sons like to brag, but the facts are, while they are out playing ball, the guys with daughters are at home..."

"Balling their wives!"

Reynolds fixated on what a great stud he was, something always suspected and now confirmed. He felt warm and proud and happy . . . and horny. He could not wait to get into Lori's bed that evening and bang her. Those big tits were going to get a workout tonight!

"I'm going to like you, kid."

Reynolds transmitted a status report. At seventy-five miles, halfway to intercept, their mission was brought sharply into focus.

"What are you going to do if we find someone, sir?" Michaels asked.

"Well, kid, we'll start by not hauling any potential Type 4's back to Omega 22, I can tell you that! One sick son of a bitch could endanger our entire operation. Hardly beneficial to the Type 1's, 2's, or 3's at the hospital. Or our support staff. Anyone alive in sector 43 is undoubtedly a carrier, part of the Typhoid Mary fraction of one percent that gets it, takes forever to die, and infects everyone they come into contact with."

"Rumor has it some pilots have killed suspected Type 4's instead of picking them up."

"I heard that, too. Terrible thing."

"Would you ever do that?"

He was reluctant to use the word "did."

"That's a tough one, kid. Hard to know how one might act with sufficient provocation."

"Not an answer," thought Michaels with foreboding.

The chopper's shadow passed over a herd of giraffes which quickly receded, their shapes fading to unidentifiable dots, finally disappearing altogether.

"When I first got here I used to circle something like that," Reynolds reminisced. "Just proves anything one sees often becomes ordinary. Except pussy." The bird angled down to four hundred feet. "One hundred and forty miles out, kid. With our GPS coordinates and a few landmarks, we shouldn't need a search pattern, just a survivor with enough sense to stay put."

"Why do you doubt that? He's the one who initiated contact."

"Because we're dealing with a dumb nigger."

Michaels bristled, hurt and angry.

"Is that what you think of me?"

"Come on, Specialist, you're an African-American and fairly intelligent, or you wouldn't have made Spec 4 in the Medical Corps. It's so obvious I'm embarrassed to say it, but since you don't seem to understand, there are whites and honkies, Vietnamese and gooks, African-Americans and... "

"I get the point! How can you work in Africa and think like that?"

142

"Why not? In my high school a fourth of the kids were white or black with a hand-full of Orientals. The rest were honkies or niggers. I'm used to it."

Michaels did not respond. Besides Reynolds being his immediate commander, talking to him was starting to screw up his mind. While all the pilots seemed heartless, from the safety of an antiseptic flight deck, this man made it into an art.

"Omega 22, MV-27 to Omega 22."

"This is Omega 22. Go ahead."

"Approaching intercept, Omega. Landmarks identified. No survivor. Copy?"

"Commence search pattern. Clear."

The olive-drab chopper descended to three hundred feet and moved at forty knots in an ever-expanding spiral. Their sweep had taken them four miles from the intercept when Reynolds asked, "See anything?"

"Negative, sir."

"I'm going to increase velocity. Keep a sharp eye!" The air speed indicator crept to fifty knots, steadied.

"We going much further out?"

"Affirmative."

"Why, if we aren't going to engage?"

"S.O.P., my friend. S.O.P."

Unsure why, a subtle change in Reynolds' manner made Michaels hope they never located the man, but before sagacity silenced his tongue, he blurted out, "Captain, look!" for to the north something was moving along the savanna-like floor toward a rise two miles away.

"Could be an animal but it looks upright," he reported, peering through binoculars.

"Roger. Let's check it out."

Rotor rpm increased, the bird jumped forward and veered right, coming on course to close on the suspected target. The altimeter wound down to two hundred feet as forward motion slowed to twenty knots. In seconds the distinct outline of a man became obvious.

"Got him."

The impersonal label, the ring of a hunter closing in on prey was unmistakable. The man looked up and waved. Airspeed dropped to zero as the helicopter eased to one hundred feet and held position, whipping light dust along the surface.

"Give me the glasses."

Michaels slipped the leather thong over his head, surrendering the binoculars. "Aren't we going in?"

Reynolds adjusted the focus. "Beats the shit out of me." He descended to fifty feet and reexamined the native.

"He doesn't *look* sick, Captain."

Not responding, Reynolds spun the tail of the chopper one hundred eighty degrees. Inching forward, the craft moved out a few feet, completed a full revolution and settled to the surface, whipping debris over a huge circular area. Feeling the skids touch, Ed switched off the engine, leaving the rotor to coast overhead, inertia maintaining its spin. Oppressive heat enveloped them, taking their breath. Reynolds adjusted his sunglasses, leaned back in his seat and peered through the dust, large particles of which were already settling on the airframe. The native stood his ground, afraid to advance, or expecting them to come to him. Reynolds issued a command. "Go talk to him."

"Aren't you coming?"

"I stay with the bird. Standing orders."

With more than a little trepidation, Specialist Fourth Class Paul Michaels unbuckled and dropped to the ground as the blades continued to rotate slowly overhead.

"Keep your distance! Don't touch him or let him touch you."

"I won't."

Reluctantly, the medic approached the statuesque African. Face to face with a man very likely to be a Type 4 carrier, knowing the briefest contact could be fatal, he wished he was safely aboard the helicopter, high above an Africa that snuffed out life at a touch, a sneeze, an errant cough. Reynolds got out, unsnapped the flap of his holster and leaned against the fuselage, a boot heel hooked over a skid. After a final flurry of spirited talk and gestures, Michaels turned and started back to safety. The native followed. Michaels halted, cautioned him to wait.

"Well?"

"With many dialects out here, I had trouble understanding

him, but near as I can tell, he needs a ride."

"No shit?"

"Says he was hunting and went too far. Tried to flag down the recon unit yesterday to take him home. He's worried about his kid, a boy about twelve who's alone over that ridge."

"What did you tell him?"

"That I had to ask you."

"Tell him, no."

"Can I at least find out where the boy is so we can make sure he's okay?"

"Good idea. What happened to the rest of his family?"

"They're dead."

"That's too bad." Reynolds knew that in all likelihood, the father and son were carriers.

Michaels returned. "His boy is in a village five miles north of the ridge. No one else is left."

"He has skin lesions."

"I noticed. What do we do?"

"Follow Captain Essell's orders."

"I thought you said you'd never pick him up."

Reynolds started away from the shade of the helicopter, an enormous, stilted grin creasing his face, wrinkling the skin around his eyes. Michaels, instantly suspicious, ran to catch up.

"What are you going to do?"

"Talk to him."

"You don't know the language."

His grin continuing to broaden, Reynolds maintained a steady pace and, without turning, ordered his medic back.

"Sir, you can't talk to him unless I interpret."

"Go the fuck back! That's an order!"

The orderly froze. Conditioned to obey yet dedicated to saving lives, his brain was in turmoil as it processed contradictory signals. Legally or morally he was going to lose.

At a safe, comfortable distance, Reynolds stopped, grinning from ear to ear. The African returned the smile to this great white man who was going to transport him in the giant metal bird to his very hungry son.

Open abscesses and the beginning of others were distinctly

visible. Ulcerated ones oozed and must have stung as the sun further damaged sensitive, exposed tissue. The native wished the large carnivorous flies, attracted to fetid flesh, would stop tormenting him, but shooing them provided no relief as they either clung tenaciously or transferred to a different ulcer before the motion of his hand was complete.

Reynolds was prepared for the human misery that stood before him, but the encounter remained unnerving. Here in the middle of this godless wasteland, a lush jungle before the ravages of twentieth-century man converted it to a near barren plain, was a contemporary. Born in America to an affluent, suburban African-American couple, he could have been flying the helicopter, not confronting its pilot.

Beyond redemption, this man was ten paces from infecting him with Type 4 AIDS and a similar wretched fate. His hand moved deftly to the service pistol at his side. In smooth, practiced movements, he removed the weapon from its holster and, planting both legs apart, brought it up in front of his chest, his left hand joining his right to stabilize the piece stiff-armed before him. Aiming directly between the man's eyes, both hands folded around the pistol grip, he squeezed the trigger in the prescribed manner.

To a prolonged "Noooo!" erupting from the orderly's throat, the firing pin flew forward, striking the outer rim of the cartridge, exploding powder, and rifling the bullet down the barrel of the automatic, hurtling it through twenty-five feet of space, into and out of the native's head.

Momentary surprise and horror flickered deep within the man's eyes before a little round spot formed on his forehead slightly left of center. His final thought was of his boy waiting alone for paternal care that as of this moment would never come. Sadness had not time to show before his brain ceased functioning. The back of his skull exploded into fragments of bone and hair, blood and brain. Jerked off his feet, he splayed backward and fell prostrate to the earth from which he had sprung.

Reynolds closed, then reopened his eyes, holstered the gun, and walked back to the helicopter and distraught medic, the echo of Michaels' scream and the sharp report of the automatic temporarily impairing his hearing.

"What in hell did you do that for?" demanded Michaels, fighting for control.

"Shut up and get on board."

"You didn't have to do that!"

"I just saved your life. Get in."

Numb, more than anything, Michaels ducked under the tail section, climbed over a strut, and ascended the rigging to his seat. Reynolds cranked the engine and engaged the rotor as Michaels found and secured his seat belt. Dust whipped across the arid land and settled over the corpse, annoying flies that deserted ulcers to feast on a fresh wound.

At four hundred feet Reynolds turned north. Cruising at fifty knots, they vectored toward the ridge two miles away.

"Where are we going?" Paul asked suspiciously, dread and revulsion welling up inside.

12

Michaels began to feel nauseous. "You didn't answer me."

"North," replied Reynolds, as if that explained everything.

"You *wouldn't.*"

Ignoring the Spec 4's mounting horror, a dispassionate Reynolds feigned incomprehension. "Wouldn't what?"

"You can't! Not a child!"

"We may not even find him."

"But if we do you'll kill him, won't you?"

"Let's look around for a while."

Michaels wracked his brain for an option. While impossible to condone murdering a child, he also realized they could not transport the boy, especially after seeing his father. Returning him to base would literally condemn all personnel to death. Now he understood the unofficial "solution."

"Why not just leave him? He's going to die anyway."

"Slowly and painfully. Alone and frightened."

"But you can't shoot him! Back home he'd be a sixth or seventh grader!"

"We're not... *back home,*" Reynolds quickly pointed out. "Look, Paul, I don't want to do this. I've never had to, and I'm not sure I have the guts . . . but it has to be done."

"Why can't you just leave him alone?"

"Because that's inhumane, goddamn it!" Reynolds exploded. "He's not a dog, *Captain*! He's a human being!"

Ed's voice grew softer. "All the more reason to alleviate his suffering."

"Oh, *shit!*"

Michaels felt powerless to argue against such logic. Since Dr. Kevorkian, euthanasia was widely accepted for the terminally ill. Perhaps a mercy killing *was* the best of many unacceptable choices. And then, from the depths of consternation, a possible alternative emerged.

"If he doesn't show symptoms, he may have a reasonably long time to live. Why can't we maintain isolation until he gets sick? Maybe there will be a cure before he has to be . . . "

His supposition trailed off; he could not say the word.

"There isn't going to be any remedy, Paul, and as a medical technician you know that better than me. AIDS is like the fucking flu. What's therapeutic for one case won't necessarily benefit another. Besides, AIDS hasn't begun to mutate."

"No one knows for sure."

"Like hell. It's evolving into new strains, related but unique, every fucking day. It's a family of diseases like cancer, which we also haven't conquered. Right?" Avoiding eye contact, Michaels remained silent as Reynolds persisted. "Right?"

" . . . Probably."

"Probably, *hell!* Besides, how would a twelve-year-old, alone, feed himself?"

"We'll airdrop supplies."

"Fly all the way out here to deliver food to one doomed little kid?"

"What's wrong with that?"

Having no immediate answer and finding the suggestion not unreasonable, Reynolds needed a more plausible excuse to put an end to this situation, *now*, before he lost his nerve and his vision of the father's diseased body faded from memory.

"He could starve before we get back."

"People exist for weeks without food and you damned well know it! Our emergency packs will sustain him until we can get approval to return."

"Suppose we crash?"

"*Goddamn* it, Captain, it's unlikely we'll crash! Even then we can call for help. And if the radio's dead and we miss three check-ins, they'll come looking for us, S.O.P.! Search-and-rescue will home in on our satellite emergency locator beacon. Have I forgotten anything?"

Michaels was proud of himself. He not only stood up to this military bastard, but shot down arguments before they were advanced. In the midst of self-congratulations, he was first to spot the outline of native dwellings growing out of the plateau floor less than a thousand meters ahead. Reynolds throttled back, not wanting to over-fly, nor get there too soon. Michaels scanned for signs of life as they closed.

"Nothing's moving," he commented.

"He's probably hiding. We'll land a ways out and go in on foot."

"Promise you won't hurt him."

Reynolds remained edgy and irritable. "I'm not promising anything!"

"I'll turn you in."

"Who the fuck would believe you?"

Immediately after the helicopter's skids touched down, the engine was shut off to conserve fuel. Without comment, both men stepped to the ground.

Thirty-odd huts were clustered in a circular pattern surrounding a barren, open space. Methodically the pair searched each shelter with Michaels peering into its entrance while Reynolds circled the perimeter. Two-thirds of the way through, in a stick and earthen hovel, the little boy cowered.

"He's in here," Michaels quietly announced, hoping to avoid further alarming the frightened child. Using a crude approximation of the father's native tongue, he offered a package of cookies, which he placed at the hut's opening before taking several steps back. The boy hesitated, then eagerly garnered the treat as Michaels confronted Reynolds. "He's surprisingly healthy and seems to understand me. We're going to make friends, leave him rations, and go. You are *not* going to kill him."

Ed noted the assertiveness his medic projected and doubted it was false bravado. The nature of this African assignment rapidly made or negated an individual's authority. If one wavered, another involved in the situation made a decision. Admiring Paul's spunk, however, did not alter his conviction.

"Tell him to come out."

"You are *not* going to kill him!"

"Follow orders, Paul."

Doubting Reynolds would go into the enclosure, Michaels parried. "*You* get him."

"Get him the fuck out! That's an order!"

Insubordination became moot. Slowly, tentatively, the boy emerged. One barely audible word escaped his mouth.

"What did he say?"

"Food," answered Michaels, discretely positioning himself between Reynolds and the boy. "He's hungry."

"He looks healthy."

"I *told* you. Sound medical practice dictates we avoid contact, but… "

"There are no 'buts', goddamn it! You act like you never saw anyone die from this shit!"

Reynolds' rage contrasted with the calm demeanor masking Michaels' inner terror as he deliberately remained in the line of fire. "We'll maintain a safe distance. I'll tell him to keep away from us. He'll understand."

Another utterance from the boy set Reynolds off again.

"Now what?"

"He's thirsty."

"Poor little bastard. Get a canteen."

Such compassion was out of character.

"You go."

"Goddamn it, Michaels, your new self-confidence may be the eighth fucking wonder of the fucking world, but I'm still in command. Get the water. And bring the emergency packs."

Their confrontation continued with Michaels holding position, uncertain how to interpret this abrupt change of heart.

"He's just a kid," Reynolds expostulated. "I don't need to further taint my immortal soul with the blood of a child. We'll leave him food and water, and go."

"I don't trust you."

"Listen, you enlisted son of a bitch, if I want him you can't stop me, so get your ass in gear so we can return to base and get the hell out of this *fucking* heat! I need a beer."

That, was the real Reynolds. Hesitantly, Michaels removed himself from the line of fire.

"Tell him where you're going and to stay the fuck put until you get back."

The boy said nothing, yet appeared to comprehend the instructions. With Reynolds' manner now non-threatening, Michaels had little choice. At the edge of the village he paused one last time in a psychological effort to intimidate his pilot and commanding officer, only to find Reynolds' automatic pointed directly at the little boy's head. Terrified, the child stood mute and motionless, perhaps mature enough to understand the seriousness of the situation, but unable to grasp its irrevocable finality. Though witnessing the deaths of family and neighbors, in his child-mind he could not comprehend his own.

Michaels realized arguing was pointless. His mind racing, he carefully avoided any unexpected movement that might result in the firearm's accidental discharge and started back between the huts. "You want me to watch?" he calmly asked.

"*Wait, there*," Reynolds precisely enunciated.

The boy froze in terror as increasing recognition of his impending demise gelled inside his youthful brain.

"No, I want to watch."

"Goddamn you, get out of here!"

Drawing nearer, Michaels reasserted, "I want to watch. You figure the back of his head will explode like his father's did?" Reynolds brought the barrel around and aimed it at Michaels. "No witnesses, Captain? An unfortunate accident? Gets easier all the time, doesn't it?"

The cold, soulless stare deep within Reynolds' eyes reflected little about the workings of his mind. "Do not move," he ordered, the unwavering barrel pointed at Michaels' chest. "Watch, if you have the stomach."

There was nothing more Michaels could do. Powerless to halt the proceedings, psychologically mismatched with a seasoned executioner, Michaels found little comfort in having tried. "Get it over with. He's petrified. And for God's sake don't miss and maim him."

After a final visual warning against interference, Reynolds

reaimed his automatic at the child. Terrified, but submitting to fate as he had succumbed to hunger and deprivation throughout his life, the youngster squatted and curled into a fetal position. Reynolds lowered the gun, training it on the top of the boy's head, fingers tightening around the grip. Sickened, Michaels looked away.

"Damn it to hell!" Reynolds exploded, rapidly spinning around and targeting a clay pot in front of a nearby hut. The automatic pistol emptied in a burst of fire, the urn disintegrating into unrecognizable shards, fragments, and chips. Reynolds holstered his piece. "Satisfied?" he asked with disdain.

Michaels ignored his comment and hurriedly moved to comfort the frightened boy. After they conversed for several minutes he turned to Reynolds. "I'm going for the canteen and food packs." With that he quickly strode away, leaving his commanding officer facing the boy who, in turn, watched him intently with a mixture of fear and awe.

As they flew south in excess of a hundred knots, Reynolds broke the silence. "What did you say to him?"

"I told him we would send more food and water tomorrow, and then supplies would be delivered on some regular basis."

"Who in hell do you think will be dumb enough to fly back there tomorrow?"

"You."

"Medevac 27; base to Medevac 27. Respond."

Reynolds acknowledged Essell's radio transmission.

"Where in hell have you been? You're in violation of communication regs."

"Stick it up your ass, Ben. We ran into trouble."

"Did you find anyone?"

"Affirmative."

"Appropriate action taken?"

"Yes and no. I'll explain when we get back."

"Anyone on board?" It sounded more like an accusation than a question.

"Negative, for Christ's sake!"

"Report to my office the minute you return. How's your fuel

supply?"

"Adequate."

"E.T.A.?"

"We'll be late for lunch. Will you call Lori and ask her to meet me a half hour later?"

"Affirmative. Position check at seventy-five miles, or I'll have one of your bars. Clear."

Reynolds nudged the controls to skirt the area where the body of the youth's father laid. It was a premonitory decision for Michaels probably would have vomited at the sight of feasting hyenas. Some things were better left unknown.

"What stopped you, Captain?" Michaels asked as Omega 22 hove into view. It was his last opportunity to broach the subject.

"I don't know," confessed Reynolds, uncharacteristically subdued and introspective. "Somewhere we all draw the line."

Reynolds landed his bird one hundred fifty feet west of the wing of stationary medevac choppers. Two others already rested there in a rudimentary formation.

"We should have parked out here from the beginning," he asserted.

"Won't most pilots balk at the additional walk in this heat?"

"Fuck'em. Essell and I make the rules."

Michaels was beginning to believe that.

"What are you going to report?" he asked.

"About what?"

"The man."

"Officially?"

Michaels gave a confirming nod.

"Never found him."

"And the boy?"

"The truth. Well . . . an expurgated version."

"I'll corroborate."

. . .

Lori Tomasini completed medical training at twenty-one and began as a floor nurse in a Minneapolis hospital. She hated the hours: nights, weekends, holidays, swing shifts, and doubles. There were hassles, paperwork, and egotistical, demanding doctors by day, and meds and boredom by night.

Quickly stressed out, Lori resigned to take a position as nurse-receptionist for a young internist with a fledgling practice. Her salary was barely adequate, but he was a nice guy and she enjoyed the work, including the inevitable intimacies. Often after the last patient had departed, Lori removed her panties, and the good doctor unzipped his fly. On occasion, he took her to dinner. Then a young woman appeared, introducing herself as Mark's fiancee from Cincinnati. Totally disenchanted and starting to care for him, Lori split.

The Omega Corps promised excitement, high adventure, and humanitarian service. It delivered drudgery, bone-weary fatigue, and the fear of contracting AIDS. Plus, there was nothing to do with one's leisure time except watch videos and drink! The only interesting thing in the entire place was Capt. Reynolds, and for weeks he did not seem to know she existed. Then, quite suddenly, he began to seek her out at the Officers' Club during the evenings and the mess hall at noon when he was not on a mission.

Handsome, exciting, and straightforward, Ed was a blessing. "I want to fuck you," he had said during their third casual lunch. He did not say, "I love you;" or, "I want to fuck *with* you;" or that non sequitur, "I want to sleep with you." All he said was a good old fashioned, "I want to fuck you." That was very refreshing and kind of cute in a barbaric sort of way. Something about him scared her. She liked that. Twenty-two years old, her doctor/lover behind her, she knew what to expect from this experienced man. Within days he got his wish.

Most of the nurses entertained "company" in their rooms and jokingly wondered why BOQ's had been constructed. Few were discrete, as if their lovers were husbands and their GI cots connubial, queen-sized beds. She and Ed walked the middle ground. He usually arrived after the others and returned to his quarters before anyone awoke.

. . .

"Thanks for waiting, Lori." Ed expressed his appreciation as they unloaded trays and sat down.

"Big sacrifice. Now I'll have a three-hour afternoon instead of four. How did it go?"

"As usual."

"Didn't find anyone?"

"Never do in a yellow zone. I think the guys are spotting apes."

He took a bite from his corned beef sandwich. Lori avoided mentioning oft-repeated rumors about unofficially sanctioned elimination of all human life in Type 4 sectors, refusing to acknowledge Ed's participation. Early in their relationship, when she questioned why he, Lt. Kolata, and a few select others were the only pilots dispatched to investigate yellow-zone contacts, he had been evasive, mumbling inconsistent and incomprehensible reasons. She decided against further probing.

"We did spot a little boy," Ed volunteered.

"Did you bring him in?"

"No. He seems healthy, but he's gotta be a Type 4 carrier. Ben wants to maintain him in his 'habitat.' I'm flying back tomorrow with enough supplies for a fortnight. How's your day going?"

"I'm tired. Let's turn in early."

"You don't mind if I show up before the rest?"

"I hardly think we're a secret, Ed, especially when the base commander calls to tell me you'll be late."

. . .

Seated across from Bill Fairchild in a small café in Little Italy, Roberta was astounded. The implications and ramifications of Secret Service protection seemed enormous. "They *watched* us? Actually *watched* us?"

"Apparently so."

"Oh, my."

"I don't think they actually *saw us* . . . I mean . . ."

"I *know* what you mean. And the way sound travels on the water . . ." He managed a weak smile over her dangling thought. "Well, what's done is done, and I certainly have no regrets, but I can't believe how tacky this whole thing is," she concluded.

"It was probably distant surveillance. Just close enough to protect us."

"From *what*?"

Fairchild shrugged. "Accidents? Muggers? Foreign terror-ists? A radical who doesn't want a cure, some religious nut who thinks AIDS is God's will? The President's rationale is that if anything happens to me, the program will be set back. We're running out of time as it is."

"Why didn't he have the courtesy to ask if you wanted bodyguards?"

"I might have declined."

"Do you believe that?"

"Yes."

She thought a moment, then answered, "That helps, although it will be a while before I'm not paranoid when we're in bed."

Fairchild leaned across the table and spoke in hushed tones. "I suspect those two men in the second booth are part of the current team. Try not to stare, but turn around and take a peek."

Roberta stole an innocuous glance. "I only see one. Is he wearing a dark blue suit?"

"Yes."

"I don't believe it! This is worse than a single-star, made-for-TV movie."

"I'm afraid it's inevitable, especially after talking with the president this morning."

Lunch arrived ... chef's salads, larger than anyone could eat at midday. Roberta removed her onions. "I forgot to ask the waitress to hold these. What did you tell McDonnell?"

"As little as possible."

Fairchild, who loved onions, reluctantly began removing them from his salad. Roberta put down her fork.

"Are we moving too fast?"

"Probably."

"Want to slow down?"

"Absolutely not."

"I don't want to scare you off," she looked away before continuing, "yet I don't want you going along with this just because . . ."

"The sex is great?"

"Blunt, but I guess that's what I meant."

"Honey, if we were kids it would be different. We aren't." He chuckled. "Especially me."

On the way out, Roberta paused beside the booth containing

the suspected Secret Service men and flashed a coy smile. "Did you gentlemen enjoy your weekend at the lake?"

"I beg your pardon, ma'am?"

"Didn't I see you at Port Clinton last weekend?" She exuded innocence.

"I don't see how." It was more an admission of stealth, than a denial.

"I'd swear I saw you, and your friend, too." Roberta unexpectedly turned to Fairchild, drawing him into her charade. "Don't you remember them, Bill?"

"I really don't, Roberta. Perhaps you were mistaken."

Attempts to nudge her to the door were unsuccessful as she held her ground, smiling demurely. "Maybe I am wrong. Sorry to have disturbed you, gentlemen."

With four quick steps she was at the register, waiting on her befuddled escort. He collected his wits and joined her.

"Cute, Roberta, real cute."

"I thought so." It was hardly a remorseful comment.

"You realize two new men will be assigned after they report this incident."

"How do you know they'll be men?"

"Roberta!"

"It doesn't matter. They'll be just as easy to spot."

"And just as easy to get rid of?"

"If I put my mind to it."

"These agents are only doing their job."

"True, but maybe they'll maintain a more discrete distance in the future. Might afford more privacy when we're . . . occupied."

He gave up. More than youth she brought vitality and the joy of living to him. He wondered what he gave her and hoped it was enough, for he wanted to marry her. The thought made him falter as he rooted for his keys. He wanted to *marry* her. How could that be? Was he that vulnerable, that lonely, or, as she so often pointed out, was this relationship less spontaneous than it seemed?

"Roberta."

"Yes?"

"Never mind. We'll talk later."

158

13

Ed Reynolds sat opposite his friend in the cool confinement of the wing commander's office.

"I couldn't do it, Ben."

"You're just putting it off."

"Find another officer for this one."

"Can't do that. How would you like it if I gave you one of Kolata's eliminations?"

"Look, I know you're right. This isn't killing; it's the alleviation of suffering, but . . ."

"Not a child?"

"That's right."

"Take the rest of the day off. We'll talk about it later." Reynolds rose to leave. "Any preference on who rides shotgun tomorrow?"

"You."

Essell smiled. "Wish I could. This place is claustrophobic."

"Give me Michaels."

"You sure?"

"I'm not sure about anything, but I think if I work with him, he'll understand and be valuable to us."

"I'll add his name to the duty roster. Top off your tanks this afternoon. After the supply drop to the boy, recon sector 42."

"Exciting, fucking life."

. . .

Securing the door after admitting Ed, Lori went to the utilitarian chest of drawers and placed her bracelet in the jewelry

159

box on top, quickly closing the lid in an attempt to prevent the incursion of ever-present dust.

"What time do you have to get up?" she inquired.

"Same as you."

Reynolds glanced at the bolt. Their ritual to ensure privacy: Lori locked, Ed checked. Slipping out of her uniform, she sat on the edge of the bed in her panties and bra while he disrobed to his Jockeys and stretched out on his stomach behind her.

"Tired?" she asked.

"Not especially. You?"

"Uh uh. I got a second wind."

"What are you thinking?"

She turned and began stroking his back. "That I'd give anything to go to a town for dinner and shop at a mall. This isolation is frightening. It's as if the rest of the world doesn't exist."

"I feel that way on every mission, though less than a month ago at the airport in Kisangani you'd never suspect anything was wrong. But just wait. In six months hardly anyone will be left."

"I can't bear to think about it. Then again, after April, I won't have to. Will you miss me?"

Her inquiry was pointed. He had never said he loved her, nor had she told him. Their total relationship was company at meals, someone to pal around with, snuggling at night, and sexual release and pleasure. Reynolds' third-lunch comment summed it up: "I want to fuck you." Now, he made an uncharacteristic admission.

"Of course I'll miss you. I don't want you to go."

"Do you *love* me?"

The L-word, finally out in the open, gave Reynolds pause. Of the many ways to love a person, only one mattered to Lori.

"Yes," he responded quietly.

"Do you love your *wife*?"

That question put him on a spot he preferred not to occupy. What did she want to hear? Which response was in his self-interest? What was the truth?

"Not like I do you."

Lori appreciated his choice of words, honest and direct.

"*How* do you love me?"

"It's . . . separate."

"How so?"

"Well, you're here and . . ."

"She's there?"

"It's not that simple."

"I'm sure it isn't."

"Lori, I told you the truth when I said I had no interest in anyone here until you came. I slept alone for over a year."

"Why me?"

Reynolds thought a long moment before the next admission, one that would forever alter their relationship. "Because I can't do it with a girl I couldn't marry." Ed paused again, looking directly into her eyes. "I could marry you."

Startled, Lori collected her wits long enough to answer, "Do you love me enough to divorce your wife?"

"Maybe."

Doubting it wise, she pursued the topic by inquiring, "If we were married, and I was back home with *our* kids, would you still shack up with someone?"

"That's not a fair question."

"Why not?"

Ed thought a minute. "Because men and women are different."

"Not *that* different. Answer the question."

"If she was as nice as you?"

"*Yes, Ed.*"

"Maybe."

"*Maybe?*"

"Probably not."

"*Probably* not? You're a strange man, Captain Reynolds."

In spite of his responses, her feelings toward him were suddenly important. "Do you love *me?*" he asked.

"Would I sleep with you every night if I didn't?"

"I don't know."

"Trust me, Ed. I wouldn't. Once in a while . . . *maybe.*"

"Are you going to re-up in April?"

"So we can make love every night?" She wasn't astonished. It was just another question.

"No, I want you to re-up because I'll miss you."

"That's months away."

"Will you?"

"Would you do it for me?"

"Yes."

"Now that's interesting. I think you would." She kissed him on the cheek. "Can we talk about it after Christmas?"

"Whenever you want."

A monumental leap in their relationship now established, Lori became introspective and analytical. "I accept that you love me in the conventional way in an unconventional situation; our microcosmic universe here. But tell me this, Ed, if you had to state the two most important reasons why you love me, aside from sex every night... that's a given... what would be number one?"

With furrowed brow, Reynolds sat upright. "You're a free spirit, not all wrapped up in yourself or a cause. You came here for a lark, same as me, and because structured life back home is a pain in the ass. Right?"

"Yeah, sort of . . . I guess. What's number two?"

"Those tiny hairs growing on the inside of your thighs. They make my cock ache."

"You're *perverted*." She sounded like it pleased her. Unhooking her bra and stepping out of her panties, she stood before him. "Well, Captain, are you going to let me be the only one naked?" Reynolds removed his shorts and pulled her down on top of him. Between nibbles, she whispered in his ear, "I wish these walls were thicker. Joyce heard us last night."

"So? Everyone in the building can hear her puffing and wheezing. She shouldn't smoke."

"Deliver us from reformed smokers." Ed ignored her taunt, so she delivered another. "And don't you moan in ecstasy?"

"I thought that was you."

Lori cuffed him. Sharing muffled laughter, he rolled on top of her on the narrow bed and proceeded to give her ample tits the workout he had promised himself earlier. With both thoroughly aroused, his hard, condom-sheathed cock slipped smoothly and quickly inside. Her legs wrapped around him as he thrust; after a minute–not more than two–she felt him ejaculate.

She loved the weight of his big body, limp and satisfied, upon her, but wished he would last longer or stimulate her to climax before entering–preferably both. "Oh, well," she thought, "someday we'll work on that." For now she was content to experience his warmth, his flaccid penis surrounded by her vulva, and for a few more minutes their closeness before uttering, "Ed . . . *Ed*!"

"What?" he mumbled sleepily.

"Get off. You're heavy."

"Sorry."

Bearing his weight with his arms, he lifted up as Lori wiggled from under him, then collapsed onto his side, almost falling from the bed. No sooner had he pulled her to spoon, when sleep reclaimed him.

Lori wasted no time positioning her right hand between her thighs. Using light, full motions she stroked between her anus and pubic hair, devoting substantial attention to stimulating her clitoris while her left hand alternated between breasts, massaging around and around each nipple.

In moments she returned to her previous level of arousal and with her pelvis rearing and her abdomen rippling, fought to remain quiet through wave after wave of ecstasy. Almost exhausted after several climaxes–each bigger than the one before–she worked toward a frenzied finale. Unrestrained ebullient outbursts aroused a groggy Ed.

"You okay?"

"Fantastic."

"Someday I'll teach you how to do that," she thought, reaching behind her and patting his hip as she spooned closer. If you become good enough, I might even re-up.

. . .

Rays from a punishing sun seared every surface as the Grants rode the moped over the camelback bridge to the main island and turned right on Bay Street. Specialty shops, the Straw Market, and the Cable Beach hotels slipped quickly by. The scooter had been rented for two hours, plenty of time to circumnavigate the twenty-two-mile-long island at their leisure. Cruising at two-thirds throttle, they passed the airport, rounded the western end of

New Providence, and approached Miller Sound, encountering a cement plant and a few nameless intersecting roads leading to the nearby sea, but little else. Made drowsy by the wind, vibration, and monotonous engine noise, they looked forward to returning to the sanctity of their room for a nap, in preparation for spending an afternoon on the beaches of Paradise Island.

As they neared the east shore, clusters of modest cottages appeared; occupied by the army of poor islanders that supported the wealthy tourist industry. And directly ahead, lay a barricade with a large yellow arrow attached that routed traffic onto a small connecting lane of dirt and loose gravel. Instead of turning onto it, Charlie brought the scooter to a halt beside the barrier. Though nothing specific appeared out of order, he sensed something amiss. For one thing, there were no signs of the usual preparations necessary to do road repair. And no people were outside in the partitioned area, either. They were not in their yards or idling time on front porches or steps. That was odd. Looking back at the block through which they had motored, he saw no one there either, so maybe the absence of activity was not unusual.

"Is something wrong?" Sarah asked, over the stumbling idle of the engine.

"What do you suppose that's all about?" He pointed east of the detour.

"Road work."

"I don't see any."

"Maybe they haven't had a chance to start."

"Then why divert traffic?"

"To start tomorrow? Maybe the barrier just went up."

Sarah could not imagine why she and her husband were sitting on a rented scooter in Nassau discussing road repairs.

"Look there; honey. See the tire marks where vehicles have turned?" Sarah nodded with no idea where this conversation was going. "The road is rutted but doesn't appear to be heavily traveled, so the barricade has apparently been up a long time. Something's not right."

Sarah removed her helmet and shook out her hair as Charlie turned off the engine. "What are you getting at?"

"I'm not sure, but something's different across the barricade when compared to this side. I just can't decide what."

Immediately comprehending, Sarah explained, "It's the level of care. All these places have junk lying around. But look, in the yards we passed, it's better organized. And over there it's… " she paused to get the right word, "random. Behind us the grass has been cut and flower beds are tended. Beyond the barricade it's unkept, almost looks abandoned."

An unwelcome reality was slowly gelling in Grant's mind. He noticed something else amiss. "Sarah, there are no children up ahead." Quizzically, she looked to him for an explanation. "We passed several yards with trikes, big wheels, assorted yard toys. Look over there; nothing."

Lightning struck simultaneously. "Oh, my God, Charlie; it's an *AIDS* compound!" With mutual horror, the truth registered.

"Part of the island has been cordoned off for AIDS victims," Charlie reasoned. "They never meant to fool anyone into thinking there was road work because they never expected tourists to be here."

"An isolation ward."

"The modern equivalent of a leper colony."

"Why would they do that if Type 4 wasn't present? Oh, my God!"

Torn between a primal urge to flee and morbid fascination, they stood mesmerized across the barricade. The scene affected a macabre hue, more closely resembling a series of crypts than a back street Caribbean slum. Charlie broke the deepening spell.

"Children must be housed elsewhere or hospitalized."

"Let's get off this awful island."

"We can't leave until Saturday."

"Pull strings! You're a congressman. *Bump* somebody!" Panic was rising.

"Honey, I'm not a congressman here. This is a foreign country, remember? Even if I could, they'd only make room for me. You'd have to stay."

"Will you *try*? Will you at least *try*? I want to go home!"

Charlie reached for her hand. "I don't think it will do any good, but I'll call as soon as we get back."

Grant raised the kick-starter and pushed down rapidly,

spinning the crankshaft and getting a weak cough in return.

"Oh, *God*," Sarah exclaimed.

Further attempts caused the little engine to sputter, but it steadfastly refused to fire. A dozen tries accomplished nothing.

"Oh *shit!*" Sarah despaired.

Charlie tried reassuring her. "The engine's probably overheated and needs to cool down."

"Why did you shut it off?" she snapped in frustration.

"Honey . . ."

"I'm sorry, but if you hadn't... Charlie, I'm scared."

"There's nothing to be afraid of. Look, I'll push it away from here, down to the next intersection."

Over the barrier an unkempt, emaciated woman, more apparitional than corporeal, materialized on the rickety porch of the nearest dwelling, apparently curious about the source of the ongoing commotion. Riveted by the sight, Sarah shrank in horror behind her husband. "Oh, God . . . Charlie! Get us *out* of here!"

Gripping the handlebars, Grant leaned into the scooter, expecting it to roll easily, but encountering resistance in the loose gravel and yielding sand of the roadbed. Seeing him straining and anxious to put distance between themselves and the moribund– whatever it was–Sarah quickly assisted.

"Thanks. When we get to the corner, we'll wait until it cools." Unaccustomed to such exertion, they inched the heavy scooter along the detour with Charlie's encouragement. "Just a little farther."

Sweaty and exhausted, they eventually succeeded in traveling the two or so hundred feet and found themselves looking down a residential street with the suspected AIDS colony beyond the back fences of houses on the south side.

"Who'd want to live here?" Sarah cynically asked, heading for the shade of a palmetto tree while attempting to purge the ghastly female specter from her mind.

"People with nowhere else to go." Charlie reset the kick-stand. Because the sandy soil was unable to support the weight, the scooter promptly fell on its side. "Fuck!"

"Leave it be."

Soaked with perspiration, Grant settled to the ground beside his disheveled wife. A bevy of chickens wandered over from the house behind them, hoping for more sustenance than their owners provided. A curious goat, tethered to the veranda, stretched its chain to the limit, hoping to share any good fortune found by the chickens.

"God, that thing stinks," Sarah complained.

Charlie waited five minutes and again spun the starter. Several futile attempts later he gave up, unleashing a string of his favorite invectives. After a long interval, his next effort was successful as the balky engine roared to life.

"Thank God!" Sarah exclaimed, then urged, "Let's get out of here!" while climbing onto the buddy seat.

As they pulled away, a woman in a nearby house moved away from the window and returned to the chipped, green-enameled, wooden chair she had occupied before noticing activity across the road. Had the Grants been able to see her, they might have estimated her age in the low forties when, in fact, she had just entered her thirty-first year the week preceding their arrival.

Once a successful waitress in a restaurant near Government House, poverty and six active children had stolen her youth. At the end of the tourist season two years ago, she had been informed her services were no longer needed. Now, American soap operas and occasional fights with an abusive husband, who appeared only to impregnate her, filled forlorn days.

"I need a bath," Sarah remarked as the scooter coasted to a stop in the path of the approaching rental clerk.

"You were gone a long time," he winked. "A romantic interlude by the sea?"

"I made the mistake of turning off the engine."

"And it failed to restart immediately? I'll send it out for service." The man turned the ticket over and jotted a notation on the back.

"Why is that street blocked?" Charlie wanted to know.

"Which one?"

Grant described the location as best he could but was unable to provide its name.

"I'm not certain. A lot of roads are being repaired."

"We didn't see any workers or equipment."

167

"Perhaps they have finished."

"Then why are the barricades still up?"

"Life moves slowly here, unlike where you are from."

"It's restricted to AIDS victims," Sarah vehemently averred.

The man's expression sobered as he studied her. Denial would be useless. "We unfortunately have several cases of the disorder you mention."

"How many?" she demanded.

The man hedged. "A house here, a house there. For the protection of us all, a rather large area was quarantined."

"I'd say so," Sarah remarked snidely.

"If we err, it must be on the side of caution. We are not trying to hide the extent of the . . . problem. You are free to roam the island. So is everyone else."

"Any Type 4's?"

"Certainly not!"

"Do you believe he is telling the truth?" Sarah asked as they crossed the street to the hotel entrance.

"About Type 4?"

"Everything."

Charlie shrugged. "This probably happened so fast there were no other options but to quarantine. Suddenly faced with large numbers of potentially contagious people, coupled with insufficient hospital facilities, they had neither the time to take a chance nor money to build more."

"We have to leave this island."

"I'll call as soon as we're upstairs." They entered the air-conditioned comfort of the lobby. "But don't expect miracles."

"I don't; I just want out of here."

. . .

Snow was falling as the Grants' plane landed on schedule at Akron-Canton. Being on time was a pleasant surprise, as typical Bahamian indifference resulted in them being predictably late leaving Nassau. Fortunately, the flight crew requested and received permission from air traffic controllers to cruise at a higher altitude to take advantage of favorable winds. Two-thirds of the deficit was made up on the leg to Atlanta. A heavy hand on the throttles between Georgia and Ohio regained the remaining twenty minutes.

"Glad to be home?" Charlie asked as they gathered their carry-on possessions.

"Am I ever!" Sarah retrieved her straw hat from the overhead compartment. "But I feel kind of silly now, making such a fuss about trying to leave early. I absolutely adore the beaches and ocean."

They arrived at baggage area 3 as the carrousel began snaking through the crush of impatient fellow passengers. Momentarily, the first suitcases nudged the thermal barrier aside. Sarah pointed to an emerging bag. "There's one of yours. When do you leave on Monday?" Already planning her week ahead.

"My meeting with Fairchild and the President is scheduled for 10:30, so I'll probably catch the 7:35. There's an earlier flight, but no way in hell am I getting up at 4 a.m. the first Monday after vacation."

"Won't you need time in D.C. to get ready?"

"There's nothing to prepare. I assume AIDS is the topic, or Fairchild wouldn't be there. More than that, I don't know."

"Maybe there's a cure."

"That'll be the day! Where in hell is the rest of our luggage?"

. . .

Highway crews had been caught napping by the storm; salt trucks and removal equipment were nowhere in sight, and Interstate 77 was slippery and snow covered. Warm air and the weight of vehicles liquified snow under tires while the frigid roadbed quickly refroze it. The combined effect made driving on the resultant slush extremely hazardous.

"Welcome to Ohio," Charlie muttered under his breath while exercising extreme caution. A rapidly moving car passed them, throwing semi-frozen grime over the windshield. Charlie said, "Bastard!" then slowed to let the wipers catch up. "You haven't mentioned the kids," he observed.

"I can't let myself think about them, or I'll start imagining all sorts of horrible things have happened."

"We can pick them up tonight if you wish."

"In this weather?"

. . .

169

Sarah picked up the library phone and pushed the preset that automatically dialed her mother's house. She was in luck. The children had been kept up.

"Daddy and I will get you right after breakfast, honey," she told Jennifer. . . . "Mommy misses you, too, but the side streets are too bad to drive on tonight. First thing in the morning, I promise. . . . Yes, my right hand is up. Now, be a good little girl and go to bed for Grandma."

Sarah's mother came back on the line as Charlie carried the last of the luggage to their upstairs bedroom.

"Mom, you won't believe what we saw. Charlie and I rented a moped on the third day and went for a ride around the island... Yes, all the way. It's not that big. . . . Twenty-some miles, I don't remember. Anyway, we came upon this detour and . . ."

Charlie passed out of hearing and then caught more of the conversation as he reentered the downstairs hall en route to the fridge for a beer.

"The shops are great! Most things cost the same as here, but if you know what you want and can remember prices, there are some fabulous bargains in upscale merchandise. I've been lusting after a particular brand of perfume... That's the one. . . . Well, of course, I bought it! Oh, and I found . . ."

Out of earshot, Charlie was sorting the mail in the kitchen when Sarah rejoined him.

"Would you like to share your beer?" She took a sip, handed it back as the phone rang. "Thanks. I'll get it. Mom probably forgot something."

Sarah returned to the library as Charlie went back to the mail.

"Barb!" she squealed into the telephone. "I've been trying to reach you for ages! I called from the airport in Atlanta a week ago today and again this afternoon when Charlie and I had a short layover. It's so nice to . . ."

Her initial excitement spent, Sarah's voice returned to normal, and Charlie could not hear any more. Expecting her to talk for a long time, he turned on the under-cabinet television, but in minutes she was back, ashen and shaken.

"The reason I haven't been able to reach Barb is because she spends all her time in the hospital. Sam has AIDS."

Sarah was devastated. Barb's husband was dying, and dying from AIDS made it doubly obscene. She searched Charlie's expression for clues to his reaction.

"You don't seem surprised."

"I'm not. Sam fucked any woman that would lie down . . . and probably some that wouldn't!"

Sarah knew it was true. Promiscuity had always been a way of life with Sam. He did not become more sexually active after marriage; he simply maintained the status quo.

"Charlie, why is this happening?" Sarah tried desperately to understand. Suddenly her color drained. A horrible and plausible probability pressed in. "Oh, my God! That bastard may have given her AIDS! Even their kids aren't safe. My God, what a mess!"

"Depends on the type."

"Charlie, as far as we know he's strictly heterosexual and probably has a more transmittable strain. I *told* her to leave, that he wouldn't change. Womanizing *bastard*! Always thought he was so cool. God's gift to women. Now we know what God's gift to *him* is!" Sarah was livid.

"Honey."

She leaned down, spontaneously kissed him on the cheek. The expression of affection not consistent with her mood, he asked, "What's that for?"

"Being a decent man."

14

Organizing the massive testing program to determine super T-cell effectiveness without raising false or unrealistic hopes was a delicate balancing act.   Fairchild labored from 7 a.m. until he could no longer think or focus his eyes–occasionally midnight–and Roberta often stayed with him.

Wednesday evening she insisted they leave at 7:30 after Bill's exhaustion was manifested in worrisome ways, and he reluctantly agreed. Leaving her car at Northcoast, they departed in the Buick with Roberta behind the wheel despite his weak protestations.

Arriving at her apartment minutes later, she settled him in the living room with the newspaper and a stiff drink, then prepared a light supper of soup, salad, and fruit.

By 10:00 they had showered and gone to bed. Enveloped in each other's arms, they silently embraced for a few moments before making love.   Bill nodded off immediately after, but Roberta fought slumber long enough to reset her alarm to seven, reasoning both needed extra rest, and he would soon be ill if he did not slow down . . . or make mistakes . . . or both. If he was upset tomorrow morning after discovering her ruse, so be it! Spooning behind him, she pressed her body close, put her arm around him, and surrendered to sleep.

. . .

The alarm woke only him. He checked the time and smiled, realizing what she had done. Gently waking her, he whispered his thanks.

"For what?" she sleepily asked.

"The additional rest."

"Oh, that. You're welcome."

. . .

"I hate re-wearing a sweaty shirt," he complained as they dressed.

"Maybe you should leave a clean one here."

. . .

It was late Friday. With Northcoast Harbor, the Rock and Roll Hall of Fame, and Lake Erie in view, Fairchild's car entered the parking garage, paused momentarily at the ticket dispenser, then rolled down the ramp into the subterranean depths beneath the mall. Spotting a choice space near the elevator, Bill parked and hurried around to open Roberta's door.

Ascending to the first floor, they strolled past exclusive shops, then entered the lobby of a companion office building and walked to a waiting elevator. No sooner had its doors closed than Bill reached over, kissed her lightly on the lips, and said, "I love you."

"What's going on?" Roberta asked, reaching into her purse for a tissue to dab lipstick from his mouth.

"Just a relaxed evening after a hard week."

"I think not."

"You're too suspicious, my love."

The elevator reached the top floor.

"Fairchild, party of two," Bill informed the pleasant hostess.

Running a finger down the reservations list, she responded, "I'll page you when a table by the west windows is available."

"Just another date, huh, Fairchild?" Roberta chided as they entered the lounge.

"As I said, you're too suspicious."

"What an absolutely *breathtaking* view. Oh, my, that's scary!" Roberta exclaimed, quickly repositioning her chair away from the wall after looking down at the street several hundred feet below. Bill moved next to her. "I have always considered this side more impressive," he remarked, gazing through the glass.

Terminal Tower, anchor of nearby Tower City, glowed with historic grandeur despite the newer, taller buildings clustered around Public Square and the lakefront, which dominated the skyline. The Shoreway—delineated in amber—snaked westward through the city, upstaging luminance emanating from neighborhoods and distant shopping centers. Running lights on pleasure boats moving along the Cuyahoga River dotted the black waters directly below. The elaborately fitted vessels circled to observe activities on shore or moored at one of the many Flats' restaurants and bars.

Dinner was superb. Elegant ambiance complemented the restaurant's fine cuisine; generous, top-shelf drinks; and exotic desserts. Mellow and full, their cares and difficult hours of the week melted away.

"When are you going to let me in on the big secret?" Roberta inquired as after-dinner liqueurs arrived.

"Now is as good a time as any."

"No, wait, let me guess. We are going to spend the night on the boat?"

"A pleasant thought, but too distant for the hour."

"A late performance at Playhouse Square?"

"Capital idea… but, no."

"We're sleeping at your house for the first time?"

"Soon. But not tonight."

"Okay. I give up."

Bill reached across the table, enveloped her hands in his. "I want you to marry me."

The balance of power had shifted and none too subtly.

"You're *proposing* to me?"

"Why does that surprise you?"

"Because we've only dated a month! Don't think I'm not flattered or unreceptive, but…"

"I didn't mean this weekend or next." Bill was amused.

"*When*?" Roberta asked suspiciously, thoroughly convinced of a greatly abridged timetable.

"Christmas would be nice." He was *serious*.

"*Bill!*"

"It doesn't *have* to be then."

"You've only dated *me*. What if . . . what if someday you regret not taking the opportunity to see other women?"

"I won't."

"I'm not so sure."

"Roberta, if you don't love me . . ."

"You *know* I love you."

Bill wisely dropped that line of reasoning.

"Bill, I'm scared. All of a sudden the tables have turned. I pursued you... sort of. Now, *I'm* the quarry."

"I'd hardly put it that way," he smiled.

"You know what I mean. I'm scared and you aren't."

"There is nothing to fear."

Roberta looked at this wonderful man she had known for years, loved for . . . she was truly uncertain at what point in time that feeling surfaced. "Maybe we can live together," she suggested.

"No."

"*No?*"

"Our relationship can remain as it is, or we can marry, but living together is unacceptable."

"Suppose I want to?"

"Sorry."

Roberta leaned back, her gaze boring into him as she analyzed the situation. "You know, my mother told me that someday I would meet a man that couldn't be pushed around and he'd be the one."

"So, say yes."

"May I qualify my acceptance?"

"That depends."

"Does it really?"

Her initiative heavily eroded, Roberta continued studying the man she had methodically courted. Conflicting emotions and motivations vying, an awful thought occurred.

"You didn't buy a ring, did you?"

"Before asking or determining your preferences?"

"Then the reason for this very special date was . . . is . . . a proposal?"

Bill responded with an affirmative nod.

"But there is no ring?"

"That is correct."

"Well, that's something."

It did not help that tonight marked the logical culmination of months of planning, being indispensable, available, and supportive. 'Scheming' was more descriptive. God punishes by granting what you want. Although she did not believe that, the phrase passed through her mind. What if sex was all Bill needed and did not realize it? If true, given enough time, commitment would fly out the window. God, she wished she was not so analytical.

"You firmly believe we're going to marry, don't you?"

"Without a doubt."

"Do you know how annoying I find that smugness?"

"I'm beginning to," Bill smiled, smugly.

"Like many little girls, I dreamed of being swept off my feet by Prince Charming. Now I'm not so sure I like it."

"Will you marry me, Roberta? I love you."

For one last moment of independence, she paused, then answered, "Yes. But when I'm ready. Please don't push."

"Agreed."

"Now I suppose you'd like to celebrate?"

"That would be nice. A perfect ending to a perfect evening. We have only to shake our bodyguards."

Intrigued, Roberta raised an eyebrow. "You can do that?"

. . .

After electronically sweeping the room, the uniformed White House Security officer posted his partner at the door, keyed the two-way radio using the microphone clipped on his shoulder, and notified the President's secretary. "Room's secure, Kim."

She buzzed the Oval Office. "The room is ready, sir."

"Thanks, Kim." McDonnell switched off, then immediately back on. "Have Grant and Fairchild taken there upon arrival."

Robert Harrison, who stood by the President's desk, wanted to know, "Any additions to the agenda?"

"Nothing I can think of. Discussing AIDS should be traumatic enough."

The intercom sounded. "Dr. Fairchild called, sir. He's behind a multi-vehicle accident fifteen blocks away. Doesn't anticipate a lengthy delay but wanted you alerted to the possibility."

"Your words or his?"

"His, sir," she laughed. "I'd have told you he'd be ten

minutes late."

"Sounds like him. Call back, and tell him not to worry. Nothing else is on the calendar until one o'clock."

McDonnell scrutinized his aide. "You've read the reports, Bob. Do you think Northcoast made a breakthrough?"

"These aren't reports, sir. Updates, perhaps."

"Goddamn it, stop sidestepping my questions! You act more like a politician every day. Let's not debate semantics. I asked if you thought Northcoast is on to something."

Harrison was unruffled. "Having read the . . . reports, I find no indication."

"I disagree," McDonnell quickly retorted. "Fairchild is a master of the King's English. He's been hedging, but from reading between the lines, I believe he's hinting at significant progress. Either a preventative vaccine or an honest-to-God cure."

"I didn't pick that up."

McDonnell slid a folder across his desk. He was annoyed and growing impatient with his usually diplomatic aide. "Page three, fourth paragraph, near the bottom. Read it."

Harrison scanned the indicated section. "When I read that before, I didn't interpret it to mean anything special."

"Goddamn it, Bob, that's how he operates! Sneak it in, then later act surprised you didn't know." McDonnell impatiently snatched back the folder. "Listen to this; and I quote: 'We are currently experimenting with specific cells which seem to sense and attack HIV with greater than normal vigor. As research on this cellular family continues, updates will be provided.' Unquote! He's got something but isn't ready to go public."

"You may be correct, Mr. McDonnell."

Harrison's lack of conviction was painfully obvious. The President carelessly tossed the manila folder on his desk with the others. "You take a lot of shit from me, don't you, Bob?"

"At times."

"How much do you make?"

"Not nearly enough, sir."

"For all the shit that's heaped upon you?"

"Yes, sir."

The President roared with laughter. "You always tell the

truth as you see it, don't you?"

"That's why I was hired, and until told otherwise, I assume that's what you want."

"Given a choice, Bob, would you prefer more money or less shit?"

Harrison smiled. Easy working for a straightforward man. "More money."

"Hopefully, you'll see it next month but you know how slow accounting can be. And exchange your staff car for something more luxurious. There's a limit on how much your position pays, but perks are another matter. When the transaction on the Key West estate is completed, my wife and I will be doing a great deal of entertaining in Florida. I want you to take someone every time we go there. Officially, she'll be invited by Karen, but you'll be the one fraternizing with her." McDonnell chuckled, taking pride in his tongue-in-cheek humor and circumvention of rules.

"In what capacity shall I list my guest?"

"Companion." Harrison rarely demonstrated such naivete.

"Sir, won't it seem unusual that one of your wife's friends is so much younger? Especially someone she doesn't know?"

"We have friends of all ages and constantly meet new people. No, Bob, it won't look funny."

"But what if she and Mrs. McDonnell have nothing in common?"

"*Jesus Christ*, Robert! Karen may never see her! She'll be *your* guest. *You* will fraternize, not my wife! Ladies are *female* in case you haven't noticed. Surely you can think of *something* to do with her! Jesus Christ! I can't do everything for you!"

Harrison fidgeted as Kim's voice came over the intercom. "Representative Grant is being escorted to the Sanctuary."

"Thank you." McDonnell returned his attention to his aide. "Has the Secret Service encountered any problems protecting the good doctor since that episode in the cafe?"

Relieved his dearth of lady friends was no longer under discussion, Harrison summarized the most recent report describing Fairchild and Curtis' two-hour disappearance from the restaurant. "It was last Friday night, sir. We have no information on where they went or why."

McDonnell was more amused than exasperated. "We may never know *where*, Bob, but *why* is rather obvious. Remind me to discuss this incident with him before he leaves." Harrison made a note. "I understand his motivation and see some humor in the affair... God knows my wife and I share the problem... but I will not tolerate staff members circumventing their protection any more than I can ignore mine. If we lose this man, the battle against HIV is in jeopardy. The lengths to which people will go for a little pussy."

"With all due respect, Mr. President, I'd say the operative words are, 'a lot of pussy'."

McDonnell laughed so hard and long, tears came to his eyes. Eventually, he regained his composure. "Well, that's nice. I'm happy for him. He lost his wife and needs someone. You need someone too, Bob!"

"I'll work on it, sir."

. . .

No more successful in bypassing the traffic tie-up than any other vehicle on the street, Fairchild's limo was four minutes late when it passed the checkpoint and entered the White House grounds. After depositing its valuable passenger, the Cadillac stretch moved to the designated waiting area where its chauffeur turned off the engine, poured a cup of black coffee from his vacuum bottle, and relaxed with the morning paper.

. . .

Notified that Dr. Fairchild had also arrived and was en route to the Sanctuary, McDonnell rose from behind his desk. "The moment of truth, Bob."

"I hope your interpretation is correct, sir. The world could use a bit of good news."

"Where's Albert?" McDonnell directed the question to his secretary as he entered the reception area.

"On vacation, sir. Agent Flanders is filling in."

Flanders nodded to his chief.

"Nobody told me."

Kim was not about to be intimidated. "I did, sir, last Thursday."

"Bob?"

"She's correct, sir. I was with you at the time."

"Must be getting old. I don't remember."

"Not old, sir, just too much to keep in mind."

"Don't bullshit me, Harrison! If I say I'm getting old, then I'm getting old!"

Kim blushed, even though accustomed to the President's occasionally crude outbursts.

"You're getting old, sir," Harrison pleasantly agreed.

"That's better. Last thing I need around here is you turning into a suck-up."

. . .

The Sanctuary was the name McDonnell assigned to a previously unoccupied room near the presidential suite. Seldom utilized by countless predecessors, its door had not been opened for years until McDonnell ordered it unlocked. Without windows, the chamber perfectly suited his purpose. On his third day in office, the Chief Executive toured White House storage facilities and selected period furniture from revolutionary times–at least the articles appeared to be from that era–and requested that the curator determine authenticity. Each bona fide item was restored and placed in the room awaiting approval. McDonnell chose pieces he liked, directed their modifications and ultimate arrangement, and ordered the remainder returned to storage.

A magnificent period armoire, into which a refrigerator had been skillfully installed, dominated the executive chamber and functioned concomitantly as a display cabinet for a fine collection of old and valuable glasses. To its left, a dry sink held an electric coffeemaker, stored within when not in use; an impressive array of antique ceramic mugs; and a priceless pewter creamer and sugar bowl set, discovered by Mrs. McDonnell in an antique barn near Boston. A roll top desk contained paper supplies and writing instruments while artfully concealing a high-capacity document shredder. Around a fireplace whose flue had been bricked shut were randomly placed chairs, a small sofa, and several tables. Walls paneled in thoroughly reconditioned, rich dark woods served as elegant backdrops to several paintings from the President's personal art collection. Only the ever present, state-of-the-art secure telephone betrayed the facade of a Jeffersonian room for computers and recording devices of all kinds were prohibited. Electronically scanned for surveillance apparatus, regularly and immediately before use, the room was secure.

"Good morning, gentlemen. Thank you for being prompt. How was your flight, Bill?"

"Uneventful, sir."

"And yours, Charlie?"

"The same."

"Glad you both arrived safely. Detest flying in general, helicopters in particular. Hate that damned vibration. It feels like the tail rotor is trying to rip off the back end, which my pilot assures me is true. How's the weather in our favorite state?"

"The same as here," Grant volunteered. "A rather mild fall."

"I miss Ohio. Do you have a promising new treatment, Bill?"

That was getting right to the point. Grant was startled by the question while Fairchild reacted candidly to such bluntness. Hearing someone else say it was an odd sensation. An abstraction in his mind became a reality.

"I'm as certain as I can be," he responded, "until further research is conducted. I need more time and hadn't planned to say anything until extensive human experimentation is completed."

"A preventative?"

"No. We will continue to see the persistent and massive spread of the disease."

"Is a cure on the horizon?"

"Sadly, no."

"Then what exactly *have* you accomplished?" McDonnell pressed.

"Nothing guaranteed, though based on limited testing it appears we have bought some time."

"How much?"

"I can't provide an exact duration at this point."

"But you have gained remission."

Fairchild hesitated. "That may or may not be true."

"Please explain."

Fairchild took a deep breath, wishing he could be more definitive. "We are conducting investigations in two areas, but it's too early to determine which will be more successful. STCs... "

"What are they?" McDonnell interrupted.

"Sorry, super T-cells. Hence STC."

"Go on." The President assumed subsequent comments would explain the designation, "super."

"A colleague, Dr. Eric Li, successfully isolated superior T-cells that have the ability to recognize HIV's before and possibly after they adopt their host cells' genetic makeup."

"Therefore, the virus can't hide."

"At least not as successfully."

"What's your second theory?"

"STCs have forced HIV into remission. Let me explain Herpes Simplex I, which is genetically related to AIDS, and what may have happened will be clear. Herpes can literally hide in the brain. At least some in the medical profession believe that. Indeterminate periods of time may pass... months, maybe years... with no patient symptoms, then stress, an excess of citric acid, even overexposure to sunlight will trigger an attack. We... Dr. Li and I, among many others... assume HIV can lurk undetected somewhere in the body. Blood cells remain likely suspects."

"The result being remission, not temporary success against individual viruses."

"That is our supposition."

"But not a cure, and certainly not a preventative."

"Correct. Palliative is the proper category."

McDonnell spent a moment in contemplative silence. "Do your STC's work against all types of AIDS?"

"It's too soon to know, but I suppose early results can be duplicated on Types 2 and 3, based on their similarity to Type 1."

"Type 4?"

"That has yet to be determined, since it is much more virile."

"What can I do to help?"

"Increase funding. We need to recruit massive numbers of HIV-positive volunteers, and technicians and clerical help will be required to keep track of them."

"Done. Bob, send an order to GAO to rubber stamp all requests. Invoke my emergency powers."

Harrison made a note as the President's gaze bore into Fairchild. "Volunteers are to be told an absolute minimum, only what is necessary to conduct tests and obtain valid results. I don't want unruly mobs descending on test sites demanding medical treatment that isn't corroborated and can't be provided. And absolutely *nothing* to the media."

Fairchild nodded assent. "I couldn't agree more."

"Mr. President, why would it make any difference if this is publicized?" asked Grant.

"Because, Charlie, with any premature media exposure, we'd be deluged by uninformed editorial pressure and public . . . clamoring. Under no circumstances can the general public or foreign powers learn anything before we have something definite."

A plausible explanation, but a subtle change in McDonnell's demeanor made it ring false.

"The president is correct, Charlie," Fairchild confirmed. "You wouldn't believe the hell I went through last time."

"We'll hold a joint press conference when the appropriate time comes," McDonnell assured Grant while settling deeper into his chair. "Bob, have you anything to add?"

"Not at the moment, sir."

"Then that concludes this portion of our meeting. Charlie, I want you to stay a few minutes."

McDonnell rose and spoke in a quiet voice as he walked his AIDS research coordinator to the door. "I've instructed Secret Service personnel to maintain a more discreet distance. I'm sorry their presence is necessary, but I can't risk some fanatic shooting you or abducting you for ransom. As of yesterday, Ms. Curtis has her own protection for similar reasons. Someone stalking you may attempt to accomplish his goal by abducting her."

"I understand. I am sure she will, too."

"Then it would be appreciated if neither of you tried to elude your protectors in the future."

Fairchild suddenly felt as a schoolboy being scolded by his unit principal. "Sorry, Mr. President. It won't happen again."

"We're all new at this, Bill. My wife and I experience comparable pressures."

"It won't happen again."

Satisfied, the President placed a hand on the doctor's shoulder and abruptly changed the subject. "Sorry you were detained in traffic. Next time I'll have you helicoptered from National. None of us can afford delays. Have a safe flight."

After Fairchild's departure, McDonnell returned to the fireplace and remained standing, looking down at Charlie. "I want an accurate population report in thirty days. Complete demographics by country, continent, hemisphere. How many estimated to be infected; who they are. The number dead; who they were. Contact Bob or me if you need assistance, clearance, money... anything. Additional funds can be transferred to your office under the AIDS research appropriation. Any questions?"

"No, sir."

"Say hello to Sarah."

Obviously dismissed, Grant stood, shook hands, and moved to the exit. As he opened the hall door, McDonnell offered some advice. "I don't want your fourteen-hour workdays causing marital problems. Coordinate and delegate."

"As much as I can."

"I understand. Just don't burn out on me. In a different way, you are as valuable as Dr. Fairchild."

After Grant left, McDonnell crossed to the liquor shelf of the antique armoire, poured half an ounce of Black Velvet, and filled his glass with ice and Seven-Up.

"Help yourself, Bob."

"It's a bit early, sir, but thank you."

"Nonsense! It's almost time for lunch."

Submitting to Presidential coercion, Harrison splashed scotch over ice, took a sip and decided he would have only one with lunch. The President settled into a corner of the sofa. "Keep on top of this, Bob. Stonewall the media should they, by some bizarre twist of fate, get wind of it."

Harrison acknowledged the directive as McDonnell finished his drink in one gulp and continued. "Just being in this room gives me a sense of our heritage and my role in shaping the future. I thought the meeting went well, didn't you?"

"Yes, sir. But I found myself questioning the requirement for secrecy. May I ask what's going on?"

"In time, Robert, in time."

15

The Governor of the Bahamas stared at his executive order enlarging the Yellow Zone, painfully aware it would have to be discreetly implemented to avoid adverse effects on tourism. Official estimates predicted new diagnoses would fill the expanded area by March, though it might be sufficient until April with an accelerated death rate–a morbid thought.

The Governor felt a labor shortage was imminent, and envisioned a near future when finding sufficient labor on New Providence for cleaning the hundreds of rooms, staffing kitchens, running front offices, and the myriad other support jobs would be impossible. Young, naive immigrants could be lured with proper incentives, but to fill skilled jobs, mature citizens must be recruited with requisite wage increases, which in turn would affect hotel rates–the only bargain on the island. Visitors might object as dinner for two often exceeded the cost of fine accommodations.

All available rooms were booked this week–a miracle–but with rumors rampant, he was not optimistic business would remain strong after the holiday season. The only good thing was, most tourists did not want to know. Ignorance *was* bliss. But that would not bring the vast numbers of guests needed to return island enterprises to profitability.

Disquieted by futility, he rose from his desk, crossed to the east window, and lit his pipe. Smoke exhaled toward the opening, curled back and dissipated, leaving the lingering sweet aroma of fine tobacco. With skill bred of patient practice, he formed a large smoke ring, blew a second smaller one through it, then returned to his desk.

Signing the document, he summoned a clerk and instructed, "Copy and distribute this."

The young man bowed and ambled off to the mailroom in the basement.

. . .

Reynolds filed his flight plan with the air controller, then called Lori from the counter phone, asking her to step outside.

"Be careful, Ed," she cautioned.

The chopper rose two hundred feet and inched toward the hospital.

As a youngster, Reynolds had fashioned parachutes from handkerchiefs spirited from his father's top dresser drawer, pieces of string his mother saved in the kitchen, and elongated stones from the garden. By throwing these crude objects into the air or, if really ambitious, tossing them from a second story window, he created reasonable facsimiles of parachutes. Last evening, while Lori was visiting with girlfriends, Ed excused himself, rounded up materials and summoned long-dormant skills to craft a special one.

Firmly secured to this makeshift device was a note. Hovering over the parade ground, he pitched it from his Blackhawk. Its brief free fall was abruptly terminated as the tiny canopy billowed, easing the missive to earth a short distance from the steps where Lori was waving. Brimming with curiosity, she ran onto the field to retrieve the envelope and examine its contents.

"I love you, Lori Tomasini! Merry Christmas! Ed."

"How sweet," she said to herself. "What a tender fake you are, Ed Reynolds." Beaming, she waved and blew a kiss. The Blackhawk's nose tipped forward, then the craft spun around, gathered airspeed, and rapidly disappeared to the north.

. . .

Hadari sensed rather than heard the pulsations before locating a dark dot in the southern sky. As the helicopter became visible, he grew concerned about its unfamiliar shape, for the closer it came the more menacing it appeared. However, if it was not his friend, hiding or running would not change the inevitable, so he steadfastly stood his ground.

From the strange craft hovering overhead, the anticipated bundle emerged, descending rapidly until slowed by its small cargo chute. A second carton averted his attention as brightly colored wrappings shredded into bits and streamers under the onslaught of rotor-generated downdrafts.

Upon impact, a random gust refilled the collapsing canopy, which dragged the light container between two huts, threatening to carry it into the bush. Fast becoming adept in these matters, Hadari ran in pursuit, pounced on the inflated fabric and forced out the air. From its sheath, the young lad took out the hunting knife delivered on an earlier mission, severed the harness lines, and dragged the box to the front of his hut.

Inside the carton, he discovered treasures beyond his imagination. There were several balls. One, strangely shaped with points on each end, bounced and bounded in unpredictable ways. He found a knife with many blades and unfamiliar implements folded inside, plus picture books of mysterious places, funny looking trees, and oddly colored people; and a tan garment similar to the one worn by the pilot, which he would try on later.

His continuing search through the popcorn styrofoam uncovered a three-foot replica of an African child that reminded him of his little brother, who had succumbed to the plague at age four. Hadari's face split into a gigantic grin and, hugging the doll to his chest, he raised a delicate black hand, waving a grateful thank you to the white man who had once intended to murder him.

"Merry Christmas, you little shit," Reynolds said quietly to himself. "May God take care of you."

. . .

Grant sent his secretary home at noon. The balance of the staff returned after lunch to put things in order for the Christmas break, but departed before Charlie left for his appointment with the president. Except for security personnel, the hallway was deserted as he locked the suite and approached the elevators. During the short trip to the ground floor, he adjusted his tie, taking advantage of the reflective, black synthetic material facing the cab walls. Seconds later, the door opened into the lobby.

Through the expansive glass facade he spotted his ride, a lone government car idling in the parking zone reserved for VIP vehicles, its white exhaust vapor condensing in the wintry air.

A cold, steady drizzle wetting streets and sidewalks quickly generated bone-numbing chills. Although fall weather conditions had been moderate by Ohio standards, an impending blizzard promised to be calamitous. An intense low-pressure cell dragging a storm front up the eastern coast was gathering copious amounts of ocean moisture, and forecasters predicted substantial quantities of heavy, wet snow would be dumped on the city within hours. As usual, the lack of adequate removal equipment guaranteed a traffic-snarling shutdown of the nation's capital.

Charlie glanced at the bleak sky as, briefcase in hand, he strode briskly across the small plaza to the waiting limo. No wonder people escaped to Florida or the Caribbean. Though he enjoyed the seasonal changes–a frosty day with bright crystalline accumulations squeaking and crunching underfoot was an experience he was unwilling to relinquish–with advancing years, the in-between days of D.C. were becoming less tolerable.

"Representative Grant?" inquired the driver, hurrying around the car to greet him.

Charlie nodded. "Trip order four-four-three."

The chauffeur opened the door. "Hop in, sir. Have you at the White House in minutes."

Grant sank into the enveloping gray leather of the spacious rear seat, cradled by luxury he had come to expect as a presidential special assistant. Adapting to creature comforts and opulence required little effort, but privileges were coupled to responsibilities not always convenient. Nearly everyone–from influential to impotent–had departed for the holidays. With official D.C. resembling a ghost town rather than the center of world power, Charlie could not fathom why this report had to be rendered now. No doubt Fairchild and Harrison were no more thrilled.

Escorted directly to the Sanctuary, Charlie was surprised to find himself alone, expecting at least one of the others to have arrived. Craving a drink, but deeming it unwise to be presumptuous, he aimlessly wandered, noting a Robinson projection of the world had been mounted on the wall to the right of the fireplace since his last visit. Walking past the sofa for the third time, he abruptly placed his briefcase on the floor and sat. How would it appear if the President entered and found him mindlessly pacing? Minutes later, McDonnell burst into the room.

"Sorry I'm late! Got tied up on the phone. Care for a beer?"

"No, thank you."

A little surprised to hear himself decline, he was relieved when the President insisted. "Have a beer, Charlie. The holiday season is upon us, and I've scheduled our meeting for a time when you'd rather be en route to your wife and children. Have a beer! You deserve it."

"It does sound good."

"Get me one, too." McDonnell headed for his favorite chair.

"Any preference?" Charlie asked, perusing the limited selection.

"Whatever's handy." Picking the nearest two, Charlie twisted both caps off.

"Glass, Mr. President?"

"Bottle's fine. Sit down. The quicker we get through this, the sooner I can pack for Florida."

"Congress approved the acquisition?" Charlie could not recall voting on that issue.

"Hardly. We aren't going to the Keys. We're staying at a friend's new estate north of Tampa. Evidently a security nightmare, but that's not my problem, is it?" The President laughed heartily. "Are you and your family going anywhere?"

"Not this year."

"Wise decision. Best to celebrate Christmas at home when you have little ones. Now to business. Give me a condition report on all significant areas; precise numbers, percentages, forecasts."

"Shouldn't we wait for the others?"

"Others?"

"Dr. Fairchild, Bob Harrison. I assumed . . ."

"Just you and me, Charlie. I sent Bob home this morning; phoned Bill last night. You're the key man today. I plan to take advantage of the holiday to review data you've compiled. After the first of the year, the four of us will draw up our battle plan."

"Then Dr. Fairchild's STC's are effective?"

"Remission in the first few Type 1 volunteers, but that's not for publication. We may be a long way from any general success. We'll discuss that in January, too. What I need now are numbers. There are certain areas of concern, so allow me to dictate questions. In view of the hour, it will be more efficient. Does that pose any problems?"

"None at all."

"Good. First: central Africa. Data from the point of origin, with some adjustments, should predict patterns elsewhere."

"That isn't always true for reasons we can discuss, but your point is logical." Charlie extracted the report from his briefcase, located the desired section, and turned to McDonnell. "These statistics are appalling. If relief in the form of a complete cure... including Type 4... isn't provided soon, virtually everyone will perish. Hostile climates, the prevalence of secondary diseases, deplorable hygienic conditions, and as you indicated, the fact that AIDS started there, are all to blame. Already overloaded immune systems were powerless against attacks from a virus as virulent as HIV."

When Charlie stopped to sip his beer, McDonnell took advantage of the pause to speed things along. "How about other areas on the continent?"

"Despite immense depletion, many remain alive and apparently well."

"Any possibility of annihilation?"

"Always."

"Assuming it would take place, when?"

"Impossible to predict."

"I understand the difficulty, but give me your best estimate. You're my most knowledgeable source."

Charlie shrugged. "Two years, three years?"

"Anything else I should know about Africa?"

"An apparently symptomless survivor, a young orphan about twelve, has turned up in a confirmed Type 4 area."

McDonnell was instantly alert. "Go on."

"He's being maintained in strict isolation, with supplies air

190

dropped by the Army pilot that discovered him. No medical exam has been performed, but the youth's health appears good, and it's assumed he has been exposed."

"Would it be possible to take him somewhere for study without infecting medical personnel?"

"My first impulse is to say, no; but you'd better ask Dr. Fairchild."

The President drifted into a contemplative state. "A biologically different survivor. Perhaps unique. Fascinating." McDonnell became lost in thought. After what seemed an interminable interval, he directed Grant to proceed.

"There's nothing further on Africa except for detailed statistics on specific countries."

"Unnecessary. Let's go to India."

Charlie flipped through his report. "Events in Africa seemed to be duplicated in India a year later. Characteristics such as racial susceptibility or resistance, while unlikely, have yet to be correlated with HIV." McDonnell's arched eyebrow indicated his desire for further explanation. "Certain diseases occur more commonly among specific races or groups, so that aspect needs to be examined. Sickle cell anemia is a case in point, predominantly afflicting blacks. Another example is Tay-Sachs. Dr. Fairchild can elaborate."

"I'm familiar with those diseases. How many are left in India?"

"Sixty million, scattered mainly over the Deccan."

"Odds of survival?"

Charlie took a deep breath. "Minimal. Most will be lost within two years."

"Are those in Pakistan and Bangladesh included?"

"No, because almost all were wiped out with the Indus-Ganges people."

"Mexico?"

"Heavy losses with an indeterminate number infected. Computer projections give Mexico until 2009."

"Too bad."

"What a bizarre response," Charlie thought. McDonnell's first remorse upon hearing these apocalyptic losses rang hollow, but maybe he was reading too much into it. Perhaps repeated attempts to remain objective finally overloaded the President's psyche. On the other hand our good neighbor to the south was being crippled. "Whatever," he mentally resolved his reaction.

"And the worst of it..." Now he was doing it! "I didn't mean that; it's a figure of speech. With so many Mexicans fleeing into Texas and California, losses in those states are expanding exponentially. San Diego is little more than a ghost town except for illegal immigrants, and they disperse to the north in days. Looters have emptied the stores, and shards of glass litter the streets."

"I'm painfully aware of those conditions. Personnel at our reactivated naval base keep me apprised of that city's sorry fate. I'm considering martial law throughout southern California. Brief me on South America."

"Very difficult to obtain accurate data. The mountains, the Amazon rain forest...what's left of it...primitive communication and transportation systems, the deplorable level of education. My guess is rural South America may parallel Australia, remaining relatively unscathed if a cure is found in the near future. We'll lose many in Central America, Venezuela, Columbia, and big South American cities, but not the farmers or the villagers."

"Let's go on. My next major concern is the Orient, particularly the Japanese."

Grant turned to the middle of his summary. Since 2002, when the first significant increase in the infection rate was recorded, numbers have skyrocketed."

"How do you account for that?"

"Population density. Japan loses an unbelievable seventy-five to eighty thousand persons daily."

"They face extinction." McDonnell's reaction sounded incredibly nonchalant. "Refresh my memory about Europe and the former Soviet Bloc countries."

"All reflect trends in the United States," Charlie responded, trying to shake an amorphous foreboding generated by the President's perplexing comments and behavior. "Ghetto areas have been hardest hit. If we lose *our* ghettos... which appears likely... similar circumstances in Europe will seem worse simply because a greater percentage of their population is affected."

"A few minutes ago you indicated racial susceptibility isn't an issue," the President commented tangentially. "Can you elaborate on that?"

"All I meant was, while it's not likely, it hasn't been substantiated one way or the other."

"But black Africans fare worse than black Americans."

"Infinitely."

"However, black and white Americans have similar infection rates."

"If living conditions are comparable, yes."

"Yet there's no evidence Negro or Caucasian blood has anything to do with it."

"No, but the American black isn't Negro, if that's what you're alluding to. Upwards of ninety percent carry white blood, a tribute to the apparent lack of bigotry on the part of southern colonial aristocracy. President Jefferson was the rule, not the exception. Mulatto children were sired by the tens of thousands, so those we refer to as black in the United States are, in reality, a new and separate race, and their incidence of the disease doesn't differ measurably from Caucasians. You might ask Dr. Fairchild."

The President nodded, then sat motionless for several minutes, deep in thought. "Charlie," he said abruptly, "barring widespread STC infusions, how much longer do you think it will be before the ... developed nations on Earth face annihilation?"

"That may never happen."

"But what if our containment of Type 4 fails? What if a Type 5 emerges, God forbid?"

"Obviously, those are two of many variables."

"How long, Charlie?"

"There is no answer, sir. Anything I say, any predictions I make, may corrupt our analysis of the situation. We may base decisions on an erroneous premise."

"I'll accept that. I chose well when I selected you. See if you agree with my analogy of our current plight:

"A fictitious ship springs a leak, small and unnoticed, below the water line. Eventually it's discovered, but to no avail, for water has inundated the hold, endangering the lives of all on board.

"The nature of the fissure is such that repair isn't possible... tools and materials necessary to stem the flow don't exist; and in addition, expansion is so rapid it's doubtful the breach can be closed in time to spare many lives even if technology and materials become available.

"A few were drowned when water first seeped in, caught sleeping, as it were. Others accidentally fell in. They too were lost, unfortunately in the wrong place at the wrong time.

"A general alarm is sounded. All that are able flee to the upper decks seeking relative, albeit temporary safety, but alas, the first class passengers seal the hold. Trapped by circumstances beyond their control, lower-order victims tacitly await their fate. Though the number perishing is alarming, life above decks temporarily goes on unimpeded. Rather like Russia before the Bolshevic revolution.

"That's where we stand now with AIDS. Will we sink, and if so, when? Depends on stemming the flow. Rapid spread, a new crack in the vessel... further mutation... and the balance is tipped. At some critical point, with too much water and insufficient buoyancy, the vessel slips below the surface. Most people are sucked down with the ship, although a handful of them are left bobbing on the surface, safe for the moment. With a life jacket... STC... survival may be possible until help arrives.

"The rescue ship in our current situation is Bill Fairchild's research lab and a potential cure not yet on the horizon. Are my parallels, conclusions, and forecasts in line with your report? With reality?"

"Frightfully so."

The President rose and stepped over to the huge world map. As he talked, he circled with yellow chalk the most heavily infected countries. "Charlie, today's discussion is strictly confidential. Communication with anyone, including Dr. Fairchild, is expressly forbidden. I need time to think, to plan."

Charlie was astonished. Bill already had access to most of this information. Why would it matter if he knew the rest?

"After the holidays we'll all get together, and you can brief Fairchild and Harrison. With updated statistics, of course." McDonnell retrieved the binder from the coffee table. "Who else has seen this?"

"The staff members that compiled the data, each assigned a specific group of countries."

"What about the summary and conclusions?"

"Marcie Warner, my chief statistician, and I prepared those sections."

"Any other copies?" The President grew more intense with each question.

"No. This is the only printout."

"What security measures have been taken?"

"It's encrypted in the computer."

"Who besides you and Ms. Warner has access to the complete report?"

"My secretary and chief of staff. Both have top level passwords and decryption keys which would allow them to retrieve it."

McDonnell's fervent gaze and facial expression was something Charlie had never seen.

"This information *has* to remain confidential. Access *must* be restricted. Can you alter the password over the network?"

"Yes, but it's a complicated procedure and... "

"Let's go to my terminal and *do* it."

. . .

"Should be secure for now. Look at the time! You'd better go. I can do a lot as President, but I doubt the airline will hold your flight for me. My helicopter's standing by. Have your best Christmas ever!"

. . .

As the chopper rose from the White House lawn into a Cimmerian sky, John McDonnell stood alone, staring at the oversize world map on the Sanctuary wall. Yellow-encircled countries stood out from unaccented land masses. Reaching into his suit coat pocket, he extracted a piece of blood-red chalk and slowly, deliberately, X'd out central Africa, the Middle East, northern India, Pakistan, Bangladesh, Iran, and Iraq.

Palming the chalk, the President of the United States went to the liquor shelf and poured two ounces of scotch over a glassful of ice. Swirling the amber fluid around and through the cubes to chill and dilute it, he retraced his steps and, with labored precision, drew additional red X's across Japan, China, and Indochina.

Surveying his handiwork, he downed the scotch in a single gulp and, in a barely audible voice, darkly uttered,

"Thy will be done."

PART III

THE PARING

"Unchecked, AIDS will winnow world population to a manageable size."*

John H. McDonnell
Forty-fifth President
of the United States

*Statement made during a weekly press conference in response to a question on the spread of AIDS.
December 14, 2004.

16

Holiday music filled the air, and profuse alcohol consumption fueled the festivities with a mellow aura as Ed and Lori wandered from group to group wishing friends and co-workers a joyous season. Gregariously affectionate by nature, she thoroughly enjoyed the opportunity to be close to people and considered it unfortunate such camaraderie did not permeate day-to-day living. Jubilant and mildly inebriated, they drifted to the back of the room for a moment of relative privacy. Lori sparkled.

"What do you think?" she asked.

"It's a nice party, honey," Ed assured her. "You did good."

"I had a lot of help."

"It's still your party."

"How's Hadari?" she inquired, asking after the child receiving supplies that Ed had airdropped earlier that afternoon.

"Great. Gaining weight with no sign of illness."

"Did he like his doll?"

"I meant to tell you! He hugged that damned thing and looked up with the biggest grin. If I was the least bit sensitive, I would have been touched."

"Right, Ed. You're hard as nails." Lori encircled his neck and pressed her lips full against his, her tongue probing the roof of his mouth. "You're such a fake!" she declared, releasing him. "Give me a few minutes. I have to keep things going."

"Take your time."

"Nice tits," Ed thought as she leaned down for a parting kiss.

· · ·

199

Tossing candy canes and chocolate kisses, Santa worked the crowd, repeatedly bellowing unconvincing "ho-ho-hos." Claude Flanders, a motor pool mechanic, had managed to stuff all two hundred sixty-five pounds into a red suit one of the secretaries whipped together during a single afternoon of R and R. Distant memories of Tailhook notwithstanding, he pinched a substantial number of nubile asses while mouthing litigious innuendoes. One particular ass tweaked by Santa, Ed would not mind a piece of. She was a sharp girl. He wondered who she was.

Lori, with Santa's help, concluded the formidable task of dispensing a mountain of presents, then wend her way to Ed through a room in total disarray. Facing each other in a warm glow of caring that evolved from the heat of sexual attraction, which originally drew them together, the two smiled. Ed pointed to her gift and said, "You first."

"No, you. I insist."

Having learned the futility of arguing with this determined young woman, Reynolds carefully removed the wrapping, uncovering a small, rectangular box. Inside, fastened to a man's neck chain, was a fourteen-carat, inlaid gold dog tag with his name engraved on the side with beveled edges.

"Turn it over. You can't see it, but it says, 'Love Always, Lori'. Maybe someday I'll be able to have that engraved."

"It's beautiful, honey. Thank you."

Leaning forward, breasts pressing against him, she looped the chain around his neck and deftly fastened the clasp. "Looks good, hunk!"

"Now open yours."

Conflicting emotions surged when, noting the size of the package, she guessed a ring. Though it would be the type and value of the stone that would please or alarm her, Lori knew she had no right to feel that way. After all, her comments about the dog tag blatantly indicated what *she* expected. Liberated, with a reverse double standard, she wanted assurance Ed was committed to a possible future together while retaining the right to repudiate her espousal. Pretty difficult remaining autonomous while wearing a valuable ring.

Ed's wife and children were disturbingly real. Here she was

exchanging expensive, meaningful gifts with someone else's husband preparatory to sleeping with him, while his wife tucked their children in bed. "Way to fuck yourself up, Lori!" she chastised herself.

Colorful paper fell away, revealing the anticipated jewelry box. "Make it be a pin, God! An obscenely expensive pin. Or a bracelet," though she knew Ed was aware she had tons of them.

It *was* a ring–so exquisite, its message could not be misconstrued. Only the diamond was missing and, in its place, was a perfectly cut and mounted birthstone.

"It means I love you," Reynolds said, expecting Lori to rush into his arms. Instead, she remained motionless, numbly staring at her present, silent tears trickling down her cheeks.

"Honey, what's wrong?"

"I think you know," she murmured, tears flowing faster.

Ed put his hand on her knee. "Honey, I don't know what will happen, but you deserve *some* evidence of how I feel."

"How do you know you aren't just caught up in the mood of the season?"

"Because I've had this for a month."

"So where does that leave us?"

"Where we've always been. Together."

"Until I ship out? Until you return to your wife and kids?"

"I can't plan that far ahead."

"Well I can, and I don't like what I see."

"Look, Lori, if you want me to apologize for falling in love with you, I won't."

"I don't expect that."

He did not deserve to be attacked. This whole untenable situation was as much her fault as his. It was not as if he forced her to have sex every night. A more willing partner, she doubted he ever had.

"Honey, I stayed away as long as I could."

"I believe you," she replied without vanity. "Besides, if you hadn't approached me, I would have found a way to meet you. Almost had my nerve up when you came over that evening at the club and bought me a drink. I don't know if I would have invited you to bed, but I was certainly receptive enough, wasn't I?"

Reynolds smiled. Holding up the ring, Lori continued, "Do you
expect me to reenlist if I accept this?"

"No . . . yeah! I want to be with you."

"That's not fair, Ed, a ring for a year of my life."

"It's the best I can do."

"So what happens now? No, don't tell me. I've seen the
movie: Brave, handsome pilot experienced in the ways of the
world continues sleeping with the young, not-so-innocent girl
until he gets transferred. Several affairs later, he settles down
with his wife and kids. Girl gets over him but, in a world with an
abundance of women and a dearth of marriageable men, wakes up
one day too old to attract another lover, too young to be satisfied
living alone." Tears gushed out of control.

"Honey, it's not like that."

"The *hell* it isn't."

"Then you'll have to do what's best for you."

Lori fought to control her emotions. "Can we leave?"

"If you want."

Unnoticed, they slipped out the back door into a night of
stifling heat, quiet except for the drone of air conditioning units
and the whine of generators. Silently, an awkward distance apart,
they walked the few yards to Lori's building.

"I'll see you in the morning... if that's all right... at
breakfast?" Ed was obviously uncomfortable.

"What are you talking about? Aren't you coming in?"

"I didn't know if you wanted me."

"*That's* not an issue, *Edward*!"

"Don't you want to be alone?"

"*On Christmas Eve?*"

The "iron man" appeared wounded by her snide comment.
"I'm sorry. I'm upset. Everything is so damned complicated."
Her voice softened. "Will you stay with me?"

"I want to."

"Good! Just promise one thing... you'll hold me when we
get into bed, but no sex. I'm too drunk, too tired, and too
confused to enjoy it."

"I promise."

Naked, they lay in a tight embrace, Reynolds' erection against

202

her tummy. "Sorry, honey," he apologized. "I can't prevent that."

"I'd be disappointed if you could."

Intertwined, tears glazing her eyes, Lori's fingers traced the gold chain, located the dog tag behind his neck, and placed it on his tangled chest hair. How could she break the news of her decision to not reenlist and bail out before being hurt any more? And why on earth had she made that daft schoolgirl remark about someday engraving the back of the dog tag? How else could he interpret that except she was in for the duration? What else could she have meant? *Damn!*

She had submitted to his advances out of loneliness and horniness and because he was virily handsome. Half the girls in camp lubricated every time he said hello. And then, to top it off, she found out how nice he was and fell in love with him . . . a married father of three! *Damn!*

"You okay?"

"How can I be okay?"

She rolled over on top, thighs and tummy pressed against him, full breasts hanging over his chest. Time to set the record straight. "I'm leaving when my hitch is up. I think it would be better." Why did she have to say, "think"?! It sounded as though she was wavering!

Ed was stunned. "I thought you would stay."

"What good would it do? Will you stop loving your wife because you love me more? Will your love for me compensate for the pain inflicted on her and your children? If you were a bastard, I'd say yes, but you're not. Otherwise, I'd never have allowed you into my bed in the first place." Lori's arms ached. Letting her full weight press against his body, her breasts flattening across his chest, she kissed him. "Ed, I lied. I'm neither drunk nor particularly tired, but I needed to know if and how willing you were to forego sex. You love me, don't you? Not just my big tits and availability." She could feel his penis hardening. It had gone flaccid when she told him she was not re-upping.

"I love you."

"Enough to stick around for a third hitch if I sign on for a second?"

"Absolutely."

"You'll put that in writing? You'll promise? You'll swear?"
"I'll write it in blood."

"Then I'll consider an extension. Just *think* about it... no promise... because I have more to lose if things don't work out."

"What about the ring?"
"What about it?"
"Will you wear it?"
"Can I decide in the morning?"
"You can decide next week."
"And you won't be pissed?"
"No. I understand your dilemma."
"Suppose I'm such a mess inside I take a month?"
"To decide about wearing the ring? Not reenlistment?"
"Yes."
"Then I'll be pissed."

"That's my boy. Wouldn't want you any other way." Lori rubbed her breasts from side to side across his chest. "Want a quickie?" She reached down, clasped a hand around his cock, and rubbed her thumb over the glans, spreading seminal fluid.

"Not tonight. You'll remember I reneged."

"I can think of a way to give you relief and technically you wouldn't be breaking your promise." She lubricated the back lip of his glans where she knew he was most sensitive, but he removed her hand and gently but firmly rolled her off.

"Go to sleep!"
"Okay, Captain. What a hard-ass."

Cupping his hand over a breast, Lori pressed her back against his chest. Ed was about under when she had a thought. "You asleep?"

"Almost," he mumbled.

"Don't forget to call your wife and kids tomorrow."

"I won't . . . that's nice of you."

"What is, is."

First thing in the morning she would have Ed put the ring on her finger. It was beautiful, thoughtful, significant. Damned right she'd wear it, no matter what the future held! Then she would treat him to the fuck of his life for being strong tonight.

Deep, peaceful slumber overtook her.

. . .

Roberta and Bill drove to Public Square to view the holiday decorations before attending the lab Christmas party. Tens of thousands of cheery, multicolored bulbs surrounded the ice rink and illuminated high rises radiating from Tower City. Always joyful and occasionally whimsical, the vivid displays sharply contrasted with the passive glow of adjacent office windows. At her insistence they circled the Soldiers' Memorial twice before heading east on Superior for a long cross-town drive to the Gates Mills restaurant reserved by the Northcoast staff.

. . .

Frozen slush clung to the wipers and was beginning to cloak road surfaces as they returned from the holiday celebration. Carefully turning onto his snow-clad driveway, Bill handed Roberta a house key and let her out to unlock the back door and turn on lights while he garaged the sedan.

Hanging up his coat, he stomped accumulated snow from his shoes before removing and placing them on a mat by the door.

"I'm in here," Roberta called from the living room. "How about building a fire?"

Fairchild seldom used his fireplace because it disrupted the heating system, and he hated carrying wood in and ashes out. Those logs on the grate had been there for . . . he could not remember the last time he had used it.

"Sure," he answered cheerfully, "it's damp in here."

Dry hickory rapidly ignited, sending sparks ricocheting off the tempered glass enclosure and up the chimney, riding tongues of flame.

"Fires are so romantic," Roberta cooed. "Make one for me often?"

"Anytime. Would you like a drink?"

"No, thank you. Fix yourself one if you like."

Roberta rarely consumed two alcoholic beverages in a row since their initial afternoon on the boat, but this was the first time he could remember her abstaining. Perhaps she did not feel well or was not in the mood. When he returned with his scotch, they talked of the party, how nice it was to have a few days off–she demanded he not go to the lab, or even drive by! They also discussed completing their Christmas shopping and picking up her brother's gift from the jewelers tomorrow.

During a lull in conversation, Bill's eyes were drawn to the area in front of the television. Last Saturday, after dinner and stopping for a rental movie, he had suggested his place instead of hers, for it seemed more secure from the ever-vigilant eyes of Secret Service personnel. Even though President McDonnell had ordered discretion, their presence remained intrusive.

They had gathered pillows and a blanket from an upstairs closet and then, like kids, stretched out on the floor. With scrolling credits and accompanying theme music in the background, friendly kisses and embraces quickly became intensely passionate. For the first time in the Fairchild house, Bill and Roberta made love. Another milestone passed, but spontaneous sex on the floor of the living room and premeditated lovemaking in the home and bed he had shared with Coletta were eons apart.

Roberta rose from the couch, went to the front window and parted the drapes. "The snow has let up but the street's a mess," she observed.

As she tried to stifle a yawn, Bill joined her, slipping both arms around her waist. "What time do you want to go shopping tomorrow?" he inquired.

"Ten?"

"Let's plan for 9:30 so we're out the door by then."

"Whose door?" she wondered, aloud.

"Do you mind if we stay here?"

Roberta turned and encircled his neck. "No, dear, not at all."

"We can use the guest bedroom on the second floor."

"That's fine. Will Mrs. Romano drop in tomorrow? I'd hate to meet her the first time, peeking over the covers in bed with you."

Bill laughed. "I hope not. My specific instructions... no, orders... were to stay away and enjoy her holiday."

Though appearing unconvinced, Roberta seemed resigned that nothing would guarantee Mrs. Romano's absence.

"Well, not everything can be controlled. I just don't want any embarrassment or to create hard feelings for the future. Now, come sit with me. We need to talk."

"Is something wrong?"

Soft and vulnerable, she emitted a glow he had not seen before. "'Wrong' is not really appropriate. I'd planned on waiting until after the holidays, but the longer we sat here tonight, the more foolish that seemed."

Nothing in her manner gave cause for alarm or prepared him for the forthcoming monumental announcement.

"Remember I left work early on Tuesday?"

"Yes."

"I went to the doctor."

Previous impressions must have been in error. Panic ensued. "Honey!"

"No, no, no," she soothed, sensing his alarm. "I'm not sick. Everything's fine."

"But you just said . . ."

"Bill, listen to me." She held his hands, looking directly into his eyes, calm, serene, Madonna-like. "I'm going to have a baby."

Dumbfounded, Bill Fairchild stared at Roberta Curtis. Many years his secretary; long the object of his interest; recently, his affections; and *very* recently–three weeks ago–recipient of his marriage proposal. But a *baby*? *His* baby? *Their* baby? He had no frame of reference to conceive–poor choice of words–such a thing.

After all those childless years with Coletta, and here he was at age–he banished the number from his mind–with a pregnant young woman sitting on his sofa telling him she was carrying his child. He half expected Roberta's father to burst into the room demanding to know his intentions.

"Now we know who was sterile all those years, don't we?"

"There's no mistake?"

"No, Bill. You're going to be a daddy."

"What are you . . . we . . . going to do?"

"Get married and have a premie, I suppose."

"Is that what you want?"

"The baby or marriage? Both, though I'd prefer the sequence reversed. You know, engagement ring... by the way, I don't have one... wedding ring, baby. But with the order already established ... yes, Bill, I want to get married. I had originally decided to accept your proposal at Easter and planned a June wedding but, considering our current situation, that schedule will be a bit awkward, since I'll be seven months pregnant."

"Have you considered . . . ?"

Gently squeezing his hands, she looked deeply into his eyes. "No, and I won't. It's not a religious thing. That's nonsense and this is no time to get philosophic . . . or maybe it is because I want you to know what's in my heart.

"The morality of an abortion doesn't dissuade me. If someone doesn't want a baby, can't afford or won't care for one, giving birth seems a greater evil than aborting a fetus because the world is too full of miserable, unwanted children now. But none of that pertains to us. I want this baby for me and because it's yours. I don't care how old we are. I'm young and healthy enough to raise him or her. And so are you, my friend."

Apparently everything had been decided.

"When did it happen? Do you know?"

"On the boat, I guess. It's the only time... times, we didn't use anything."

"Our first time?"

"Like a couple of teenagers, weren't we? You at least had an excuse, thinking it impossible. I figured it was a safe time of the month. Obviously, I was wrong."

"That's why you didn't drink tonight."

"Very good, Doctor. By the way, you don't have to marry me. I'm prepared to raise this child alone."

"Roberta!"

"I just thought you should know I don't want a shotgun wedding."

"We should marry soon. People will talk as it is."

"Let's discuss that in the morning. Would you care to share a glass of wine? A touch won't hurt our son or daughter."

Dazed, Bill poured Chablis from a chilled decanter obtained from the refrigerator and handed it to Roberta.

"To us... you, me, and our perfect offspring," she toasted, taking a sip, and returning the glass to Bill. "You finish it."

Her calm acceptance and contentment worked its magic and he began to relax. What had been shocking and alien, moments before, was becoming part of their joint destiny. Roberta hugged him and kissed his cheek. "You are such a dear man."

Bill smiled, basking in the glow of happiness she exuded. "I love you," he murmured.

"Are you ready for this line? *Prove it*, Doctor!"

. . .

Roberta glanced one final time at the drift-covered scene. Powdered snow swirled about the house, dancing in eddies before spinning wildly across the lawn. The streetlight two houses away was but a dim glow, nearly obliterated by icy flakes touching the earth, only to be swept hurriedly away by a capricious wind.

"It's a good thing we didn't go out. Shall we wave good night to our protectors across the street?"

"Roberta, close the drapes!"

"Just a thought."

. . .

Afterwards, intimately comfortable and serene, Roberta whispered, "When I'm big and fat, you'll wonder what you saw in me."

"Pregnant is not big and fat."

"It's nice to hear a man say that."

"I wish you had a ring."

"We can look for one tomorrow . . . if you feel like it."

"Do you have anything specific in mind?"

"Something gaudy and expensive would be nice."

"You aren't the gaudy type," Bill observed with obvious satisfaction.

"I notice you didn't say I wasn't expensive."

"Do be quiet, Roberta."

Mock alarm rang out in the darkness. "Oh, now that we are betrothed, you start ordering me around. Barefoot and pregnant. Is that all I have to look forward to?"

"Good night, Roberta."

Safe and warm, lulled by the staccato tapping of sleet against the windows, they drifted off to sleep. A windrow of snow accumulated across the end of the driveway, symbolically sealing them from the world.

17

Air Force One received immediate clearance and landed at St. Petersburg-Clearwater International Airport. Taxiing across the tarmac adjacent to Old Tampa Bay, it rolled to a stop beside a remote service gate. The President and First Lady deplaned and promptly entered the previously delivered armored limousine.

The gate swung open and motorcycle officers halted traffic in both directions, enabling two black GMC Suburbans bristling with antennas and filled with Secret Service personnel to move quickly onto the street. Followed immediately by the limo, several more black Suburbans, and then the remainder of the presidential entourage, they were soon out of sight.

An agent in the lead vehicle, seated before a dazzling array of communications equipment and data terminals, referred to his electronic map display and simultaneously relayed instructions to his driving partner and all other units. Route "C" was to be followed.

"This vacation should get Congress off their fat, procrastinating asses," McDonnell said, gloating at his wife. "They stonewalled an acquisition of the Bruggemeister estate, and the Secret Service wouldn't let us go home. Now they'll *have* to do something. This villa is less secure than either."

The President smiled at his symbolic victory, thumbing the Executive nose at regulations designed to protect him. Karen, well aware of all the assassinations and attempts tainting the twentieth century, was visibly concerned.

"It *is* safe where we're going, isn't it? You promised it was."

"I wouldn't take you anywhere it wasn't, but members of Congress don't have to know. Besides, who would want to harm a nice old man like me?"

"A goodly number of affluent people since you're hell-bent on raising their taxes to help the disadvantaged."

"Good point, but they only want to; they won't actually perform the deed."

"Whereas the unfortunate masses might?"

McDonnell nodded.

"If people knew how terrible you are . . ."

The motorcade proceeded at high speed along a familiar four-lane highway en route to Alt. U.S. 19, north of Clearwater.

"Remember our last vacation here, John? Traffic was slowed by cars just dawdling along. We almost missed our plane."

"The curse of the aging population. Old farts taking over the roads."

"*Must* you be so graphic? You carry this Harry Truman correlation too far."

"I *am* the new Harry Truman. All the media say so."

"Well, I don't like it, and I'm sure Bess didn't either."

McDonnell tapped his driver on the shoulder. "Can we go a little faster?"

"We're doing sixty now, sir, and I have to follow the escort," the agent helplessly replied.

"Get on the radio and tell them to get the lead out of their..."

"John!"

" ...to stop driving like a bunch of old wo... "

"That's *worse*!"

"Tell them to speed it up, Victor."

"I'll try, sir."

Karen admonished her husband. "Is it *so hard* to be *civil*?"

"It was just a figure of speech."

"So is, 'old fart,' but I doubt you'd want *me* saying it."

"Stop grinning, Victor. If my wife says something funny, I'll let you know."

"Yes, sir." The agent suppressed his amusement to acknowledge radio traffic that the convoy's pace was about to increase.

"Anyway, it hardly matters because this may be our last time anywhere." Her expression was deadly serious, but McDonnell's raised eyebrow indicated a lack of comprehension. "This AIDS thing could run rampant at any moment," she elaborated. "I wake up thinking about it, afraid it will escalate in the U.S. as it's done so many other places."

"That's possible," he conceded.

"Have you talked with Dr. Fairchild, lately?"

"Yesterday."

"Any more to report on his new treatment?"

"Hard to tell."

Confused, she commented, "You told me it worked."

"Well, in a limited way on a handful of volunteers. An unproven serum can't be rushed into distribution."

"Not even for AIDS? What could be worse?"

"It's very complicated." McDonnell exhibited discomfort, as if he wanted to avoid further discussion.

"Why don't you authorize production? If it doesn't work, how are the patients any worse off?"

"There are laws, Karen, even for the President. They can't be circumvented." Now visibly irritated, he rationalized, "I don't know what's worse than AIDS, but something could be. Look at Thalidomide."

"Well, I'm sorry, but I don't understand why Congress couldn't grant special dispensation for testing in some poor country which has experienced catastrophic losses. I'll bet there are lots of Third World people who would gladly volunteer as guinea pigs."

"Karen, we can't do that!" His tone and manner were unduly harsh. Traits normally hidden, occasionally flared and frightened her.

"I just think we should do everything possible as soon as we can," she insisted, both piqued and reticent.

McDonnell checked his response. Because they were on vacation, his guard was down. He must never let that happen.

"I'm sorry I snapped," he apologized. "I'm on edge over this all the time. Honey," he took a deep breath, "if we give an untested serum to a Third World country and anything bad results, we'll be crucified by world opinion, accused of racially motivated behavior and economic arrogance... the poor can be guinea pigs, as you put it, but not the affluent. Then, if and when we verify STC's potential and/or discover a successful treatment, no one will trust us. I'm sorry if my decisions seem arbitrary."

Such conciliatory remorse, sincere or not, helped.

"It's all right, dear. I know you're under pressure."

"Thank you. I *am* sorry."

"John?"

"Yes, dear?"

"What is, 'the winnowing'?"

"Why do you ask *that*?" McDonnell snapped.

He had the look of a carnivore flushed from its den. Almost as if he harbored some deep, evil secret and if cornered, would protect it unto death.

"You *do* need a vacation!"

McDonnell heard himself apologizing once more. Karen was right, about his needing a break. Repetition of this behavior before the media or an unfriendly colleague . . . he shuddered to think of the consequences. Apprehensively, he glanced at his wife. She was too angry and alarmed to be soothed; however, as the minutes ticked by, she chastised herself for having an overly vivid imagination. Her poor husband was exhausted after being continually hassled from every direction! Even this vacation began on a stressful note when the Secret Service resisted after he presented his plans un fait accompli. As always, she softened and exuded understanding.

"I asked because you've been saying it over and over in your sleep. Not every night, but often enough to make me wonder."

"Saying what?"

"'The winnowing'. At first I wasn't sure. It took time to understand your nocturnal mumbling... I don't mean that to be offensive because when you're awake, your speech is very precise... but after hearing it repeated so often, even indistinctly, there is no misunderstanding."

A beleaguered look flashed . . . or did it?

"You must be mistaken. That word is vaguely familiar, but I'm unsure of its meaning."

"*Damn*! Why did I say that?" he thought. "The word is in

my course syllabus of 'The Bible as Literature.'" She might find that out. It was *another* slip. Well, too bad. He would have to muddle through, for backtracking and admitting comprehension might make her more suspicious. He hoped Victor was not paying attention.

"I wasn't sure either, so I looked it up," she continued. "It's a threshing term, means eliminating the chaff, the useless, and sorting out, keeping the grain. Why would you say a thing like that? Do you have a latent desire to be a farmer, or is there some agricultural legislation on the Hill that's on your mind?"

"I have no idea. I was probably mumbling in my sleep as you said, and it just sounded like that."

"I'm *quite* certain what I heard."

"Well, next time wake me and perhaps I'll remember."

"You usually say it in conjunction with some reference to AIDS. Does that help?"

"Can't you leave it alone?" McDonnell said to himself. Battling frustration, he desperately sought to end this incriminating conversation or at least redirect its thrust to his advantage. Suddenly, he had an inspiration.

"I remember! One of my staff used the term in observing how AIDS seems to be more prevalent in ghettos and Third World countries, and he mentioned something about winnowing out the bottom of society." He felt that statement should be general enough. "I don't recall it making that much of an impression at the time. Now, in context, I know what the word means. I do need rest."

"What a dreadful idea! As if it's somehow acceptable that the least fortunate among us bear the burden."

"I couldn't agree more. The concept must have shaken me more than I realized."

"That's terrible. What kind of person conceives such a thought?"

"An intellectual. Sounds pragmatic. Perhaps no moral judgment was being made."

"I understand, but don't let anyone else hear you. The media would certainly misconstrue it. They'd have you approving of winnowing out human beings or some other ghastly thing. You didn't hear any of this, Victor."

"I've heard nothing, ma'am."

The point vehicle turned left onto a sandy, coral lane leading to the Gulf of Mexico.

"We're here. Merry Christmas, Karen!"

"You too, dear." She leaned over to kiss him. "You're a good man, John. I wish you'd consider getting rid of the awful person who came up with such a disgusting analogy. Winnowing! It's macabre!"

"He's a valuable member of my team, but I'll give it some thought."

The limo passed through a forest of bramble-like mangrove trees. Another hundred yards and a huge house appeared, rising on concrete pilings from the coral sands.

"Do you like it, Karen?"

"It's lovely; I can't wait to walk the beach."

Victor got out and stood in front of the car, admiring the ocean and amber sun that rode high above the waters. His absence afforded the McDonnells a rare moment of privacy.

"Do you love me?" the President suddenly queried.

"Of course. Why do you ask?"

"Sometimes I'm called upon to make unpopular decisions."

"John, we don't always agree, but I will always love you . . . unless you decide to go around winnowing the planet's population."

Chilled by something in her husband's reaction to her warning, Karen's affectionate smile quickly faded. As she stepped from the limousine into the balmy gulf-stream air, a shiver shot up her spine.

. . .

With both children asleep, the Grants began the tedious task of assembling toys and arranging presents under their tree. Earlier that day, a last-minute shopping trip was necessary despite gallant efforts to avoid one, for when gift lists were reviewed, the amount spent on each child was comparable, but the number of presents was not. Although Matt and Jennifer had little comprehension of value, they could count with a vengeance, so the only solution to achieving parity was buying cheap supplementary items.

"I thought we'd never get them to bed," Charlie bemoaned. "Why does it seem Christmas comes every year?"

"Now don't be a Scrooge!"

"Damn!"

"What are you looking for?"

"One of those pressure nuts that secures the wheel."

"What's that?"

"A pressure nut. Ah so."

"Stop that! Lots of things aren't imported anymore. McDonnell has seen to that."

"This was."

"So why did you buy it?"

"It's the one the kids wanted."

"You're a good daddy. Selling out your principles for your son and daughter."

"Why does everything come knocked down or up?"

"I didn't come knocked up. Not that you didn't try. Is the tree okay?"

"Fine." He hardly cared one way or another.

"We've had better, but I couldn't drag myself out alone to get one before you got here. Maybe I should have. It's kind of skaggy."

"They were picked over. It's my fault for not telling McDonnell to go fuck himself and getting home earlier."

Intermittent sparks, generated by bits and pieces from the last log dropping through the iron grate, escaped up the chimney. With an old flannel robe wrapped snugly around her, Sarah curled up on Charlie's lap, and together they surveyed the obscene number of gifts surrounding the tree. He gently patted her knee. "What are you thinking?"

"That this is the culmination of two months of planning, frustration, and financial flagellation to provide our kids with a lifetime of memories."

Charlie smiled at the wisdom of her remark, then said, "It's great to be home. I get sick of being alone in Washington."

"Any chance you'll be called back before New Year's?"

"None, barring a crisis. McDonnell's in Clearwater."

"How did your meeting go?"

"Weirdly. Something strange is going on."

"What do you mean?"

"The President asked the damnedest questions. He's more interested in when a country will be depopulated than how soon we can send a cure, and he refuses to acknowledge how successful STC's are. I'm almost convinced he's deliberately delaying treatment to ensure perpetuation of the AIDS epidemic."

"That's preposterous!"

"Before yesterday's relentless interrogation I would have agreed, but he seemed obsessed trying to ascertain when the depopulation of India and the Orient will match that of Africa, and you know how he hates the Japs."

"Japanese."

"Whatever."

"You're accusing our esteemed President of withholding serum until people he hates or considers undesirable are eliminated?"

"Uh-huh, and nature is playing into his hands. In McDonnell's new world only Caucasians and an elite few from other races will survive."

"That's bizarre!"

"And precisely what is happening."

"Do you believe this?"

"I'm beginning to."

"What are you going to do?"

"At this point I'm not sure, but I need to discuss it with someone in authority that I can trust."

"Bob Harrison?"

"Too much of a gamble. Loyalty to his President might cloud his judgement."

"Contact Bill Fairchild."

. . .

Cuddling in bed, exhausted beyond the point of falling directly asleep, Sarah poked her husband into a semiconscious state. "I've been thinking about your meeting. I understand what you're saying, but I still think you're crazy. We're talking about the President of the United States, not some militia nutcake or

217

radical elitist."

"Seems impossible, doesn't it?" he mumbled, barely functional and immediately dozing back under.

Within moments the grandfather clock in the foyer chimed the hour, further waking an already alert Sarah.

"Charlie." She nudged him again. "I can't sleep."

He rolled over and embraced her. "A quickie help? I'm willing if you are."

"You're such a humanitarian."

. . .

Lunch seemed a good idea, but neither Roberta nor Bill had an appetite. Food was nervously picked over and rearranged on their plates, but little was consumed and the garbage disposal became its final repository.

Within an hour, in a tasteful ceremony in the chapel off the narthex, with only the officiating minister and his wife looking on as a witness, they were married. Reconsummating the union was furthest from their minds. Consistent with the reversed order of events marking most of their courtship, celebratory coitus had taken place that morning before the wedding, rather than after.

The newlyweds drove directly to Roberta's brother's garage and broke the news. Mildly surprised, he would be again a month later when informed he was going to be an uncle. Next, they proceeded to Mrs. Romano's house. Though Roberta was not on Marie's list of possible mates for her employer, to the woman's credit she was polite and open-minded.

"How did we do?" Bill asked as they left.

"My brother thinks you're stuffy, but otherwise okay. Mrs. Romano wishes I was fat and fifty, but she'll come around."

"That was easier than I anticipated."

"Me, too. That's one advantage of expecting the worst!"

. . .

Bill was not thrilled with the prospect of a long drive, but their ride to Akron was pleasant.

"I'm glad we were invited," Roberta stated upon spotting the Grants' house number. "We need to cultivate new and common friends. What better place to meet interesting people than at a congressman's party?"

Charlie waited until all the guests had arrived, and festivities were in full swing, before maneuvering Fairchild into the library to broach the subject of the President's perceived aberration. The doctor listened, but appeared uncomfortable and confirmed nothing. Disappointed, Grant dropped the subject.

Midnight came and went and with it the passing of the old year and the beginning of the new. Everyone kissed everyone else; especially Fairchild's new bride. "Did you really get married this afternoon?" one particularly curious individual asked.

At a quarter after one, Sarah and Roberta chatted in the foyer while Charlie assisted Bill with his coat. To Grant's surprise, Fairchild indicated he would be in touch to discuss the President's unorthodox actions. Then, not wanting to become embroiled at the moment and uncertain how much information should be shared with Rep. Charles Grant–an acquaintance he did not know well enough to confide in–he abruptly ushered Roberta out.

. . .

Ed's wife expressed deep displeasure upon being informed that his presence in Africa was crucial and an extension was a distinct possibility. Surely she understood. Surely she did not. "We'll talk later," he soothed. She hotly told him the result would be the same, not going so far as to suggest finding a way to be home in June or not bothering to return, but the inference was unmistakable in her voice. Raising three children alone was frequently overwhelming. It was not fair while he played "Top Gun" in central Africa, riding herd on wild animals . . . or was he riding something else? Before he could respond, the line went dead.

Ed elected not to relay substantial parts of the conversation to Lori. He did not have to. His obvious distress fueled her frustration, for decision time was only weeks away, and if she re-upped and he did not, she would be stuck in this hellhole months after he left. Shit!

Her situation notwithstanding, she recognized the incredibly complicated dilemma Ed faced. If he stayed in Africa, his wife might divorce him; and the kids–who hardly knew him now– would be deprived of their father even more. Was he deeply enough in love with her to justify the sorrow they would surely endure, or would he conclude she was merely a convenient sexual outlet, temporarily return to his family, and then eventually find another paramour?

Lori had seen him scoping Cheryl's ass during the Christmas party, an act confirming her decision to keep them apart because she feared he lacked sufficient self-control to resist should an opportunity to bed her new acquaintance arise. Face it, Cheryl exceeded Ed's stringent criteria for a desirable woman! If indeed he slept alone until she came along because he intuitively sensed he could fall in love with her, might not her oversexed pilot have a similar but accelerated reaction to Cheryl? The key to her April decision hinged on Ed's feelings and level of commitment to her as a person, not a sex object! It had taken a while, but she finally knew what she wanted. What he really thought and wanted was unknown, and she did not have a clue how to find out! Shit!

. . .

Roberta rearranged rooms with Bill's blessing and assistance. Her prized possessions–pictures and statuary, lamps, end tables, and one Oriental rug–were placed throughout the house. Except for a few cherished belongings from both sides, she wanted to sell everything and buy new, but events occurred so quickly, they had not discussed preferences. What if she liked something Bill could barely tolerate?

She wondered how he would react to her getting pregnant again; she doubted he would be thrilled considering their ages and his commitment to AIDS research. But STC's looked promising, they both enjoyed good health and financial security, and with one child to raise, what possible difference could a second baby make?

No cutting comments reached her at work, directly or indirectly, concerning their marriage, but tongues would wag when she started to show, since a math degree was not required to count back to their wedding and come up short the requisite number of months from conception. She determined to tolerate any raised eyebrows and get on with it.

18

"I had intended we meet weeks ago, Charles," Fairchild disclosed. "How did it get to be February?"

"Charlie. Call me Charlie."

"And I'm Bill. William only to select women when I displease them; my dear departed mother... I can still hear the ice in her voice when she addressed me by that name... and *both* wives."

Grant and Fairchild occupied a rather isolated booth in a small restaurant near Playhouse Square, less than a block from the refurbished Hanna Theatre on 14th Street. The Hanna, complementing the previously restored Ohio, State, Palace, and Allen Theatres around the corner on Euclid Avenue, completed the entertainment complex. Niceties out of the way, the doctor backtracked to his opening statement.

"We need to discuss our common . . . suspicion . . . regarding the individual to whom you referred New Year's Eve. I must confess to being thunderstruck when you approached me."

"Too ridiculous?"

"Quite the contrary. A frightening confirmation of what Roberta and I had spent a great deal of time deliberating."

"Sarah and me, too. I felt more than a little paranoid when I initially told her of my . . . misgivings, but after explaining and defending every apprehension and impression, my conclusions solidified."

"Charlie, I felt it important to follow up quickly and in

relative privacy, but with my responsibilities and recent marriage... you see what happened to my intentions. I did try to contact you in mid-January, but you didn't return my call." It was simply a statement, not a censure.

"Sorry. I should have responded, but by then I began having reservations, started feeling foolish. Even a bit traitorous."

"Don't apologize. I brushed you off New Year's Eve. Your reasons may be the root of my procrastination as well. The foolish feelings haven't gone away, but I'm troubled by the unanswered questions."

"Which are?"

"Why can't my serum be produced and made available to all volunteers willing to assume the risk? Early test results have been encouraging." An afterthought: "And why did the... our man ... become suddenly inaccessible?"

"I'm not sure. Plus, why would a person with his background and responsibilities devise a plan to withhold treatment?"

"I'd like to know that, too; because some type of scheme *is* being implemented. Otherwise, substantial numbers of AIDS victims would be receiving STC's now."

"Then we... may I use the word 'we'?"

Fairchild nodded.

"Then we are not paranoid?"

"Charlie, I have considered that possibility daily, and you can put your mind at ease. We are as sane as human beings can be. Since early January I have been attempting to arrange a meeting among the four of us... you, me, the individual in question, and his aide; whose role also must be ascertained. We'll address that in a minute.

"Prior to last week my requests went nowhere. Each excuse would have been plausible if AIDS control and eradication were not the world's top priorities. Finally, this past Tuesday, I succeeded in pinning him down. You seem unaware of that. We are all scheduled to meet in the Sanctuary at 3 p.m., a week from today."

"I haven't been notified."

"You will be, although I predict that a day or two before you'll receive a second call postponing the session."

"Surely he doesn't think he can avoid us forever."

"He's not concerned about forever, only avoiding face-to-face encounters until . . . his goal is achieved. In a meeting we might seize upon some nuance and see through his machinations."

"And when he can no longer evade our requests?"

"Many options are available. He could pressure the FDA into issuing stringent guidelines, order more testing, inhibit production, delay distribution... to name but a few. Then, when he's damned good and ready, accelerate everything."

"Why?" Charlie knew the answer. He sought validation.

"I think... and this is only conjecture, mind you... that our friend is using AIDS to selectively reduce the world's population. When all the 'weeds' are gone and 'good' people begin dying, he will step in to stop the plague."

"What I alluded to New Year's Eve."

"And I was not ready to acknowledge. He keeps us at bay where all we can do is surmise and suspect, probably realizing he's not a good enough actor to survive direct confrontation."

"So now that we know, what do we do?"

"We only suspect. Correct me if I'm wrong, but if some new piece of evidence to the contrary surfaced, we would stumble over each other for the chance to believe it first! I know I would. Currently, we lack proof. With even a smattering of hard evidence, I would blow the whistle and he knows it! I'm no eccentric, introverted researcher cloistered in a subterranean lab, nor am I without influence. Denying access to STC's, banning them by fiat . . . our friend is either evil incarnate or a madman."

"Neither, Bill. He's an errant visionary. If racial overtones are removed... can you do that?"

"I've done it all my life."

"So you have. Disregarding racial overtones and human suffering caused by the delay, one might conclude the world *would* be a better place." Fairchild, the scientist, was seemingly nonplussed by this thesis. "Fewer people, less pollution, decreased depletion of natural resources, no children born into poverty and want. The planet could heal." Grant continued to elaborate. "This situation parallels Truman's decision to drop atomic bombs. Premeditatively kill several tens of thousands to prevent one to

223

two million deaths resulting from a conventional assault."

"Wherein lies the greater sin?" Fairchild pondered. "Sacrifice a few to save the many . . . or in this case, the many to save a few."

"See how easy it is to accept?"

Fairchild's eyes bore into Grant. "Theoretically the concept is not without merit, and I could reluctantly support it on intellectual grounds with one exception."

Grant was unprepared for such an admission. "Which is?"

"First, understand I am just extrapolating on a theme, same as you."

"I do. If I didn't feel you shared my revulsion at what we presume is happening, I'd have never confided in you." Hearing his own words, Grant discovered to his dismay an anticipated depth of conviction was lacking. No wonder the premise seduced McDonnell.

"Your faith in me will not be betrayed, but perhaps for a reason you may not approve."

"Go on."

"I could almost... almost, mind you... live with what our man is allegedly attempting. Even tolerate the devastating loss of most of my race... few remain outside America as it is... if convinced future children, regardless of color, would no longer be born into abject, grinding poverty in the Third World or the ghettos of developed nations.

"Unfortunately, the human race has done little to earn such credit. I fear people haven't the sense to capitalize on any optimum conditions they may encounter in the near future. I doubt the species that raped a virgin Earth... God, I hate cliches and I just uttered one of the more insipid... would be capable of maintaining a reasonable population level.

"Religions of the world wouldn't get the point. Some hypocritical evangelical or misguided mainline cleric would capture the intellect of the masses, and the mindless cycle would be reestablished. Too few practice birth control now. What incentive would there be on a depopulated planet? World pulpits would cry, 'Go forth and multiply!' The average person would be only too happy to do his or her religious best. Oh, things might not be set back for a century or two, but given enough time, the old stupidity would reassert itself, followed by a new, debilitating population explosion."

Before Grant could react to the deluge of radical information, Fairchild continued. "By the way, lest you think I'm a pompous ass harboring thoughts of superiority, I must tell you . . . Roberta is pregnant."

That announcement was as earthshaking as anything Fairchild delivered during his bombast. Charlie hesitated, unsure how to respond. "That's . . . that's wonderful!"

"We think so... especially Roberta. I see you are having a bit of trouble ingesting the news."

"No, no. I'm happy for you, Bill. It's great." Reaching across the table, he pumped his friend's hand.

"That may not be a majority opinion. Being on the far side of middle age as my dear wife enters it hardly qualifies us as ideal parents."

"Nonsense. You obviously love each other. You're both intelligent. The baby should be very fortunate."

"Thank you, but we are a trifle old for this sort of thing."

"I don't see how that can make a difference." Grant was being supportive, subliminally delineating many complications.

"I'm not so certain, but I appreciate your kindness. Suppose it wakes at night?" Fairchild was being facetious. "I've never had to get up. Nor has Roberta for that matter."

"They're only little a short time, Bill," Charlie said with amusement. "You'll do fine."

"Well, I hope you are right. If it's a boy and I die before he's raised, Roberta has promised to haunt me through eternity."

"You might give her the same warning."

"Good grief! I hadn't thought of that! Maybe I wouldn't feel so ambivalent if one of us was younger."

"Then you should have married a twenty-year-old."

Fairchild roared with pleasure. "Roberta said you were quick. I love dry humor."

"Sarah will be thrilled when I tell her. How does Roberta feel?"

"Fine, if I can believe her. She *looks* great."

"Pregnancy has that effect on some women."

"Her waistline is disappearing, but unlike mine, will return. Do you realize we chased the waitress away and haven't ordered? *Drinking lunch,* won't do."

"I'm not hungry, but if you are and have time, I can stay."

"Good. Roberta knows I'm here and why. She'll cover my absence."

"By the way, since we're not supposed to be in communication, how did you elude the Secret Service?"

"Roberta engaged them in conversation. Pregnant or not, she's quite a distraction. How they explain their failure to keep track of me is their problem."

"Never underestimate the power of a woman, huh?"

"Something like that," Fairchild winked. "At any rate, it's good we're here. We need to discuss our common problem."

"If there is one. After feeding each other's fantasies, we may be wrong."

"I think not. Action must be taken and don't misread from my previous comments any support for this genocide. As a doctor, I take my oath very seriously. If by default we allow this to happen, the blood of millions will also stain our hands."

"But if there's any possibility of being wrong, perhaps we should proceed slowly."

"Allow me to reaffirm my position. Make no mistake Representative Grant, we are right and must exercise all possible haste."

. . .

"We couldn't have anticipated this, Ed. My father's never been sick."

They sat in an otherwise deserted mess hall, discussing the call notifying Lori Tomasini that her father was terminally ill with cancer. Early detection would have made a difference in the treatment, but not in the prognosis. Determined to cope, her mother nevertheless left no doubt that Lori's help and moral support would ease the burden. "Please come home," she had pleaded. "A second tour in that awful place? What possible attraction could there be?"

"All right, mother, A.S.A.P., depending on connections and

when the Army releases me."

"I don't know what else to do, Ed. If I reenlist, I may never see him alive again because the Corps will furlough me only for his funeral. That's not fair to him or mother."

"Or yourself. You have to go."

"But what about us?" Lori paused to blow her nose. "I wouldn't have left you. Isn't that a pisser, Ed? Having to leave makes me realize I couldn't have done it voluntarily. Does that suck or what?" She dabbed her eyes with a fresh tissue and blew her nose again. "Oh, Ed. I love you! I don't want to go. This kind of separation can be deadly to a relationship."

Reynolds gripped her small hands tightly in his. "June's only two months away. My hitch is up on the eighth. Or tenth... Jesus, I can't even remember! I'll take leave time before my next assignment to be with you."

"How will I introduce you to my parents? As my friend, boyfriend, fiance? Do I tell them you're married?"

"Your boyfriend, I guess."

"Are you married?"

"Jesus, I don't know!"

"And what explanation will you give your wife for being on leave, but not going home?"

"I won't tell her."

"Oh, Ed, that's so dumb! Suppose she calls here?"

"She doesn't call. Hell, she rarely writes."

"We need to talk. We'll steal every spare minute before . . .". Fighting a resurgence of tears, her voice trailed off.

"Honey, I'll write every day and call twice a week. Before you know it, we'll be together again."

"You sure you don't want to kiss me goodbye and find a new girl?" Lori's eyes brimmed with tears.

"Positive. And I'll be at your side in June trying like hell to make it permanent."

Lori took a deep breath. "Okay. I guess that's the best we can do. Believe it or not, I have to go to work. You done for the day?"

"I wish. Essell wants a quick recon of sector 26. Some idiot reported evidence of human life, but no sightings have been confirmed since we found Hadari. One of these days Washington will wise up and pull our funding."

"Rumor has it India Command is about to supersede the African Command except in strategic places in the North and South. There may be no AFCOM to re-up in. How are you at flying through monsoons?"

"Won't happen as long as Hadari's out there."

"Some day they'll bring him in for tests."

"Never. He makes Typhoid Mary look like Florence Nightingale."

"The only way to study him is in a lab. And guess which dummy will volunteer to transport him?"

"As much as I . . . care about that little bastard, he'll never ride in my bird."

"You say that now, but you'll change your mind. You're a closet crusader, Reynolds. I have to go. I'm late and the sooner you leave, the sooner you'll be back. Besides, if we stay much longer, I may start thinking how hopeless everything is and start crying again."

Lori rose on tiptoe, and kissed him squarely on the mouth. "You come back safe. I hate those ugly machines and the ominous noise they make." Reynolds reacted as if his mother had been slandered. "Worship them if you want. You probably do in your juvenile way, but loving you doesn't mean I have to like those 'angels of death.'"

"Why do you call them that?"

"Because I know what happens to anyone found out there!" Startled, Reynolds opened his mouth to speak, was silenced by her rationalization. "It's okay. I realize the necessity for this . . . practice. Protects *my* life."

"Not true, honey. None of us... "

"It's too late to pretend. Has the reason you or Kolata or one of your tight-lipped buddies follow up after initial recons affected my feelings for you?"

"No." It was an oblique admission of guilt.

"Ed, no one is fooled. All that ammunition isn't expended target shooting or hunting protected wildlife. For all I know, you have the President's blessing. Go do what you have to."

. . .

When Ed shut the door of his BOQ, life closed in as well. How could a woman he had known less than a year, do this to him? It had nothing to do with sex. Sex, he could get anytime.

Fifteen minutes ago she was in his arms, ardently expressing her love. Now he was alone, his uniform damp with her tears, make-up permeating his shirt where she burrowed her face. After a final poignant kiss, with feminine acquiescence she had accepted unnecessary assistance boarding the shuttle that would carry her on the first leg of her journey. At Omega 23 she would transfer to a battalion chopper en route to the Kisangani airfield, which could accommodate long-range 747's.

Reynolds clutched the sealed envelope she pressed into his hand prior to departure. He stared numbly at his last link to the girl he had grown to love. Finding nothing to use as an opener–when was anything ever around this shit-hole of a duty station when one needed it?–Ed held the envelope to the light, tapped it to shift the letter inside, and carefully tore off the end. Depression plummeting to new depths, he lay his head on the pillow and read:

My dearest loving Ed,

How strange it is to type this, my first letter to you. The circumstances that necessitate writing instead of talking fill me with infinite sadness. This forced separation has made me aware of how much I love you. More than I ever thought possible, enough to hurt others to get what I want. I'm not terribly proud of that, but there it is.

At least you'll have company; my replacement, Cheryl Fletcher, currently assigned to O-23. The shuttle that takes me from you will return with her. You saw her when she was here on TDY the latter part of December. She has long chestnut hair, is four or five inches taller than me, and is in her late twenties. You were staring at her ass. It's okay. You tried not to.

As for me, with nursing my father, comforting my mother, and working full time God knows where, I doubt I'll have time to fraternize with the opposite

229

sex. Call me; write me. Hold me in your heart.

Love forever,
Lori

Ed reread every word with quiet despondency, then folded the letter and put it in his breast pocket. He had another search and destroy mission. Two females had been spotted in sector 32, probably fleeing the plague further north. Both showed advanced symptoms of the disease. It was a lousy, fucking way to make a living.

. . .

Appreciative eyes remained transfixed until it became awkward not to look away. A handful recalled her previous visit, nodded and smiled. Ed, following her progress through the line, recognized her immediately. Upon spotting him she smiled slightly, flashed an expression that said, "Oh, there you are. I'll be right over," and wended her way across the room.

Her casually styled hair flowed in gentle waves over graceful shoulders. One could sense quickening male pulses. Moving with elegance enhanced by a charming touch of naivete, she blushed slightly at a restrained whistle. Accustomed to such attention, she managed an amiable, polite acceptance, instinctively pleased while simultaneously wishing such exhibitions would not occur.

"Hi," she smiled. "Ed Reynolds?" She knew precisely who he was, but felt proper etiquette demanded verification. When he started to rise, she waved off his gesture. "Don't get up."

Placing her tray opposite his, she turned to an unoccupied table for salt and pepper. A fitted, white satin uniform molded to her buttocks and the back of her thighs, an innocent display of an incredible figure.

"I shouldn't use these, but breaking the habit is difficult. My family salted everything before tasting it." Thus apologizing, she gracefully settled onto the chair. "Let me introduce myself. I'm Cheryl Fletcher, Lori's friend."

"I noticed you at the Christmas party. You were due yesterday."

"The helicopter was grounded. Something about the

electronics, I don't know. Do you mind me joining you?"

Ed's expression indicated she was more than welcome. Cheryl was the most incredibly sexy woman he had ever met. Hauntingly beautiful, modesty and substance beneath the carnal attraction made her irresistible.

"Good! Sorry I didn't get to meet you in December. Guess our schedules were different."

"Must have been. How long have you been on active duty?" He felt a need to say something to draw attention from his poorly suppressed scrutiny of her breathtaking physical attributes.

"Since October. Got the usual hurry-up training. Three weeks at Fort Bragg. There's a place! Have you been to Fayetteville?"

"Several times."

"And once is too often, right?"

"Like any army town."

"I escaped every week-end to Carolina Beach. Do you like to swim."

"It's okay."

"Lori does. We talked about it a lot when I was here at Christmas."

"I didn't know that," Ed confessed, wondering what else he did not know about his girl friend.

"She says you're leaving in June."

"The eighth. Unless they extend me. It happens."

"That would be good. Leaving in June, I mean. I'm stuck until October. I said that, didn't I? Well, if you want a friend until you go, whenever that is, I'm available. Do you have any plans for dinner?"

"I have reservations at the Ritz."

Cheryl laughed. "May I join you?"

"I'd like that."

19

With calls held and the calendar cleared, John McDonnell ceased admiring the grounds and swiveled to face his chief of staff. Recognizing the act as a non-verbal signal to start the briefing, Harrison opened the folder on his lap. The scheduled topic was Hadari, the Type 4 symptomless African boy maintained in isolation in northwestern Congo.

Silent until now, the Chief Executive opened the session by courteously inquiring, "And how are you this morning, Robert?"

"Fine, sir. And you?"

"The usual aches and pains associated with growing old, but other than that, fine. Well, what do you have to report on this remarkable lad?"

With the President's attention, focused on the issue at hand, Harrison commenced. "Outwardly, his health continues to improve."

"A tribute to American nutrition, much as that's maligned."

"But no evaluation has taken place, nor will it until you give the order. It occurs to me, sir, when the time comes, it may be difficult to find someone willing to examine the young man."

"We'll use a military doctor."

"You expect anyone to volunteer?"

"Bob, there is always some gung-ho fatalist."

"I hope so." Harrison thought his chief a bit naive and overly optimistic on this one. More likely, he would have to draft some poor bastard too impuissant to refuse.

"Is there any reason to maintain the majority of the Omega

units in central Africa much longer?" the President proceeded, intent on making some hard decisions this morning.

Since asked, Harrison offered his opinion. "Not at present strength."

"I agree." Leaning forward, McDonnell tapped his pencil on his desk several times, then stopped. "Is INCOM ready for activation?"

"We have sufficient equipment deployed in three coastal areas."

Pencil tapping intermittently resumed. "Okay, Bob; here's what I want. Initiate personnel reductions as soon as practicable at all Omega units within twenty degrees of the equator. RIF to maintenance-level crews. Tentative shutdown, 30 June; for all units except 22 and 23. Reassign anyone with six months or longer, as of this date, to India Command. Get the Secretary of Defense and Chairman of the Joint Chiefs on it right away. Now, this pilot that found the kid... what's his name?"

"Reynolds. Ed Reynolds."

"He's to remain in his current assignment until further notice... Executive Order." Harrison started flipping through papers in the boy's folder. "Is that a problem?"

"Sir?"

"You look concerned."

"I'm trying to locate information about this officer. Seems to me, he's had back-to-back hardship tours. Extending him, even with your Executive Order, may be a little sticky."

McDonnell reached for his intercom. "Kim, pull up the records of Army Captain Edward Reynolds, R-E-Y-N-O-L-D-S. ... That's right ... Middle initial? Just a minute." Harrison shrugged. McDonnell resumed his instructions. "Unknown, if any. Shouldn't be hard to locate. AFCOM, Omega 22. D of D, Priority One. I'll wait." In seconds the information appeared on McDonnell's video desktop. "Got it, Kim. Thank you."

"There it is." Harrison pointed to the relevant data. "Due out 8 June. Two consecutive hardships. Wife and three children. This may be tough, sir. Army regulations... "

"Do you think I give a fuck what the regs say, Bob! The boy knows and trusts him. Upgrade my Executive Order to 'Most

Urgent.' Double his re-up bonus."

"You know we'd never get away with that, sir. Ever since Nixon and Reagan; Iran-Contra; Watergate; the congressional bank scandal, Rubbergate; and GOPAC the media sniff out this sort of thing in days. Their computers... "

"All right, all right. Let me think. ... Put him on hazardous duty pay."

"He already is."

The President grew impatient. "Then just do it! I'll write him and his wife a letter, emphasizing patriotic duty. If neither objects we're home free. In addition, I'll promote him to major immediately and make him an acting lieutenant colonel after he delivers the boy. I can do that, can't I? Under battlefield promotions?"

"Considering the perilous nature of his assignment, I should think so."

"Then it's settled. Goddamn it! No wonder I can't get anything done. Fucking legal bullshit!"

"When will you order the boy picked up?"

McDonnell became evasive. "Months . . . months. That's why I need Reynolds' extension."

"Sir, isn't Northcoast ready for a Type 4? When Dr. Fairchild called last week, he indicated the serum works well against the first three and... "

"He called, and you didn't tell me?"

"You were busy and always seem annoyed when he does."

"Did he ask for me?"

"Yes, but it seemed routine."

"*Nothing* concerning AIDS is routine, Harrison!"

"Sorry, sir."

Harrison's status as hired help was abruptly reestablished, too much so.

"Put him through *immediately* in the future! AIDS is so important I must deal one to one! Bob, not until *I'm* satisfied STC's are one hundred percent effective against the first three strains do I dare allow anyone to risk exposure to Type 4. I receive reports you haven't seen, and my most recent information... from all sources, not just Dr. Fairchild... suggests additional testing is required."

"Yes sir," Harrison said; but wondered, "*What* other sources? There aren't any." Perhaps he would check with Fairchild later. Perhaps he would be searching for a new job if he did!

"Look at that mountain of paperwork. Most of it bullshit! Tell Kim to continue holding my calls, short of an emergency, until I tell her otherwise."

Obviously their consultation was terminated. Harrison rose and returned his chair to its original location. "I'll get right on this, sir." His hand was on the doorknob to the outer office when McDonnell stopped him.

"Bob, just a minute. Keep this close to your chest, but since you asked, I'm thinking of bringing the boy in around October."

"Will do, sir," Harrison assured his chief, while thinking, "So the old boy does have a plan. But what is it and why October?"

"And check with Ralph Nolin on contract negotiations between the UAW and Autotech. Last thing I need right now with this AIDS crisis and the Japanese on the run is a strike against the country's biggest auto maker."

"I'll inquire this afternoon. Anything else?"

"Not unless I call you."

His aide departed, and with no interference, the President stared vacantly into space for almost a quarter of an hour before settling down to work.

. . .

"Thank God!"

Hastily cradling the phone, Cheryl hurried from her office and raced across the parade ground to the landing field. Ben Essell, standing outside the air traffic control office, expressed words of caution as she ran past. "Don't get too close," he ordered.

"I won't."

Trailing bluish-brown vapor, the wounded bird struggled to the vicinity of the maintenance hangar, then abruptly descended to earth. Cheryl turned aside, attempting to avoid dirt particles pecking sharply at her face and settling onto her hair and clothes. To the metered swish of coasting blades, she mustered one last burst of energy to sprint the remaining distance to Ed's Huey.

"I was worried to death," she gushed as he stepped onto the

compacted earth. "Why didn't you report in?"

"I tried. On top of everything else, the damned radio went out." Her arm around his waist, they started across the barren ground. "When the engine malfunctioned I was afraid of a stall, so I landed," Ed reported. He then went on to explain that warning annunciators failed to pinpoint the problem and, upon restarting, the engine ran smoothly without a load but stumbled again at lift off. A second, lengthy shutdown and further diagnostics proved no more fruitful. However, after the third startup, the craft seemed steady enough to ascend and remain airborne, so he took a chance and flew it back.

"What happened?" Ben asked when they were within earshot.

Reynolds brought him up to date, concluding, "I knew you'd look for me, but the lower the sun got the more determined I was to avoid spending the night in that damned thing."

"Harvey can work on it in the morning. Get cleaned up. You and Lt. Fletcher are a mess. No offense, Lieutenant." Ben entered the building to tell the air controller to shut down the radar and close up for the day.

"What did you do all evening?" Ed inquired.

"Paperwork... what else? Worrying about you prevented accomplishing much."

For a brief moment she brushed against him and both were sensually aware of the contact.

"You smell good," he commented.

"I didn't know you ever noticed."

. . .

In the dimly lit passageway outside her quarters, Cheryl unexpectedly embraced Ed, drawing his body tightly against hers. "I was so afraid today." She pressed closer. "Afraid you crashed in some awful place and were never coming back." Uncertain, appearing vulnerable and younger than her years, she whispered, "Will you come in?"

"I'd like to," he answered, but the tone of his voice conveyed an unmistakable hesitancy.

" . . . Nevermind. It was a bad idea."

"Nothing wrong with the idea, just the timing."

"You'll be gone in three weeks, anyway. Sorry if I made you

uncomfortable . . . and I'm not sure I could have gone through with it. Wouldn't that have been mean?" She gave him a peck on the cheek. Entering her room, she turned and, silhouetted by moonlight streaming through the window, she asked, "Breakfast at the Ritz?"

"Zero-seven-thirty."

. . .

Alone in his townhouse and contrary to his usual lack of interest, Bob Harrison longed for female companionship. His high-profile government position placed him in frequent proximity to scores of intelligent, attractive women, many of whom were seduced by the aura of power associated with someone close to the President and willing to stretch personal moral standards to be included. But neither the women nor the pleasures offered were appealing.

Compelled to attend charitable functions on Washington's expansive social circuit, he begrudgingly allowed well-meaning friends to fix him up, but rendezvous were invariably short and reserved. When he was not fortunate enough to arrange meeting a date at their designation, he generally countered by arriving at the girl's apartment late. Once at the affair, he found frequent quasi-official reasons to desert her, but if she continually sought him out, and there was no pressing need to stay, they departed early. If she indicated a desire to spend more time with him at some future event, rain checks were offered; but never honored.

Robert E. Harrison was not homosexual. The thought of men together revolted him. Robert Elsworth, as his mother called him, was asexual and usually resigned to his fate—but not this evening, for he desperately needed someone he could trust, just for a while, to sort things out. He should have asked his secretary to stay. An enthusiastic listener, Bonnie made no special demands, realizing he was different and accepting it.

Today had been particularly grueling with McDonnell's behavior more unorthodox than usual. Predictably, when HIV was mentioned, tension filled the air. Harrison dreaded the topic and learned to put anything remotely related to AIDS last on the agenda, for the easy rapport carefully cultivated with his boss vanished the moment the subject was introduced. McDonnell became combative, so totally unreceptive to suggestions on dealing with the crisis that Harrison judiciously offered none.

No discussion with Dr. Fairchild or Representative Grant had taken place since . . . it had been so long, Harrison would have to consult his notes. The situation was tantamount to not conferring with one's general staff during wartime. When informed of Fairchild's or Grant's requests for meetings, the President, contrary to his previous insistence that he would take their calls, brusquely replied he was too busy.

Over and over Harrison relived that fateful morning when McDonnell abruptly ended the briefing and hustled him out. Their discussion had been rife with odd inferences. Then, without warning, a momentary hardness flashed in the President's eyes, followed immediately by an expression of uncompromising determination. It was a fanatical look, but about what?

Why in hell did McDonnell refuse contact with Fairchild, the one man that had it within his power to impede the progress of AIDS? Did he want the world depopulated? How absurd! Maybe he was only waiting until certain people or countries were decimated. Good God, that was *it*!

Harrison sat upright in his chair, realizing he had not imagined any of it. Those smoldering emotions, kept tightly under rein, occasionally spilled from McDonnell's eyes for an instant before they could be reburied. This man was a monster . . . a mass murderer!

How ironic it all was. He was the only decent President since . . . what did it matter? They all appeared saintly by comparison. The most powerful person in the world presiding over the selective demise of tens of millions of innocent souls, a crime of omission, for AIDS committed the atrocity while all McDonnell did was withhold orders that could retard it. Through AIDS he was purging the planet of all those who did not fit his conception of how human life should be: people in India, central Africa, and urban ghettos everywhere. But why include the Japanese? The world depended on their industry, now crippled by loss of manpower.

He wanted revenge! Everything fit! He hated the Japanese for what they did to American industry, and now he was getting even by allowing a race to be annihilated. He was not necessarily enjoying it, but he was fanatically convinced it was proper.

Millions were dying unnecessarily . . . women, children. The President was a Vlad III, the Wollechian prince the fictitious Dracula was patterned after. The story of *The Feast of the Beggars* globally reenacted in the year 2005. It was Transylvania: circa 1460. Assemble all undesirables in one building, lock them in, and set fire to the structure. AIDS was the conflagration. Africa, China, India, Japan–can not forget the ghettos–were the banquet halls. Purge the world of the lame, the poverty-stricken, the drug-addicted, the super-competitive. In McDonnell's mind there were no innocent bystanders. The poor would beget children destined to be poor, and their children would mature and procreate, perpetuating the cycle of suffering ad infinitum.

Someone must be told, but whom? Who would believe him and have the power to stop it? "Grant!" he thought. No, he was too young, too inexperienced. And what if he was in on it? Both men were from Ohio. He was a protege of the man. No, Grant could not be trusted. "Fairchild!" The name exploded in his brain. He must contact Fairchild, who was older, respected, and a member of one of the victimized races. The man whose life's work was tabled so the greatest perversion of all time could gobble up lives at an unprecedented, incomprehensible rate. Fairchild was perfect! A doctor, sworn to protect life.

Fairchild would listen. With a scientist's mind, he would sift the evidence, and arrive at the same correct conclusion. The man moved in multiple worlds: medicine, politics . . . and was no stranger to the media. Somehow he could bypass the President, convince reporters, and enlist the aid of colleagues. Somehow he would get his serum distributed.

Harrison's first impulse was to pick up his phone, but with no idea where the doctor would be at this late hour, he could not take a chance on not reaching him and receiving a return call at an inopportune time. McDonnell might be standing beside him. He must be patient. He would wait until 10:00 or 10:30. At the very least, he would talk to Fairchild's wife.

The microwave's digital clock took an eternity advancing to the next minute. Harrison picked at some fruit. He warmed a piece of leftover pizza, but the cheese melted and burned on the glass tray. He ate what was salvageable.

9:45 . . . 9:46 . . . 9:46 . . .

He must stop watching the clock. He turned on the small countertop television, turned it off; picked up the newspaper, put it down.

9:50 . . . 9:51 . . . 9:52 . . . 9:52 . . .

At 9:53 he could tolerate it no longer and entered the spare bedroom used as a study, picked up the phone and punched in the numbers, 1-2-1-6, before abruptly hanging up. What was he to say? "Hello, Dr. Fairchild? This is Bob Harrison. I'm calling to tell you why the President won't meet with you or authorize use of your marvelous serum. You see, he's waiting until all the disgusting people on Earth are dead."

Frustrated, Harrison returned to the kitchen, opened a wine cooler, took a sip, set it down. He must not drink.

9:57 . . . 9:58 . . .

"Goddamn it, it has to be done!" With righteous resolve Robert Harrison strode through the short connecting hall and back into his study. Retrieving the phone, he pressed: 1-2-1-6- . . . the remaining numbers following in close succession. Placing the handset to his ear, he listened impatiently as network-switching equipment completed his call.

It was ringing! Once . . . twice . . . three times.

"Come on. Be there!"

Four . . . five . . . six . . .

"Hello." It was the rich, melodic baritone voice of the man capable of ending this madness.

Harrison stared blankly at his most recent art acquisition, a watercolor of an old mill, complete with waterwheel, race, and millpond. Several wild ducks splashed across the surface. One was on the verge of touching down, wings spread, feet in position to break its entrance into the water . . . a good picture, well executed, acquired at a fair price.

"Hello," Dr. Fairchild repeated.

Harrison hung up. This whole thing was ludicrous. It was all supposition. Fairchild would notify the President, and McDonnell would fire him. Even if true, the slaughter would continue because governments grind slowly. Dejected, Harrison returned to his kitchen and snapped on the mini-TV. He needed a distraction.

. . .

"Who was that?" Roberta asked.

"I don't know. The caller ID was blocked," Bill answered. He was too tired to be annoyed. "Someone was on the line but said nothing."

"It couldn't have been important. Probably a wrong number." She returned to her reading.

"How do you feel?"

She placed his hand on her tummy. "Pregnant. *Very* pregnant."

. . .

Sarah and Charlie were extracting winter debris from one of several flower gardens behind their house. Charlie, having returned from D.C. at 11:45 the night before, was not rested and would not be when he flew back, Tuesday.

"Do you have any idea what your schedule will be around the Fourth?" she inquired, wanting desperately to have a family holiday.

"No. Depends on who calls." Grant stood stiffly, straightened his back, then returned to his labors, this time on one knee.

"You should say, 'no,' more often."

"I can't. It goes with the territory."

Sarah sighed with resignation. "I'm not convinced I want you to be president some day."

"A view shared by millions of others, no doubt."

"How did your meeting go?"

"We were stood up."

"*What?*" Sarah rose to her feet.

"He postponed. Sent Harrison to break the news. Bill and I had been waiting in his outer office for close to half an hour."

"*How frustrating.* After you made a special trip. Charlie, I think it's time to involve the media."

"Sarah, I *can't*! I'd sound like a fool!"

"Well, you have to do *something!*"

"On the flight home, Bill and I discussed camping outside McDonnell's door until it's impossible to ignore us, but that's

241

impractical. Besides, Roberta is due in three months. The man's a mess, Sarah, torn between devoting time and attention to his wife and literally saving the world . . . or what's left of it."

"Let me call Roberta. The four of us can have dinner and go to Blossom. You and Bill can talk more."

"I don't know what else we can say, but I'm willing."

"What do you have going next weekend?"

"I can arrange to be here. What if Bill and Roberta can't?"

"They will."

Grant did not doubt it for a minute. When Sarah put her mind to something, it usually happened.

. . .

"All set," she announced, cradling the phone. "The Fairchilds will arrive about 5:30. I got pavilion instead of lawn seats because Roberta is pregnant."

"Good. I hate sitting on the fucking grass."

"Now all I have to do is find a sitter."

"Easier to save the world."

20

On the fifth of June, in the year of our Lord, twenty hundred and five, Capt. Benjamin Essell, Omega 22 commander, sat at his desk in company headquarters. Before him lay an official packet containing the fate of his unit.

Breaking the seal, he extracted the contents, noting the first document promoted him to major, effective 1 May 2005. Next was the new table of organization and equipment for a downsized Omega 22. Bundle three held orders for the new permanent party assigned to the shrunken unit, and a fourth rather sizeable parcel delineated reassignments for remaining personnel.

Essell studied the reorganization information. He would have the manpower to support two helicopters—a mission craft and one for backup. There would be two pilots and an air controller, plus a factory trained and certified Blackhawk mechanic—a civilian also familiar with Hueys—two cooks, a clerk/secretary, one nurse, a doctor, and himself. Everyone else was to be transferred as of... "Holy` *shit*!" he said, under his breath, "12 June 2005! *One fucking week*! Jesus` *Christ*!" He was starting to sound like Reynolds.

Essell thumbed through the ten sets of orders that included his own: Ann Hemminger, Cheryl Fletcher, Norman Rosemond, M.D.... "What's this?" he muttered to himself, "Edward Reynolds? *Son* of a *bitch*! Ed will just *shit* when he finds out!" But, affixed to the document was Ed's majority as of 1 June. "That should ease the pain," thought Essell.

With eight men and two women, it was going to be one hell

of a party or the kind of close-quarter boredom scientific groups encounter wintering in Antarctica. There would be little to do, and there would be ten to do it—but only after this week. For the next seven days he would have to work the asses off of everyone. Entire buildings had to be cleaned; equipment and furniture had to be inventoried and crated for shipment to INCOM. Wanting to get the touchiest detail out of the way, he paged Reynolds.

. . .

He was initially angry, but the longer Ed brooded over his assignment, the more it appeared to be the answer to his prayers. Now an irrevocable decision could be postponed for months. Life was a bitch, but one that took care of you. Lori would understand and wait, proud of his role in conquering AIDS. His kids could boast their dad took care of the boy that was studied in the effort to cure Type 4 AIDS. He might even have a place in history.

The only problem was his wife would be pissed, thinking he engineered the whole thing. He would try to pacify her by sending his re-up bonus, writing her and the kids more often, and providing frequent presents. All in all, his ass had been saved again!

Reynolds left company headquarters, walked across the parade ground through the usual inhuman heat, entered his BOQ, and proceeded to compose the letter that would hopefully smooth things over and maintain his life on hold.

Dear Janet,

I hope this letter finds you and the children happy and safe because I have some unfortunate news . . .

. . .

With everyone milling around, Captain—now Major—Essell began. Most found seats; a few remained standing. It was hardly a time to enforce strict military discipline, at the death knell of the organization. General orders reducing the unit to a survivable minimum were read. A surprise to no one, the demise of Omega 22 was received with equanimity. Individual orders were handed out accompanied by requisite bitching. Though few wanted to remain at O-22, the majority dreaded completing tours in India.

Essell expressed his condolences but made it clear that the transfers were irrevocable and inevitable, and individuals would not be released until he personally conducted inspections of their workstation and quarters. Without a signed clearance stapled to their orders, permission to board the shuttle would be denied, and if they did not report to INCOM on time, their asses would be in a sling.

"Any questions? . . . Okay, clean meticulously," he advised. "In seven days I expect this place to look like it did when the contractor signed it over." Hesitating momentarily, he fumbled through his papers before resuming. "There are two more things. One order that arrived today promoted me to major . . ."

The room burst into applause followed by a round of mildly irreverent remarks.

"We really *are* happy for you, Ben," a senior nurse assured him.

"Thank you, Althea. Ed Reynolds also advanced in rank. Congratulations, *Major*."

Another eruption of approval accompanied by a bombardment of lewd and pithy repartee caused Reynolds to redden.

"How'd you kiss ass at the Pentagon from here, Ed?"

"Be glad they didn't make him a bird colonel. He'd shit on us even more!"

"It's the Peter Principle!"

"Couldn't be. He doesn't have one."

"That's not what Kolata says!"

"It *could* have happened to a nicer guy."

When the room quieted, Ben observed, "They love you, Ed. Imagine what it would be like if they didn't."

"Someday with luck, every last mother of them will end up in my command," Reynolds winked. "Thanks, everyone!"

Becoming introspective, Essell continued. "I'm grateful for your perseverance and devotion to assignments. This is not a particularly pleasant place, with the odds of contracting a fatal disease many times what they would be almost anywhere else. Since I have been CO, none of us have been infected, by the grace of God and due to your diligence and care. Finally, thank you for your friendship. Dismissed."

Reynolds sat meditating as the room emptied. One table away, Cheryl wanted to offer sympathy but was reluctant to intrude until he looked up.

"Sorry, Ed."

"For what?"

"Getting stuck here. I know you were counting on seeing Lori."

"When you've been in the military as long as me, you get used to it."

"That doesn't mean you like it." She rose and approached his table saying, "Let me know if I can do anything for you." Then she leaned down to kiss his cheek. Reynolds watched as she turned and walked to the door. "What a great ass," he thought. "Damned shame, no one is getting any of it."

. . .

Authorized by Congress in February 2001 and activated in March of the following year, the Omega system had steadily downsized. Soon, ten people designated by presidential fiat would carry out the sole mission of sustaining one unique boy in his habitat, or at an isolation facility on site, until he could be safely transported to Cleveland, Ohio.

A destiny to discreate was implicit in the original mission: 'To preside over and alleviate the suffering of a potentially terminal population.' Initially, thriving villages dotted the countryside. Standing procedure sent two or three Hueys and a couple of Blackhawks, loaded to capacity with personnel, food, and medical supplies, into a stricken area. Doctors routinely checked everyone. Symptoms were medicated, and those in need of institutional care were loaded into now partially empty Blackhawks for transport to the hospital.

After the first confirmed diagnosis of the incredibly contagious Type 4, contact was broken off. The sector was designated yellow, and supply airdrops superseded landings and personal contact. As the resultant new patient hospitalizations declined, staffing levels were adjusted, surplus wards disinfected and closed, and helicopters idled.

Concurrently, Reynolds and Kolata, plus an elite few others, were issued weapons and ammunition and began flying follow-up missions alone or with carefully selected noncoms.

. . .

"Ed," Cheryl called out quietly into the darkness of the Officers' Club, her eyes not adjusted from the brightly lit entrance.

"Over here," he whispered.

In flickering light emanating from the huge projection television screen, she vaguely discerned his silhouette along the left wall.

"You okay?" he asked, as she sat beside him.

"I dropped a contact. Took forever to find it."

"I was getting worried."

"What could happen to me here?" She touched his forearm.

When he reached to return the gesture, his hand accidentally brushed her breast. "Sorry."

"Don't be."

The movie over, Ed escorted Cheryl to her room and started to leave. She took his hand. "I want you to stay."

"Me, too. That's why I'm going."

Outside, the night was beautiful. Warm breezes brushed his face; stars were everywhere. Getting accustomed to different constellations and shifted positions of familiar clusters in the equatorial sky had taken some time, but after two years the heavens looked familiar.

A couple walked past. "Good night, Ed." They looked sad. Only six more nights before she would be heading home and he was en route to the Indus Valley. The end of an affair was as emotionally draining as the death of a mate. In divorce at least one partner feels relief. Here, both were distressed.

Reynolds entered the BOQ, threw his clothes over a chair and, supremely conscious of being alone, climbed into bed as emotionally spent as the night Lori left. Wide awake and staring into the darkness, he attempted to filter out the grinding whir of his old electric clock, concentrating instead on intruding sounds from the African night. Beyond the distant trumpeting of a lone bull elephant, he discerned eerie, distinctive laughter from a pack of hyenas on the prowl. The animal population seemed to be escalating, a good sign.

The camp quieted as personnel settled down for the night. Traffic decreased in the hall and doors discreetly shut, until the only audible human activity emanated from the club across the parade ground where diehard drinkers congregated. Time passed slowly, minute by wide-eyed, interminable minute.

The nocturnal tranquility was suddenly interrupted as the exterior door to the building opened and closed, followed by the approach of delicate footsteps. Some lucky guy was getting a late caller. Part of him wished it was Cheryl. He felt both relief and disappointment as the muffled sounds passed down the hall.

. . .

A quarter of the world away John McDonnell tossed and turned. It was one of those evenings when he was too tired to stay up, but the depth of his fatigue inhibited sleep. As Karen snored lightly beside him, he considered mixing a nightcap and going to the library to read but rejected both ideas. While alcohol might rapidly induce sleep, he would awake in the middle of the night, more insomniac than ever. Eventually, he drifted off.

Around 3 a.m., sweating profusely while coming out of his REM phase, he mumbled the words repeatedly and, with a violent, involuntary jerk, was suddenly awake. "Damn!" he thought. "The third time in two weeks!" Karen remained asleep, thank God! McDonnell crept from under the covers and changed pajamas, then placed a towel over the damp sheets, flipped his wet pillow and lay back down.

Something kept disturbing him; what, he could not remember. Had she been awake, Karen could have told him, often hearing the word as he sweated and thrashed about. McDonnell was under the impression it had happened thrice in a fortnight, those times he remembered. It occurred nightly.

"The winnowing," he'd mumble. "The winnowing, the winnowing . . ."

. . .

The children were at grandma's house, and the Fairchilds were due any minute. Sarah was applying finishing touches to hors d'oeuvres she would serve with drinks before they left for dinner at Lock 16 in the Merriman Valley. Ostensibly a social evening, clandestine undercurrents dominated her thoughts when somewhere outside an automobile door slammed.

"Charlie! I heard a car. Will you check and see if they're

248

here?"

"It's them," he confirmed, passing through the kitchen. "I'll get the door."

"Leave your beer."

"Why?"

"It's tacky and rude."

"Who says?"

"Civilized people. You wouldn't know, dear." She kissed him on the cheek, then set the confiscated can on the counter after guiltily sneaking a sip. The voices of Charlie and their guests filtered into the kitchen from the foyer. Moments later, Roberta stuck her head around the corner.

"Hi. Can I help?"

"No, thanks; I just finished up." Sarah placed the platter of canapes on the table, gave her guest a big hug–awkward because of Roberta's advanced pregnancy–and said, "How are you?"

"Fine, except nothing fits; and total strangers think my tummy is community property."

"I remember that. I couldn't go anywhere without people patting me and telling horror stories about delivery."

Bill appeared in the doorway.

"We're so glad you two could make it," Sarah greeted him as she ushered everyone into the living room.

"We always look forward to charming fellowship and a performance of the Cleveland Orchestra. Even on a chilly preseason evening such as this."

Minutes later, Charlie abruptly altered the mood by briefly explaining an ulterior motive behind their sincere invitation.

"Bill and I suspected as much," Roberta said.

Sarah voiced her concerns, reviving Charlie's earlier suggestion that the men camp outside the Oval Office until the President granted an audience.

"Without his concurrence, we wouldn't get through the front gate, let alone near the office," countered Fairchild the scientist, prepared for all contingencies.

"Then I have several alternate plans: send the President an ultimatum through Harrison; appeal directly to either the Speaker of the House or the Secretary of State; or go public."

"I'm against involving the media." Fairchild was adamant.

"That would be our last resort," Sarah assured.

"Did you consider approaching the Vice President?"

"We discussed that, Bill," Charlie injected. "But McDonnell has never granted the man any real authority and, to the best of my knowledge, seldom confides in him. We can't put the VP in a position to look foolish or challenge his running mate. Besides, if we're right and can prove it, we have no choice but to go for impeachment. If successful, we'll need a squeaky clean Vice President."

"Which leaves us with . . ."

"Bob Harrison, the Secretary of State, and the Speaker of the House." Grant completed Fairchild's thought.

Silent up to this point, Roberta weighed in. "The Speaker belongs to the opposition party. People would suspect political motivations. If Harrison won't deliver our ultimatum, or the President obstinately refuses to grant an audience, I suggest contacting the Secretary of State. He's cognizant of the problem and has worldwide connections. Pressure could be brought to bear that I doubt McDonnell could resist."

"Echoes my thoughts," Fairchild said. "Any opposing views?"

Hearing none, Grant volunteered, "I'll initiate action by calling Bob. I suspect he shares our suspicions, but is leery of confiding in us for the same reasons we don't go to him."

"Namely?" Fairchild wanted confirmation.

"Fear of ridicule? Retaliation in the form of job loss? Professional isolation? Physical harm? Hell, I worry about those things. Anyone who could countenance the preventable deaths of multitudes could . . . no, he couldn't. That's melodramatic. The multitudes are statistics. McDonnell isn't capable of . . . murder. He *is* capable of tolerating massive numbers of deaths by default if they are foreigners, racially different, or their continued existence is perceived as a threat to Americans."

"Ergo the Japanese," Fairchild reasoned. "They meet all three criteria."

"And he won't initiate treatment until few, if any, remain."

"Or," Roberta suggested, "Americans start to succumb at alarming rates, whichever comes first."

"If those Americans are white," Sarah stated tersely.

"Probably true," her husband agreed.

Fairchild addressed Grant. "I don't have the clout to get to the Secretary of State, but I'd be willing to bet you do."

"Then that can be our contingency plan, although I expect McDonnell will grant us an audience fairly quickly once he realizes we mean business. He needs to defuse this situation."

With everyone in agreement, they selected Thursday morning of the following week for the confrontation.

"What are we going to do about the Secret Service?" Roberta injected. "If they report you two traveling together, the President may figure it out before Harrison delivers the message, and he may find a way to circumvent or retaliate."

"Oh, *shit*," Charlie exclaimed.

"That never entered *my* mind," Bill admitted.

"Let's not panic," Sarah cautioned. "We obviously erred in thinking you two could travel together and share our apartment. What we need is a good reason for Bill to be in D.C. Is there anyone in Washington, you need to see?"

"Regrettably, no."

"Do either of you have relatives near the Capital that might suddenly become ill?"

"Alas, all our relatives are west of the Alleghenies and in disgustingly good health."

"Any medical peers you might consult with, someone working with you on AIDS research?"

"Frances Coleman!"

"At Walter Reed! Bill, that's *perfect!*" Roberta was jubilant.

"Who's Frances Coleman?" Sarah inquired.

"She's a civilian research scientist pursuing a separate line of inquiry involving T-cells," Roberta answered excitedly. "Bill flew down to see her . . . when was it? February? March?"

"February."

"Then I don't see any problems," Sarah commented. "Call her early next week. Tell her you need to schedule a consultation Thursday and cancel at the last minute."

Grant posed a legitimate question. "Is she in a position to insist on a different day or telecommunications conference?"

"No. Everyone in AIDS research answers to me, and she can't refuse granting exactly what I request." Fairchild looked uneasily about the room. "I know that sounds egotistical, and so much power makes me uncomfortable, but it's true."

"And necessary," Charlie confirmed.

"Apparently all that remains," Sarah continued, "is to make the necessary calls Monday to Dr. Coleman and for plane and room reservations."

"I could stay at Walter Reed, but I don't think that's wise, since Frances might contact me early, and I have nothing to discuss with her."

"Then everything's settled." Sarah was proud of her role in engineering the meeting and its decisions. "Shall we go?"

"What's on the program?" Roberta asked as they rose to leave for the restaurant before going to Blossom Music Center.

"Mozart."

"How utterly superb," Fairchild commented.

. . .

Sunday morning dawned clear and crisp over Washington. John and Karen McDonnell sat at the rear of the church, Secret Service personnel on all sides. As the minister droned on, McDonnell's mind drifted to the topic that increasingly weighed on his mind–how much longer could he avoid Fairchild and Grant? Both were intelligent, decent men. If they had not figured out what he was up to, they soon would. And when absolutely certain, their innate sense of decency would compel intervention.

He was decent, too, but in a way he feared would be misunderstood. No person ever on Earth had been given the opportunity to improve the human condition as had befallen him. If he was successful, the outcomes were beyond belief: an end to suffering, the surcease of want, and the elimination of strife. He only needed four to six months. Please, God, I'm doing what you want. Give me four to six months.

"Are you all right, dear?" Karen whispered. "You look bothered."

"Just the usual pressures. I'm fine."

She reached over and patted his hand.

21

John McDonnell nodded to his Secretary of Labor to start the meeting. The cabinet members looked expectantly at Ralph Nolin.

"President McDonnell," he began, "was kind enough to call this special session because a chronically troublesome situation has suddenly become untenable."

Nolin, a small distinguished-looking man in his late sixties, had been appointed by the previous administration. One of the few holdovers, he was highly regarded by both parties.

"As you know, we have been trying for months to avoid a strike against Autotech. It appears our efforts have been futile, and the United Auto Workers are going to reject the proposed contract."

Consternation filled the room.

"At issue is executive pay. The union doesn't feel the company is equitably sharing the windfall profits that have accumulated since import quotas were enacted. Triggered yesterday by *Time's* disclosure of CEO Owens' compensation last year, the union is in full-blow rebellion." Not prone to theatrics, Nolin nevertheless paused for effect before reporting, "He received $887 million, take or leave a few hundred thousand."

The cabinet was astounded.

"We all know this has been going on for more than a decade, but the disparity between rich and poor continues to grow, and the public has had a belly full of it. Garnered in the form of salary, bonuses, and exercised stock options, Owens' windfall is perfectly legal but understandably unethical to employees asked to moderate their demands. And it makes us look like accomplices or incompetents, since it was our quotas and tariffs that enabled the profits that generated the money."

"What's Farotini's response?" the Secretary of Human Services inquired. Michael Farotini was the head of the UAW.

"Outrage, but he has no love for Walter Owens, anyway."

"This has been brewing a long time," McDonnell injected. "Ever since the nineties when numerous individuals regularly earned incomes in the low hundreds of millions. Merit and history notwithstanding, Owens' compensation is without precedent and in my mind, indefensible."

"What we've done so far," Nolin continued, "is call in a mediator, and if that fails, a federal arbitrator is standing by."

"I've also scheduled a meeting at Camp David with Owens and a couple of his officers." McDonnell announced. "We're hoping the casual surroundings will facilitate a mood of conciliation."

"With that background," Nolin stated, "The President and I would like your input."

. . .

Earlier that day, loitering out of habit in the air traffic control building, Reynolds had sat with his feet propped on the radar console. Coffee in hand, and the taste of breakfast still on his palate, he yearned for a drink. Consumption had been increasing as habit turned into want, and want became need. Never hung over during his twenties, he now experienced morning sluggishness, which occasionally persisted until supper. That alone was cause for concern, but most disconcerting were recent sexual encounters with Lori. His erections were not as hard, and climaxes were less explosive . . . classic signs, of too much booze. A constant glow was no tradeoff for a less-than-sated dick! Taking advantage of a clear head the night before, he promised himself and his cock that beer consumption would be less and straight shots eliminated.

Now, having embarked on his resolution, he lay in darkness craving a drink. Someone entered the BOQ, probably Ben. It sounded like it was at that end of the building. He looked at the lighted face of the old clock: zero-zero-forty hours. Seven hours difference would make it 5:40 p.m. in Minneapolis, and Lori should be home from work. Overwhelmed by a desire to hear her voice, he dressed and tiptoed from the room and down the hall. Ben's door opened as he passed.

"You okay?" his friend and commander asked.

"I'm fine."

"Going for a nightcap?"

"Going to make a phone call."

"Lori?"

"Yeah."

"Say hello; for me."

"I will. She often asks about you."

"Your zipper's down."

"Thanks." Ed corrected the problem.

"You've got enough women; you don't need to advertise."

"Fuck you, Ben."

"Just trying to save a little nookie for the rest of us."

"You wouldn't know what to do with it."

"Use my office phone."

"Thanks."

. . .

"Lori, it's me."

"Ed!" Squeals of delight surged over the line. "How nice! You never call on weekdays."

"How are you, honey?"

"Tired. I'm working full time. They had me on three days a week... that was the deal... but you know how it goes. 'Could you fill in here? Someone's sick; or someone's quit.' With forty hours, occasional overtime, and my dad, I'm a wreck."

"I'm sorry, honey. How is he?"

"Failing."

"I'm sorry."

"Thanks. Me, too. Can't change anything, though."

"Your mom okay?"

"Coping. She'll have her breakdown when it's over. I'm having mine now."

"Can I help?"

"You have with your support, even from seven thousand miles."

"I love you, Lori."

"I love you, too . . . are you okay?"

"I miss you."

"You don't sound right. What's wrong?"

"I miss you, that's all."

Unconvinced. "Tell me if it isn't?"

"I promise. Do you mind that I'm thirty-six?"

"Why do you ask?"

"Do you *care*?" he persisted.

"Does it bother you I'm twenty-two?"

"I kind of like it that way."

"Me too. Does that answer your question?"

"As soon as I get out of here, I'm coming to you."

"I'd like that. I need to be held."

"I hope your dad has peace."

"He will . . . soon."

"Good night, honey."

"Take care of yourself."

. . .

The telephone on Bill's desk warbled. Looking through the glass partition, Roberta noted he had not returned. "Dr. Fairchild's office," she responded, tapping in on the line.

"Hi, mom! This is Charlie Grant. How ya doin'?"

"What if somebody else had answered?"

"No sweat. Ninety-one percent of American women are mothers. Odds are in my favor."

"That's not true, and you know it."

"You're right. I made it up. Is Bill available?"

"He stepped out a few minutes ago without telling me where he was going. Should I find him or have him return your call?"

"Neither. I'd rather talk to a pretty girl."

"Flattery, sir, will get you everywhere. You're certainly in a good mood!"

"You will be, too, when I tell you the news. Harrison called."

"He *didn't*!"

"Ah, but he did. Our efforts at subterfuge were unnecessary. Bill and I have an appointment two weeks from next Monday at

10:30 sharp in the Sanctuary."

"You know what Bill will say: 'I'll believe it when I see it!'"

"Tell him not to worry. Our foot is in the door."

"What makes you so sure?"

"Harrison's attitude. More *how* he delivered the message than anything he said."

"Woman's intuition?"

"Something like that. Anyway, I'd bet money... and you know I don't gamble... that McDonnell will show up. Once he does, I'll get a hook into him. We aren't going through this sh... crap again."

"*Much* better choice of words, Charlie. When did he phone?"

"Just now. Bill should be getting his message any minute."

"Hang on. Another call's coming in. It might be Harrison."

Roberta put Charlie on hold for a moment, then returned. "False alarm. Accounts payable wanted to confirm delivery of an order so they could process the invoice."

"Someone anxious to pay a bill? Tell my constituents at tax time. Listen, I have to go. I'll be at my Akron office all week. Call me here or at home if you need anything." He had an afterthought; "Any names picked out?"

"Charles Grant Fairchild if it's a boy."

"Good one, Roberta. Planning on filing a paternity suit?"

"Bye, Charlie. Say, hello; to Sarah."

Less than a minute later, Bob Harrison phoned with notification of the scheduled meeting. Charlie's prediction looked good. Roberta wondered what changed the President's mind to make him suddenly accessible.

When her subsequent call to Charlie's office was answered by a volunteer she could hear him in the background asking who it was before coming on the line. "Hi, Babe. What's up?"

"You were right. Harrison called. I got the same impression. What do you suppose precipitated this magical transformation?"

"Beats me. We need to analyze it. Thanks for the message. I owe you a big kiss."

"I'll collect it from Bill if you don't mind."

"Damn! So much for improved race relations."

"Honestly, Sarah was right. You *are* terrible."

Roberta was dying to tell Bill the good news. When he had not returned in fifteen minutes, she considered instituting a telephone search, then decided against it to avoid the appearance of being a hovering wife. Leaving his pager behind–it was on top of his desk–meant he did not want to be bothered. Still, it was unlike him to be gone so long. Returning to her computer, Roberta wondered if the baby might recognize its characteristic sounds after birth, familiarity being one reason a mother's voice was more soothing than a father's.

"I'm back," Bill announced, pausing at her desk. "Can you believe Schleider's wife hasn't delivered?"

"Schleider?"

"In Oncology. She's two weeks overdue. Poor man."

"Poor man?" Roberta arched an eyebrow, then hurried on. "Can you believe Bob Harrison called and you and Representative Grant have an appointment with the President at 10:30 a.m. two weeks from Monday?"

Bill did not seem impressed. "We'll see."

"Charlie's in Akron. Do you want to talk with him?" Roberta reached for her phone.

"Not now. Remind me after lunch." Turning to enter his office, he mumbled, "I feel so sorry for Schleider."

Bill sounded *serious* in his concern for the husband! Until that moment a righteously indignant Roberta had been willing to ignore his misdirected sympathy.

"*One moment*, Doctor. What is this 'poor Schleider' routine? Don't you suppose his wife is the *least bit* uncomfortable?"

"No, I'm sure she's fine," Bill replied with a twinkle in his eye. "She's only pregnant!"

"You set me up!" A wad of paper heaved squarely at his back scored a direct hit as he retreated to the haven of his office. "Don't count on *another* chance to get me in this condition!" A second barrage flew through the air.

"Those aren't classified, are they?"

"Get to work!"

. . .

Hanging up the phone, Harrison faced the President. "Dr. Fairchild was unavailable, but his secretary... wife... took the

258

message."

"Thanks, Bob. Should have scheduled this, weeks ago. Always so much to do. Presidents need a teenager's body, the organizational skills of a fifty-year-old, and wisdom accrued over at least seventy years. Unfortunately, I fall short in each category."

"You do fine in all respects, sir."

"Thank you. I appreciate your kindness and confidence, but I'm not sure I share your conclusion. Now, where's the file on this lad, Hadari?"

Harrison produced a packet from his briefcase.

"I presume he's healthy?"

"We should be in such good condition. Latest observations indicate stable weight, clear skin, no apparent abnormalities."

McDonnell thumbed through the thin report. "Wonderful. Summary?"

"Hadari is checked once a week by... "

"Double that. Give those poor devils at Omega 22 something to do, and keep closer tabs on the boy."

Harrison dictated a note into his microcassette recorder before he resumed his briefing. "Supplies are replenished weekly. Is that sufficient?"

"That's up to them. What else?"

"There's no one who can communicate with him since the interpreter was transferred out on 12 June."

The President was astounded. "How in hell did that happen?"

"A detail apparently overlooked by the Pentagon." Harrison's wry expression did not go unnoticed.

"Have that man returned A.S.A.P. No, wait. What a great opportunity for a little affirmative action. Assign an African-American woman."

"Locating one fluent in such an obscure dialect may be difficult. Seems to be an uncommon form of Lingala. We were lucky to locate the man we had."

"*Do* it, Robert."

"I'll contact the State Department."

"Good. Those two women currently assigned will appreciate

additional company, and the men might enjoy another female presence." The President winked, then commented, "We both know what goes on at those camps. The Romans married women who lived near frontier posts throughout the Empire, the French married Indians in Canada, and our twentieth century GIs returned with war brides from every country after every war. Undoubtedly various participants in the Biosphere II experiment paired off as well."

McDonnell flipped through the report. "What else is here?"

"Not much. He has no symptoms. Correction... none that are externally apparent. No cough, no skin lesions, no runny nose. We still assume he's Type 4 positive."

"Must have an amazing immune system. Can't wait to learn how it differs. May unlock the door to an honest-to-God cure."

"He did have a cold three weeks ago. Omega personnel were concerned enough to request a specialist flown in."

"I should think so. Where's it say that?"

"Page six and top of seven."

Harrison waited as the President read.

"Appears to have run its course. Amazing. Type 4 infection and he shakes the common cold in a week. Mine hang on a month."

"With all respect, sir, Hadari is a bit younger than you."

"And *you*, Harrison, can be *replaced*!"

"Not very easily, sir."

"That's true." McDonnell chewed on a pencil. "It's time, Bob," he mused, "to bring the lad in. I want an isolation facility constructed at Omega 22."

"You've changed your mind about transporting him directly to Cleveland?"

"Not one of my better ideas. The chance of infecting the general population is alarmingly high. Something could go amiss en route, at the airport, even in the antiseptic conditions at Northcoast. We can't risk Type 4 running rampant throughout northeastern Ohio. Preliminary assessments must be made in the field.

"This isolation chamber should be large enough to support life for an extended period while two distinct problems are overcome. One is ridding the boy of all traces of Type 4, and the other is eradicating the virus from his environment. Frankly, I don't know if either can be accomplished, but until they are he must remain isolated. Perhaps prolonged exposure to air will be sufficient for decontamination, but we don't know that. These things require discussion with Dr. Fairchild. Make a note."

Dutifully, Harrison did as instructed while the President continued. "Find out what clean rooms are available, and if they can be modified for our purpose. I want this lad to have a bathroom, bedroom, and a reasonably large living area."

Harrison interrupted. "These facilities are normally used for research and manufacturing and installed inside another building, sir. The free-standing outdoor unit you propose will require a custom design which may take months. Couldn't we make do with one room assembled in an existing building and add a shower and toilet facility? It's far more than he has now."

"No. He's accustomed to freely roaming outside. A pre-adolescent boy can't be expected to thrive in a tiny box for what may be weeks. His quarantine is tantamount to imprisonment, complete with a locked door, because a twelve-year-old can't be trusted to stay put.

"In addition, if something happens to him, we may never find another Type 4 carrier with such incredible immunity. He may be unique except for those two African prostitutes in 1997 and the six or seven HIV-positive people in Australia. And the latter aren't scientifically useful because they have an attenuated strain." McDonnell was emphatic. "I want a sizeable free-standing unit. We must make the boy comfortable and safe-guard those who examine him."

"But testing could be expedited by using an existing facility."

"*Damn* the time it takes, Harrison!"

"Sir, with accelerated tests a substantial percentage of the Orient might be saved."

The President switched off the recorder, an increasingly common occurrence. "We can't save *shit*, Bob. It's too late! That's reality! And it's their damned fault! Besides that, there are too many of them! Always have been. Good God, a thousand years ago they numbered over a hundred million, and as recently

as 1989, they were producing forty thousand babies a day! *A day!*
And they kept it up throughout the nineties. Jesus Christ, Bob,
that's a football stadium full of people every forty-eight hours, a
city the size of Akron or Toledo every week! Jesus Christ! Who
needs it? There is no way *I* nor *anyone else* can treat the Chinese
or Japanese in time to forestall the inevitable."

Harrison surrendered. Right or wrong, McDonnell's mind
was made up, and argument was pointless.

"Bob, one misstep now and we lose the ballgame. I'm sorry
the world will come out of this with few blacks and fewer
Orientals, but at least the human race will continue. I could give a
shit what color the survivors are!"

Begrudgingly, "I do see your point."

"The media will be covering events at Omega 22. How will it
look, now or in retrospect, if we confine a twelve-year-old black
kid to a little box with a potty for weeks, possibly months?

"Our first consideration is curing AIDS, but I have to look
further down the road to when this over. Remember what
happened following World War I? We shit on the Germans,
providing them a rationale for World War II. And think about
what the Japs did to us subsequent to that conflagration. After
quietly rebuilding the Empire, they repaid us by crippling our
economy... with our help, I admit. Jesus Christ, they once owned
an incredible percentage of America!"

"I don't see where that's relevant, sir."

"Goddamn it, Bob, they aren't going to do it to us again! I
want posterity to record what we did was right, in the correct
way, to perpetuate the species. I can see us saving six hundred
million Chinese and Japanese and them being pissed off because
we didn't save seven hundred million. Americans are going to be
saved first, for a change! I can imagine them suing us in Federal
Court to get STC's before all of our citizens are treated, and some
asshole judge ruling in their favor!"

"Sir, that's so unlikely."

"Unlikely, *hell*! Americans ruling against their own self-
interest used to be the norm! Look what happened with the free-
trade bullshit in the eighties and early nineties! And most favored
nation status after that! I don't trust them, Bob, those Japs and

some of our own.

"Unfortunately, I'm not a dictator. I don't mean that literally, but too many Americans in high places have a distorted view of fairness. We saw it years ago when criminals were coddled and corporate raiders were permitted to plunder unimpeded. Hell, some of them were foreigners! And the masses weren't any better. It was the same profane time that juries freed murderers! Do you realize how fucking dumb some people are?"

Harrison listened, trying to appear noncommittal. Although he agreed with much McDonnell said, the President's fervor and rationale were alarming.

"Bob, I don't trust the Japs. They haven't played by the rules for fifty years. And that doesn't count Pearl Harbor! I *am* sorry they're dying." The President became soft spoken. "I realize the average person suffering is not at fault. I'm aware women, children, and babies are dying horrible, lingering deaths. I know only a relative handful of wealthy industrialists and politicians cause the grief, but as a race they have been responsible for so much misery in America since 1941 that I hate the yellow fuckers!"

Harrison blanched at the vehemence and implications of his Chief's comments.

"For far too long the world has careened out of control. History indicates it's always been that way, but we now have the capability and expertise to rein it in. And it's time we did.

"Obviously, none of this conversation is to leave this room," McDonnell concluded with quiet restraint. "But I mean every word."

"Yes, sir," Harrison responded, while thinking, "Who would believe it anyway?"

As if his last few statements had never been uttered, McDonnell activated the recorder and abruptly switched subjects. "Determine which vendors are capable of supplying the required equipment, including life-support systems with multiple levels of redundancy, and a complete inventory of spare parts. Not a single mechanical or electrical malfunction can be tolerated, especially climate control. He'd cook in there without air conditioning.

"Next, compile a list of construction firms with overseas

operating experience and capable of mobilizing rapidly. Send an order to the commander of Omega 22 to prepare barracks for technicians and construction workers and beef up the kitchen help and ancillary services.

"Factory engineering personnel must conduct exhaustive test procedures after the chamber and auxiliaries are assembled. Service crews will be needed to maintain the unit around the clock when it's in operation."

"Give me a few seconds to get that down." Harrison looked up from his laptop, indicating he was ready for more information.

"I want the facility operated and monitored a minimum of ninety-six hours; after which, all nonessential personnel are to be evacuated. Only then, can Hadari be picked up and delivered to the site. I don't want a bunch of people around if something goes wrong.

"That reminds me. Call Fairchild and tell him to set aside sufficient T-cell serum to treat all personnel that will be present the day we bring the boy in. Have I overlooked anything?"

"If you did I'll get back to you." Harrison shut down his computer.

"Bob," McDonnell deactivated his transcription unit, "if I could save the Orientals, I would."

"I know, sir."

"He doesn't believe me," McDonnell thought as Harrison left, "but there's nothing he can do about it. He's a loyal aide, and he'll do what I tell him, even if he has to shove ethical and moral considerations aside."

Convinced this isolation facility would get Fairchild and Grant off his ass until he could think of something else, the President contentedly settled down to accomplish more mundane tasks. Four more months . . . if Grant's projections were correct, he only needed four more months.

22

Low level cloud banks blanketed west central Maryland as the ebony limousine passed the check-point and rolled quietly to the complex of buildings that was Camp David. With heavily tinted windows concealing passenger identities, the E-3 member of a brace of special detachment marines halted the vehicle while an E-4 cautiously approached the driver's side. The faintly audible whir of a power window broke the stillness of the bucolic countryside.

"Where do I park?" the chauffeur inquired.

Temporarily ignoring the question, the sentry leaned forward, his right hand resting lightly on a government-issue automatic with the safety catch off, and reconnoitered the interior.

"Lower the barrier," he impassively requested.

The glass partition separating the chauffeur from the occupants in the rear compartment disappeared into a pocket behind the front seat. The sergeant's eyes scanned from left to right, alert for irregularities. Finding none, he ordered, "Open the trunk," while nodding to the corporal to move to the rear and perform the required inspection. The young marine did as instructed, found nothing suspicious, signaled all clear, and retreated several steps to narrow his field of fire.

Satisfied no danger existed, the sergeant directed, "Park over there," and resumed a wary parade rest beside the driveway.

Irritated by the delay and incensed at the indignity, Walter Owens sat impatiently in the limo's plush interior beside his first vice president, Philip Campbell, and the company's chief legal counsel, Dave Johnson.

"Dragged out on a Saturday afternoon by a retired college professor," he complained under his breath as his driver opened the rear door. Disdain filled Owens' voice. "I wouldn't hire the son of a bitch to clean the executive washroom."

Once inside the house, pleasantries were quickly dispensed with and the President got down to business.

"Gentlemen, we have a nasty strike on our hands. You, Walter, are going to find it expensive; I find it a major embarrassment. Indulge me while I chronicle my dilemma, and then I'll listen to yours.

"One: My quota system eked through Congress. The swing votes will desert to the free-traders at the first crack in the dike. Two: Foreign manufacturers are furiously seeking situations to discredit me. Three: The average consumer will only support his neighbor by buying American so long as value is equivalent, and his checking account isn't raided. The least inkling of Detroit taking advantage of its favored position, and he'll bolt once more to foreign goods. I'm sure you understand this."

Noncommittal expressions greeted the President's opening salvo.

"My policies have halted the unilateral trade war by taking control of the means of battle... money. Millions and billions of American dollars. The day we stopped sending it overseas for imports was the day we got the ball back in our court. Without our purchases the opposition is checkmated."

He paused to let that sink in.

"Detroit... Autotech... turns out a fine array of products. With your cooperation and that of the union, I can help maintain and improve our position in domestic and world markets. But you didn't come here to listen to a speech. Sorry, gentlemen, the professor in me sometimes controls the politician."

Owens took advantage of the pause to nudge things along. "What do you propose to do about the strike?" he asked.

"Strongly recommend to the union that they settle for three-and-a-half percent, a two-year contract... not three... and a frozen fringe package. You hold the line on prices a year. We'll look at the possibility of increases before the '07's come out."

Owens glanced at his first VP. "Can we absorb an additional half percent?"

"I doubt it but I'll sit down with the comptroller."

Ignoring the blatant parrying, McDonnell resumed, "And, before we discuss this, there are two more things. One; stay the hell out of Mexico with future expansions... "

"Where we put plants is none of your business."

"Perhaps not, but you didn't object when I bullied congress into a protective tariff. Have to take the good with the bad, Walter."

"What's the other issue?"

"You made $887 million last year, and your officers split an additional $675 million. As an act of good faith, you, and they, are going to give most of it back. Smile, you're about to become a hero!"

. . .

The President's interview on CBS, emphasizing executive compensations at Autotech and the CEO's adamant refusal to return any of it to the company, was completed and the network had switched to an angry picket line outside the Tennessee assembly plant. Walter Owens brusquely pushed the red button on the television remote control. The screen went black.

"Who does that cock-sucker think he is?" he demanded of the men seated in his library. Owens had assembled his key executives at his Grosse Point home shortly after jetting to Detroit.

Silence greeted his question.

. . .

As much as he wanted to visit with his wife on Sunday evening, an exhausted Charlie Grant retired at a quarter to ten. With the children also in bed, Sarah straightened the library, then did her nails before curling up naked next to her husband. She needed the time alone: no children, no noise, no hassles. The alarm was set for 4:30 a.m. so they could make love before he left for D.C. For many moments she remained contentedly awake, savoring the solitude and Charlie's assurance that tomorrow's meeting with the President marked the beginning of the end of the AIDS crisis. Soon, he promised, they would share more time together. She believed him and, when she drifted off, she was more relaxed than she had been in weeks.

. . .

Silence reigned between the two men throughout the flight; for 6:30 in the morning was not considered a reasonable time by Charlie Grant. He hoped Fairchild would understand his aversion to conversation and not take offense. In contrast, Bill loved the early hour. Alert and rested, he was amused by his catatonic colleague. Morning and evening people, he was convinced, were genetically determined. To the steady, high-pitched whine of the engines and the ever-present hiss of frigid air hurtling over the aluminum skin, Fairchild settled back and contentedly stared at the brightening mantle of clouds.

"Sorry I wasn't much company," Grant apologized as touchdown jarred the 737. "It's too early for me to function."

"Ah, the zombie moves, the zombie speaks. You should have been a bartender. Stay up half the night, then sleep until noon."

"I was and did my last year of college. Had only afternoon classes. Loved it."

"Why am I not surprised?"

. . .

As they entered the Sanctuary, the President was sitting in his familiar spot left of the non-functional fireplace with Harrison across the hearth nonchalantly smoking a yellow-stained, hand-carved Meershaum. McDonnell oozed hospitable goodwill. "Welcome, gentlemen. Good of you to be prompt."

"We could hardly keep the President waiting," Dr. Fairchild sagely observed.

"But of course you can! Happens all the time!" McDonnell rose in greeting, returned to his chair, and immediately resumed speaking. "I apologize for any inconvenience you have suffered at my hands. At times you must have felt purposely avoided. Let me assure you that that was *not* the case. Before my election I had no comprehension of the demands on the Chief Executive's time.

"Rationally, nothing should take precedence over AIDS, but sadly, many other things demand attention. I can only compare it to parenting a dying child; the tragedy is overwhelming. While it seems logical to devote all efforts to tending the ailing youngster, one must also care for others, go to work, steal a personal moment. In short, gentlemen, life must go on. AIDS is no different. The American people are my children and come first, their lives proceeding without interruption. As President, I must stand above it all as unemotional as my humanity permits.

"No, gentlemen, I have not been malingering or avoiding you, and most importantly I am not insensitive to the alarming statistics you, Charlie, have so diligently provided. Nor have I been passively sitting by. The wheels are in motion to take corrective action, but first, Bill, bring me up to date. What is the status of your T-cell serum? Have any curative properties surfaced?"

"No," replied Fairchild.

"Most unfortunate. One always hopes… " With a disappointed sigh, he let the thought dangle. "But it does greatly retard the progress of the first three types of AIDS?"

"That seems to be true. During these few months of experimentation, some remarkable remissions have been recorded."

"Good. How long have you been convinced of STC's effectiveness?" McDonnell had not completed his question before regretting it–a tactical faux pas of the first order.

"With the success in treating Type 1 and the basic similarity of the first three, I was fairly sure by March and rather positive by May," Fairchild stated. The accusatory tone directed at the President was unmistakable, but he deflected the inculpation by changing tack.

"Any side effects?"

"None that are observable."

"Which brings us to the reason for this meeting." McDonnell skirted the quicksand of questionable secrecy and his rationale for not authorizing treatment weeks ago. "I'm not comfortable releasing STC's until they have been successfully tested on a Type 4 patient. I fear people will think the plague is at bay and if Type 4 doesn't respond to medication, it will ravage the planet before we have a prayer of stopping it. Fortunately, the perfect subject is waiting for us in central Africa."

"*What* perfect subject?" Fairchild dumbfoundedly asked.

"Hadari, the young native boy seemingly immune to Type 4.

Bob and I were..."

"Begging your pardon, Mr. President, but am I to understand an individual with apparent Type 4 immunity has been located?"

"Yes. Surely you knew."

"How would I?"

"I assumed Charlie told you."

Fairchild looked askance at his friend.

"Sorry, Bill. It never occurred to me you didn't know."

"Apparently, each of us thought the other had informed you, but it doesn't matter now."

The doctor's booming voice interrupted. *"Doesn't matter,* Mr. President?"

"Bill, what's done is done. We all apologize, but I fail to see how your lack of knowledge about this lad's existence changes anything."

"He could have been studied. How long have you known?"

The President's evasiveness continued. "That's inconsequential. What *is* relevant is I'm ready to initiate tests on him. Bob, update Bill and Charlie."

Ignoring Dr. Fairchild's frustration, Harrison methodically detailed the President's plan, explaining what would be done and why. When, never surfaced.

After Harrison finished, Fairchild pointedly observed, "No timetable was mentioned. Representative Grant and I need prior notification to get our affairs in order before departing."

"Departing to where?" the President asked.

"Africa. I assumed we'd go."

"There's nothing Charlie's qualified to do. Why expose him to danger?"

Surprised by his friend's exclusion, Fairchild nevertheless concurred with the logic while insisting, "I still need to know."

"Actually you don't, because you aren't going either."

"Excuse me, Mr. President. Research is my responsibility. I *must* be there."

"No, Bill. Any doctor can perform these simple procedures. You are too valuable to imperil. Suppose all become infected and have to be quarantined? Suppose, God forbid, they die!" Feeling angry and betrayed, Fairchild remained silent. "You agree, don't you?" McDonnell pressed.

Disparaged, but unbowed, Fairchild belatedly uttered, "Reluctantly." but not before fuming inside, "*Damn* this man! With expertise sufficient to buttress good intuition, his logic on this point is also sound."

"As long as there's any possibility of failure," McDonnell insisted, "I cannot place you at risk. There is no other Dr. Fairchild to which the world can turn if you become a victim. Sound too melodramatic?"

"While I appreciate your confidence, I'm rather uncomfortable being so important."

"'Crucial' is more aptly descriptive. By the way, have you selected a name for this serum, or are you sticking with STC?"

"I've given it no thought whatsoever." Fairchild remained upset over being excluded from the President's plans and especially his withholding information on the existence of an apparently HIV-immune individual.

"May I recommend you incorporate a variation of your name. If STC were mine, I'd want my identity attached to it, but then I'm a politician with a political ego. Take it under advisement."

Fairchild's response was icy. "My wife and I will discuss it."

"As well you should." McDonnell turned to his aide. "Bob, brief Bill and Charlie on the status of the isolation facility."

Harrison absentmindedly tamped and lit his pipe before saying, "I have received quoted delivery dates from several interested manufacturers, all in late August or early September."

"So far away." Fairchild expressed deep disappointment as inside he continued to seethe with rage.

"Afraid so, Doctor. Manufacturers and fabricators can't easily accelerate delivery when we have imposed so many stringent specifications. Quality control standards are similar to those of space vehicles. We all saw what happened years ago with the Challenger tragedy. We'd like to avoid equipment failure. Lost a bright young woman from your area as I recall."

"Judy Resnick," the President injected. "Didn't she attend the same high school as you, Charlie?"

"Firestone," Grant supplied, nodding his head.

"That's what I thought. Well, the stakes are infinitely higher here. We cannot afford viral escape!"

Fairchild sighed. Once again the logic was irrefutable.

"Next, we had to decide on the mode of transportation," Harrison continued. "Access to the area is difficult at best. Two options were considered.. One involved landing strip improvements at Omega 22, to accommodate a C-141 cargo plane. The other employed the existing air facility at Kisangani with trucks hauling the components overland." Harrison paused to relight his pipe before going on. "It's a rather circuitous route, and while the roads are terrible, they *are* open, and the rivers are sufficiently bridged to support the weights we'll be dealing with. That alternative is cheaper, more flexible, probably faster. President McDonnell, with my concurrence, opted for number two."

"What if it rains?" Dr. Fairchild was becoming increasingly distraught and confrontational.

"What if it does?" the President challenged, equally irritated.

"Won't the roads become impassable?"

"Probably. The same is true of an airfield we construct in such a place. We aren't talking about a paved surface."

"But . . ."

"But, *nothing*! Do you expect me to control the weather?"

Quietly listening until now and hoping to defuse an escalating confrontation, Grant leaned forward with a query, "When will testing commence, Bob?"

"Five or six days after the contractor... yet to be selected... certifies the chamber complete and properly functioning. There will be a ninety-six-hour dry run to verify seal integrity and reliability of components. On the fifth day, Hadari will be transported to the unit and placed inside. The helicopter will be temporarily abandoned in a remote area and the pilot quarantined until we know what we are up against."

Harrison's pipe went out. He put it down and solicited questions. Ignoring Harrison, Fairchild addressed the President. "Assuming that through this boy we learn to control Type 4, what time frame are you considering for STC distribution?"

"Distribution where?" McDonnell countered, an edge in his voice.

"Worldwide, I assume."

"Never happen. We will not distribute internationally until sufficient serum is produced to treat, simultaneously, everyone in the United States."

"*Simultaneously?*"

"Yes, simultaneously! Or would you like to prioritize?" Sarcasm hung heavy in the air. "That puts us at the end of September or early October. Add another week for national transshipment and distribution to medical facilities and temporary treatment centers."

"Once that has been accomplished, what countries will receive it next?" the doctor demanded.

"Whoever is left and needs it the most. Impossible to determine until the time comes."

"You never intended to save the Orient, did you?"

McDonnell bristled, his eyes boring into Fairchild. "I never intended on anything interfering with saving American lives. That's an entirely different statement. If you are asking if I willfully took steps to insure the depopulation of the Orient . . . most emphatically, no!"

Fairchild settled back, not believing him and beyond caring if the President knew.

"Bill, we have to stay on target. There is the ever-present potential of AIDS killing every soul on Earth with the exception of Hadari and others similarly constituted, assuming they exist. If I could only save a dozen people in extracting a guarantee that mankind would survive, I'd do it. The history of this planet is rife with examples of extinct species. I do not intend for people to join that list! If ultraconservatism has doomed untold millions..."

"Hundreds of millions."

"If you insist. Perhaps I *have* unnecessarily doomed the Orient. So be it. Hindsight is wonderful, also useless. This plague is unique. The stakes involve no less than the continuation of human life on this planet, and whatever happens, I would do *exactly* the same thing again. I can glibly make that statement while being deeply saddened over every person who has died or will die from this mindless scourge."

Fairchild remained unconvinced.

"Come here, Doctor. Look at this." McDonnell rose and

moved between the marble mantle and Harrison's chair to stand beside the giant wall map of the world. "See these yellow encirclements? Months ago I outlined potentially depopulated areas. Later, in red, I X'd out places where annihilation was inevitable: Africa, northern India, China, Japan, and Southeast Asia. Sheer numbers and the wildfire spread of AIDS in those locations precluded help arriving in time or sufficient quantity to stem the tide."

"Sorry, but I don't believe that," Fairchild interrupted dispassionately.

"Believe what you want, Doctor!" McDonnell snapped. "I'm sorry if I seem arbitrary or impatient, but I resent your continued inferences. You take no risks in your labs at Northcoast Medical. Why do you expect me to do less with the fate of mankind hanging in the balance?"

Fairchild retreated to the sofa. "Nothing will be gained from further argument."

"On that we can agree. If Hadari's blood is clear or improves after STC's are administered, I was wrong. If not... I will be vindicated. For as long as anyone's left to care."

"Is there any way to speed up the process in the future?" Grant interceded, seeking conciliation.

"We'll pull out all the stops, Charlie. I guarantee it! It's late. Anything else on your minds?"

"Just that from now on we stay in constant touch and Representative Grant and I are kept abreast of all further developments."

"I thought we were. Hadari's existence slipped between the cracks. Such things happen, Doctor!" the President sharply retorted. "If I have erred in not consulting with you often enough, let us rectify that now. Suppose we schedule a closed-circuit teleconference Mondays at 10:30 and meet as the need arises."

"I'd be more comfortable meeting bi-weekly."

"Fine! Bob, make note. Teleconference next Monday, meeting here in two weeks. Anything else?"

"No," Charlie answered.

"Not at this time," said Bill.

"Then I must be going."

With a final nod the President left the room.

Harrison stood, retrieved his pipe and relit it, then turned to Fairchild. "I started to call you several weeks ago."

His comment piqued Fairchild's curiosity. "About what?"

"A theory. By the next day it didn't seem important."

"Perhaps you should have contacted me."

"Probably so. Have a safe trip."

. . .

"What was that all about?" Charlie asked as they walked to the waiting limo.

"I have a suspicion. We'll talk about it later. If I'm right, all three of us fumbled the ball, and it may have cost us the game."

. . .

In North American Consolidated's VIP lounge, away from the prying ears of the Secret Service, Fairchild and Grant settled in for a leisurely lunch. Two hours remained until departure.

Propelled by quiet rage, the doctor's pent-up frustration erupted. "You and I, Charlie, just met with the most unprincipled bastard that ever lived, and there is nothing we can do about it! Hitler pales in comparison to this monster. We have witnessed the greatest depravity ever visited upon the Earth, and I do not mean AIDS. I am referring to that murderous bastard's refusal to take action until all those he wants purged are, in fact, dead. Without doubt, John McDonnell is the most morally evil human that ever held a position of power."

Grant was taken back. "A little strong, don't you think?"

"Not nearly strong enough! The English language does not contain words that describe the magnitude of his depravity! That amoral son of a bitch is presiding, and will continue to preside, over the annihilation of sixty to seventy percent of human race, and except for Africa, the flood plains of India, and a few other places, I think it could have been prevented. And do you know the worst part? You and I and Bob Harrison... that's what his aborted call was about if I'm not mistaken... suspected what he was doing, but through doubts, indecision, and cowardice, procrastinated and let it happen. I will carry that burden to my grave."

"We were powerless to prevent it."

"Since no attempt was made, we'll never know."

"Nothing we could have done would have saved a single life."

"A very comforting thought, my friend, but I disagree. Many Germans undoubtedly said the same after World War II."

"And it was true then. Don't kid yourself about how much we could have accomplished. Self-flagellation doesn't become the man that developed STC's. What has happened was destined to be."

Cynically, "God's will?"

"If you wish."

"You can't believe that."

"Part of me does."

"God didn't do this, Charlie! John McDonnell did."

"And I can speculate on several reasons why."

"To slaughter millions?"

"'Let die,' not 'slaughter.'"

"Semantics." Disapproving, but intellectually curious, he requested, "State your reasons."

"To get even with and eradicate the Japanese; to reduce the strain on the world's resources; to be rid of pains in the ass like southeastern Europe, the Middle East, or big city slums."

Snidely, "Any others?"

"Many others: To curb overpopulation; reduce pollution; restore the ozone layer..."

Fairchild raised a hand to stop further enumeration. "You made your point. And make his goals sound clinically desirable."

"Maybe they are. What's better, Doctor... notice I didn't say 'worse'... aborting a fetus or condemning to misery for eternity the progeny of the person allowed to be born?"

"A living person is not a fetus."

"Is the result any different for their descendants?"

"You are being facetious."

"Not really. The suffering goes on to infinity."

"Charlie, you can't condone his actions!"

"No, but I begrudgingly respect his vision of the future. The world is chaotic and the masses miserable . . . mostly because uninhibited population growth."

"A utopian vision! Utopia never came to pass."

"Granted, but in his mind, there are probably only two scenarios from which to choose: vast premeditated misery now, with less misery later; or reduced misery now, with chronic, escalating misery forever. If you were in his position, what choice would you make?"

"Certainly not his."

. . .

Bill remotely unlocked the Buick and tossed his briefcase on the passenger seat. "Keep in touch," he reminded Charlie as they parted in the shuttle service's parking lot.

"God bless."

"If there is one."

23

Last evening, having exhausted delaying tactics and knowing he had not fooled Fairchild or Grant, McDonnell had difficulty falling asleep. He no longer woke at night mumbling, 'the winnowing,' but with being tired and the late hour he had overslept and arrived late at the Oval Office. If not careful, he would get Reagan's reputation. Then again it hardly mattered, for besides covering for him and compensating as necessary for his idiosyncrasies and impetuosity, Harrison ran the executive branch smoothly in his absence. The President found it hard to believe he once hesitated hiring the man.

Within minutes of arrival, a blinking light indicated his secretary wished to converse with him. "Yes, Kim?"

"Line two, Mr. President," she reported. "Bob said you didn't want to be disturbed, but it's Walter Owens. Says it's important. I thought you might want to take the call."

McDonnell smiled to himself. Apparently he'd waited the pompous bastard out.

"You were correct to notify me. Put him through."

"Good morning, Walter," the President said, warmly greeting his adversary. "What may I do for you?"

"My executives and I spent many days discussing our differences with you. Meeting until the wee hours last night, we came up with a plan that hopefully will be acceptable to all parties. We want to resolve this. It's not proper for us to criticize you publicly, and we wish to avoid a repeat of your television interview censuring us. That sort of thing does no one any good."

"I agree. And since you've been candid, I must admit that part of me is sorry for going public and embarrassing you. I apologize, though at the time I didn't see an alternative."

"I don't concur you had no choice. You'll understand if I don't care to discuss it."

"Certainly."

"We are both chief executives and can settle this in private. Because we don't like each other doesn't mean we can't work together."

"I agree. It's not personal. I don't approve of anyone financially raping their company and the American people."

"You have a right to your opinions," Owens replied rather stiffly, "but I'd rather not get into that, either."

"That's fine. What's your proposal?"

"Is this line secure?"

"Tighter than a rat's ass, Walter. Do I look like Nixon?"

Owens smiled in spite of himself. Besides being a formidable foe, the asshole had a sense of humor. "No, John, and I doubt you keep a diary like Packwood did, either. Now, in order for my staff and me to not appear guilty of something, which we aren't, here is what I propose: Instead of returning part of last year's compensation to the company treasury, the nine of us will establish a trust to improve education. The funds can be earmarked for equipment not ordinarily affordable, create special programs, grant scholarships, or any other damned thing you want. Hell, you can construct a model school rivaling a sports arena for all I care."

"Named after you?"

This time Owens laughed out loud. "Named after anyone you want. Kids win; we save face. What do you think?"

"Not what I wanted, but I'm intrigued. How much are you talking about?"

"We hadn't thought about that."

"Think about it."

"We're open to suggestions."

"Throw out a number."

Owens hesitated before saying, "a hundred million."

"From you or everyone?"

"All of us for Christ's sake!"

"Bye, Walter."

"Wait! I'll double it."

"Chicken feed, but I appreciate your choice of charities in view of my pre-political career."

"What will satisfy you?"

"One billion with you kicking in half."

"No way!"

"Then make a counter-offer that is not insulting and swear you'll run next year's figures by me before deciding on executive compensations so none of us have to go through this again."

"You have no authority to fix our pay. I'll never agree to that."

"I wouldn't expect you to. But a cap is not unreasonable. I want salary input to protect us from adverse publicity in the future."

"What about our Mexican operations."

"What's done is done, but no more."

Owens hesitated a moment. "I think we can work this out. Will you stay off the air until I get back to you?"

"How long?"

"Two or three days, no more."

"That will be fine. You know where to reach me."

"I'll get back to you, Friday, latest."

"Take your time. I appreciate your willingness to compromise. Goodbye, Walter."

The President hung up and glanced across the room at Bob Harrison, who had been intently following what he could of the conversation.

"Did you hear enough to understand?"

"I think so."

"We got the son of a bitch, Robert."

"Congratulations, sir."

"That was fun. Apparently my wife was right."

"About what, sir?"

"She told me I like a good fight. I do. Especially winning."

Later that day, McDonnell's jubilant mood was shattered.

Shortly after lunch, Harrison hurriedly entered the Oval Office without his customary polite knock, hastily secured the remote and turned on the television. Sound immediately filled the room.

"What is it, Bob?" the President asked, noting his aide's agitated state.

"Fairchild called a press conference in Cleveland. It's in progress."

"He *what*?!"

"He called a press conference."

"God *damn* it!"

In seconds the TV screen became luminous and definition improved. In what appeared to be a hospital conference room, a determined Bill Fairchild squarely faced the cameras. He was in the midst of complimenting the President for an understandable hesitancy to release Northcoast Medical's newly developed AIDS treatment while simultaneously bemoaning the fact that future procrastination would result in additional millions of preventable deaths.

"How did you find out about this?" McDonnell demanded, trying to listen at the same time.

"The Press Secretary's office monitors and records major network and PBS newscasts. The woman on duty thought it was inappropriate that Fairchild would discuss this without you or me or someone from her office present. She said some of the material sounded politically sensitive, so she paged me. A complete tape will be delivered as soon as the broadcast is over."

Fairchild was expanding upon the President's reluctance to release the serum at home or abroad, couching his comments in terms that implied top level caution was likely based on a fear of possible side effects. He made it clear, however, that while respecting McDonnell's concern, he felt STC's safely exceeded FDA guidelines. Safer, he insisted, than many drugs that won approval and certainly preferable to more deaths.

"Get Grant on the line," McDonnell brusquely ordered, while raptly attentive to Fairchild.

Harrison punched the pre-set that dialed Grant's secure direct-link to the White House. The call not answered during the first four rings, the equipment switched to his assistant's companion phone.

"Representative Grant's office. Marcie Warner speaking."

"Marcie, it's Bob Harrison. I need Charlie."

"He's out of the office. I'm uncertain where, but I expect him any minute. Can I help?"

"Not this time. Patch me through to his mobile. Scramble it."

"Hang on."

"Grant, here," came a curt response.

"Charlie, it's Bob Harrison. The President wants to talk to you."

The phone was handed over.

"Are you near a television set?" McDonnell barked.

"No, why?"

"Fairchild's holding a news conference on AIDS. Did you know about it?"

"No."

"That's what I wanted to hear. Get over here."

Not waiting an answer, the President hung up and returned his full attention to the screen. Fairchild was hinting that if foreign governments and the American people would assume the risks inherent in an experimental drug, the executive branch might be willing to provide it. Of course that was presumptuous, for he was only the National HIV/AIDS Coordinator, and the ultimate authority rested with the Chief Executive. Nevertheless, he concluded, the President's reluctance to distribute the serum might be overcome with proper encouragement and shared responsibility.

"He may have a point, sir," Harrison injected. "Perhaps it is better if the public has input. Take some of the heat off of you."

McDonnell's look scalded his chief of staff.

"Perhaps it isn't," he quickly recanted.

The question and answer period took an additional half hour and commentator recap many minutes more. Finally, the treacherous horror was over.

McDonnell slumped into his seat as Harrison waved the remote in the general direction of the TV, turning off the set.

"What did I miss, Bob?"

"Just a quick history of the development of STC's."

"Nothing else?"

Harrison shook his head. "Not really."

"I'll still need to watch the beginning."

"It should be here any minute."

McDonnell turned to face his beloved White House grounds. "Fairchild's good," he admitted, staring through the window. "I underestimated his resolve and ingeniousness." Harrison remained silent. "He's publicly challenged my decisions and authority and put me in a corner. Fire him."

"Begging your pardon, sir, that isn't the way to handle this."

The President spun 180 degrees and angrily ordered, "Fire the son of a bitch!"

"Sir . . . "

"Fire him or I'll fire you!"

"You won't, sir."

"Do not, 'sir me,' Robert! I want that traitorous son of a bitch fired, now!"

"I won't do it, sir. It's the wrong way to handle this."

"Get out! Get your personal things and be off the grounds immediately."

"I'm not fired, and I'm not going."

The President sighed and rotated his chair to resume his scrutiny of the manicured scene outside. "Why not?"

"Because you aren't thinking clearly. I'll come back in an hour. If you feel the same, I'll resign." Harrison rose and gathered his papers.

"Sit down!" the President commanded, returning his attention to the matter at hand. "You're right as usual, you prissy bastard!" Harrison sat, trying not to gloat in his victory. McDonnell pressed the intercom key that alerted his secretary. "No calls, Kim."

"Yes, sir."

"*None.*"

"Yes, sir."

"Except the Press Secretary. Bob will take those. Oh, and I'm expecting a tape. Bring that in when it comes." McDonnell switched off and faced his aide. "First, we'll issue a statement on how much the world and I owe Bill Fairchild, the disloyal prick! Next, we'll defuse the situation by taking the initiative. Here's how. I plead caution was my motive."

"Which it was, sir."

"Be quiet, Robert. I may still fire your ass."

"Being quiet, sir."

A scathing look and the President resumed his oration. "I will insist I had no choice but to go slowly and must continue to do so. Without making that ungrateful cock-sucker look bad, I'll infer he doesn't know his ass from a hole in the ground on this issue and is in error on several points. Next, we'll bring in world leaders or their representatives and I'll project an internationalism I could give a shit about! Within reason, I'll promise them anything they want. We'll finish with a press conference that will make the second coming look like a rerun!" Becoming suddenly quiet, McDonnell pensively stared into space for several moments before expostulating, "I'm going to cut that black-hearted, black-assed bastard's nuts off." Once more in control, he turned to Harrison. "Your cool head prevailed. Thank you."

"My pleasure, sir."

The intercom light summoned the President.

"Yes?"

"The Press Secretary, sir. Seems urgent."

"Put him through; Bob will take it."

"And the tape arrived."

"Bring it in."

Harrison took the call and listened a moment, then muted the instrument and reported, "Ray wants specific instructions, says it's getting ugly. You want to talk to him?"

"No. Tell him to respond to all queries with: 'an official White House announcement is forthcoming.'"

Harrison relayed the message, promised to get back to the Press Secretary's office and hung up.

"What else did he say?" McDonnell asked.

"That the White House lines are melting down and little of it is positive."

"Oh, well. I never did care what the public thought. Get on this. Discredit Fairchild and save my ass."

"Yes, sir." Harrison turned to go, only to be stopped by the President suggesting, "And give yourself another raise."

Harrison smiled. "You know I can't do that."

"Did you get a better staff car?"

"The biggest fucking Lincoln they make, sir."

It was the President's turn at levity. "I'd get you a woman, but I know you don't want one."

Harrison broke into a broad grin. "You're right about that," he replied, and left the room.

. . .

A diverse assemblage of foreign dignitaries and diplomats were gathered in the White House press room. Not sure what to expect, they nervously chatted among themselves until McDonnell, twenty minutes late, entered. He apologized and unceremoniously launched into his prepared text, stating the White House position against distributing a less than thoroughly tested new treatment. After assuring them the AIDS serum would be available on an as needed basis as soon as its safety was established, he invited their questions.

"Does that mean ample supplies will be provided to foreign countries before less ill Americans are treated?" the Japanese ambassador opened the period.

"There might be some disagreement on what's ample, but that's a reasonable assumption," the President parried.

"When can we expect delivery?" he pressed.

"There's no way to answer that. We will keep you and everyone else informed."

"But just two days ago Dr. Fairchild announced the serum was safe to administer," objected the Chinese envoy.

"He was wrong. While privy to most research and development, I have access to information he does not."

"But he seemed so certain of his facts," the United Arab Emirates' emir insisted.

"I think," the President responded, carefully choosing his words, "his enthusiasm and desire to cure AIDS led to impetuosity. It happened before. A few years ago, his lab falsely reported a major breakthrough. Then, it was a technician making unfounded statements; this time it's the director. That makes it more unfortunate . . . but no less human. I apologize . . . for him and myself as the responsible individual, for the false alarm. To prevent a repeat of this in the future, disregard all reports that do not originate in this office."

"Any chance of having the serum in its current state of development if we assume the risks?" the Philippine Health Minister inquired.

"None. It might make your people suffer more, and I won't be a party to that. Nor do I think federal agencies with the jurisdictional authority to give approval would do it."

"Why weren't we kept abreast of Dr. Fairchild's progress?" the Mexican president demanded.

"Because there was nothing to report. All of this has been blown out of proportion."

"Can we send our scientists into your labs to learn and assist?" the Indian ambassador requested.

"No."

"Isn't that up to Dr. Fairchild?"

"Hardly. I am in charge, and where would I draw the line? Dr. Fairchild needs to conduct research without interference."

"Will you promptly and completely disclose all developments in the future?" It was China asking the question.

"We have been and will continue to."

The briefing took another forty minutes. Finally, the President was able to excuse himself and turn the affair over to Ray and his PR staffers by promising to stay accessible. Escorted by the Secret Service, he went directly to the Rose Garden and spent an additional hour with the White House Press Corps, answering their questions.

"How do you feel the international briefing went?" Simmons of CBS asked.

"Very well."

"Can you explain how you and Dr. Fairchild arrived at such wildly different conclusions from the same data?"

"Obviously our facts are not the same."

"What are your 'other sources,' Mr. President?"

"What are yours, Melissa?"

"Seriously, Mr. President."

"I *am* serious. The information you seek isn't classified, but I don't want my people bothered. Next question."

NBC jumped in. "Will foreigners really get the serum before Americans when it is approved?"

"That, Harold, is a sticky problem. I know what I said a few minutes ago at the international briefing and intend to honor my pledge, but conditions change. Ask me again when I announce the serum's release."

"When do you estimate that will be?"

"I don't play the lottery, and I don't forecast the future."

"Why don't we share our current medical advances, so foreign powers can build on them or conduct their own research?"

"When there is something to share, we will."

ABC had been silent up to now. "Why did Dr. Fairchild hold a news conference without your knowledge?"

"I've been asking myself the same question."

"Could it be he thought he was right, and you disagreed so strongly you wouldn't sanction it?"

"I thought of that, but something else occurs to me. Do you recall Newt Gingrich?"

"Yes."

"Remember how difficult it was for him to realize that while he had an important job, he wasn't president?" The crowd laughed. "I'm afraid Dr. Fairchild may have the same delusion. Plus, he's not a young man. He has been overworked, and that is partly my fault. As soon as things slow down, I'm going to see to it he gets a much deserved, long vacation."

"Is that a threat?"

The President laughed. "That doesn't deserve an answer. Without him, we'd be nowhere near a cure."

"When do you expect to bring in this African boy who apparently is immune to AIDS?"

"Whenever it's practicable."

"But when?"

"If I could answer, I would."

"But Dr. Fairchild says he's ready for a Type 4."

"Dr. Fairchild is exhausted. And so am I. Contact my press secretary or chief of staff for updates. Thank you all."

In the privacy of the Oval Office–while the reporters were

racing to beat each other into printed or electronic mediums–John McDonnell collapsed into his chair. Sipping Black Velvet and ginger ale as Bob Harrison nervously paced, he muted the recorder and mused, "One down, one to go. Now all I have to do is get this UAW strike settled. Fortunately Owens is smart enough to know I have him by the short hairs, even if his executives aren't. He won't like it, but he'll deal and keep his people in line. I figure he'll demand some pissy-assed concession to save face and then capitulate." The President heaved a sigh of relief and stated, "Thank God this Fairchild bullshit is over."

"You did good, sir," Harrison complimented, nursing Cutty Sark, straight up. "But you seemed a little vague about when you intended sharing medical information and Fairchild's serum with foreigners. Off the record, when do you think that will be?"

"When hell freezes over, Robert. And not one minute before."

. . .

As if McDonnell's troubles were not sufficiently calamitous, the phone warbled at six-thirty a.m. the next morning, wrenching him from a fitful slumber. Groggily groping for the instrument, he irritatedly barked, "Yes?"

"It's Harrison, sir. We've got another problem. Somebody shot Owens."

"Jesus Christ!" McDonnell was awake. "How is he?"

"Dead. Three rounds in the face, point blank."

"Jesus Christ! When did it happen?"

"A half hour ago. Owens was coming out of his house to get into the company limo, and this guy appeared out of nowhere. He apparently disabled the security system during the night and was crouched behind the foundation plantings on the driveway side of the mansion. When Owens came around the corner, the assailant stood up and did it."

"Where's the man now?"

"On the way to the morgue. He stuck the gun in his mouth and shot himself."

"Wonderful."

Karen rolled over. "What's wonderful, John?" Only partly awake, the ring of sarcasm in his voice was lost. She raised from her pillow, noticing even in the dim morning light that her husband was chalky white. "John, what is it?"

"Shh!"

Harrison was talking again.

"The man carried identification. He was a mid-level manager in his early forties. Got 'RIFed' eight months ago. Four children. Wife left him, recently divorced."

McDonnell sighed heavily.

"John, what's the matter?" Karen asked.

"Some white collar asshole just shot an executive asshole."

"John!"

"Shh!"

"President McDonnell, are you still there?"

"I'm here."

"That's not the worst of it. He had a letter on him: 'To whom it may concern.' In it he wrote that your aggressive stance in regard to executive pay inspired his actions."

"Jesus criminy!" McDonnell tried to think. "Do the media know that?" The line was oddly silent. "How in hell did that happen?!"

"It was no one's fault. Things happened too fast. I need direction. This could damage your presidency worse than the Fairchild fiasco."

McDonnell was fully functional. "Call public relations, get Ray, and get over here. And try not to worry. If we buy time, some other atrocity will undoubtedly divert public attention."

"I'm on my way. I'll phone from my car."

"Scramble it. The journalistic buzzards will be monitoring every frequency they can think of."

"I will." Harrison rang off.

McDonnell sat on the edge of the bed looking at the telephone in his hand. It never brought good news, and the longer he held office the more offensive the instrument became. He cradled it as if it were an evil being.

24

After recklessly making up time on the interstate, Sarah parked in the first spot she could find at the fringe of Lot A, then hurried to the enclosed walkway which separated that area from the rather new short-term parking deck beyond. Rejecting the speedwalk as too slow, she strode rapidly beside it, took a waiting elevator to the promenade beneath the street which serviced arrival passengers, only to be stymied by a large family dawdling on the escalator to the ticket lobby. With progress temporarily impeded, she had no choice but to bide her time until the schedule information monitors appeared at the top. Impatient eyes scanned for Charlie's flight.

>739~D.C. to Cleveland~on schedule<

Damn! Any other time! Picking up the pace, she rushed past restaurants, gift shops, and a shoeshine stand–anachronistic in an age of polymers and synthetics–plus restrooms and numerous mini-bars strategically located to undermine one's abstinent resolve. Weaving through the crowds she rapidly traversed concourse C, arriving at the circular cluster of gates which served Charlie's carrier. Her arm waving attracted his attention as he entered through the double doors of the boarding ramp.

Meeting halfway and embracing, Sarah said, "I missed you!"

"You too, honey." He planted an affectionate kiss on her lips. "Where are the kids?"

"At mother's. I wanted us to have some privacy first."

. . .

With WKSU's classical selections softly emanating from

concealed speakers, Charlie nursed a beer while Sarah sipped a glass of chilled Chablis. They sat before the living room fireplace. The kids–retrieved from grandma's house after a lengthy carnal session–were playing downstairs in the game room.

Charlie had been in Washington three weeks and looked it.

"How are things going?" she inquired, knowing the answer.

"Terrible. Owens' death was the last straw. I've never seen McDonnell so distraught."

The phone rang in the library.

"I'll get it." Sarah motioned for her husband to stay put. "Thanks. If it's for me, I'm not here."

"Hello. . . . Oh, hi. . . . Just a second." Returning to the living room, she handed him the cordless. "It's Marcie. Sounds important."

"Damn!" Charlie muttered under his breath, then with resignation bred of years as a public servant, answered pleasantly, "Hi. What's up? . . . Maybe it's a virus. . . . Did someone input the wrong data? . . . Then I don't know. Can you work on something else until I get back? . . . Yeah, do that. I'll take the heat if he bitches about the delay. He's pretty hard to please these days, anyway, one more problem hardly matters. . . . Tuesday; Wednesday for sure. I'll call before I leave, and you call me if you have to. . . . No, it's okay. . . . Yeah. . . . Bye."

"What is it?" a concerned Sarah asked as he lay the phone on the end table beside him. She was afraid of losing her husband just as he arrived home.

"An irregularity with some rather critical data. You heard what I told her."

"Will that be okay?"

"Hell, yes. Everything is critical! I'm tired of it."

A relieved Sarah visibly relaxed. "How's Marcie doing with both jobs?"

"Phenomenal. If it weren't for her, I'd be calling for an airline ticket right now. When Gail quit because her husband retired and I made Marcie my special assistant, I planned to hire a new statistical supervisor, but she insisted she could delegate the grunt work and handle both jobs. And damned if she can't. McDonnell said to promote her to the highest GS category allowed to make sure it was fair."

"When's her birthday?"

"I don't know."

"Find out. We have to do something special and that could be a good excuse. If it's too far away, we'll think of some other reason to reward her."

"That's nice."

"And selfish. We see little of each other as it is. If her being there can free you to come home once in a while, she deserves whatever we can afford to give her."

. . .

Summer passed quickly for Bill Fairchild, who sublimated the sting of his press conference gone awry by staying busy at the lab. The season dragged for an increasingly uncomfortable Roberta. "If this baby waits one more day to be born!" she began thinking, during the last week of August. A week overdue, she experienced breathing difficulties, waddled instead of walked, and only with concentration remembered not being pregnant.

Bill looked up from his morning paper. "How do you feel?"

"No different than five minutes ago," she snapped.

"A bit testy, my love?"

"Do you want to carry it for a while?"

"I'll pass."

"Fortunately it can't be long. This child of yours is playing soccer in here."

"Girl soccer or boy soccer?"

"Does it *matter*?!"

"Honey, you *know* it doesn't. Touchy, touchy."

"It was touchy-touchy that got me into this condition!"

Bill returned to his newspaper, thinking it best to ignore her comment.

"Then why did you ask?" she persisted.

"Just making conversation."

He tried to read.

"You're the one that didn't want an ultra-sound."

"Honey . . ."

"Well, if it makes you feel any better, no girl would go through these gymnastics."

"*Roberta!*"

"You're right. I'm being bitchy. It's not your fault. Well, actually it is but we've discussed that."

"Honey, you're pregnant, and I love you for it." He leaned over and kissed her.

"You're sweet." She struggled to her feet and started across the room.

"Where are you going?"

"Where do I usually go every ten minutes?"

"Sorry I asked."

"You should be. Now I can't rag you when we travel and have to stop twice on the way to the boat!"

Roberta disappeared down the hall.

"*Bill!*" A blood-curdling scream was followed by the muffled sound of knees dropping to the carpeted floor. He rushed to her side. Roberta was bent over holding her stomach.

"What's wrong?"

"This must be it," she uttered between spasms, looking up with an expression of concerned relief. "I feel like someone slugged me in the midriff with a baseball bat. Get something. I think my water broke."

Fairchild flew into the bathroom, grabbed the nearest towel, and rushed back.

"Not that one. It's for guests and not big enough. Get an old one from the linen closet."

"Here."

She stuffed it under her skirt. "Help me into the bathroom and wait outside."

"Should I call the doctor?"

"No. We need to time the contractions first. Get your stopwatch."

A few minutes later he heard moaning. "Are you okay?" he asked through the closed door.

"I'm having a second contraction. How long?"

Bill pushed the red button. "Six minutes. Can I help?"

"Only if you can have this baby."

"I'll call the doctor."

"Let me. Get my bag and bring the car to the back door."

Fairchild took the stairs two at a time, grabbed her suitcase, and raced to the garage. He suddenly reappeared, hurrying past his wife, who was on the phone. "Forgot the keys."

"Take it easy. We don't need you with a heart attack the day our baby is born."

. . .

"Dr. Fairchild? I'm Nurse Warton. Your wife's in Labor Room 6."

"Thanks."

"She's dilated three centimeters and doing well."

Bill walked past Rooms 2 and 4, both of them empty, then hesitated before tentatively peeking into number 6. "Roberta?"

"Come in."

"How are you doing, honey?"

She looked drawn and worn. "I'm glad I'm here. This baby is going to come quickly."

"Have they given you anything?"

"Not yet. Oh, here comes another one. Did you bring the watch?" He extracted it from his coat pocket. "Time me. Oh, God, hold my hand! Oh, God! There must be a better way!"

. . .

Lolita Roberta Fairchild was born at 11:47 p.m. on the second day of September in the year 2005. Eight pounds, seven ounces, twenty-one inches long, she was her mother's clone.

. . .

"Isn't she precious? It's a miracle. I lay here by the hour and stare at her."

With pillows bunched behind her, Roberta was propped up in bed nursing the baby. Fairchild bent down and kissed his wife. "She's adorable," he said, "just like her mother."

"I'll bet her mother is adorable! How did you get away?"

"I snuck out."

"Nothing like being boss, is there?"

"My secretary wasn't there to stop me, either. When can you go home?"

"When I feel like it. I wanted to feed her once more. Did you bring an outfit?"

Bill produced a bag. "Right here."

"I bought a generic one so we wouldn't have to fuss with two, then forgot to pack it. You're a good daddy."

"We'll soon find out."

"Hush. Let's put her in the nursery while I dress, and then the Fairchild family can go home. Look, she's asleep. Nursing does that."

"Funny, it wakes me up."

"Retract your horns, Doctor! I'm hardly in condition to accommodate you, but perhaps one of those young nurses is available."

"Roberta!"

"Go to your daddy, Lolita." Bill pulled back. "She won't break. Just support her little head." With surgical care, Fairchild took his infant daughter into his arms. Roberta beamed with pride. "See? She's just a little person, that's all."

. . .

"How are the test preparations going?" she asked upon Bill's return from the nursery.

"The convoy should be transporting components of the isolation facility to Omega 22 as we speak."

"That's gratifying," she observed, adjusting a loose skirt around her waist.

"It is, though we *are* a week behind."

"How did that happen? All was going so well."

"Guess."

"El Presidente gummed it up?"

"Give that lady a cigar. I'd choose a stronger word than 'gummed,' but you have the idea. He insisted the damned thing be assembled and operated at the plant. By the time tests were completed and the chamber disassembled and crated for shipment, eight days were lost."

"Maybe he was just being careful." Roberta pulled a mauve jersey over her head.

"Perhaps not enough undesirables had perished."

"Honey, think of the lives your efforts will prolong, not those he's throwing away."

"I try." Fairchild had no desire to engage in further discussion, not on this special day. Roberta put on shoes and crammed the last few items into her suitcase.

"Do you like her name?"

"I love it."

"You don't know how skittish I felt using my first name as her middle one."

"Men do that all the time."

"I know, and I'm glad we did. I can't think of her any other way. Do you really think she looks like me?"

"From the top of her pretty head to the tips of her delicate toes."

"My toes aren't delicate! Do you mind that she's a girl?"

"Roberta, how could I mind? I never thought I'd have any children. She's a gift from God and you."

"Kiss me." Fairchild planted a lingering kiss on his wife's loving lips. "The technology's good," she volunteered. "I'll give you a boy in about eighteen months."

"Let's see how we do with Lolita first."

"We'll do fine. You'll have your son in 2007."

. . .

The expanded party at Omega 22 milled about as the lead Kenworth ground to a halt with an accompanying hiss of air brakes, and the driver reluctantly emerged from his climate-controlled cab into the stifling afternoon heat. Harold Durr, factory rep in charge of assembly, strode from the gathered personnel to issue unloading instructions.

"Durr," he identified himself.

The burly teamster extended a callous hand. "Bavaro. Where do you want this shit?"

"On the near side of those yellow streamers."

Grabbing the cab's handrail as the driver climbed back in and closed the door, Durr hoisted himself onto the narrow access step. Bavaro instructed the other operators by radio, engaged the transmission, and crept off the dirt road onto the field where brightly colored flags hung limply from canted stakes.

"If you'll leave us a driver," Durr suggested, "to pull up the trucks as we need them, the rest of you can settle into your quarters. Lt. Fletcher will show you."

"Let me know when you need a rig moved. These guys don't

like no one fuckin' with their tractors."

"As you wish."

"Where's the beer?"

"Lt. Fletcher will take you to the club."

Durr assembled his civilian crew for job assignments. "Palmatier, release the tie-downs. I'll help get the tarps off. Novarese, bring the crane up on this side. Space the crates about fifty feet apart. And be careful!" he called after him. "As far was this stuff has come, we can't afford to bust anything now."

. . .

Assembly of the isolation facility proceeded smoothly, and an hour before dinner on day two, the three-room structure had been bolted together, fasteners torqued to specifications, and life support equipment readied for installation.

By the fourth day all that remained was to test the equipment and seals and stock the shelves and refrigerator with food. Durr, with Major Essell's concurrence, declared a happy hour celebration that lasted until 0130 hours the next morning.

. . .

Durr roused his men at dawn. Hung over, they ate a scanty breakfast, drank urns of coffee, and arrived at the construction site by 0710 hours. One of two diesel-generators was started, brought up to operating temperature, and loaded by energizing in sequence the air conditioning units, filtration plant, and compressor for the pressurized reserve water tank. Instruments monitoring the electrical system fluctuated with each increase in demand, then quickly returned to the desired setting as the computer-controlled governor stabilized engine rpm.

"Yeah!" exclaimed Durr to no one in particular. "Evan, go inside and bleed those water lines."

A sun-burned, heavily freckled technician entered the chamber, opened faucets one at a time to the predictable thumps and chatters of air forced from pipes, then flushed the toilet to check its operation. Unseen, water sped through drains to the waste treatment and filtration plant, eventually emerging into a giant underground holding tank.

Durr spoke through the voice-activated intercom. "Can you hear me, Evan?"

"Roger."

"Activate the vials and get out."

"Wilco."

Evan extracted several small canisters from his toolbox and set them in the living room, sleeping compartment, and bathroom. Depressing triggers that released an invisible inert gas, he quickly retreated through the airlock, firmly closing both doors behind him. The gas expanded rapidly. Special vapor detectors registered its presence in all parts of the chamber in seconds. Technicians pressurized the inner structure to test specifications, then gathered around their instruments to monitor seal integrity. If no traces of gas were detected between inner and outer shells during the next twenty-four hours, the facility would be considered airtight. Inside air would be purged and redundant life-support equipment operated an additional seventy-two hours. If all systems performed as expected, the unit would be certified operational and turned over to the military and medical personnel. It would then be time to pick up Hadari.

One wall of each room, including the bath, had full-height electrochromic "smart windows" sandwiched between transparent polycarbonate layers. The opacity of these windows could be varied electronically to provide privacy for the occupant while allowing observation when required. No problems developed with these or any electrical or mechanical system, but gaskets leaked in three places due to slightly over-torqued bolts. After service personnel made adjustments and conducted follow-up tests the unit was ready for occupancy. Along with closed-circuit television and a radio inside the capsule, picture books and native crafts abounded. For a short time the facility would be tolerable, but over an extended period become what it literally was–a prison.

. . .

Reynolds' Huey ascended into darkness at 0510 hours on the morning of 18 October 2005. Dr. Wyant, chief medical officer and project coordinator, had recommended an earlier departure to ensure maximum daylight in the event of site contamination upon the boy's arrival, but Major Essell had abrogated that request. Wyant was willing to bet he was rubber-stamping Reynolds' wishes. The arrogant prick probably wanted an extra hour in the sack to hump that gorgeous nurse. Rumor had it he was dicking her every night and had some twenty-two-year-old waiting in the States. Some guys had it all.

. . .

Hadari was ready. He stripped and stepped into the disposable tub of tepid water. Reynolds prayed the kid remembered previous instructions relayed by interpreter Gisele Rotkin because there was no way in hell he could communicate with him. The boy lathered with antiseptic soap, scrubbed vigorously, rinsed off, and toweled dry. Donning the western clothing provided, he pulled on crew socks and sport shoes, lapping the Velcro fasteners. "Good kid," thought Reynolds.

After loading empty water cans into the Huey, Reynolds motioned for Hadari to board and go directly to his seat. Though drilled repeatedly on fastening and adjusting the safety harness, he made no progress and looked helplessly at Reynolds.

"Don't cough or sneeze," Ed cautioned, securing the belt.

Uncomprehending, Hadari grinned from ear to ear. "Hi, Major Ed."

"Good kid. Time to teach you something else."

"Hi, Major Ed."

Fearing the lad might panic at liftoff, Reynolds very gradually increased rpm and rotor pitch, but to his surprise, the more noise and vibration, the wider the boy's grin.

"You like?" Reynolds shouted over his shoulder as the ground fell away.

Hadari beamed. "Hi, Major Ed."

. . .

With strategically placed videocams recording the event, all Omega personnel were outside staring north as the helicopter came into view. Ed landed east of the complex where the Huey would be temporarily abandoned until the heat and lack of moisture killed on board viruses.

With gentle persuasion from Gisele, Hadari reluctantly passed through the airlock and into the isolation chamber as Reynolds simultaneously skirted the group. Upon entering Building D, he performed decontamination procedures, placed the nozzle of an inoculator containing STC's against his midriff, and pulled the trigger. Medicine shooting through tender tissue would leave a small bruise, nothing more.

"Now what?" he thought, arriving at his designated room. Drinking was prohibited so as not to affect the serum's efficacy, and isolation was mandatory. "First, no pussy; now, no beer. The fucking sacrifices one makes for one's country!"

Early afternoon was spent putting Hadari at ease, orientating him to new surroundings and answering his unending barrage of questions. Gisele talked him through the use of all the strange things in his new, hopefully temporary, home.

The toilet fascinated him. Flushing as instructed, he watched the water swirl around and then disappear, wondering where it went. Gisele tried unsuccessfully to provide a simple explanation. It was great fun. Joyously, he flushed again, spitting into the bowl and visually following the bubbles' downward spiral until they too vanished.

Rivaling the toilet in appeal were the electrically operated smart windows. These he continuously cycled from transparent to opaque and back until an override on the external control panel was locked out so his attention could be focused elsewhere.

At 1725 hours they broke for supper. Gisele explained once more where food was located, suggesting a nourishing, well-balanced menu. He chose cookies, potato chips, and a soft drink.

By early evening Roger Powell, the medical technician who volunteered to extract blood, donned protective clothing, picked up a respirator and prepacked medical bag and reported to Dr. Wyant, who was nervously waiting outside the chamber.

"Got everything, Roger?"

"I guess. I feel like I'm going on a kamikaze mission."

"You may be. Do you want to back out?"

"At this stage? With a videocam in my face? Thanks, anyway."

Wyant paused to ascertain Powell's level of commitment, then stated, "Let's review the procedure one last time. Obtain samples as quickly as possible, then inject the boy with STC's. Upon exiting the facility go directly to the Building D decontamination room, entering through the exterior door. Place the samples in the isolock and discard your clothing, respirator, and medical equipment in the appropriate hazardous biowaste containers. Shower, scrub, and dress in one of the sterile uniforms provided. Run prescribed tests in triplicate, checking results after each stage. If you hit a snag, call me. If we've forgotten anything or you need something, it will be placed in the hall outside the far entry door. Any questions?"

"Nope. Let's get it over with."

"You don't have to do this, Roger. I'll go in."

"Would you really? I'm impressed, Doc, truly I am, but a deal's a deal. So long as you don't mind I'm scared shitless."

"We all are."

Powell turned to the camera crew and requested they edit out his last statement.

"No problem, Roger. Good luck."

Taking a deep breath, Powell put on his headgear and stoically waited as a technician in a contamination suit checked the integrity of the completed outfit. Pronouncing it bacterially and virally impregnable, the young woman unlocked the outer door and stepped aside for him to enter the airlock. With the external door resealed, he waited impatiently for completion of the decontamination/purge cycle. He then greeted the boy upon entering through the inner closure.

"Hi, Hadari."

"Hi, Roger."

Over the intercom Gisele reiterated the procedure. Hadari smiled and cooperated until spotting the needle in Powell's right hand whereupon he shrank away.

"Wait, Roger," Wyant cautioned quietly.

Gisele calmly explained how cooperation was essential, assuring him it would barely prick. Unconvinced, he retreated into the bathroom. Fortunately, the door had no lock.

"Now what?" Powell's frustration was apparent.

Dr. Wyant could only shrug. "He's afraid of needles. Why is it always the obvious?"

No one offered a solution.

Wyant seldom confronted this aspect of his profession. A doctor quickly learned to make subordinates the heavies. Write an order; have the nurse draw blood or administer the shot. Ask any pediatrician.

"Tell him we are going to make the bathroom window transparent," he requested.

Gisele relayed his message. Medical personnel watched, as the window became clear. Hadari was sitting on the lid of the toilet, frightened and forlorn. For forty minutes, Wyant's and various team members' impassioned pleas failed to convince him to submit. Addressing no one in particular, a frustrated Wyant voiced his decision. "We'll send others in and overpower him."

He was about to ask for volunteers when Cheryl offered her services. "Let me try." Wyant shrugged and stepped aside.

"Hadari," she said through Gisele, "remember the doll Major Ed gave you?" As he looked out the window, she thought he was going to cry. "You had to leave him. That was very brave." Embarrassed, a tear rolled down his cheek. "Hadari, I know it hurts, but his brother is on the way. If you let Roger take blood, I'll make sure the new doll arrives before you sleep tomorrow." There was no response. "You can stay in this room. Roger will come to you." There was a hesitant response.

"What did he say?" Wyant demanded.

"He asked how much it will hurt," Gisele interpreted.

"Only a little," Cheryl replied. "A brave warrior like you will hardly feel it." Hadari stared suspiciously through the window. "I promise." He uttered one syllable. Cheryl pleaded to Gisele with fingers crossed, "Tell me that means 'yes.'"

"It does."

"Get the sample, Roger," Wyant urged, "before he loses his nerve." Then, turning to Cheryl, he whispered, "Where in hell are we going to get a doll?"

"We'll find one. I'll get on the radio immediately."

Powell's voice came over the intercom after joining Hadari in the bathroom. "Ask him to bare his arm, hold still, and look away. Remind him it may prick a little." Hadari flinched as the needle went in. "Damn it," exclaimed the medic, under his breath.

"What's wrong?" asked Wyant.

"I missed the vein. Tell him we have to try again."

"He says it's okay," Gisele relayed. "Nothing for a brave

warrior to bear."

Hadari said something else.

"Now what?" Powell asked, fearful the boy was changing his mind.

"He wants this done in private."

"Fine, darken the window."

One of the videographers objected. "We need to get this on disk."

"Darken the window," Powell insisted.

"Do it," Wyant ordered.

A tense hush fell over the crowd. Interminable seconds of silence ticked by becoming one minute and then two, before the intercom transmitted Powell's quiet yet triumphant exclamation. "Got it!"

"Will you please make that window transparent?" the videographer pleaded, annoyed he was unable to capture the moment. Wyant nodded, and the technician pushed the button.

Powell held a rack with several vials of red blood as Hadari stood proudly beside him, a finger on cotton gauze in the crook of his arm. Looking out at Gisele, Powell requested, "Explain about the inoculator."

That done, and after setting the samples on the countertop, he removed the device from his medical bag, placed it against the boy's stomach and pulled the trigger.

25

His hair matted, having neither shaved nor showered in thirty-six hours and wearing the scrubs into which he had changed upon entering isolation, Roger Powell adjusted a high-resolution electron microscope in the Building D lab.

Required to be one hundred percent sure, Powell reexamined every aspect of the magnified blood sample. Satisfied nothing had escaped his eye and his judgement was sound, he turned off the instrument and began recording his findings.

. . .

Bill Fairchild hung around the house all morning playing with the baby and getting in Roberta's and Mrs. Romano's way. He needed to pass the hours until leaving for D.C., but he did not feel like going to Northcoast, and it was too cold to be outside.

Bored, yet enjoying this idle time, he pondered retirement. If all went well in Africa, he had certainly earned the right! Let others bear the burden so he and Roberta could enjoy life. There were plenty of places to visit that AIDS had not ravaged. They had the boat on Lake Erie, and they could easily afford a second home in North Carolina, Florida, or his favorite locale–Jekyll Island off the southeast coast of Georgia.

Such a life style had a definite, if shallow, appeal. But it was a pipe dream, for STC's brought only remission. The world needed a cure or preventative, and he was best qualified to co-ordinate necessary research. Fate did indeed have a way of withdrawing the carrot, as one was about to grasp it. For even if something unusual and easily duplicated *was* discovered in

Hadari's blood or genetic makeup, many frustrating months or years lay ahead before the secrets of his immunity were uncovered and put to practical use.

His trapeziuses were killing him! He called to Roberta in the next room. "Honey, will you give me a back rub?"

. . .

Making little progress after toiling all morning in his Washington office, Charlie canceled a strategy session with a colleague–scheduled concurrently with lunch–and sent Marcie out for sandwiches. With her help, if they ate in and worked through the afternoon and early evening, he might make a dent in the backlog of legislative proposals that required his attention. The amount of paperwork was monstrous, and computers had made it worse. How was anyone to get anything done when every son of a bitch in the world wanted a copy of this, a justification for that, an addition here or a deletion there? And then there were the conferences, the fucking useless conferences!

He tolerated it until 6:30; then could not stand it another moment. With a "screw-them-all" attitude, he sent Marcie home, put everything away, locked his desk, and phoned Sarah.

"Hi, babe!"

"Hi! I called earlier. Did you just get in?"

"No, I'm at the office. What's up?"

"Nothing. I just wanted to tell you, I love you."

"You too, Sarah."

"And since you'll be up half the night, to insist you eat a decent, but light, dinner; not fast food."

"Would I do that?"

"Not more than four or five times a week!"

"I'll stop and have a real meal. Salad, fruit for dessert."

"Yeah, right! At least don't order something heavy."

"I promise. Now, how are you?"

"Okay, but I miss you. Are you coming home tomorrow?"

"I have no idea."

"Call me when you know."

"I will. Kiss the kids."

"For both of us. Hope all goes well."

"Based on the call from the on-site doctor, we should know

305

by 2 a.m."

"Well, good luck."

"Thanks, honey. Bye."

Securing his attache case, Charlie left the building and drove to the apartment. As soon as he stepped inside, the solitude closed in. No wonder people had affairs. Recalling that from the beginning Marcie Warner dropped hints she was available and willing, he picked up the phone. It would be fun to watch television, visit, and share pizza and a few drinks with her. She could go home when he left for the White House. What was the harm? But after fingering the first three digits, Charlie abruptly hung up, realizing he wanted to have sex with her, and that's exactly what would happen! There was no way he would do that to his wife!

He ordered a pizza delivered, got a beer from the refrigerator, and then settled in front of the TV. Lying about dinner was bad enough. Inviting a woman to the apartment was unconscionable.

Later, setting his alarm for 11 p.m., he stretched out on the sofa for a nap but found he was unable to avoid erotic thoughts of a naked Marcie. He must stop having lunch with her so often.

. . .

Harrison could never escape the demands of his position, particularly encounters with the media.

"What's going on in Africa?"

"Can you elaborate on the intended use of a sterile, sealed compartment equipped for human habitation?"

"Why is Dr. Fairchild refusing interviews?"

"There are allegations American pilots are executing infected people in India. Would you care to comment on that?"

"Why is the President reneging on promises to inform other nations of the latest advances in AIDS research?"

McDonnell personally avoided such problems through inaccessibility and a simple five-word instruction: "Take care of it, Bob."

By 7:30 Harrison was exhausted, and tomorrow the pressure would be unrelenting. At a quarter to ten, he ordered the answering machines activated, dismissed his staff, and collapsed on the office couch hoping to catch a few winks before going to the Sanctuary at 1 a.m. Regardless of what happened in Africa,

306

tomorrow was going to be hell!

. . .

Catching a late flight out of Hopkins, Fairchild arrived first. A marine helicopter met him at National and flew him to the White House where he was escorted to the Sanctuary. At 12:40 Grant entered. In a comfortable silence, they waited. At two minutes to one, McDonnell came through the door, followed by Harrison. He motioned for them to remain seated and went to his chair. Everything had been said or never would be. McDonnell's actions and rationale were history and recriminations useless. Convinced he had done the right thing despite how it had been accomplished, his conscience was clear.

Bill Fairchild was seething; he wanted to punish this man. But why bother, for amoral individuals had always existed. McDonnell was the current one; others would follow. The pogroms, the Kent States, were better forgotten, for remembrances kept animosities alive, reopened wounds, prevented no recurrence. Recalling did nothing to punish unrepentant perpetrators and more deeply scarred tormented victims and their families. Tired of thinking about it and experiencing personal guilt, Fairchild had more important items on his agenda, not the least of which was being able to provide remission for those currently infected should his serum proved successful in Africa. He had made his peace with God–sort of. Let McDonnell burn in hell by himself.

Charlie Grant was beyond caring but prayed for good news. If not . . . he was unsure he had the guts to continue compiling such grim statistics. How field personnel coped day to day escaped him, and he would not have blamed any for resigning. All he wanted to do was go home, curl up next to Sarah, and sleep! He glanced at Harrison. The poor bastard resembled a zombie. But he did not look bothered. Ethical qualms must have been sublimated months ago. Willing to serve anyone, pre-side over anything, he was the perfect bureaucrat, driven by habit and loyalty.

"Won't be long, gentlemen," the President dispassionately assured them.

. . .

Scruffy and fatigued, flanked by Dr. Wyant on the sun-bleached wooden steps of Building D, Roger Powell surveyed the assembled group, searching for something momentous to say. Lacking inspiration, he made his announcement with an expression of disbelief. "The boy has no trace of HIV. He possesses the expected antibodies and some immune system abnormalities which bear further study, but no active AIDS."

. . .

Hadari was instructed to shower and dress in the conventional pre-teen clothing provided. Twenty minutes later he entered the chamber's airlock and awaited release.

"Let him out," Dr. Wyant directed when the green light indicated the purge cycle was complete.

Emerging through the outer door, he stepped into an antiseptic footbath and, after drying, slipped into new sport shoes. He was disinfected, noncontagious, and free. Wyant asked Gisele to escort the boy to his new quarters, then get Reynolds.

"Shouldn't we run a blood test on Ed, first?"

"Roger took care of it before the announcement," Wyant responded, then turned to Essell. "Ready? We have to notify the President."

. . .

The call came through at 1:23 a.m., EDT. McDonnell ordered a 7:15 meeting, got up and left. Harrison stumbled back to his office, locked the door, and crashed. Fairchild and Grant spent the night in Charlie's apartment.

. . .

Shortly after 9 a.m. a huge crowd of media correspondents—but only a fraction of those who applied for credentials—were waiting as the group emerged from seclusion following a lengthy strategy session. Midmorning was spent fielding questions after which McDonnell retired to nap so he would be rested before delivering a televised speech that evening. By noon all press conferences had ended, and Bill and Charlie were helicoptered to the airport to return home for much needed rest.

. . .

Preempting network programming, McDonnell confirmed earlier announcements: An individual had been found with a natural immunity to HIV, and a remissive serum would soon be available for AIDS victims. He assured the distraught and dying that medication would be distributed by early December when blood testing and treatment centers throughout the country were scheduled to open. The world at large was promised immediate access to technology for producing STC's, offered the options of producing their own or awaiting shipment from the United States as quantities became available.

"For twenty years this plague rained death upon us for reasons each of you may surmise," he concluded. "Though it is not cured, we have remission; and that is no small accomplishment. God bless each of you. May you and your fallen relatives and friends have a measure of peace."

. . .

Bill Fairchild relaxed in his living room with Roberta and Lolita, his luggage carelessly dropped at the foot of the stairs. His flight had been delayed, baggage retrieval slow, crosstown traffic congested. He arrived home only minutes before the broadcast.

"I watched you all morning," Roberta announced. "You were very impressive."

"I don't know how. Tired, and constantly bombarded by reporters. We were pestered at National, surrounded on board the plane, and attacked by another contingent at Hopkins when we entered the terminal."

"The price of fame, my love. Here." She handed him a double scotch. "I have to change Lolita and rock her to sleep. Relax and enjoy your victory."

. . .

Roberta entered their bedroom as Bill started unpacking.

"I can't wait to get my hands on that kid," he stated.

"Lolita couldn't stay up later. You can play with her tomorrow."

"I was referring to Hadari."

"Oh... When's he coming?" Roberta asked as she changed into a gown and robe.

"In three days. McDonnell made arrangements to send a military transport out of Germany for him."

"Just a second. I hear the baby."

Roberta returned bearing Lolita. "She's hungry. Go on

while I feed her." Sitting in the rocker, back to the front window, she opened her gown and exposed a breast.

"He'll be shuttled to Kisangani."

Roberta pushed down above her left nipple so the baby could breathe more easily.

"From there he'll be flown to London, lay over for a few hours, and then on to Wright-Patterson in Dayton. I expect they'll feed and quarter him overnight. He should arrive at Burke Lakefront before noon."

"Are you excited?"

"Yes, but mostly full of hope. This child's immune system is a gift from God, honey. With his body and our previous discoveries, I'm going to conquer this curse!"

. . .

Bending over, Cheryl strapped Hadari into a jump seat while Dr. Wyant struggled unsuccessfully to avert his eyes. He was envisioning her in a skimpy swimsuit, exquisite ass gracefully curving to her firm flanks in one direction, and the backs of well-formed thighs in the other.

With Roger and Gisele, he would escort Hadari to the States for exhaustive examination and testing. He asked to participate but, this no longer being a military affair, his request was denied.

Roger and Gisele approached, Powell toting his gear and part of hers. Cheryl waited beside Hadari until all were safely on board, blithely unaware of the impact she was having on Wyant.

"Tell him he'll have fun in the United States, Gisele," she requested.

Hadari beamed and said something.

"What did he say?"

"He wants to marry you."

"Too young."

"He disagrees."

"That's hilarious! Tell him I'm too old for him."

A serious expression accompanied Hadari's lengthy response.

"What did he come up with this time?"

"Age doesn't matter. You are very well preserved and will do fine as the first of several wives. His father's first two mates were much older and not nearly as dark as the other women."

310

Cheryl suppressed a laugh. "Inform our little bundle of emerging testosterone he'll have to find someone else."

"That will hurt his feelings. I'll tell him you're spoken for."

"Bite your multilingual tongue! I have to go. Bye, buddy."

"Bye," Hadari said clearly.

"That's *so cute!*" Cheryl moved to the front of the compartment, placed a hand on Ed's forearm. "Be careful!"

"I will. Back tomorrow."

She patted his shoulder, went to the edge of the decking, and stepped down. When she was clear, Ed engaged the rotor and lifted off, totally unaware Wyant hated his ass for a non-existent sexual relationship with Cheryl.

. . .

Preparations were complete in the suite where Hadari would be housed over the next . . . no one knew how long. Orientation and training of his tutor and three nannies was finished, and plans to provide peer companionship were under way.

. . .

The day after his worldwide broadcast, McDonnell sat at his desk in the Oval Office with a sheaf of paper and a supply of well-honed pencils. Kim was instructed to hold calls, and Harrison was dismissed.

"Unplug the phones and sleep," the President had advised him. "Take two days. I won't send for you."

Harrison gratefully obeyed.

McDonnell reached for a sheet of paper and began to write. This document had to be composed while events and motivations were fresh in his mind, and he wanted no electronic record!

. . .

Enveloped in darkness, Cheryl stood beyond the reach of building lights that reflected off the angled surfaces of the sole remaining Blackhawk. Resembling an evil bird of prey ready to pounce from the shadows and devour her, its terrifying image was the least of her worries. Ed was overdue, and uneasiness fostered a threatening deja vu as she remembered standing in the same spot several months ago awaiting his uncertain return. The office door opened and closed, bright interior lights momentarily casting her shadow across the field.

"Relax," Ben suggested, coming up behind her in the dark. "I just talked with him. The tail rotor linkage required adjustment. He's airborne and will be here shortly."

"Thank God! I knew I was being silly," she admitted, "but I was worried to death. Your pipe smells good."

"Flying Dutchman, and your concern isn't silly.   The worrying..."

"Listen! . . . Do you hear it?"

Ben shrugged. "Piloting the damn things for years affected my hearing."

They stood silently, searching the black eastern sky, the warm and cheery glow from Ben's pipe suggesting a tranquility Cheryl did not feel. Eventually, the rotor's distinctive pulsing was unmistakable, and she noticeably relaxed. "Now, do you see it?" She pointed to a moving spot of light east of the complex.

Essell indicated he did, then gazing paternally at Cheryl, pointedly asked, "What are you going to do?"

Startled by the intimate nature of the question–one more indication the end was near for Omega 22–Cheryl was momentarily dumbstruck. The base commander's inquisitiveness about her personal life was improper and out of character, but his compassion deserved an honest answer. Her response tinged with sadness, she candidly admitted, "I wish I knew," then regained her composure and commented, "It wasn't supposed to be this way."

"But it usually is."

"Camp romances, Major?"

"I prefer to call them escape valves." Cheryl shrugged her shoulders. "Things seldom go as planned," he added. "Sometimes it's better that way."

"Turned philosopher, Ben?" she asked with affection. The use of his first name at this juncture seemed appropriate.

"He cares for you."

"I know. But he loves Lori. I could win against an incompatible wife. Married too young, poor, kids right away... the whole bit. But against Lori, his first real love . . ."

"Giving up?"

"Not without a fight! I have as much invested as she does! In the final analysis, Ben, we're all selfish. I want him!"

Landing lights pierced the darkness. With Ed's safe return, this conversation with her commanding officer would never resume.

That night, Cheryl was quieter than usual.

"What is it?" Ed inquired.

"I'm bummed. How much longer do you think we have?"

"A month; six weeks. We'll be out before Christmas."

"Now that it's near, I'm not sure I want to go."

"Me, either. People ruined everything, and now that they're gone, Africa will rejuvenate; the jungle, the game animals north and east on the true savannas. There are signs of it already. Some day... three or four decades, tops... it will be like it must have been around 1900."

"I didn't mean *that*. I could give a damn about the jungle and the filthy animals. I'll miss *you*." Cheryl moved within inches of him. "She's too young for you, Ed."

"I know," he introspectively acknowledged.

"And I'm just right!"

It was out in the open. Ed fumbled for the right thing to say. "I like you and you're beautiful . . . and I want to sleep with you . . . but if I do, it will ruin it with her."

"It won't ruin anything, Ed." She closed the remaining distance between them.

"It will."

"Look, we won't make love." She kissed him. "We'll just have sex."

"I can't."

"Lori will understand."

"Maybe she would, but I won't. Listen to me, Cheryl. I *want* to, but I *can't*, because for the first time in my life, I'm going to do the right thing."

PART IV

FRUITATION

"Because of the huge reduction in population
wrought by AIDS, given sufficient resources
and time, every diligent person on the Earth
can have a decent standard of living. If
family size is limited, and the excesses of the
past are avoided, we can safely take that for
granted."*

John H. McDonnell
Forty-fifth President
of the United States

*Special Oval Office broadcast.
December 20, 2005

26

Oncoming traffic cleared, and the front wheels bit into furrowed snow as Reynolds turned off the thoroughfare onto Woodbine Avenue.

When her father died in July, Lori, without assistance, arranged for the funeral, comforted her mother, and hosted out-of-town relatives. Declining Ed's offer to take leave and help, she had explained she could not deal with the silent disapproval and raised eyebrows that would greet his arrival.

Besides, they could not be intimate. Because her mom's house was small, even if they waited until she was asleep before sneaking into bed together, she would wake and hear them. How many times during childhood had she heard her parents fighting, quietly visiting at the end of a busy day, or making love? To be so close, yet have to abstain, would be torment. Thanks, honey, but no thanks.

She wrote him an extra long letter after the funeral. Sad, but it was time. Her father had suffered greatly, and she was approaching the breaking point. Coming home each night to chaos–a messy house, dinner not started and her mother unable to cope–she was glad it was over. Grieving was behind, having occurred each interminable day as her invincible dad failed.

Mother would just have to survive. Though it would be practical from a financial standpoint to live at home, she needed privacy and independence. Spending the Saturday after the funeral looking at apartments, she narrowed her choices to three and selected the roomiest. A bit far from work, she had written, but

317

well tended and worth the drive.

The stop sign was partially obscured by snow-laden bushes. His mind elsewhere, Ed braked too late and skidded halfway across the slippery intersection, fortunate there was no cross traffic.

He entered an older section of town. It looked pleasant in spots, poor in others. The yards were the size of postage stamps. Dilapidated and shabby cars, purchased second and third-hand, usurped much of the open areas that should have been lawns. He never considered Lori as being poor, and it bothered him to think of her that way.

Five hours ago he had said goodbye to Cheryl at La Guardia. They had flown out of Kisangani, refueled in Cairo, and continued on to Paris for the night. After sharing dinner and drinks, they awkwardly retired to separate rooms. Meeting for breakfast the next morning in the hotel coffee shop, both found it difficult to believe they might never see each other again.

"Will you be okay?" he inquired.

"You have my number. Call and find out."

Parting in New York was distressing. He did not know what to say, and finally settled on, "Good luck in Louisville."

"Give my best to Lori," was all she could think of. Reaching up–eyes moist with emerging tears–she kissed his cheek, then hurried through the jetway and was gone.

After pensively staring down the empty corridor for a moment, he turned, wove through the crush of friends and relatives awaiting the flight's departure, and headed down the concourse to his gate.

Entering the eight hundred block ended his reverie. Midway, he spotted number 856, a four-unit red brick, architecturally dated though perhaps newer than surrounding buildings. Reynolds followed the driveway to a small parking area at the rear–someone's backyard, before the original house and garage were razed to make room for apartments. Salty slush squirted from the front tires as his rental rolled to a stop beside an old '96 Chevy.

Frigid December air rolling across the Great Plains to blanket Minneapolis knifed through his uniform while he retrieved suitcases from the trunk. It reminded him that two and a half years had lapsed since experiencing such bitter cold.

The enclosed vestibule was only a little warmer than outside, for the meager output from a small space heater quickly escaped through a quarter-inch crack under the ill-fitting outer door, where weather-stripping had frozen to the concrete floor and pulled away. He put down his bags and pushed "D."

"Ed?"

Even the mediocre intercom system's distortion could not mask her joy. Mashing the push-to-talk button, he responded, "Hello, honey."

"Ed!" she squealed excitedly. "Oh, my God! You're here! Right door at the top of the stairs. I'll buzz you in!"

To the prolonged rasp of the remote lock release, he shoved the door open a crack and placed a foot on the threshold to prevent it from closing, but before he could pick up his luggage, Lori bounded down the steps and into his arms.

"Oh, God, you're here! I'm so glad to see you!" She smothered him with affection, kissing his mouth, his neck, his cheeks, and then began to cry. "Oh, God, I missed you so much. I was afraid something would happen to you, afraid you weren't coming, afraid you'd never come. Oh, God. I love you so much!" She buried her face in his neck, kissing him all over as he enveloped her in his arms.

"I'm here. I'm here. Let me look at you." He gently repositioned her a few inches away, his eyes expressing approval.

"Come upstairs," she urged. "You must be freezing. Don't you have a coat?"

"No, I..."

"We'll go shopping tomorrow. There's this great coat outlet at the plaza." She led him upstairs. "Supper's almost ready."

"I planned to take you out."

"In this weather? After I slaved all day over a hot stove?"

"Our first home-cooked meal?"

"Exactly. I made a *fantastic* supper. Everything you like, plus a fifth of J.B., a six-pack, and a bottle of my favorite wine. We're going to party, Ed!"

"I don't drink much anymore. I'll have a beer, maybe sip some whisky after supper."

"I'm glad. I was starting to worry."

"Me, too."

Lori's apartment was larger than expected. The decor an expanded version of her room at Omega 22–the pictures, the colors–a collage of memories came flooding back.

"Where did you get the furniture, honey?"

"I bought some, and Mom gave me stuff from her place."

"How is she?"

"Depressed. I'm not sure she'll ever adjust."

"Sorry."

"Me, too, but there's nothing anyone can do. How's Hadari?"

"I don't know. They took him to Cleveland."

"And Ben and Cheryl?"

"Fine."

At that moment, everything came into focus, and Ed made his decision. He could not go home to his wife. Something was wrong between them and always had been. Furthermore, he was not going to contact Cheryl. In a weak moment, the urge for such a fine piece of ass might cloud his judgment. Confident that he would not change his mind, he gazed at the only woman he had ever met with whom he was willing to be monogamous. She looked so young . . . younger than in Africa. There, Omega 22 was the world. Lots of people shacked up; there was no tomorrow; age did not matter. Now he saw her through the eyes of others. She was *definitely* young! Well, *fuck* whoever did not like it! He loved her and was not going to screw this up! He envisioned waking up next to her each morning for the rest of his life and could not imagine anything else.

"Lori, sit down," he requested.

"What is it?" She was terrified. He was going back to his wife! Oh, God, he looked so serious. No, it was Cheryl! She was waiting in a nearby motel, letting him have one last night to say goodbye. Tomorrow he would be gone, flying off with her to God knows where.

"Nothing's wrong. Please sit."

Lori sat.

"Honey, although you're a lot younger than me, and that might cause some problems, I love you and I want you to marry me. It will take some…"

He did not get any further before she collapsed crying into his arms.

"Honey, *what's* wrong?"

"I'm finally happy," she burst out between sobs, "*that's* why I'm crying. I haven't been happy in eight months. Ever since leaving Africa my life's been a wreck! Dad died, Mom's sad, I worried that Cheryl would steal you. It's been *so* damned hard. I never took off my ring, my link to you." Everything poured out. "I've *never* felt so alone."

"Honey …"

"Don't *ever* tell me what happened between you and her! I don't want to know. Oh, Ed, I need you."

"Nothing happened." He was glad it was true. Lori's clinging was uncharacteristic . . . the desperation it revealed. Sobbing slowed to intermittent bursts of sniffles.

"You *did* say you wanted to marry me, didn't you?"

"Lori Tomasini, will you marry me?"

"Yes!" She embraced him, kissed him. "God, you smell good! You're sure you want to do this? I'm only twenty-three."

"You're in luck. I'm still thirty-six. Now I'm only thirteen years older."

"Gee, maybe some day I'll catch up!"

"I hope not. I kind of like robbing the cradle."

"Interesting you would say that. Come here; I have something to show you." She took his hand, led him to the bedroom opposite hers. "Shh. If we're lucky, we can celebrate our reunion and engagement before he's up."

"Who?" Ed had not the slightest idea what she was talking about as she guided him to a crib next to the only window.

"You like?"

"He's cute." It was nice of her to watch someone's kid. Ed feigned interest. "Who is he?"

"He's your son, Ed."

Disbelieving, he regained enough composure to respond, "Why didn't you tell me?"

"Because I didn't want you out of a sense of guilt or obligation. I wanted you after we'd been apart, after I'd had

321

some . . . competition. If you preferred me, you'd come. If not, I was better off alone."

"Honey . . ."

She began to cry again. "I was *so* afraid."

"Honey, don't cry." Ed enveloped her in his arms to comfort and assure her. "How old is he?"

"Three weeks."

"And you look like this?" He scanned her body.

"I only gained nineteen pounds. Aren't you proud? Even my mother didn't suspect until the fourth month."

"Does she know about us?"

"Yes."

"Bet she loves *me*."

"Don't count on it... now or later."

"What's his name?"

"He doesn't have one, but there are two or three I like. I waited so you could help choose." She took his hand. "Come on. We need time alone that we won't get if he wakes." They tiptoed from the room, leaving the door ajar. "Ed, thank you for him."

"He's beautiful, honey."

She pushed him into her bedroom.

"More surprises?"

"There's nothing in here you haven't seen. Proof of that is across the hall! We can't do much after only three weeks, but I need to be close. And I'll figure out some way to satisfy you," she winked. Demanding sounds emanated from the nursery. "He can wait," Lori emphatically stated. "We've been apart for almost a year!"

Outside, the wind picked up, swirling snow about the building and obliterating the tire tracks from Ed's rental.

. . .

The massive stone church on St. Clair, an architectural masterpiece rivaling many medieval European structures, had been chosen despite their preference for a neighborhood congregation. Precisely laid, elegantly weathered stone blocks–in stark contrast to randomly flawed stained glass–complemented its ethereal interior where the high vaulted ceiling dwarfed intricately carved pews. Espousing a religious philosophy similar to their own,

Roberta and Bill liked the tribute to God that this immense structure symbolized. It also partially satisfied joint aspirations to support downtown activities and revitalization.

Although sparsely attended throughout the year, typical of mainline churches near the heart of most major cities, its sanctuary was filled to capacity on Christmas Eve. The Fairchilds, arriving late, were fortunate to find seats.

"Try as we might"–the sermon was in progress–"to understand what God has in mind, we are often confused. Though granted a reprieve in the battle against AIDS, we wonder why untimely death intrudes in any form. Perhaps it helps to remember our Savior died for us, and that was not an end, but a beginning, an incarnate second chance for humanity. And might eternal life be so much more precious than our brief stay on Earth, that what appears catastrophic to us, is not in the eyes of the Lord? Have faith, my friends; have faith.

"For survivors, life will not simply continue but dramatically improve. Many of us may feel guilty about that, but there is no need to. As you and I enjoy the benefits of fewer individuals upon the Earth, we will also suffer infirmities of the flesh and the slings and arrows of misfortune, conditions spared our fallen brethren of all faiths and races, already joyfully united with a loving, omnipotent God.

"Yes, the timing of death is often inexplicable. The loss of a small child, the seemingly endless tolls extracted by warfare and plagues that ravage the planet. What purpose the random plucking of one or millions of souls serves the Creator we can contemplate, but not know.

"Premature death is difficult to understand on a small scale. The devastation wrought by AIDS is beyond human comprehension; therefore, we can only accept, believe, and go forth. That is what I challenge you to do. Go forward with grace and optimism and joy. The blackest night is followed by the dawn, the most violent storm by a glorious sun breaking through the clouded sky. Hope returns and is justified.

"On this Christmas Eve, I ask each of you to pray for the fallen and dedicate your lives to the living; to a better future next year, the year after, and for eternity. Return to your homes in peace and love. May God bless and guide you, now and forever. Amen."

. . .

For Cheryl, Africa had been a spontaneous lark, born of boredom. Intrigued after investigating the overseas program, she signed up for a tour of duty only to find it neither as exotic or fulfilling as the recruiter's representations. At some level, she knew it would not be, and took comfort in knowing life was what one made of it.

Upon returning to Louisville, AFCOM became surreal–except for memories of Ed. Those remained *disturbingly* fresh! The level of unreality was so intense the experience slipped out of order. It did not belong in her twenty-eighth year, so her mind filed the events out of sequence, placing them after college, but preceding her stint at the hospital. That is where flings should be–following the completion of formal education and before professional commitment.

She resumed her hospital duties with mature expectations, foreseeing few challenges and accepting the monotonous routine. Her personal life was no more exciting, though that was by choice, as numerous men requesting dates were politely turned down. It was, however, mid-May, and Ed had failed to call. If he did not contact her soon, she might feel differently.

Loving the water and swimming since the age of two, Cheryl had selected her apartment complex because of the large pool. As a graceful, mature, and statuesque fourteen-year-old, she devoted a brief period preparing for the Olympics, but the rigorous training and time commitment distressed her. Quitting after three months, she launched a more satisfying social career, though never giving up recreational swimming, the activity she missed most in Africa.

Cheryl had recently worked a double and, learning years ago that comp time not promptly taken was conveniently forgotten, she informed her supervisor she would not be in the next day.

She slept until 10:00 and, between cleaning her apartment and doing laundry, went grocery shopping. Chores completed, she arrived at the pool shortly before 3:00, did twenty laps, covered herself with sunscreen, donned sunglasses, and stretched out on a chaise.

Waking shortly before 5:15, she swam an additional ten laps. Gathering possessions while toweling her hair, she started the long walk across the parking lot to her building. Shaking out matted tresses as she crested the last flight of stairs, she saw him.

"Well, hi! What a surprise!"

"Hello, Cheryl. I came in with one of your neighbors. I hope you don't mind." Uncertain he should be there, he seemed ill at ease. "Perhaps I should have called first."

"It's okay, I'm just surprised to see you." Unlocking the door, she preceded him. "Come in."

"Thank you." His nervousness was increasing.

Cheryl motioned toward the couch. "Take a seat. I took advantage of a day off by spending it at the pool. Pretty obvious, huh?" A white beach towel covered her bikini, tucked in at the bodice to hold it up.

Awkwardly sitting, he wondered if he made the right decision calling on her, or was he destined to be a fool?

"What brings you to Louisville?" she asked.

"I bought a practice."

"How nice. Welcome to our city."

"Thanks."

"I'll be right back."

She returned clutching an ankle-length Oriental silk robe about her neck for warmth. He caught the slightest glimpse of inner thigh as she curled up on the chair opposite and folded the garment around her legs. "What can I do for you?"

Avoiding eye contact, he cleared his throat. "It took a while to summon the courage to contact you. I called information my first day in town and picked the phone up a dozen times since, but I always lost my nerve. Wednesday office hours end at noon so when I locked up today I thought, why not? The worst she can say is, no."

"To what?"

He was squirming like an insecure schoolboy trying to date a popular cheerleader. How refreshing, after all those throbbing egos at the hospital.

"May I take you to dinner tonight?"

"How sweet! Yes, if you don't mind waiting for me to get

ready."

"It would be my pleasure."

"How should I dress?"

"We'll be going to a four star restaurant."

"'Four stars,' take a while. Would you like to stay? There's beer in the refrigerator. I acquired a taste for it in Africa."

"No, thanks. Eight, okay?"

"Fine. Have you made reservations? On the chance that I might go?"

"For 9:00," he sheepishly admitted.

"Good. That will give us time for a drink before dinner. We can get reacquainted."

"More like, 'acquainted.'"

"You're right. We barely know each other."

He rose to go. "I'll be back at 8:00."

"Delightful."

. . .

After returning to his condo and quickly changing, he drove around the city, stopped at his office intending to catch up on dictation–but was unable to concentrate–and found himself in the parking lot outside her building at 7:45 with nothing to do. To avoid appearing overly eager, he waited in his car, impatiently listening to music and contemplating his good fortune.

. . .

The bolt in the electric door lock retracted. Unable to control escalating excitement, he hurried up the stairs, pausing momentarily to catch his breath before rapping. The door opened immediately, revealing a goddess in a green sheath slit up one side to mid-thigh. A single strand of pearls lay loosely in spectacular cleavage.

"You're absolutely breathtaking!" It was out before he could stop it.

"More likely it's those two flights of stairs," she modestly joked, standing aside to admit him. "Thank you for asking me out. I'm really looking forward to our evening together. I haven't dated since I got here."

"You haven't?" He was dumbstruck.

"I haven't wanted to. Until now," she added.

"Oh."

"Would you like a drink before we go?"

"No, thanks."

"Then I'll fix you a nightcap when we get back." Cheryl picked up a small sequined clutch bag. "I don't know your first name. How embarrassing."

"No reason you should and rude of me not to tell you. Chester. It's a family tradition. I'm the fourth."

"A strong name. Chester Wyant." She put the two together to fix them in her mind. Are all the other Chester Wyants doctors?"

"Yes, but I'm the black sheep. Or was until a month ago. First to make a career out of the military. I just retired... well, didn't actually retire. I resigned my commission. After the short stint in Africa, they sent me to INCOM. God, what a hellhole India is! I couldn't stand it so I got out. Served thirteen years."

"What made you select Louisville?"

"I was raised here."

"No!"

"Afraid so."

"Small world."

"Everyone has to be from somewhere . . ."

"But this place is nowhere!"

They laughed. The old Omega 22 joke was still funny. It was going to be a wonderful evening. Wyant basked in his good fortune.

"Ever hear from Ed Reynolds?" he asked as Cheryl pulled the locked door closed.

After a millisecond flicker of what he could only interpret as longing, she confidently responded, "No," mentally closing a chapter. Slipping her arm inside his, she let him help her down stairs she took two at a time when alone and in a hurry. "This is so pleasant," she smiled, tightening the hold on his forearm.

. . .

"Phagocytes," Eric Li postulated as he leaned against the doorjamb leading into Fairchild's office. "Ravenously aggressive phagocytes, unusual helper T-cells, and rare DNA patterns. Our efforts to stymie HIV come down to this, a kid with a unique immune system. Do you realize virtually every avenue any of us tried except T-cells was a dead-end?"

"The nature of medical research, my friend. Do you have enough chromosome modification volunteers?"

"A thousand for every one I need."

"Good." Fairchild studied his research colleague and declared, "With diligence and barring the unforeseen, if we can't eradicate AIDS, at least we can control it."

"I'd bet on it. These procedures are hardly routine, but we have learned enough about genetic targeting and alteration during the last decade to successfully create any CGNA sequence we want."

"From super T-cells to super phagocytes to DNA changes. It is amazing."

"Speaking of which, it's too soon to know if they are relevant, but I've found more abnormalities in the boy's blood."

"That's great." Fairchild became philosophic. "After all our trials and defeats, it seems God felt sorry for us and gave us this kid as a present."

Li shrugged. "I don't know about that, but without him, I doubt we would ever find a cure."

"Perhaps he holds the key to conquering cancer."

"Don't count on it. His bout with the flu last month suggests he is no more resistant to other diseases than anyone else."

"Possibly, but worth pursuing."

Li nodded agreement. "Well, I must get back to work."

Alone, Fairchild meditated. How could it be so simple? It made a mockery of years of human endeavor. No, that was too harsh an indictment of his profession and personal efforts. While it was true HIV might be conquered because of a unique young man, success would not be possible without previous scientific research.

So the species might survive after all . . . but with so few left relative to the onslaught of AIDS! If God was going to provide a moratorium, why did he wait so long? An awful thought occurred: perhaps because His delay solved a number of persistent human problems–pollution, natural resources depletion, and starvation to name a few–McDonnell was right. When the Supreme Being decided that through over-population we had made a hopeless mess of life and the planet, He intervened with a surgical solution using the President as the facilitating agent. What a horrible premise, that was!

. . .

Medical progress was more rapid than anticipated. On December 15, 2006, Dr. William Fairchild called the President of the United States, informing him that while DNA alteration was inefficient and unrealistic for the mass of humanity, Hadarium–as the serum containing the young man's super phagocytes and helper T-cells was named–was ready for mass production. Based in part on mutation research in CD-4 cells in 1995, the assault on HIV had another potent weapon in its arsenal.

McDonnell broadcast the news globally, via satellite. Within a few years, he informed the world, HIV might be relegated to the annals of medical history. At the very least, it was stymied.

. . .

Fairchild tabled thoughts of retirement. Roberta enjoyed working, the baby deserved the role model of an employed father, and there were doctors at Northcoast many years his senior actively employed. But he would cut back: leave earlier each day, no more Saturdays, frequent three-day weekends, and six to eight weeks of vacation each year. Lolita would know her father, and so would their next child. Fairchild was not comfortable with that, but Roberta would cuddle up some evening, lure him into bed, tease until he could not... did not want to resist. She would insure the baby was a boy. They would have one of each. What the hell!

. . .

Though sequestered in the Oval Office with calls held and no appointments, President McDonnell still found it difficult to concentrate. Heavy equipment rumbling outside and the whine of power tools within distracted him. His sensitivity to noise increasing with each passing year, he tolerated the intrusion because a national treasure was being saved.

While cheaper to abandon the presidential complex than restore it, the preservationists had rightly prevailed. Tradition mattered more than economics and modern accommodations, for a chief executive and those fortunate or unfortunate enough to be assisting him.

A glance at the indicator beneath his desk assuring him the access doors were locked, he energized the voice activated security mechanism on his personal safe. Responding with the required password requested by the synthetic voice, he listened for the audible that signaled the device was unlocked. Opening the door, he extracted a manila envelope. Little else was there.

Slitting open the sealed packet with the gold letter opener presented by his wife the day he won re-election, he set aside the dated and signed cover letter. Determined to ignore the invasive cacophony, he began to read. Soon, the construction din faded.

'I, John H. McDonnell, 45th President of the United States, did premeditatively, willfully, and singularly, contribute to the demise of over one billion people by delaying the introduction of treatment that could have prevented many, if not most, of the losses.

My act was of omission, not commission. I could not deliberately take life but found it relatively easy to ignore death. That statement, I trust, will provide legions of historians and mental health professionals with years of speculation and analysis.

Initially appalled by the exploding numbers and apocalyptic suffering they represented, as the population declined, the benefits of fewer souls dominated my thoughts.

With God as my judge–or partner–I took the necessary steps to guarantee the annihilation of individuals, cultures, and countries that in my opinion blighted the earth.'

The letter went on to delineate specific delaying tactics from January 2004, until the manufacture and distribution of Hadarium in late 2005 and early 2006. It closed with an exoneration of his closest advisors.

Pensively setting the indicting document aside, the sounds of construction crept back into McDonnell's consciousness. He heard the rhythmic beep-beep-beep of a backing front-end-loader, the bone shattering chatter of an air hammer, and the unmistakable thump of a nail gun. Temporary dividers were being erected, compressing the usable West Wing space to a bare minimum until a portion of the facility was refurbished and returned to service.

The President's quandary was obvious. If his "confession" surfaced before his death, he would be indicted, impeached, removed from office, and in some manner, punished. Released after his death, the multitudes thinking AIDS was God's will would realize much of the loss of human life was his fault, not God's, and therefore preventable. They might begin to feel guilty living in a better, less populated world and become lax about limiting family size.

Nixon was a fool to make tapes and a bigger one to not destroy them. How was he any wiser? Whatever prompted him to create this "confession"–an unrealized need to cleanse his soul or an academic desire to "right" history in the distant future–the short-term risk was unacceptable.

Without further consideration, the President reached behind him, activated the document disintegrator, and inserted the ill-conceived, damning memoir. How ludicrous it was to be re-elected by the biggest majority in history and then plant a "smoking gun."

The faint smell of burning paper emitted by the voracious machine was soon carried away by the ventilation system. McDonnell swiveled his chair the few remaining degrees necessary to face the windows, view the gently falling snow beyond the glass, and serenely murmur,

"Thy will was done."